# The Miracles of Antichrist

## A NOVEL

# The Miracles of Antichrist

A NOVEL

SELMA LAGERLÖF

*translated by*
*Pauline Bancroft Flach*

# ÆGYPAN PRESS

From the 1915 Little, Brown, and Company edition; that edition
bore a 1899 copyright, also by Little, Brown.

Selma Lagerlöf lived from 1858 until 1940.

*The Miracles of Antichrist*
A publication of
ÆGYPAN PRESS
www.aegypan.com

"When Antichrist comes, he shall seem as Christ. There shall be great want, and Antichrist shall go from land to land and give bread to the poor. And he shall find many followers."

SICILIAN LEGEND

# INTRODUCTION

*"When Antichrist comes, he shall seem as Christ"*

# I

## THE EMPEROR'S VISION

*I*t was at the time when Augustus was emperor in Rome and Herod was king in Jerusalem.

It happened once upon a time that a very great and holy night sank down over the earth. It was the darkest night ever seen by man; it seemed as if the whole earth had passed under a vault. It was impossible to distinguish water from land, or to find the way on the most familiar paths. And it could not be otherwise, for not a ray of light came from the sky. All the stars stayed in their houses, and the fair moon kept her face turned away.

And just as intense as the darkness was the silence and the calm. The rivers stood still in their course; the wind did not stir, and even the leaves of the aspen ceased to tremble. Anyone walking by the sea would have found that the waves no longer broke on the shore, and the sand of the desert did not crunch under the wanderer's foot. Everything was as if turned to stone and without motion, in order not to disturb the holy night. The grass did not dare to grow, the dew could not fall, and the flowers feared to exhale their perfume.

During that night the beasts of prey did not hunt, the serpents did not sting, the dogs did not bay. And what was even more wonderful, none of the inanimate things would have disturbed the holiness of the night by lending themselves to an evil deed. No false key could open a lock, and no knife could shed blood.

In Rome, on that very night, a little group of people came down from the emperor's palace on the Palatine and made their way over the Forum to the Capitol. During the day just completed his councilors had asked the emperor if they might not raise a temple to him on Rome's holy mountain. But Augustus had not immediately given his consent. He did not know if it would be pleasing to the gods for him to possess a temple next to theirs, and he had answered that he wished first to discover by a nocturnal sacrifice to his genius what their wishes were. Followed by a few faithful retainers, he was now on his way to perform that sacrifice.

Augustus was carried in his litter, for he was old, and the long stairs to the Capitol fatigued him. He held the cage of doves which was his offering. Neither priests, nor soldiers, nor councilors accompanied him; only his nearest friends. Torch-bearers walked in front of him, as if to force a way through the darkness of the night, and behind him followed slaves, carrying the tripod, the charcoal, the knives, the holy fire, and everything needed for the sacrifice.

On the way the emperor chatted gaily with his retainers, and none of them noticed the infinite silence and calm of the night. It was only on reaching the open place on the top of the Capitol, which had been thought of for the new temple, that it was revealed to them that something unusual was occurring.

It could not be a night like any other, for on the edge of the cliff they saw the strangest being. They thought at first that it was an old twisted olive trunk; then they thought that an ancient statue from the temple of Jupiter had wandered out on the cliff. At last they saw that it could only be the old sibyl.

They had never seen anything so old, so weather-beaten, and so gigantic. If the emperor had not been there, they would have all fled home to their beds. "It is she," they whispered to each other, "who counts as many years as there are grains of sand on her native shores. Why has she come out of her cave tonight? What does she foretell to the emperor and to the country, she who writes her prophecies on the leaves of trees, and knows that the wind carries the words of the oracle to him who needs them?"

They were so terrified that all would have fallen on their knees with their foreheads to the ground had the sibyl made the slightest movement. But she sat as still as if she had been without life. Crouched on the very edge of the cliff, and shading her eyes with her hand, she stared out into the night. She sat there as if she had gone up on the hill the better to see something, happening far away. She alone could see something in the black night!

At the same moment the emperor and all his suite perceived how intense the darkness was. Not one of them could see a hand's-breadth in front of him. And what a calm, what silence! They could not even hear the rippling murmur of the Tiber. The air seemed to choke them; a cold sweat came out on their foreheads, and their hands were stiff and powerless. They thought that something dreadful must be impending.

But no one liked to show that he was afraid, and everybody told the emperor that it was a good omen; nature herself held her breath to greet a new god.

They urged Augustus to hurry, and said that the old sibyl had probably come up from her cave to greet his genius.

But the truth was that the old sibyl, engrossed in a vision, did not even know that Augustus had come to the Capitol. She was transported in spirit to a far distant land, where she thought she was wandering over a great plain. In the darkness she kept striking her foot against something, which she thought to be tufts of grass. She bent down and felt with her hand. No, they were not tufts of grass, but sheep. She was walking among great sleeping flocks of sheep.

Then she perceived the fire of the shepherds. It was burning in the middle of the plain, and she approached it. The shepherds were lying asleep by the fire, and at their sides they had long, pointed staves, with which they defended their flocks from wild beasts. But the little animals with shining eyes and bushy tails, which crept forward to the fire, were they not jackals? And yet the shepherds did not throw their staves at them; the dogs continued to sleep; the sheep did not flee; and the wild beasts lay down to rest beside the men.

All this the sibyl saw, but of what was going on behind her on the mountain she knew nothing.

She did not know that people were raising an altar, lighting charcoal, strewing incense, and that the emperor was taking one of the doves out of the cage to make a sacrifice to her. But his hands were so benumbed that he could not hold the bird. With a single flap of her wings the dove freed herself, and disappeared into the darkness of the night.

When that happened, the courtiers looked suspiciously at the old sibyl. They thought that it was she who was the cause of the misfortune.

Could they know that the sibyl still thought she was standing by the shepherds' fire, and that she was now listening to a faint sound which came vibrating through the dead silence of the night? She had heard it for a long time before she noticed that it came from the sky, and not from the earth. At last she raised her head, and saw bright, glistening forms gliding about up in the darkness. They were small bands of angels, who, singing, and apparently searching, flew up and down the wide plain.

While the sibyl listened to the angels' song, the emperor was preparing for a new sacrifice. He washed his hands, purified the altar, and grasped the other dove. But although he now made a special effort to hold it fast, the bird slipped through his fingers, and swung itself up into the impenetrable night.

The emperor was appalled. He fell on his knees before the empty altar and prayed to his genius. He called on him for strength to avert the misfortunes which this night seemed to portend.

Nothing of all this had the sibyl heard. She was listening with her whole soul to the angels' song, which was growing stronger and stronger. At last it became so loud that it wakened the shepherds. They raised themselves on their elbows, and saw shining hosts of silvery angels moving in the darkness in long, fluttering lines, like birds of passage. Some had lutes and violins in their hands; others had zithers and harps, and their song sounded as gay as children's laughter, and as free from care as the trilling of a lark. When the shepherds heard it they rose up to go to the village which was their home, to tell of the miracle.

They went by a narrow, winding path, and the sibyl followed them. Suddenly it became light on the mountain. A great, bright star kindled over it, and the village on its top shone like silver in the starlight. All the wandering bands of angels hastened thither with cries of jubilation, and the shepherds hurried on so fast that they almost ran. When they had reached the town they found that the angels had gathered over a low stable near the gate. It was a wretched building, with roof of straw, and the bare rock for one wall. Above it hung the star, and more and more angels kept coming. Some of them placed themselves on the straw roof, or settled down on the steep cliff behind the house; others hovered over it with fluttering wings. High, high up, the air was lighted by their shining wings.

At the moment when the star flamed out over the mountain-village all nature awoke, and the men who stood on the top of the Capitol were conscious of it. They felt fresh, but caressing breezes; sweet perfumes streamed up about them; the trees rustled; the Tiber murmured, the stars shone, and the moon stood high in the heaven and lighted the world. And out of the sky the two doves flew circling down, and lighted on the emperor's shoulders.

When this miracle took place Augustus rose up with proud joy, but his friends and his slaves fell on their knees. "Hail, Caesar!" they cried. "Your genius has answered you! You are the god who shall be worshipped on the heights of the Capitol."

And the tribute which the men in their transport offered the emperor was so loud that the old sibyl heard it. It waked her from her visions. She rose from her place on the edge of the cliff, and came forward toward the people. It seemed as if a dark cloud had risen up from the abyss and sunk down over the mountain. She was terrifying in her old age. Coarse hair hung in thin tufts about her head, her joints were thickened, and her dark skin, hard as bark, covered her body with wrinkle upon wrinkle.

Mighty and awe-inspiring, she advanced towards the emperor. With one hand she seized his wrist, with the other she pointed towards the distant east.

"Look," she commanded, and the emperor raised his eyes and saw. The heavens opened before his eyes and he looked away to the far east. And he saw a miserable stable by a steep cliff, and in the open door some kneeling shepherds. Within the stable he saw a young mother on her knees before a little child, who lay on a bundle of straw on the floor.

And the sibyl's big, bony fingers pointed towards that poor child.

"Hail, Caesar!" said the sibyl, with a scornful laugh. "There is the god who shall be worshipped on the heights of the Capitol."

Augustus shrank back from her as if from a maniac.

But upon the sibyl fell the mighty spirit of the prophetess. Her dim eyes began to burn, her hands were stretched towards heaven, her voice did not seem to be her own, but rang with such strength that it could have been heard over the whole world. And she spoke words which she seemed to have read in the stars: —

"On the heights of the Capitol the redeemer of the world shall be
    worshipped,
    Christ or Antichrist, but no frail mortal."

When she had spoken she moved away between the terrified men, went slowly down the mountain, and disappeared.

Augustus, the next day, strictly forbade his people to raise him any temple on the Capitol. In its place he built a sanctuary to the newborn godchild and called it "Heaven's Altar," Aracoeli.

# II

## ROME'S HOLY CHILD

On the summit of the Capitol stood a monastery occupied by Franciscan monks. It was, however, less a monastery than a fortress. It was like a watchtower by the seashore, where watch was kept for an approaching foe.

Near the monastery stood the magnificent basilica "Santa Maria in Aracoeli." The basilica was built because the sibyl had caused Augustus to see Christ. But the monastery was built because they feared the fulfillment of the sibyl's prophecy; that Antichrist should come to be worshipped on the Capitol.

And the monks felt like warriors. When they went to church to sing and pray, they thought that they were walking on ramparts, and sending showers of arrows down on the assaulting Antichrist.

They lived always in terror of Antichrist, and all their service was a struggle to keep him away from the Capitolium.

They drew their hats down over their eyes and sat and gazed out into the world. Their eyes grew feverish with watching, and they continually thought they discovered Antichrist. "He is here, he is there!" they cried. And they fluttered up in their brown robes and braced themselves for the struggle, as crows gather on a crag when they catch a glimpse of an eagle.

But some said: "What is the use of prayers and penitence? The sibyl has said it. Antichrist must come."

Then others said, "God can work a miracle. If it was of no avail to struggle, He would not have let the sibyl warn us."

Year after year the Franciscans defended the Capitol by penitences, and works of charity, and the promulgation of God's word.

They protected it century after century, but as time went on, men became more and more feeble and lacking in force. The monks said among themselves: "Soon the kingdoms of the earth can stand no longer. A redeemer of the world is needed as in the time of Augustus."

They tore their hair and scourged themselves, for they knew that he who was to be born again must be the Antichrist, and that it would be a regeneration of force and violence.

As a sick man is tormented by his pain, so were they hunted by the thought of Antichrist. And they saw him before them. He was as rich as Christ had been poor, as wicked as Christ had been good, as honored as Christ had been humiliated.

He bore powerful weapons and marched at the head of bloody evil-doers. He overturned the churches, murdered the priests, and armed people for strife, so that brother fought against brother, and each feared his neighbor, and there was no peace.

And for every person of power and might who made his way over the sea of time, they cried out from the watchtower on the Capitol: "Antichrist, Antichrist!"

And for everyone who disappeared, and went under, the monks cried: "Hosanna!" and sang the "Te Deum." And they said: "It is because of our prayers that the wicked fall before they succeed in scaling the Capitol."

It was a hard punishment that in that beautiful monastery its monks could never feel at rest. Their nights were heavier than their days. Then they saw wild beasts come into their cells and stretch themselves out beside them on their beds. And each wild beast was Antichrist. But some of the monks saw him as a dragon, and others as a griffin, and others as a sphinx. When they got up from their dreams they were as weak as after a severe illness.

The only comfort of these poor monks was the miracle-working image of Christ, which was kept in the basilica of Aracoeli. When a monk was frightened to desperation, he went into the church to seek consolation from it. He would go through the whole basilica and into a well-guarded chapel at the side of the great altar. There he lighted the consecrated wax candles, and spoke a prayer, before opening the altar shrine, which had double locks and doors of iron. And as long as he gazed at the image, he remained upon his knees.

The image represented a little babe, but he had a gold crown upon his head, gold shoes upon his feet, and his whole dress shone with jewels, which were given to him by those in distress, who had called on him for help. And the walls of the chapel were covered with pictures, which showed how he had saved from dangers of fire and shipwreck, how he had cured the sick and helped all those who were in trouble. When the monk saw it he rejoiced, and said to himself: "Praise be to God! As yet it is Christ who is worshipped on the Capitol."

The monk saw the face of the image smile at him with mysterious, conscious power, and his spirit soared up into the holy realms of confidence. "What can overthrow you in your might?" he said. "What can overthrow you? To you the Eternal City bends its knees. You are Rome's Holy Child. Yours is the crown which the people worship. You come in your might with help and strength and consolation. You alone shall be worshipped on the Capitol."

The monk saw the crown of the image turn into a halo, which sent out rays over the whole world. And in whatever direction he followed the rays he saw the world full of churches, where Christ was worshipped. It seemed as if a powerful conqueror had shown him all the castles and fortresses which defended his kingdom. "It is certain that you cannot fall," said the monk. "Your kingdom will be everlasting."

And every monk who saw the image had a few hours of consolation and peace, until fear seized him again. But had the monks not possessed the image, their souls would not have found a moment's rest.

Thus had the monks of Aracoeli, by prayers and struggles, worked their way through the centuries, and there had never lacked for watchers; as soon as one had been exhausted by terror and anxiety, others had hurried forward to take his place.

And although most of those who entered the monastery were struck down by madness or premature death, the succession of monks never diminished, for it was held a great honor before God to wage the war on Aracoeli.

So it happened that sixty years ago this struggle still went on, and in the degenerate times the monks fought with greater eagerness than ever before, and awaited the certain coming of Antichrist.

At that time a rich Englishwoman came to Rome. She went up to the Aracoeli and saw the image, and he charmed her so that she thought she could not live if she did not possess him. She went again and again up to Aracoeli to see the image, and at last she asked the monks if she might buy him.

But even if she had covered the whole mosaic floor in the great basilica with gold coins, the monks would not have been willing to sell her that image, which was their only consolation.

Still the Englishwoman was attracted beyond measure by the image, and found no joy nor peace without it. Unable to accomplish her object by any other means, she determined to steal the image. She did not think of the sin she was committing; she felt only a strong compulsion and a burning thirst, and preferred to risk her soul rather than to deny her heart the joy of possessing the object of her longing. And to accomplish her end, she first had an image made exactly like the one on Aracoeli.

The image on Aracoeli was carved from olive wood from the gardens of Gethsemane; but the Englishwoman dared to have an image carved from elm wood, which was exactly like him. The image on Aracoeli was not painted by mortal hand. When the monk who had carved him had taken up his brushes and colors, he fell asleep over his work. And when he awoke, the image was colored, — self-painted as a sign that God loved him. But the Englishwoman was bold enough to let an earthly painter paint her elm image so that he was like the holy image.

For the false image she procured a crown and shoes, but they were not of gold; they were only tin and gilding. She ordered ornaments; she bought rings, and necklaces, and chains, and bracelets, and diamond suns — but they were all brass and glass; and she dressed him as those seeking help had dressed the true image. When the image was ready she took a needle and scratched in the crown: "My kingdom is only of this world." It was as if she was afraid that she herself would not be able to distinguish one image from the other. And it was as if she had wished to appease her own conscience. "I have not wished to make a false Christ image. I have written in his crown: 'My kingdom is only of this world.'"

Thereupon she wrapped herself in a big cloak, hid the image under it, and went up to Aracoeli. And she asked that she might be allowed to say her prayers before the Christchild.

When she stood in the sanctuary, and the candles were lighted, and the iron door opened, and the image showed itself to her, she began to tremble and shake and looked as if she were going to faint. The monk who was with her hurried into the sacristy after water and she was left alone in the chapel. And when he came back she had committed the sacrilege. She had exchanged the holy, miracle-working image, and put the false and impotent one in his place.

The monk saw nothing. He shut in the false image behind iron doors and double locks, and the Englishwoman went home with the treasure of Aracoeli. She placed him in her palace on a pedestal of marble and was more happy than she had ever been before.

Up on Aracoeli, where no one knew what injury they had suffered, they worshipped the false Christ image as they had worshipped the true one, and when Christmas came they built for him in the church, as was the custom, a most beautiful niche. There he lay, shining like a jewel, on Maria's knees, and about him shepherds and angels and wise men were arranged. And as long as he lay there children came from Rome, and the Campagna, and were lifted up on a little pulpit in the basilica of Aracoeli, and they preached on the sweetness and tenderness and nobleness and power of the little Christchild.

But the Englishwoman lived in great terror that someone would discover that she had stolen the Christ image of Aracoeli. Therefore she confessed to no one that the image she had was the real one. "It is a copy," she said; "it is as like the real one as it can be, but it is only copied."

Now it happened that she had a little Italian servant girl. One day when the latter went through the room she stopped before the image and spoke to him. "You poor Christchild, who are no Christchild," she said, "if you only knew how the real child lies in his glory in the niche in Aracoeli and how Maria and San Guiseppe and the shepherds are kneeling before him! And if you knew how the children place themselves on a little pulpit just in front of him, and how they courtesy, and kiss their fingers to him, and preach for him as beautifully as they can!"

A few days after the little maid came again and spoke to the image. "You poor Christchild, who are no Christchild," she said, "do you know that today I have been up in Aracoeli and have seen how the true child was carried in the procession? They held a canopy over him, all the people fell on their knees, and they sang and played before him. Never will you see anything so wonderful!"

And mark that a few days later the little maid came again and spoke to the image: "Do you know, Christchild, who are not a real Christchild, that it is better for you to stand where you are standing? For the real child is called to the sick and is driven to them in his gold-laced carriage, but *he* cannot help them and they die in despair. And people begin to say that Aracoeli's holy child has lost his power to do good, and that prayers and tears do not move him. It is better for you to stand where you are standing than to be called upon and not to be able to help."

But the next night a miracle came to pass. About midnight a loud ringing was heard at the cloister gate at Aracoeli. And when the gate-keeper did not come quickly enough to open, someone began to knock. It sounded clear, like ringing metal, and it was heard through the whole monastery. All the monks leaped from their beds. All who had been tortured by terrible dreams rose at one time, and believed that Antichrist was come.

But when they opened the door — when they opened it! It was the little Christ image that stood on the threshold. It was his little hand that had pulled the bell-rope; it was his little, gold-shod foot that had been stretched out to kick the door.

The gatekeeper instantly took the holy child up in his arms. Then he saw that it had tears in its eyes. Alas, the poor, holy child had wandered through the town by night! What had it not seen? So much poverty and so much want; so much wickedness and so many crimes! It was terrible to think what it must have experienced.

The gatekeeper went immediately to the prior and showed him the image. And they wondered how it had come out into the night.

Then the prior had the church bells rung to call the monks to the service. And all the monks of Aracoeli marched into the great, dim basilica in order to place the image, with all solemnity, back in its shrine.

Worn and suffering, they walked and trembled in their heavy home-spun robes. Several of them were weeping, as if they had escaped from some terrible danger. "What would have happened to us," they said, "if our only consolation had been taken from us? Is it not Antichrist who has tempted out Rome's holy child from the sheltering sanctuary?"

But when they came to set the Christ image in the shrine of the chapel, they found there the false child; him who wore the inscription on his crown: "My kingdom is only of this world."

And when they examined the image more closely they found the inscription.

Then the prior turned to the monks and spoke to them: —

"Brothers, we will sing the 'Te Deum,' and cover the pillars of the church with silk, and light all the wax candles, and all the hanging lamps, and we will celebrate a great festival.

"As long as the monastery has stood it has been a home of terror and a cursed dwelling; but for the suffering of all those who have lived here, God has been gracious. And now all danger is over.

"God has crowned the fight with victory, and this that you have seen is the sign that Antichrist shall not be worshipped on the Capitol.

"For in order that the sibyl's words should be carried out, God has sent this false image of Christ that bears the words of Antichrist in its crown, and he has allowed us to worship and adore him as if he had been the great miracle-worker.

"But now we can rest in joy and peace, for the sibyl's mystic speech is fulfilled, and Antichrist has been worshipped here.

"Great is God, the Almighty, who has let our cruel fear be dispelled, and who has carried out His will without the world needing to gaze upon the false image made by man.

"Happy is the monastery of Aracoeli that rests under the protection of God, and does His will, and is blessed by His abounding grace."

When the prior had said those words he took the false image in his hands, went through the church, and opened the great door. Thence he walked out on the terrace. Below him lay the high and broad stairway with its hundred and nineteen marble steps that leads down from the

Capitol as if into an abyss. And he raised the image over his head and cried aloud: "Anathema Antikristo!" and hurled him from the summit of the Capitol down into the world.

# III

## ON THE BARRICADE

W hen the rich Englishwoman awoke in the morning she missed the image and wondered where she should look for him. She believed that no one but the monks of Aracoeli could have taken him, and she hurried towards the Capitol to spy and search.

She came to the great marble staircase that leads up to the basilica of Aracoeli. And her heart beat wildly with joy, for on the lowest step lay he whom she sought. She seized the image, threw her cloak about him, and hurried home. And she put him back on his place of honor.

But as she now sank into contemplation of his beauty, she found that the crown had been dented. She lifted it off the image to see how great the damage was, and at the same moment her eyes fell on the inscription that she herself had scratched: "My kingdom is only of this world."

Then she knew that this was the false Christ image, and that the right one had returned to Aracoeli.

She despaired of ever again getting it into her possession, and she decided to leave Rome the next day, for she would not remain there when she no longer had the image.

But when she left she took the forged image with her, because he reminded her of the one she loved, and he followed her afterwards on all her journeys.

She was never at rest and traveled continually, and in that way the image was carried about over the whole world.

And wherever the image came, the power of Christ seemed to be diminished without anyone rightly understanding why. For nothing could look more impotent than that poor image of elm wood, dressed out in brass rings and glass beads.

When the rich Englishwoman who had first owned the image was dead, he came as an inheritance to another rich Englishwoman, who also traveled continually, and from her to a third.

Once, and it was still in the time of the first Englishwoman, the image came to Paris.

As he passed through the great city there was an insurrection. Crowds rushed wildly screaming through the streets and cried for bread. They plundered the shops and threw stones at the houses of the rich. Troops were called out against them, and then they tore up the stones of the street, dragged together carriages and furniture, and built barricades.

As the rich Englishwoman came driving in her great traveling-carriage, the mass of people rushed towards it, forced her to leave it, and dragged the carriage up to one of the barricades.

When they tried to roll the carriage up among all the thousand things of which the barricade consisted, one of the big trunks fell to the ground. The cover sprang open, and among other things out rolled the rejected Christ image.

The people threw themselves upon him to plunder, but they soon saw that all his grandeur was imitation and quite worthless, and they began to laugh at him and mock him.

He went from hand to hand among the agitators, until one of them bent forward to look at his crown. His eyes were attracted by the words which stood scratched there: "My kingdom is only of this world."

The man called this out quite loudly, and they all screamed that the little image should be their badge. They carried him up to the summit of the barricade and placed him there like a banner.

Among those who defended the barricade was one man who was not a poor working-man, but a man of education, who had passed his whole life in study. He knew all the want that tortured mankind, and his heart was full of sympathy, so that he continually sought means to better their lot. For thirty years he had written and thought without finding any remedy. Now on hearing the alarm bell he had obeyed it and rushed into the streets.

He had seized a weapon and gone with the insurgents with the thought that the riddle which he had been unable to solve should now be made clear by violence and force, and that the poor should be able to fight their way to a better lot.

There he stood the whole day and fought; and people fell about him, blood splashed up into his face, and the misery of life seemed to him greater and more deplorable than ever before.

But whenever the smoke cleared away, the little image shone before his eyes; through all the tumult of the fight it stood unmoved high up on the barricade.

Every time he saw the image the words "My kingdom is only of this world" flashed through his brain. At last he thought that the words wrote themselves in the air and began to wave before his eyes, now in fire, now in blood, now in smoke.

He stood still. He stood there with gun in hand, but he had stopped fighting. Suddenly he knew that this was the word that he had sought after all his life. He knew what he would say to the people, and it was the poor image that had given him the solution.

He would go out into the whole world and proclaim: "Your kingdom is only of this world.

"Therefore you must care for this life and live like brothers. And you shall divide your property so that no one is rich and no one poor. You shall all work, and the earth shall be owned by all, and you shall all be equal.

"No one shall hunger, no one shall be tempted to luxury, and no one shall suffer want in his old age.

"And you must think of increasing everyone's happiness, for there is no compensation awaiting you. Your kingdom is only of this world."

All this passed through his brain while he stood on the barricade, and when the thought became clear to him, he laid down his weapon, and did not lift it again for strife and the shedding of blood.

A moment later the barricade was stormed and taken. The victorious troops dashed through and quelled the insurrection, and before night order and peace reigned in the great city.

The Englishwoman sent out her servants to look for her lost possessions, and they found many, if not all. What they found first of all on the captured barricade was the image ejected from Aracoeli.

But the man who had been taught during the fight by the image began to proclaim to the world a new doctrine, which is called Socialism, but which is an Antichristianity.

And it loves, and renounces, and teaches, and suffers like Christianity, so that it has every resemblance to the latter, just as the false image from Aracoeli has every resemblance to the real Christ image.

And like the false image it says: "My kingdom is only of this world."

And although the image that has spread abroad the teachings is unnoticed and unknown, the teachings are not; they go through the world to save and remodel it.

They are spreading from day to day. They go out through all countries, and bear many names, and they mislead because they promise earthly happiness and enjoyment to all, and win followers more than any doctrine that has gone through the world since the time of Christ.

# FIRST BOOK

*"There shall be great want"*

# I

## MONGIBELLO

*T*owards the end of the seventies there was in Palermo a poor boy whose name was Gaetano Alagona. That was lucky for him! If he had not been one of the old Alagonas people would have let him starve to death. He was only a child, and had neither money nor parents. The Jesuits of Santa Maria i Jesu had taken him out of charity into the cloister school.

One day, when studying his lesson, a father came and called him from the school-room, because a cousin wished to see him. What, a cousin! He had always heard that all his relatives were dead. But Father Josef insisted that it was a real Signora, who was his relative and wished to take him out of the monastery. It became worse and worse. Did she want to take him out of the monastery? That she could never do! He was going to be a monk.

He did not at all wish to see the Signora. Could not Father Josef tell her that Gaetano would never leave the monastery, and that it was of no avail to ask him? No, Father Josef said that he could not let her depart without seeing him, and he half dragged Gaetano into the reception-room. There she stood by one of the windows. She had grey hair; her skin was brown; her eyes were black and as round as beads. She had a lace veil on her head, and her black dress was smooth with wear, and a little green, like Father Josef's very oldest cassock.

She made the sign of the cross when she saw Gaetano. "God be praised, he is a true Alagona!" she said, and kissed his hand.

She said that she was sorry that Gaetano had reached his twelfth year without any of his family asking after him; but she had not known that there were any of the other branch alive. How had she found it out now? Well, Luca had read the name in a newspaper. It had stood among those who had got a prize. It was a half-year ago now, but it was a long journey to Palermo. She had had to save and save to get the money for the journey. She had not been able to come before. But she had to come and see him. *Santissima madre,* she had been so glad! It was she, Donna Elisa, who was an Alagona. Her husband, who was dead, had been an Antonelli. There was one other Alagona, that was her brother. He, too, lived at Diamante. But Gaetano probably did not know where Diamante was. The boy drew his head back. No, she thought as much, and she laughed.

"Diamante is on Monte Chiaro. Do you know where Monte Chiaro is?"

"No."

She drew up her eyebrows and looked very roguish.

"Monte Chiaro is on Etna, if you know where Etna is."

It sounded so anxious, as if it were too much to ask that Gaetano should know anything about Etna. And they laughed, all three, she and Father Josef and Gaetano.

She seemed a different person after she had made them laugh. "Will you come and see Diamante and Etna and Monte Chiaro?" she asked briskly. "Etna you must see. It is the greatest mountain in the world. Etna is a king, and the mountains round about kneel before him, and do not dare to lift their eyes to his face."

Then she told many tales about Etna. She thought perhaps that it would tempt him.

And it was really true that Gaetano had not thought before what kind of a mountain Etna was. He had not remembered that it had snow on its head, oak forests in its beard, vineyards about its waist, and that it stood in orange groves up to its knees. And down it ran broad, black rivers. Those streams were wonderful; they flowed without a ripple; they heaved without a wind; the poorest swimmer could cross them without a bridge. He guessed that she meant lava. And she was glad that he had guessed it. He was a clever boy. A real Alagona!

And Etna was so big! Fancy that it took three days to drive round it and three days to ride up to the top and down again! And that there were fifty towns beside Diamante on it, and fourteen great forests, and two hundred small peaks, which were not so small either, although Etna was so big that they seemed as insignificant as a swarm of flies on a church roof. And that there were caves which could hold a whole army, and hollow old trees, where a flock of sheep could find shelter from the storm!

Everything wonderful was to be found on Etna. There were rivers of which one must beware. The water in them was so cold that anyone who drank of it would die. There were rivers which flowed only by day, and others that flowed only in winter, and some which ran deep under the earth. There were hot springs, and sulfur springs, and mud-volcanoes.

It would be a pity for Gaetano not to see the mountain, for it was so beautiful. It stood against the sky like a great tent. It was as gaily colored as a merry-go-round. He ought to see it in the morning and evening, when it was red; he ought to see it at night, when it was white. He ought also to know that it truly could take every color; that it could be blue, black, brown or violet; sometimes it wore a veil of beauty, like a signora; sometimes it was a table covered with velvet; sometimes it had a tunic of gold brocade and a mantle of peacock's-feathers.

He would also like to know how it could be that old King Arthur was sitting there in a cave. Donna Elisa said that it was quite certain that he still lived on Etna, for once, when the bishop of Catania was riding over the mountain, three of his mules ran away, and the men who followed them found them in the cave with King Arthur. Then the king asked the guides to tell the bishop that when his wounds were healed he would come with his knights of the Round Table and right everything that was in disorder in Sicily. And he who had eyes to see knew well enough that King Arthur had not yet come out of his cave.

Gaetano did not wish to let her tempt him, but he thought that he might be a little friendly. She was still standing, but now he fetched her a chair. That would not make her think that he wanted to go with her.

He really liked to hear her tell about her mountain. It was so funny that it should have so many tricks. It was not at all like Monte Pellegrino, near Palermo, that only stood where it stood. Etna could smoke like a chimney and blow out fire like a gas jet. It could rumble, shake, vomit forth lava, throw stones, scatter ashes, foretell the weather, and collect rain. If Mongibello merely stirred, town after town fell, as if the houses had been cards set on end.

Mongibello, that was also a name for Etna. It was called Mongibello because that meant the mountain of mountains. It deserved to be called so.

Gaetano saw that she really believed that he would not be able to resist. She had so many wrinkles in her face, and when she laughed, they ran together like a net. He stood and looked at it; it seemed so strange. But he was not caught yet in the net.

She wondered if Gaetano really would have the courage to come to Etna. For inside the mountain were many bound giants and a black castle, which was guarded by a dog with many heads. There was also a big forge and a lame smith with only one eye in the middle of his forehead. And worst of all, in the very heart of the mountain, there was a sulfur sea which cooked like an oil kettle, and in it lay Lucifer and all the damned. No, he never would have the courage to come there, she said.

Otherwise there was no danger in living there, for the mountain feared the saints. Donna Elisa said that it feared many saints, but most Santa Agata of Catania. If the Catanians always were as they should be to her, then neither earthquake nor lava could do them any harm.

Gaetano stood quite close to her and he laughed at everything she said. How had he come there and why could he not stop laughing? It was a wonderful signora.

Suddenly he said, in order not to deceive her, "Donna Elisa, I am going to be a monk." — "Oh, are you?" she said. Then without anything more she began again to tell about the mountain.

She said that now he must really listen; now she was coming to the most important of all. He was to follow her to the south side of the mountain so far down that they were near the castle of Catania, and there he would see a valley, a quite big and wide oval valley. But it was quite black; the lava streams came from all directions flowing down into it. There were only stones there, not a blade of grass.

But what had Gaetano believed about the lava? Donna Elisa was sure that he believed that it lay as even and smooth on Etna as it lies in the streets. But on Etna there are so many surprises. Could he understand that all the serpents and dragons and witches that lay and boiled in the lava ran out with it when there was an eruption? There they lay and crawled and crept and twisted about each other, and tried to creep up to the cold earth, and held each other fast in misery until the lava hardened about them. And then they could never come free. No indeed!

The lava was not unproductive, as he thought. Although no grass grew, there was always something to see. But he could never guess what it was. It groped and fell; it tumbled and crept; it moved on its knees, on its head, and on its elbows. It came up the sides of the valley and down the sides of the valley; it was all thorns and knots; it had a cloak of spider's-web and a wig of dust, and as many joints as a worm. Could it be anything but the cactus? Did he know that the cactus goes out on the lava and breaks the ground like a peasant? Did he know that nothing but the cactus can do anything with the lava?

Now she looked at Father Josef and made a funny face. The cactus was the best goblin to be found on Etna; but goblins were goblins. The cactus was a Turk, for it kept female slaves. No sooner had the cactus taken root anywhere than it must have almond trees near it. Almond trees are fine and shining signoras. They hardly dare to go out on the black surface, but that does not help them. Out they must, and out they are. Oh, Gaetano should see if he came there. When the almond trees stand white with their blossoms in the spring on the black field among the grey cacti, they are so innocent and beautiful that one could weep over them as over captive princesses.

Now he must know where Monte Chiaro lay. It shot up from the bottom of that black valley. She tried to make her umbrella stand on the floor. It stood so. It stood right up. It had never thought of either sitting or lying. And Monte Chiaro was as green as the valley was black. It was palm next palm, vine upon vine. It was a gentleman in a flowery dressing gown. It was a king with a crown on his head. It bore the whole of Diamante about its temples.

Some time before Gaetano had a desire to take her hand. If he only could do it. Yes, he could. He drew her hand to him like a captured treasure. But what should he do with it? Perhaps pat it. If he tried quite gently with one finger, perhaps she would not notice it. Perhaps she would not notice if he took two fingers. Perhaps she would not even notice if he should kiss her hand. She talked and talked. She noticed nothing at all.

There was still so much she wished to say. And nothing so droll as her story about Diamante!

She said that the town had once lain down on the bottom of the valley. Then the lava came, and fiery red looked over the edge of the valley. What, what! was the last day come? The town in great haste took its houses on its back, on its head, and under its arms, and ran up Monte Chiaro, that lay close at hand.

Zigzagging up the mountain the town ran. When it was far enough up it threw down a town gate and a piece of town wall. Then it ran round the mountain in a spiral and dropped down houses. The poor people's houses tumbled as they could and would. There was no time for anything else. No one could ask anything better than crowding and disorder and crooked streets. No, that you could not. The chief street went in a spiral round the mountain, just as the town had run, and along it had set down here a church and there a palace. But there had been that much order that the best came highest up. When the town came to the top of the mountain it had laid out a square, and there it had placed the city hall and the Cathedral and the old palazzo Geraci.

If he, Gaetano Alagona, would follow her to Diamante, she would take him with her up to the square on the top of the mountain, and show him what stretches of land the old Alagonas had owned on Etna, and on the plain of Catania, and where they had raised their strongholds on the inland peaks. For up there all that could be seen, and even more. One could see the whole sea.

Gaetano had not thought that she had talked long, but Father Josef seemed to be impatient. "Now we have come to your own home, Donna Elisa," he said quite gently.

But she assured Father Josef that at her house there was nothing to see. What she first of all wished to show Gaetano was the big house on the corso, that was called the summer palace. It was not so beautiful as the palazzo Geraci, but it was big; and when the old Alagonas were prosperous they came there in summer to be nearer the snows of Etna. Yes, as she said, towards the street it was nothing to see, but it had a beautiful courtyard with open porticos in both the stories. And on the roof there was a terrace. It was paved with blue and white tiles, and on every tile the coat of arms of the Alagonas was burned in. He would like to come and see that?

It occurred to Gaetano that Donna Elisa must be used to having children come and sit on her knees when she was at home. Perhaps she would not notice if he should also come. And he tried. And so it was. She was used to it. She never noticed it at all.

She only went on talking about the palace. There was a great state suite, where the old Alagonas had danced and played. There was a great hall with a gallery for the music; there was old furniture and clocks like small white alabaster temples that stood on black ebony pedestals. In the state apartment no one lived, but she would go there with him. Perhaps he had thought that she lived in the summer palace. Oh, no; her brother, Don Ferrante, lived there. He was a merchant, and had his shop on the lower floor; and as he had not yet brought home a signora, everything stood up there as it had stood,

Gaetano wondered if he could sit on her knees any longer. It was wonderful that she did not notice anything. And it was fortunate, for otherwise she might have believed that he had changed his mind about being a monk.

But she was just now more than ever occupied with her own affairs. A little flush flamed up in her cheeks under all the brown, and she made a few of the funniest faces with her eyebrows. Then she began to tell how she herself lived.

It seemed as if Donna Elisa must have the very smallest house in the town. It lay opposite the summer palace, but that was its only good point. She had a little shop, where she sold medallions and wax candles and everything that had to do with divine service. But, with all respect to Father Josef, there was not much profit in such a trade nowadays, however it may have been formerly.

Behind the shop there was a little workshop. There her husband had stood and carved images of the saints and rosary beads; for he had been an artist, Signor Antonelli. And next to the workshop were a couple of small rat-holes; it was impossible to turn in them; one had to squat down, as in the cells of the old kings. And up one flight were a couple of small hen-coops. In one of them she had laid a little straw and put up a few hooks. That would be for Gaetano, if he would come to her.

Gaetano thought that he would like to pat her cheek. She would be sorry when he could not go with her. Perhaps he could permit himself to pat her. He looked under his hair at Father Josef. Father Josef sat and looked on the floor and sighed, as he was in the habit of doing. He did not think of Gaetano, and she, she noticed nothing at all.

She said that she had a maid, whose name was Pacifica, and a man, whose name was Luca. She did not get much help, however, for Pacifica was old; and, since she had grown deaf, she had become so irritable that she could not let her help in the shop. And Luca, who really was to have been a wood-carver, and carve saints that she could sell, never gave himself time to stand still in the workshop; he was always out in the garden, looking after the flowers. Yes, they had a little garden among the stones on Monte Chiaro. But he need not think it was worth anything. She had nothing like the one in the cloister, that Gaetano would understand. But she wanted so much to have him, because he was one of the old Alagonas. And there at home she and Luca and Pacifica had said to one another: "Do we ask whether we will have a little more care, if we can only get him here?" No, the Madonna knew that they had not done so. But now the question was, whether he was willing to endure anything to be with them.

And now she had finished, and Father Josef asked what Gaetano thought of answering. It was the prior's wish, Father Josef said, that Gaetano should decide for himself. And they had nothing against his going out into the world, because he was the last of his race.

Gaetano slid gently down from Donna Elisa's lap. But to answer! That was not such an easy thing to answer. It was very hard to say no to the signora.

Father Josef came to his assistance. "Ask the signora that you may be allowed to answer in a couple of hours, Gaetano. The boy has never thought of anything but being a monk," he explained to Donna Elisa.

She stood up, took her umbrella, and tried to look glad, but there were tears in her eyes.

Of course, of course he must consider it, she said. But if he had known Diamante he would not have needed to. Now only peasants lived there, but once there had been a bishop, and many priests, and a multitude of monks. They were gone now, but they were not forgotten. Ever since that time Diamante was a holy town. More festival days were celebrated there than anywhere else, and there were quantities of saints; and even today crowds of pilgrims came there. Whoever lived at Diamante could never forget God. He was almost half a priest. So for that reason he ought to come. But he should consider it, if he so wished. She would come again tomorrow.

Gaetano behaved himself very badly. He turned from her and rushed to the door. He did not say a word of thanks to her for coming. He knew that Father Josef had expected it, but he could not.

When he thought of the great Mongibello that he never would see, and of Donna Elisa, who would never come again, and of the school, and of the shut-in cloister garden, and of a whole restricted life! Father Josef never could expect so much of him; Gaetano had to run away.

It was high time too. When Gaetano was ten steps from the door, he began to cry. It was too bad about Donna Elisa. Oh, that she should be obliged to travel home alone! That Gaetano could not go with her!

He heard Father Josef coming, and he hid his face against the wall. If he could only stop sobbing!

Father Josef came sighing and murmuring to himself, as he always did. When he came up to Gaetano he stopped, and sighed more than ever.

"It is Mongibello, Mongibello," said Father Josef; "no one can resist Mongibello."

Gaetano answered him by weeping more violently.

"It is the mountain calling," murmured Father Josef. "Mongibello is like the whole earth; it has all the earth's beauty and charm and vegetation and expanses and wonders. The whole earth comes at once and calls him."

Gaetano felt that Father Josef spoke the truth. He felt as if the earth stretched out strong arms to catch him. He felt that he needed to bind himself fast to the wall in order not to be torn away.

"It is better for him to see the earth," said Father Josef. "He would only be longing for it if he stayed in the monastery. If he is allowed to see the earth perhaps he will begin again to long for heaven."

Gaetano did not understand what Father Josef meant when he felt himself lifted into his arms, carried back into the reception-room, and put down on Donna Elisa's knees.

"You shall take him, Donna Elisa, since you have won him," said Father Josef. "You shall show him Mongibello, and you shall see if you can keep him."

But when Gaetano once more sat on Donna Elisa's lap he felt such happiness that it was impossible for him to run away from her again.

He was as much captured as if he had gone into Mongibello and the mountain walls had closed in on him.

# II

## FRA GAETANO

Gaetano had lived with Donna Elisa a month, and had been as happy as a child can be. Merely to travel with Donna Elisa had been like driving behind gazelles and birds of paradise; but to live with her was to be carried on a golden litter, screened from the sun.

Then the famous Franciscan, Father Gondo, came to Diamante, and Donna Elisa and Gaetano went up to the square to listen to him. For Father Gondo never preached in a church; he always gathered the people about him by fountains or at the town gates.

The square was swarming with people; but Gaetano, who sat on the railing of the court-house steps, plainly saw Father Gondo where he stood on the curb-stone. He wondered if it could be true that the monk wore a horse-hair shirt under his robes, and that the rope that he had about his waist was full of knots and iron points to serve him as a scourge.

Gaetano could not understand what Father Gondo said, but one shiver after another ran through him at the thought that he was looking at a saint.

When the Father had spoken for about an hour, he made a sign with his hand that he would like to rest a moment. He stepped down from the steps of the fountain, sat down, and rested his face in his hands. While the monk was sitting so, Gaetano heard a gentle roaring. He had never before heard any like it. He looked about him to discover what it was. And it was all the people talking. "Blessed, blessed, blessed!" they all said at once. Most of them only whispered and murmured; none called aloud, their devotion was too great. And everyone had found the same word. "Blessed, blessed!" sounded over the whole marketplace. "Blessings on thy lips; blessings on thy tongue; blessings on thy heart!"

The voices sounded soft, choked by weeping and emotion, but it was as if a storm had passed by through the air. It was like the murmuring of a thousand shells.

That took much greater hold of Gaetano than the monk's sermon. He did not know what he wished to do, for that gentle murmuring filled him with emotion; it seemed almost to suffocate him. He climbed up on the iron railing, raised himself above all the others, and began to cry the same as they, but much louder, so that his voice cut through all the others.

Donna Elisa heard it and seemed to be displeased. She drew Gaetano down and would not stay any longer, but went home with him.

In the middle of the night Gaetano started up from his bed. He put on his clothes, tied together what he possessed in a bundle, set his hat on his head and took his shoes under his arm. He was going to run away. He could not bear to live with Donna Elisa.

Since he had heard Father Gondo, Diamante and Mongibello were nothing to him. Nothing was anything compared to being like Father Gondo, and being blessed by the people. Gaetano could not live if he could not sit by the fountain in the square and tell legends.

But if Gaetano went on living in Donna Elisa's garden, and eating peaches and mandarins, he would never hear the great human sea roar about him. He must go out and be a hermit on Etna; he must dwell in one of the big caves, and live on roots and fruits. He would never see a human being; he would never cut his hair; and he would wear nothing but a few dirty rags. But in ten or twenty years he would come back to the world. Then he would look like a beast and speak like an angel.

That would be another matter than wearing velvet clothes and a glazed hat, as he did now. That would be different from sitting in the shop with Donna Elisa and taking saint after saint down from the shelf and hearing her tell about what they had done. Several times he had taken a knife and a piece of wood and had tried to carve images of the saints. It was very hard, but it would be worse to make himself into a saint; much worse. However, he was not afraid of difficulties and privations.

He crept out of his room, across the attic and down the stair. It only remained to go through the shop out to the street, but on the last step he stopped. A faint light filtered through a crack in the door to the left of the stairs.

It was the door to Donna Elisa's room, and Gaetano did not dare to go any further, since his foster mother had her candle lighted. If she was not asleep she would hear him when he drew the heavy bolts on the shop door. He sat softly down on the stairs to wait.

Suddenly he happened to think that Donna Elisa must sit up so long at night and work in order to get him food and clothes. He was much touched that she loved him so much as to want to do it. And he understood what a grief it would be to her if he should go.

When he thought of that he began to weep.

But at the same time he began to upbraid Donna Elisa in his thoughts. How could she be so stupid as to grieve because he went. It would be such a joy for her when he should become a holy man. That would be her reward for having gone to Palermo and fetched him.

He cried more and more violently while he was consoling Donna Elisa. It was hard that she did not understand what a reward she would receive.

There was no need for her to be sad. For ten years only would Gaetano live on the mountain, and then he would come back as the famous hermit Fra Gaetano. Then he would come walking through the streets of Diamante, followed by a great crowd of people, like Father Gondo. And there would be flags, and the houses would be decorated with cloths and wreaths. He would stop in front of Donna Elisa's shop, and Donna Elisa would not recognize him and would be ready to fall on her knees before him. But so should it not be; he would kneel to Donna Elisa, and ask her forgiveness, because he had run away from her ten years ago. "Gaetano," Donna Elisa would then answer, "you give me an ocean of joy against a little brook of sorrow. Should I not forgive you?"

Gaetano saw all this before him, and it was so beautiful that he began to weep more violently. He was only afraid that Donna Elisa would hear how he was sobbing and come out and find him. And then she would not let him go.

He must talk sensibly with her. Would he ever give her greater pleasure than if he went now?

It was not only Donna Elisa, there was also Luca and Pacifica, who would be so glad when he came back as a holy man.

They would all follow him up to the marketplace. There, there would be even more flags than in the streets, and Gaetano would speak from the steps of the town hall. And from all the streets and courts people would come streaming.

Then Gaetano would speak, so that they should all fall on their knees and cry: "Bless us, Fra Gaetano, bless us!"

After that he would never leave Diamante again. He would live under the great steps outside Donna Elisa's shop.

And they would come to him with their sick, and those in trouble would make a pilgrimage to him.

When the syndic of Diamante went by he would kiss Gaetano's hand.

Donna Elisa would sell Fra Gaetano's image in her shop.

And Donna Elisa's god-daughter, Giannita, would bow before Fra Gaetano and never again call him a stupid monk-boy.

And Donna Elisa would be so happy.

*A*h. . . Gaetano started up, and awoke. It was bright daylight, and Donna Elisa and Pacifica stood and looked at him. And Gaetano sat on the stairs with his shoes under his arm, his hat on his head and his bundle at his feet. But Donna Elisa and Pacifica wept. "He has wished to run away from us," they said.

"Why are you sitting here, Gaetano?"

"Donna Elisa, I wanted to run away." Gaetano was in a good mood, and answered as boldly as if it had been the most natural thing in the world.

"Do you want to run away?" repeated Donna Elisa.

"I wished to go off on Etna and be a hermit."

"And why are you sitting here now?"

"I do not know, Donna Elisa; I must have fallen asleep."

Donna Elisa now showed how distressed she was. She pressed her hands over her heart, as if she had terrible pains, and she wept passionately.

"But now I shall stay, Donna Elisa," said Gaetano.

"You, stay!" cried Donna Elisa. "You might as well go. Look at him, Pacifica, look at the ingrate! He is no Alagona. He is an adventurer."

The blood rose in Gaetano's face and he sprang to his feet and struck out with his hands in a way which astonished Donna Elisa. So had all the men of her race done. It was her father and her grandfather; she recognized all the powerful lords of the family of Alagona.

"You speak so because you know nothing about it, Donna Elisa," said the boy. "No, no, you do not know anything; you do not know why I had to serve God. But you shall know it now. Do you see, it was long ago. My father and mother were so poor, and we had nothing to eat; and so father went to look for work, and he never came back, and mother and we children were almost dead of starvation. So mother said: 'We will go and look for your father.' And we went. Night came and a heavy rain, and in one place a river flowed over the road. Mother asked in one house if we might pass the night there. No, they showed us out. Mother and children stood in the road and cried. Then mother tucked up her dress and went down into the stream that roared over the road. She had my little sister on her arm and my big sister by the hand and a big bundle on her head. I went after as near as I could. I saw mother lose her footing. The bundle she carried on her head fell into the stream, and mother caught at it and dropped little sister. She snatched at little sister and big sister was whirled away. Mother threw herself after them, and the river took her too. I was frightened and ran to the shore. Father Josef has told me that I escaped because I was to serve God for the dead, and pray for them. And that was why it was first decided that I was to be a monk, and why I now wish to go away on Etna and become a hermit. There is nothing else for me but to serve God, Donna Elisa."

Donna Elisa was quite subdued. "Yes, yes, Gaetano," she said, "but it hurts me so. I do not want you to go away from me."

"No, I shall not go either," said Gaetano. He was in such a good mood that he felt a desire to laugh. "I shall not go."

"Shall I speak to the priest, so that you may be sent to a seminary?" asked Donna Elisa, humbly.

"No; but you do not understand, Donna Elisa; you do not understand. I tell you that I will not go away from you. I have thought of something else."

"What have you thought of?" she asked sadly.

"What do you suppose I was doing while I sat there on the stairs? I was dreaming, Donna Elisa. I dreamed that I was going to run away. Yes, Donna Elisa, I stood in the shop, and I was going to open the shop door, but I could not because there were so many locks. I stood in the dark and unlocked lock after lock, and always there were new ones. I made a terrible noise, and I thought: 'Now surely Donna Elisa will come.' At last the door opened, and I was going to rush out; but just then I felt your hand on my neck, and you drew me in, and I kicked, and I struck you because I was not allowed to go. But, Donna Elisa, you had a candle with you, and then I saw that it was not you, but my mother. Then I did not dare to struggle anymore, and I was very frightened, for mother is dead. But mother took the bundle I was carrying and began to take out what was in it. Mother laughed and looked so glad, and I grew glad that she was not angry with me. It was so strange. What she drew out of the bundle was all the little saints' images that I had carved while I sat with you in the shop, and they were so pretty. 'Can you carve such pretty images, Gaetano?' said mother. 'Yes,' I answered. 'Then you can serve God by it,' said mother. 'Do I not need to leave Donna Elisa, then?' 'No,' said mother. And just as mother said that, you waked me."

Gaetano looked at Donna Elisa in triumph.

"What did mother mean by that?"

Donna Elisa only wondered.

Gaetano threw his head back and laughed.

"Mother meant that you should apprentice me, so that I could serve God by carving beautiful images of angels and saints, Donna Elisa."

# III

## THE GOD-SISTER

*I*n the noble island of Sicily, where there are more old customs left than in any other place in the south, it is always the habit of everyone while yet a child to choose a god-brother or god-sister, who shall carry his or her children to be christened, if there ever are any.

But this is not by any means the only use god-brothers and sisters have of one another. God-brothers and sisters must love one another, serve one another, and revenge one another. In a god-brother's ear a man can bury his secrets. He can trust him with both money and sweetheart, and not be deceived. God-brothers and sisters are as faithful to each other as if they were born of the same mother, because their covenant is made before San Giovanni Battista, who is the most feared of all the saints.

It is also the custom for the poor to take their half-grown children to rich people and ask that they may be god-brothers and sisters to their young sons and daughters. What a glad sight it is on the holy Baptist's day to see all those little children in festival array wandering through the great towns looking for a god-brother or sister! If the parents succeed in giving their son a rich god-brother, they are as glad as if they were able to leave him a farm as an inheritance.

When Gaetano first came to Diamante, there was a little girl who was always coming in and out of Donna Elisa's shop. She had a red cloak and pointed cap and eight heavy, black curls that stood out under the cap. Her name was Giannita, and she was daughter of Donna Olivia, who sold vegetables. But Donna Elisa was her god-mother, and therefore thought what she could do for her.

Well, when midsummer day came, Donna Elisa ordered a carriage and drove down to Catania, which lies full twenty miles from Diamante. She had Giannita with her, and they were both dressed in their best. Donna Elisa was dressed in black silk with jet, and Giannita had a white tulle dress with garlands of flowers. In her hand Giannita held a basket of flowers, and among the flowers lay a pomegranate.

The journey went well for Donna Elisa and Giannita. When at last they reached the white Catania, that lies and shines on the black lava background, they drove up to the finest palace in the town.

It was lofty and wide, so that the poor little Giannita felt quite terrified at the thought of going into it. But Donna Elisa walked bravely in, and she was taken to Cavaliere Palmeri and his wife who owned the house.

Donna Elisa reminded Signora Palmeri that they were friends from infancy, and asked that Giannita might be her young daughter's god-sister.

That was agreed upon, and the young signorina was called in. She was a little marvel of rose-colored silk, Venetian lace, big, black eyes, and thick, bushy hair. Her little body was so small and thin that one hardly noticed it.

Giannita offered her the basket of flowers, and she graciously accepted it. She looked long and thoughtfully at Giannita, walked round her, and was fascinated by her smooth, even curls. When she had seen them, she ran after a knife, cut the pomegranate and gave Giannita half.

While they ate the fruit, they held each other's hand and both said: —

"Sister, sister, sister mine!
  Thou art mine, and I am thine,
  Thine my house, my bread and wine,
  Thine my joys, my sacrifice,
  Thine my place in Paradise."

Then they kissed each other and called each other god-sister.

"You must never fail me, god-sister," said the little signorina, and both the children were very serious and moved.

They had become such good friends in the short time that they cried when they parted.

But then twelve years went by and the two god-sisters lived each in her own world and never met. During the whole time Giannita was quietly in her home and never came to Catania.

But then something really strange happened. Giannita sat one afternoon in the room back of the shop embroidering. She was very skillful and was often overwhelmed with work. But it is trying to the eyes to embroider, and it was dark in Giannita's room. She had therefore half-opened the door into the shop to get a little more light.

Just after the clock had struck four, the old miller's widow, Rosa Alfari, came walking by. Donna Olivia's shop was very attractive from the street. The eyes fell through the half-open door on at baskets with fresh vegetables and bright-colored fruits, and far back in the background the outline of Giannita's pretty head. Rosa Alfari stopped and began to talk to Donna Olivia, simply, because her shop looked so friendly.

Laments and complaints always followed old Rosa Alfari. Now she was sad because she had to go to Catania alone that night. "It is a misfortune that the post-wagon does not reach Diamante before ten," she said. "I shall fall asleep on the way, and perhaps they will then steal my money. And what shall I do when I come to Catania at two o'clock at night?"

Then Giannita suddenly called out into the shop. "Will you take me with you to Catania, Donna Alfari?" she asked, half in joke, without expecting an answer.

But Rosa Alfari said eagerly, "Lord, child, will you go with me? Will you really?"

Giannita came out into the shop, red with pleasure. "If I will!" she said. "I have not been in Catania for twelve years."

Rosa Alfari looked delightedly at her; Giannita was tall and strong, her eyes gay, and she had a careless smile on her lips. She was a splendid traveling companion.

"Get ready," said the old woman. "You will go with me at ten o'clock; it is settled."

The next day Giannita wandered about the streets of Catania. She was thinking the whole time of her god-sister. She was strangely moved to be so near her again. She loved her god-sister, Giannita, and she did it not only because San Giovanni has commanded people to love their god-brothers and sisters. She had adored the little child in the silk dress; she was the most beautiful thing she had ever seen. She had almost become her idol.

She knew this much about her sister, that she was still unmarried and lived in Catania. Her mother was dead, and she had not been willing to leave her father, and had stayed as hostess in his house. "I must manage to see her," thought Giannita.

Whenever Giannita met a well-appointed carriage she thought: "Perhaps it is my god-sister driving there." And she stared at everybody to see if any of them was like the little girl with the thick hair and the big eyes.

Her heart began to beat wildly. She had always longed for her god-sister. She herself was still unmarried, because she liked a young wood-carver, Gaetano Alagona, and he had never shown the slightest desire to marry her. Giannita had often been angry with him for that, and not least had it irritated her never to be able to invite her god-sister to her wedding.

She had been so proud of her, too. She had thought herself finer than the others, because she had such a god-sister. What if she should now go to see her, since she was in the town? It would give a luster to the whole journey.

As she thought and thought of it, a newspaper-boy came running. *"Giornale da Sicilia,"* he called. "The Palmeri affair! Great embezzlements!"

Giannita seized the boy by the neck as he rushed by. "What are you saying?" she screamed. "You lie, you lie!" and she was ready to strike him.

"Buy my paper, signora, before you strike me," said the boy. Giannita bought the paper and began to read. She found in it without difficulty the Palmeri affair.

"Since this case is to be tried today in the courts," wrote the paper, "we will give an account of it."

Giannita read and read. She read it over and over before she understood. There was not a muscle in her body which did not begin to tremble with horror when she at last comprehended it.

Her god-sister's father, who had owned great vineyards, had been ruined, because the blight had laid them waste. And that was not the worst. He had also dissipated a charitable fund which had been entrusted to him. He was arrested, and today he was to be tried.

Giannita crushed the newspaper together, threw it into the street and trampled on it. It deserved no better for bringing such news.

Then she stood quite crushed that this should meet her when she came to Catania for the first time in twelve years. "Lord God," she said, "is there any meaning in it?"

At home, in Diamante, no one would ever have taken the trouble to tell her what was going on. Was it not destiny that she should be here on the very day of the trial?

"Listen, Donna Alfari," she said; "you may do as you like, but I must go to the court."

There was a decision about Giannita. Nothing could disturb her. "Do you not understand that it is for this, and not for your sake, that God has induced you to take me with you to Catania?" she said to Rosa Alfari.

Giannita did not doubt for a moment that there was something supernatural in it all.

Rosa Alfari must needs let her go, and she found her way to the Palace of Justice. She stood among the street boys and riff-raff, and saw Cavaliere Palmeri on the bench of the accused. He was a fine gentleman, with a white, pointed beard and moustache. Giannita recognized him.

She heard that he was condemned to six months' imprisonment, and Giannita thought she saw even more plainly that she had come there as an emissary from God. "Now my god-sister must need me," she thought.

She went out into the street again and asked her way to the Palazzo Palmeri.

On the way a carriage drove by her. She looked up, and her eyes met those of the lady who sat in the carriage. At the same moment something told her that this was her god-sister. She who was driving was pale and bent and had beseeching eyes. Giannita loved her from the first sight. "It is you who have given me pleasure many times," she said, "because I expected pleasure from you. Now perhaps I can pay you back."

Giannita felt filled with devotion when she went up the high, white marble steps to the Palazzo Palmeri, but suddenly a doubt struck her. "What can God wish me to do for one who has grown up in such magnificence?" she thought. "Does our Lord forget that I am only poor Giannita from Diamante?"

She told a servant to greet Signorina Palmeri and say to her that her god-sister wished to speak to her. She was surprised when the servant came back and said that she could not be received that day. Should she be content with that? Oh, no; oh, no!

"Tell the signorina that I am going to wait here the whole day, for I must speak to her."

"The signorina is going to move out of the palace in half an hour," said the servant.

Giannita was beside herself. "But I am her god-sister, her god-sister, do you not understand?" she said to the man. "I must speak to her." The servant smiled, but did not move.

But Giannita would not be turned away. Was she not sent by God? He must understand, understand, she said, and raised her voice. She was from Diamante and had not been in Catania for twelve years. Until yesterday afternoon at four o'clock she had not thought of coming here. He must understand, not until yesterday afternoon at four o'clock.

The servant stood motionless. Giannita was ready to tell him the whole story to move him, when the door was thrown open. Her god-sister stood on the threshold.

"Who is speaking of yesterday at four o'clock?" she said.

"It is a stranger, Signorina Micaela."

Then Giannita rushed forward. It was not at all a stranger. It was her god-sister from Diamante, who came here twelve years ago with Donna Elisa. Did she not remember her? Did she not remember that they had divided a pomegranate?

The signorina did not listen to that. "What was it that happened yesterday at four o'clock?" she asked, with great anxiety.

"I then got God's command to go to you, god-sister," said Giannita.

The other looked at her in terror. "Come with me," she said, as if afraid that the servant should hear what Giannita wished to say to her.

She went far into the apartment before she stopped. Then she turned so quickly towards Giannita that she was frightened. "Tell me instantly!" she said. "Do not torture me; let me hear it instantly!"

She was as tall as Giannita, but very unlike her. She was more delicately made, and she, the woman of the world, had a much more wild and untamed appearance than the country girl. Everything she felt showed in her face. She did not try to conceal it.

Giannita was so astonished at her violence that she could not answer at first.

Then her god-sister lifted her arms in despair over her head and the words streamed from her lips. She said that she knew that Giannita had been commanded by God to bring her word of new misfortunes. God hated her, she knew it.

Giannita clasped her hands. God hate her! on the contrary, on the contrary!

"Yes, yes," said Signorina Palmeri. "It is so." And as she was inwardly afraid of the message Giannita had for her, she began to talk. She did not let her speak; she interrupted her constantly. She seemed to be so terrified by everything that had happened to her during the last days that she could not at all control herself.

Giannita must understand that God hated her, she said. She had done something so terrible. She had forsaken her father, failed her father. Giannita must have read the last account. Then she burst out again in passionate questionings. Why did she not tell her what she wished to tell her? She did not expect anything but bad news. She was prepared.

But poor Giannita never got a chance to speak; as soon as she began, the signorina became frightened and interrupted her. She told her story as if to induce Giannita not to be too hard to her.

Giannita must not think that her unhappiness only came from the fact of her no longer having her carriage, or a box at the theater, or beautiful dresses, or servants, or even a roof over her head. Neither was it enough that she had now lost all her friends, so that she did not at all know where she should ask for shelter. Neither was it misfortune enough that she felt such shame that she could not raise her eyes to anyone's face.

But there was something else much worse.

She sat down, and was silent a moment, while she rocked to and fro in agony. But when Giannita began to speak, she interrupted her.

Giannita could not think how her father had loved her. He had always had her live in splendor and magnificence, like a princess.

She had not done much for him; only let him think out delightful things to amuse her. It had been no sacrifice to remain unmarried, for she had never loved anyone like her father, and her own home had been finer than anyone else's.

But one day her father had come and said to her, "They wish to arrest me. They are spreading the report that I have stolen, but it is not true." Then she had believed him, and helped him to hide from the *Carabinieri*. And they had looked for him in vain in Catania, on Etna, over the whole of Sicily.

But when the police could not find Cavaliere Palmeri, the people began to say: "He is a fine gentleman, and they are fine gentlemen who help him; otherwise they would have found him long ago." And the prefect in Catania had come to her. She received him smiling, and the prefect came as if to talk of roses, and the beautiful weather. Then he said: "Will the signorina look at this little paper? Will the signorina read this little letter? Will the signorina observe this little signature?" She read and read. And what did she see? Her father was not innocent. Her father had taken the money of others.

When the prefect had left her, she had gone to her father. "You are guilty," she said to him. "You may do what you will, but I cannot help you anymore." Oh, she had not known what she said! She had always been very proud. She had not been able to bear to have their name stamped with dishonor. She had wished for a moment that her father had been dead, rather than that this had happened to her. Perhaps she had also said it to him. She did not rightly know what she had said.

But after that God had forsaken her. The most terrible things had happened. Her father had taken her at her word. He had gone and given himself up. And ever since he had been in prison he had not been willing to see her. He did not answer her letters, and the food that she sent him he sent back untouched. That was the most dreadful thing of all. He seemed to think that she wished to kill him.

She looked at Giannita as anxiously as if she awaited her sentence of death.

"Why do you not say to me what you have to say?" she exclaimed. "You are killing me!"

But it was impossible for her to force herself to be silent.

"You must know," she continued, "that this palace is sold, and the purchaser has let it to an English lady, who is to move in today. *Some* of her things were brought in already yesterday, and among them was a little image of Christ.

"I caught sight of it as I passed through the vestibule, Giannita. They had taken it out of a trunk, and it lay there on the floor. It had been so neglected that no one took any trouble about it. Its crown was dented, and its dress dirty, and all the small ornaments which adorned it were rusty and broken. But when I saw it lying on the floor, I took it up and carried it into the room and placed it on a table. And while I did so, it occurred to me that I would ask its help. I knelt down before it and prayed a long time. 'Help me in my great need!' I said to the Christchild.

"While I prayed, it seemed to me that the image wished to answer me. I lifted my head, and the child stood there as dull as before, but a clock began to strike just then. It struck four, and it was as if it had said four words. It was as if the Christchild had answered a fourfold *yes* to my prayer.

"That gave me courage, Giannita, so that today I drove to the Palace of Justice to see my father. But he never turned his eyes toward me during the whole time he stood before his judges.

"I waited until they were about to lead him away, and threw myself on my knees before him in one of the narrow passages. Giannita, he let the soldiers lead me away without giving me a word.

"So, you see, God hates me. When I heard you speak of yesterday afternoon at four o'clock, I was so frightened. The Christchild sends me a new misfortune, I thought. It hates me for having failed my father."

When she had said that, she was at last silent and listened breathlessly for what Giannita should say.

And Giannita told her story to her.

"See, see, is it not wonderful?" she said at the end. "I have not been in Catania for twelve years, and then I come here quite unexpectedly. And I know nothing at all; but as soon as I set my foot on the street here, I hear your misfortune. God has sent a message to me, I said to myself. He has called me here to help my god-sister."

Signorina Palmeri's eyes were turned anxiously questioning towards her. Now the new blow was coming. She gathered all her courage to meet it.

"What do you wish me to do for you, god-sister?" said Giannita. "Do you know what I thought as I was walking through the streets? I will ask her if she will go with me to Diamante, I thought. I know an old house there, where we could live cheaply. And I would embroider and sew, so that we could support ourselves. When I was out in the street I thought that it might be, but now I understand that it is impossible, impossible. You require something more of life; but tell me if I can do anything for you. You shall not thrust me away, for God has sent me."

The signorina bent towards Giannita. "Well?" she said anxiously.

"You shall let me do what I can for you, for I love you," said Giannita, and fell on her knees and put her arms about her.

"Have you nothing else to say?" asked the signorina.

"I wish I had," said Giannita, "but I am only a poor girl."

It was wonderful to see how the features of the young signorina's face softened; how her color came back and how her eyes began to shine. Now it was plain that she had great beauty.

"Giannita," she said, low and scarcely audibly, "do you think that it is a miracle? Do you think that God can let a miracle come to pass for my sake?"

"Yes, yes," whispered Giannita back.

"I prayed the Christchild that he should help me, and he sends you to me. Do you think that it was the Christchild who sent you, Giannita?"

"Yes, it was; it was!"

Then God has not forsaken me, Giannita?"

"No, God has not forsaken you."

The god-sisters sat and wept for a while. It was quite quiet in the room. "When you came, Giannita, I thought that nothing was left me but to kill myself," she said at last. "I did not know where to turn, and God hated me."

"But tell me now what I can do for you, god-sister," said Giannita.

As an answer the other drew her to her and kissed her.

"But it is enough that you are sent by the little Christchild," she said. "It is enough that I know that God has not forsaken me."

# IV

## DIAMANTE

$M$icaela Palmeri was on her way to Diamante with Giannita.

They had taken their places in the post-carriage at three o'clock in the morning, and had driven up the beautiful road over the lower slopes of Etna, circling round the mountain. But it had been quite dark. They had not seen anything of the surrounding country.

The young signorina by no means lamented over that. She sat with closed eyes and buried herself in her sorrow. Even when it began to grow light, she would not lift her eyes to look out. It was not until they were quite near Diamante that Giannita could persuade her to look at the landscape.

"Look! Here is Diamante; this is to be your home," she said.

Then Micaela Palmeri, to the right of the road, saw mighty Etna, that cut off a great piece of the sky. Behind the mountain the sun was rising, and when the upper edge of the sun's disc appeared above the line of the mountain, it looked as if the white summit began to burn and send out sparks and rays.

Giannita entreated her to look at the other side.

And on the other side she saw the whole jagged mountain chain, which surrounds Etna like a towered wall, glowing red in the sunrise.

But Giannita pointed in another direction. It was not that she was to look at, not that.

Then she lowered her eyes and looked down into the black valley. There the ground shone like velvet, and the white Simeto foamed along in the depths of the valley.

But still she did not turn her eyes in the right direction.

At last she saw the steep Monte Chiaro rising out of the black, velvet-lined valley, red in the morning light and encircled by a crown of shady palms. On its summit she saw a town flanked with towers, and encompassed by a wall, and with all its windows and weather-vanes glittering in the light.

At that sight she seized Giannita's arm and asked her if it was a real town, and if people lived there.

She believed that it was one of heaven's cities, and that it would disappear like a vision. She was certain that no mortal had ever passed up the path that from the edge of the valley went in great curves over to Monte Chiaro and then zigzagged up the mountain, disappearing through the dark gates of the town.

But when she came nearer to Diamante, and saw that it was of the earth, and real, tears rose to her eyes. It moved her that the earth still held all this beauty for her. She had believed that, since it had been the scene of all her misfortunes, she would always find it grey and withered and covered with thistles and poisonous growths.

She entered poor Diamante with clasped hands, as if it were a sanctuary. And it seemed to her as if this town could offer her as much happiness as beauty.

# V

## DON FERRANTE

*A* few days later Gaetano was standing in his workshop, cutting grape-leaves on rosary beads. It was Sunday, but Gaetano did not feel it on his conscience that he was working, for it was a work in God's honor.

A great restlessness and anxiety had come over him. It had come into his mind that the time he had been living at peace with Donna Elisa was now drawing to a close, and he thought that he must soon start out into the world.

For great poverty had come to Sicily, and he saw want wandering from town to town and from house to house like the plague, and it had come to Diamante also.

No one ever came now to Donna Elisa's shop to buy anything. The little images of the saints that Gaetano made stood in close rows on the shelves, and the rosaries hung in great bunches under the counter. And Donna Elisa was in great want and sorrow, because she could not earn anything.

That was a sign to Gaetano that he must leave Diamante, go out into the world, emigrate if there was no other way. For it could not be working to the honor of God to carve images that never were worshipped, and to turn rosary beads that never glided through a petitioner's fingers.

It seemed to him that, somewhere in the world, there must be a beautiful, newly built cathedral, with finished walls, but whose interior yet stood shivering in nakedness. It awaited Gaetano's coming to carve the choir chairs, the altar-rail, the pulpit, the lectern, and the shrine. His heart ached with longing for that work which was waiting.

But there was no such cathedral in Sicily, for there no one ever thought of building a new church; it must be far away in such lands as Florida or Argentina, where the earth is not yet overcrowded with holy buildings.

He felt at the same time trembling and happy, and had begun to work with redoubled zeal in order that Donna Elisa should have something to sell while he was away earning great fortunes for her.

Now he was waiting for but one more sign from God before he decided on the journey. And this was that he should have the strength to speak to Donna Elisa of his longing to go. For he knew that it would cause her such sorrow that he did not know how he could bring himself to speak of it.

While he stood and thought Donna Elisa came into the workshop. Then he said to himself that this day he could not think of saying it to her, for today Donna Elisa was happy. Her tongue wagged and her face beamed.

Gaetano asked himself when he had seen her so. Ever since the famine had come, it had been as if they had lived without light in one of the caves of Etna.

Why had Gaetano not been with her in the square and heard the music? asked Donna Elisa. Why did he never come to hear and see her brother, Don Ferrante? Gaetano, who only saw him when he stood in the shop with his tufts of hair and his short jacket, did not know what kind of a man he was. He considered him an ugly old tradesman, who had a wrinkled face and a rough beard. No one knew Don Ferrante who had not seen him on Sunday, when he conducted the music.

That day he had donned a new uniform. He wore a three-cornered hat with green, red, and white feathers, silver on his collar, silver-fringed epaulets, silver braid on his breast, and a sword at his side. And when he stepped up to the conductor's platform the wrinkles had been smoothed out of his face and his figure had grown erect. He could almost have been called handsome.

When he had led *Cavalleria,* people had hardly been able to breathe. What had Gaetano to say to that, that the big houses round the marketplace had sung too? From the black Palazzo Geraci, Donna Elisa had distinctly heard a love song, and from the convent, empty as it was, a beautiful hymn had streamed out over the marketplace.

And when there was a pause in the music the handsome advocate Favara, who had been dressed in a black velvet coat and a big broad-brimmed hat and a bright red necktie, had gone up to Don Ferrante, and had pointed out over the open side of the square, where Etna and the sea lay. "Don Ferrante," he had said, "you lift us toward the skies, just as Etna does, and you carry us away into the eternal, like the infinite sea."

If Gaetano had seen Don Ferrante today he would have loved him. At least he would have been obliged to acknowledge his stateliness. When he laid down his baton for a while and took the advocate's arm, and walked forward and back with him on the flat stones by the Roman gate and the Palazzo Geraci, everyone could see that he could well measure himself against the handsome Favara.

Donna Elisa sat on the stone bench by the cathedral, in company with the wife of the syndic. And Signora Voltaro had said quite suddenly, after sitting for a while, watching Don Ferrante: "Donna Elisa, your brother is still a young man. He may still be married, in spite of his fifty years."

And she, Donna Elisa, had answered that she prayed heaven for it every day.

But she had hardly said it, when a lady dressed in mourning came into the square. Never had anything so black been seen before. It was not enough that dress and hat and gloves were black; her veil was so thick that it was impossible to believe that there was a face behind it. Santissimo Dio! it looked as if she had hung a pall over herself. And she had walked slowly, and with a stoop. People had almost feared, believing that it was a ghost.

Alas, alas! the whole marketplace had been so full of gayety! The peasants, who were at home over Sunday, had stood there in great crowds in holiday dress, with red shawls wound round their necks. The peasant women on their way to the cathedral had glided by, dressed in green skirts and yellow neckerchiefs. A couple of travelers had stood by the balustrade and looked at Etna; they had been dressed in white. And all the musicians in uniform, who had been almost as fine as Don Ferrante, and the shining instruments, and the carved cathedral façade! And the sunlight, and Mongibello's snow top — so near today that one could almost touch it — had all been so gay.

Now, when the poor black lady came into the midst of it all, they had stared at her, and some had made the sign of the cross. And the children had rushed down from the steps of the town-hall, where they were riding on the railing, and had followed her at a few feet's distance. And even the lazy Piero, who had been asleep in the corner of the balustrade, had raised himself on his elbow. It had been a resurrection, as if the black Madonna from the cathedral had come strolling by.

But had no one thought that it was unkind that all stared at the black lady? Had no one been moved when she came so slowly and painfully?

Yes, yes; one had been touched, and that had been Don Ferrante. He had the music in his heart; he was a good man and he thought: "Curses on all those funds that are gathered together for the poor, and that only bring people misfortune! Is not that poor Signorina Palmeri, whose father has stolen from a charitable fund, and who is now so ashamed that she dares not show her face?" And, as he thought of it, Don Ferrante went towards the black lady and met her just by the church door.

There he made her a bow, and mentioned his name. "If I am not mistaken," Don Ferrante had said, "you are Signorina Palmeri. I have a favor to ask of you."

Then she had started and taken a step backwards, as if to flee, but she had waited.

"It concerns my sister, Donna Elisa," he had said. "She knew your mother, signorina, and she is consumed with a desire to make your acquaintance. She is sitting here by the Cathedral. Let me take you to her!"

And then Don Ferrante put her hand on his arm and led her over to Donna Elisa. And she made no resistance. Donna Elisa would like to see who could have resisted Don Ferrante today.

Donna Elisa rose and went to meet the black lady, and throwing back her veil, kissed her on both cheeks.

But what a face, what a face! Perhaps it was not pretty, but it had eyes that spoke, eyes that mourned and lamented, even when the whole face smiled. Yes, Gaetano perhaps would not wish to carve or paint a Madonna from that face, for it was too thin and too pale; but it is to be supposed that our Lord knew what he was doing when he did not put those eyes in a face that was rosy and round.

When Donna Elisa kissed her, she laid her head down on her shoulder, and a few short sobs shook her. Then she looked up with a smile, and the smile seemed to say: "Ah, does the world look so? Is it so beautiful? Let me see it and smile at it! Can a poor unfortunate really dare to look at it? And to be seen? Can I bear to be seen?"

All that she had said without a word, only with a smile. What a face, what a face!

But here Gaetano interrupted Donna Elisa. "Where is she now?" he said. "I too must see her."

Then Donna Elisa looked Gaetano in the eyes. They were glowing and clear, as if they were filled with fire, and a dark flush rose to his temples.

"You will see her all in good time," she said, harshly. And she repented of every word she had said.

Gaetano saw that she was afraid, and he understood what she feared. It came into his mind to tell her now that he meant to go away, to go all the way to America.

Then he understood that the strange signorina must be very dangerous. Donna Elisa was so sure that Gaetano would fall in love with her that she was almost glad to hear that he meant to go away.

For anything seemed better to her than a penniless daughter-in-law, whose father was a thief.

# VI

## DON MATTEO'S MISSION

One afternoon the old priest, Don Matteo, inserted his feet into newly polished shoes, put on a newly brushed soutane, and laid his cloak in the most effective folds. His face shone as he went up the street, and when he distributed blessings to the old women spinning by the doorposts, it was with gestures as graceful as if he had scattered roses.

The street along which Don Matteo was walking was spanned by at least seven arches, as if every house wished to bind itself to a neighbor. It ran small and narrow down the mountain; it was half street and half staircase; the gutters were always overflowing, and there were always plenty of orange-skins and cabbage-leaves to slip on. Clothes hung on the line, from the ground up to the sky. Wet shirt-sleeves and apron-strings were carried by the wind right into Don Matteo's face. And it felt horrid and wet, as if Don Matteo had been touched by a corpse.

At the end of the street lay a little dark square, and there Don Matteo saw an old house, before which he stopped. It was big, and square, and almost without windows. It had two enormous flights of steps, and two big doors with heavy locks. And it had walls of black lava, and a "loggia," where green slime grew over the tiled floor, and where the spider-webs were so thick that the nimble lizards were almost held fast in them.

Don Matteo lifted the knocker, and knocked till it thundered. All the women in the street began to talk, and to question. All the washer-women by the fountain in the square dropped soap and wooden clapper, and began to whisper, and ask, "What is Don Matteo's errand? Why does Don Matteo knock on the door of an old, haunted house, where nobody dares to live except the strange signorina, whose father is in prison?"

But now Giannita opened the door for Don Matteo, and conducted him through long passages, smelling of mold and damp. In several places in the floor the stones were loose, and Don Matteo could see way down into the cellar, where great armies of rats raced over the black earth floor.

As Don Matteo walked through the old house, he lost his good-humor. He did not pass by a stairway without suspiciously spying up it, and he could not hear a rustle without starting. He was depressed as before some misfortune. Don Matteo thought of the little turbaned Moor who was said to show himself in that house, and even if he did not see him, he might be said to have felt him.

At last Giannita opened a door and showed the priest into a room. The walls there were bare, as in a stable; the bed was as narrow as a nun's, and over it hung a Madonna that was not worth three soldi. The priest stood and stared at the little Madonna till the tears rose to his eyes.

While he stood so Signorina Palmeri came into the room. She kept her head bent and moved slowly, as if wounded. When the priest saw her he wished to say to her: "You and I, Signorina Palmeri, have met in a strange old house. Are you here to study the old Moorish inscriptions or to look for mosaics in the cellar?" For the old priest was confounded when he saw Signorina Palmeri. He could not understand that the noble lady was poor. He could not comprehend that she was living in the house of the little Moor.

He said to himself that he must save her from this haunted house, and from poverty. He prayed to the tender Madonna for power to save her.

Thereupon he said to the signorina that he had come with a commission from Don Ferrante Alagona. Don Ferrante had confided to him that she had refused his proposal of marriage. Why was that? Did she not know that, although Don Ferrante seemed to be poor as he stood in his shop, he was really the richest man in Diamante? And Don Ferrante was of an old Spanish family of great consideration, both in their native country and in Sicily. And he still owned the big house on the Corso that had belonged to his ancestors. She should not have said no to him.

While Don Matteo was speaking, he saw how the signorina's face grew stiff and white. He was almost afraid to go on. He feared that she was going to faint.

It was only with the greatest effort that she was able to answer him. The words would not pass her lips. It seemed as if they were too loathsome to utter. She quite understood, she said, that Don Ferrante would like to know why she had refused his proposal. She was infinitely touched and grateful on account of it, but she could not be his wife.

She could not marry, for she brought dishonor and disgrace with her as a marriage portion.

"If you marry an Alagona, dear signorina," said Don Matteo, "you need not fear that anyone will ask of what family you are. It is an honorable old name. Don Ferrante and his sister, Donna Elisa, are considered the first people in Diamante, although they have lost all the family riches, and have to keep a shop. Don Ferrante knows well enough that the glory of the old name would not be tarnished by a marriage with you. Have no scruples for that, signorina, if otherwise you may be willing to marry Don Ferrante."

But Signorina Palmeri repeated what she had said. Don Ferrante should not marry the daughter of a convict. She sat pale and despairing, as if wishing to practice saying those terrible words. She said that she did not wish to enter a family which would despise her. She succeeded in saying it in a hard, cold voice, without emotion.

But the more she said, the greater became Don Matteo's desire to help her. He felt as if he had met a queen who had been torn from her throne. A burning desire came over him to set the crown again upon her head, and fasten the mantle about her shoulders.

Therefore Don Matteo asked her if her father were not soon coming out of prison, and he wondered what he would live on.

The signorina answered that he would live on her work.

Don Matteo asked her very seriously whether she had thought how her father, who had always been rich, could bear poverty.

Then she was silent. She tried to move her lips to answer, but could not utter a sound.

Don Matteo talked and talked. She looked more and more frightened, but she did not yield.

At last he knew not what to do. How could he save her from that haunted house, from poverty, and from the burden of dishonor that weighed her down? But then his eyes chanced to fall on the little image of the Madonna over the bed. So the young signorina was a believer.

The spirit of inspiration came to Don Matteo. He felt that God had sent him to save this poor woman. When he spoke again, there was a new ring in his voice. He understood that it was not he alone who spoke.

"My daughter," he said, and rose, "you will marry Don Ferrante for your father's sake! It is the Madonna's will, my daughter."

There was something impressive in Don Matteo's manner. No one had ever seen him so before. The signorina trembled, as if a spirit voice had spoken to her, and she clasped her hands.

"Be a good and faithful wife to Don Ferrante," said Don Matteo, "and the Madonna promises you through me that your father will have an old age free of care."

Then the signorina saw that it was an inspiration which guided Don Matteo. It was God speaking through him. And she sank down on her knees, and bent her head. "I shall do what you command," she said.

*B*ut when the priest, Don Matteo, came out of the house of the little Moor and went up the street, he suddenly took out his breviary and began to read. And although the wet clothes struck him on the cheek, and the little children and the orange-peels lay in wait for him, he only looked in his book. He needed to hear the great words of God.

For within that black house everything had seemed certain and sure, but when he came out into the sunshine he began to worry about the promise he had given in the name of the Madonna.

Don Matteo prayed and read, and read and prayed. Might the great God in heaven protect the woman, who had believed him and obeyed him as if he had been a prophet!

Don Matteo turned the corner into the Corso. He struck against donkeys on their way home, with traveling signorinas on their backs; he walked right into peasants coming home from their work, and he pushed against the old women spinning, and entangled their thread. At last he came to a little, dark shop.

It was a shop without a window which was at the corner of an old palace. The threshold was a foot high; the floor was of trampled earth; the door almost always stood open to let in the light. The counter was besieged by peasants and mule-drivers.

And behind the counter stood Don Ferrante. His beard grew in tufts; his face was in one wrinkle; his voice was hoarse with rage. The peasants demanded an immoderately high payment for the loads that they had driven up from Catania.

# VII

## THE BELLS OF SAN PASQUALE

*T*he people of Diamante soon perceived that Don Ferrante's wife, Donna Micaela, was nothing but a great child. She could never succeed in looking like a woman of the world, and she really was nothing but a child. And nothing else was to be expected, after the life she had led.

Of the world she had seen nothing but its theaters, museums, ball-rooms, promenades, and race courses; and all such are only play places. She had never been allowed to go alone on the street. She had never worked. No one had ever spoken seriously to her. She had not even been in love with anyone.

After she had moved into the summer palace she forgot her cares as gaily and easily as a child would have done. And it appeared that she had the playful disposition of a child, and that she could transform and change everything about her.

The old dirty Saracen town Diamante seemed like a paradise to Donna Micaela. She said that she had not been at all surprised when Don Ferrante had spoken to her in the square, nor when he had proposed to her. It seemed quite natural to her that such things should happen in Diamante. She had seen instantly that Diamante was a town where rich men went and sought out poor, unfortunate signorinas to make them mistresses of their black lava palaces.

She also liked the summer-palace. The faded chintz, a hundred years old, that covered the furniture told her stories. And she found a deep meaning in all the love scenes between the shepherds and shepherdesses on the walls.

She had soon found out the secret of Don Ferrante. He was no ordinary shop-keeper in a side street. He was a man of ambition, who was collecting money in order to buy back the family estate on Etna and the palace in Catania and the castle on the mainland. And if he went in short jacket and pointed cap, like a peasant, it was in order the sooner to be able to appear as a grandee of Spain and prince of Sicily.

After they were married Don Ferrante always used every evening to put on a velvet coat, take his guitar under his arm, and place himself on the stairway to the gallery in the music-room in the summer-palace and sing canzoni. While he sang, Donna Micaela dreamed that she had been married to the noblest man in beautiful Sicily.

When Donna Micaela had been married a few months her father was released from prison and came to live at the summer palace with his daughter. He liked the life in Diamante and became friends with everyone. He liked to talk to the bee-raisers and vineyard workers whom he met at the Café Europa, and he amused himself every day by riding about on the slopes of Etna to look for antiquities.

But he had by no means forgiven his daughter. He lived under her roof, but he treated her like a stranger, and never showed her affection. Donna Micaela let him go on and pretended not to notice it. She could not take his anger seriously any longer. That old man, whom she loved, believed that he would be able to go on hating her year after year! He would live near her, hear her speak, see her eyes, be encompassed by her love, and he could continue to hate her! Ah, he knew neither her nor himself. She used to sit and imagine how it would be when he must acknowledge that he was conquered; when he must come and show her that he loved her.

One day Donna Micaela was standing on her balcony waving her hand to her father, who rode away on a small, dark-brown pony, when Don Ferrante came up from the shop to speak to her. And what Don Ferrante wished to say was that he had succeeded in getting her father admitted to "The Brotherhood of the Holy Heart" in Catania.

But although Don Ferrante spoke very distinctly, Donna Micaela seemed not to understand him at all.

He had to repeat to her that he had been in Catania the day before, and that he had succeeded in getting Cavaliere Palmeri into a brotherhood. He was to enter it in a month.

She only asked: "What does that mean? What does that mean?"

"Oh," said Don Ferrante, "can I not have wearied of buying your father expensive wines from the mainland, and may I not sometimes wish to ride Domenico?"

When he had said that, he wished to go. There was nothing more to say.

"But tell me first what kind of a brotherhood it is," she said. — "What it is! A lot of old men live there." — "Poor old men?" — "Oh, well, not so rich." — "They do not have a room to themselves, I suppose?" — "No, but very big dormitories." — "And they eat from tin basins on a table without a cloth?" — "No, they must be china." — "But without a tablecloth?" — "Lord, if the table is clean!"

He added, to silence her: "Very good people live there. If you like to know it, it was not without hesitation they would receive Cavaliere Palmeri."

Thereupon Don Ferrante went. His wife was in despair, but also very angry. She thought that he had divested himself of rank and class and become only a plain shop-keeper.

She said aloud, although no one heard her, that the summer palace was only a big, ugly old house, and Diamante a poor and miserable town.

Naturally, she would not allow her father to leave her. Don Ferrante would see.

When they had eaten their dinner Don Ferrante wished to go to the Café Europa and play dominoes, and he looked about for his hat. Donna Micaela took his hat and followed him out to the gallery that ran round the courtyard. When they were far enough from the dining room for her father not to be able to hear them, she said passionately: —

"Have you anything against my father?" — "He is too expensive." — "But you are rich." — "Who has given you such an idea? Do you not see how I am struggling?" — "Save in some other way." — "I shall save in other ways. Giannita has had presents enough." — "No, economize on something for me." — "You! you are my wife; you shall have it as you have it."

She stood silent a moment. She was thinking what she could say to frighten him.

"If I am now your wife, do you know why it is?" — "Oh yes." — "Do you also know what the priest promised me?" — "That is his affair, but I do what I can." — "You have heard, perhaps, that I broke with all my friends in Catania when I heard that my father had sought help from them and had not got it." — "I know it." — "And that I came here to Diamante that he might escape from seeing them and being ashamed?" — "They will not be coming to the brotherhood." — "When you know all this, are you not afraid to do anything against my father?" — "Afraid? I am not afraid of my wife."

"Have I not made you happy?" she asked. — "Yes, of course," he answered indifferently. — "Have you not enjoyed singing to me? Have you not liked me to have considered you the most generous man in Sicily? Have you not been glad that I was happy in the old palace? Why should it all come to an end?"

He laid his hand on her shoulder and warned her. "Remember that you are not married to a fine gentleman from the Via Etnea!" — "Oh, no!" — "Up here on the mountain the ways are different. Here wives obey their husbands. And we do not care for fair words. But if we want them we know how to get them."

She was frightened when he spoke so. In a moment she was on her knees before him. It was dark, but enough light came from the other rooms for him to see her eyes. In burning prayer, glorious as stars, they were fixed on him.

"Be merciful! You do not know how much I love him!" Don Ferrante laughed. "You ought to have begun with that. Now you have made me angry." She still knelt and looked up at him. "It is well," he said, "for you hereafter to know how you shall behave." Still she knelt. Then he asked: "Shall I tell him, or will you?"

Donna Micaela was ashamed that she had humbled herself. She rose and answered imperiously: "I shall tell him, but not till the last day. And you *shall* not let him notice anything."

"No, I *shall* not," he said, and mimicked her. "The less talk about it, the better for me."

But when he was gone Donna Micaela laughed at Don Ferrante for believing that he could do what he liked with her father. She knew someone who would help her.

*I*n the Cathedral at Diamante there is a miracle-working image of the Madonna, and this is its story.

Long, long ago a holy hermit lived in a cave on Monte Chiaro. And this hermit dreamed one night that in the harbor of Catania lay a ship loaded with images of the saints, and among these there was one so holy that Englishmen, who are richer than anybody else, would have paid its weight in gold for it. As soon as the hermit awoke from this dream he started for Catania. In the harbor lay a ship loaded with images of the saints, and among the images was one of the holy Madonna that was more holy than all the others. The hermit begged the captain not to carry that image away from Sicily, but to give it to him. But the captain refused. "I shall take it to England," he said, "and the Englishmen will pay its weight in gold." The hermit renewed his petitions. At last the captain had his men drive him on shore, and hoisted his sail to depart.

It looked as if the holy image was to be lost to Sicily; but the hermit knelt down on one of the lava blocks on the shore and prayed to God that it might not be. And what happened? The ship could not go. The anchor was up, the sail hoisted, and the wind fresh; but for three long days the ship lay as motionless as if it had been a rock. On the third day the captain took the Madonna image and threw it to the hermit, who still lay on the shore. And immediately the ship glided out of the harbor. The hermit carried the image to Monte Chiaro, and it is still in Diamante, where it has a chapel and an altar in the Cathedral.

Donna Micaela was now going to this Madonna to pray for her father.

She sought out the Madonna's chapel, which was built in a dark corner of the Cathedral. The walls were covered with votive offerings, with silver hearts and pictures that had been given by all those who had been helped by the Madonna of Diamante.

The image was hewn in black marble, and when Donna Micaela saw it standing in its niche, high and dark, and almost hidden by a golden railing, it seemed to her that its face was beautiful, and that it shone with mildness. And her heart was filled with hope.

Here was the powerful queen of heaven; here was the good Mother Mary; here was the afflicted mother who understood every sorrow; here was one who would not allow her father to be taken from her.

Here she would find help. She would need only to fall on her knees and tell her trouble, to have the black Madonna come to her assistance.

While she prayed she felt certain that Don Ferrante was even at that moment changing his mind. When she came home he would come to meet her and say to her that she might keep her father.

*I*t was a morning three weeks later.

Donna Micaela came out of the summer palace to go to early mass; but before she set out to the church, she went into Donna Elisa's shop to buy a wax candle. It was so early that she had been afraid that the shop would not be open; but it was, and she was glad to be able to take a gift with her to the black Madonna.

The shop was empty when Donna Micaela came in, and she pushed the door forward and back to make the bell ring and call Donna Elisa in. At last someone came, but it was not Donna Elisa; it was a young man.

That young man was Gaetano, whom Donna Micaela scarcely knew. For Gaetano had heard so much about her that he was afraid to meet her, and every time she had come over to Donna Elisa he had shut himself into his workshop. Donna Micaela knew no more about him than that he was to leave Diamante, and that he was always carving holy images for Donna Elisa to have something to sell while he was earning great fortunes away in Argentina.

When she now saw Gaetano, she found him so handsome that it made her glad to look at him. She was full of anxiety as a hunted animal, but no sorrow in the world could prevent her from feeling joy at the sight of anything so beautiful.

She asked herself where she had seen him before, and she remembered that she had seen his face in her father's wonderful collection of pictures in the palace at Catania. There he had not been in working blouse; he had had a black felt hat with long, flowing, white feathers, and a broad lace collar over a velvet coat. And he had been painted by the great master Van Dyck.

Donna Micaela asked Gaetano for a wax candle, and he began to look for one. And now, strangely enough, Gaetano, who saw the little shop every day, seemed to be quite strange there. He looked for the wax candle in the drawers of rosaries and in the little medallion boxes. He could not find anything, and he grew so impatient that he turned out the drawers and broke the boxes open. The destruction and disorder were terrible. And it would be a real grief to Donna Elisa when she came home.

But Donna Micaela liked to see how he shook the thick hair back from his face, and how his gold-colored eyes glowed like yellow wine when the sun shines through it. It was a consolation to see anyone so beautiful.

Then Donna Micaela asked pardon of the noble gentlemen whom the great Van Dyck had painted. For she had often said to them: "Ah, signor, you have been beautiful, but you never could have been so dark and so pale and so melancholy. And you did not possess such eyes of fire. All that the master who painted you has put into your face." But when Donna Micaela saw Gaetano she found that it all could be in a face, and that the master had not needed to add anything. Therefore she asked the noble old gentlemen's pardon.

At last Gaetano had found the long candle-boxes that stood under the counter, where they had always stood. And he gave her the candle, but he did not know what it cost, and said that she could come in and pay it later. When she asked him for something to wrap it in he was in such trouble that she had to help him to look.

It grieved her that such a man should think of traveling to Argentina.

He let Donna Micaela wrap up the candle and watched her while she did it. She wished she could have asked him not to look at her now, when her face reflected only hopelessness and misery.

Gaetano had not scrutinized her features more than a moment before he sprang up on a little step-ladder, took down an image from the topmost shelf, and came back with it to her. It was a little gilded and painted wooden angel, a little San Michele fighting with the arch-fiend, which he had created from paper and wadding.

He handed it to Donna Micaela and begged her to accept it. He wished to give it to her, he said, because it was the best he had ever carved. He was so certain that it had greater power than his other images that he had put it away on the top shelf, so that no one might see and buy it. He had forbidden Donna Elisa to sell it except to one who had a great sorrow. And now Donna Micaela was to take it.

She hesitated. She found him almost too daring.

But Gaetano begged her to look how well the image was carved. She saw that the archangel's wings were ruffled with anger, and that Lucifer was pressing his claws into the steel plate on his leg? Did she see how San Michele was driving in his spear, and how he was frowning and pressing his lips together?

He wished to lay the little image in her hand, but she gently pushed it away. She saw that it was beautiful and spirited, she said, but she knew that it could not help her. She thanked him for his gift, but she would not accept it.

Then Gaetano seized the image and rolled it in paper and put it back in its place.

And not until it was wrapped up and put away did he speak to her.

But then he asked her why she came to buy wax candles if she was not a believer. Did she mean to say that she did not believe in San Michele? Did she not know that he was the most powerful of the angels, and that it was he who had vanquished Lucifer and thrown him into Etna? Did she not believe that it was true? Did she not know that San Michele lost a wing-feather in the fight, and that it was found in Caltanisetta? Did she know it or not? Or what did she mean by San

Michele not being able to help her? Did she think that none of the saints could help? And he, who was standing in his workshop all day long, carving saints! — would he do such a thing if there was no good in it? Did she believe that he was an impostor?

But as Donna Micaela was just as strong a believer as Gaetano, she thought that his speech was unjust, and it irritated her to contradiction.

"It sometimes happens that the saints do not help," she said to him. And when Gaetano looked unbelieving, she was seized by an uncontrollable desire to convince him, and she said to him that someone had promised her in the name of the Madonna that, if she was a faithful wife to Don Ferrante, her father should enjoy an old age free of care. But now her husband wished to put her father in a brotherhood, which was as wretched as a poor-house and strict as a prison. And the Madonna had not averted it; in eight days it would happen.

Gaetano listened to her with the greatest earnestness. That was what induced her to confide the whole story to him.

"Donna Micaela," he said, "you must turn to the black Madonna in the Cathedral."

"So you think that I have not prayed to her?"

Gaetano flushed and said almost with anger: "You will not say that you have turned in vain to the black Madonna?"

"I have prayed to her in vain these last three weeks — prayed to her, prayed to her."

When Donna Micaela spoke of it she could scarcely breathe. She wanted to weep over herself because she had awaited help each day, and each day been disappointed; and yet had known nothing better to do than begin again with her prayers. And it was visible on her face that her soul lived over and over again what she had suffered, when each day she had awaited an answer to her prayer, while the days slipped by.

But Gaetano was unmoved; he stood smiling, and drummed on one of the glass cases that stood on the counter.

"Have you only *prayed* to the Madonna?" he said.

Only prayed, only prayed! But she had also promised her to lay aside all sins. She had gone to the street where she had lived first, and nursed the sick woman with the ulcerated leg. She never passed a beggar without giving alms.

Only prayed! And she told him that if the Madonna had had the power to help her, she ought to have been satisfied with her prayers. She had spent her days in the Cathedral. And the anguish, the anguish that tortured her, should not that be counted?

He only shrugged his shoulders. Had she not tried anything else?

Anything else! But there was nothing in the world that she had not tried. She had given silver hearts and wax candles. Her rosary was never out of her hand.

Gaetano irritated her. He would not count anything that she had done; he only asked: "Nothing else? Nothing else?"

"But you ought to understand," she said. "Don Ferrante does not give me so much money. I cannot do more. At last I have succeeded in getting some silk and cloth for an altar cloth. You ought to understand!"

But Gaetano, who had daily intercourse with the saints, and who knew the power and wildness of enthusiasm that had filled them when they had compelled God to obey their prayers, smiled scornfully at Donna Micaela, who thought she could subjugate the Madonna with wax candles and altar-cloths.

He understood very well, he answered. The whole was clear to him. It was always so with those miserable saints. Everybody called to them for help, but few understood what they ought to do to get their prayers granted. And then people said that the saints had no power. All were helped who knew how they ought to pray.

Donna Micaela looked up in eager expectation. There was such strength and conviction in Gaetano's words that she began to believe that he would teach her the right words of salvation.

Gaetano took the candle lying in front of her on the counter and threw it down into the box again, and told her what she had to do. He forbade her to give the Madonna any gifts, or to pray to her, or to do anything for the poor. He told her that he would tear her altar-cloth to pieces if she sewed another stitch on it.

"Show her, Donna Micaela, that it means something to you," he said, and fixed his eyes on her with compelling force. "Good Lord, you must be able to find something to do, to show her that it is serious, and not play. You must be able to show her that you will not live if you are not helped. Do you mean to continue to be faithful to Don Ferrante, if he sends your father away? I know you do. If the Madonna has no need to fear what you are going to do, why should she help you?"

Donna Micaela drew back. He came swiftly out from behind the counter and seized her coat sleeve.

"Do you understand? You shall show her that you can throw yourself away if you do not get help. You shall throw yourself into sin and death if you do not get what you want. That is the way to force the saints."

She tore herself from him and went without a word. She hurried up the spiral street, came to the Cathedral, and threw herself down in terror before the altar of the black Madonna.

That happened one Saturday morning, and on Sunday evening Donna Micaela saw Gaetano again. For it was beautiful moonlight, and in Diamante it is the custom on moonlight nights for all to leave their homes and go out into the streets. As soon as the inhabitants of the summer palace had come outside their door they had met acquaintances. Donna Elisa had taken Cavaliere Palmeri's arm, and the syndic Voltaro had joined Don Ferrante to discuss the elections; but Gaetano came up to Donna Micaela because he wished to hear if she had followed his advice.

"Have you stopped sewing on that altar-cloth?" he said.

But Donna Micaela answered that all day yesterday she had sewn on it.

"Then it is you who understand what you are doing, Donna Micaela."

"Yes, now there is no help for it, Don Gaetano."

She managed to keep them away from the others, for there was something she wished to speak to him about. And when they came to Porta Etnea, she turned out through the gate, and they went along the paths that wind under Monte Chiaro's palm groves.

They could not have walked on the streets filled with people. Donna Micaela spoke so the people in Diamante would have stoned her if they had heard her.

She asked Gaetano if he had ever seen the black Madonna in the Cathedral. She had not seen her till yesterday. The Madonna perhaps had placed herself in such a dark corner of the Cathedral so that no one should be able to see her. She was so black, and had a railing in front of her. No one could see her.

But today Donna Micaela had seen her. Today the Madonna had had a festival, and she had been moved from her niche. The floor and walls of her chapel had been covered with white almond-blossoms, and she herself had stood down on the altar, dark and high, surrounded by the white glory.

But when Donna Micaela had seen the image she had been filled with despair; for the image was no Madonna. No, she had prayed to no Madonna. Oh, a shame, a shame! It was plainly an old heathen goddess. She had a helmet, not a crown; she had no child on her arm; she had a shield. It was a Pallas Athene. It was no Madonna. Oh, no; oh, no!

It was like the people of Diamante to worship such an image. It was like them to set up such a blasphemy and worship it! Did he know what was the worst misfortune? Their Madonna was so ugly. She was disfigured, and she had never been a work of art. She was so ugly that one could not bear to look at her.

And to have been deceived by all the thousand votive offerings that hung in the chapel; to have been fooled by all the legends about her! To have wasted three weeks in praying to her! Why had she not been helped? She was no Madonna, she was no Madonna.

They walked along the path on the town wall running around Monte Chiaro. The whole world was white about them. A white mist wreathed the base of the mountain, and the almond trees on Etna were quite white. Sometimes they passed under an almond tree, which arched them over with its glistening branches, as thickly covered with flowers as if they had been dipped in a bath of silver. The moonlight shone so bright on the earth that everything was divested of its color, and became white. It seemed almost strange that it could not be felt, that it did not warm, that it did not dazzle the eyes.

Donna Micaela wondered if it was the moonlight that subdued Gaetano, so that he did not seize her, and throw her down into Simeto, when she cursed the black Madonna.

He walked silent and quiet at her side, but she was afraid of what he might do. In spite of her fear, she could not be silent.

What she had still to say was the most dreadful of all. She said that she had tried all day long to think of the real Madonna, and that she had recalled to her mind all the images of her she had ever seen. But it had all been in vain, because as soon as she thought of the shining queen of heaven, the old black goddess came and placed herself between them. She saw her come like a dried-up and officious old maid, and stand in front of the great queen of heaven, so that now no Madonna existed for her any longer. She believed that the latter was angry with her because she had done so much for the other, and that she hid her face and her grace from her. And, on account of the false Madonna, her father was now to suffer misfortune. Now she would never be allowed to keep him in her home. Now she would never win his forgiveness. Oh, God! oh, God!

And all this she said to Gaetano, who honored the black Madonna of Diamante more than anything else in the world.

He now came close up to Donna Micaela, and she feared that it was her last hour. She said in a faint voice, as if to excuse herself: "I am mad. Grief is driving me mad. I never sleep."

But Gaetano's only thought had been what a child she was, and that she did not at all understand how to meet life.

He hardly knew himself what he was doing when he gently drew her to him and kissed her, because she had gone so astray and was such a helpless child.

She was so overcome with astonishment that she did not even think of avoiding it. And she neither screamed nor ran away. She understood instantly that he had kissed her as he would a child. She only walked quickly on and began to cry. That kiss had made her feel how helpless and forsaken she was, and how much she longed for someone strong and good to take care of her.

It was terrible that, although she had both father and husband, she should be so forsaken that this stranger should need to feel sympathy for her.

When Gaetano saw her trembling with silent sobs, he felt that he too began to shake. A strong and violent emotion took possession of him.

He came close to her once more and laid his hand on her arm. And his voice, when he spoke, was not clear and loud; it was thick and choked with emotion.

"Will you go with me to Argentina if the Madonna does not help you?"

Then Donna Micaela shook him off. She felt suddenly that he no longer talked to her as to a child. She turned and went back into the town. Gaetano did not follow her; he remained standing in the path where he had kissed her, and it seemed as if never again could he leave that place.

For two days Gaetano dreamed of Donna Micaela, but on the third he came to the summer palace to speak to her.

He found her on the roof-garden, and instantly told her that she must flee with him.

He had thought it out since they parted. He had stood in his workshop and considered everything that had happened, and now it was all clear to him.

She was a rose which the strong sirocco had torn from its stem and roughly whirled through the air, that she might find so much the better rest and protection in a heart which loved her. She must understand that God and all the saints wished and desired that they should love one another, otherwise these great misfortunes would not have brought her near to him. If the Madonna refused to help her, it was because she wished to set her free from her promise of faithfulness to Don Ferrante. For all the saints knew that she was his, Gaetano's. She was created for him; for him she had grown up; for him she was alive. When he kissed her in the path in the moonlight he had been like a lost child who had wandered long in the desert and now at last had come to the gate of his home. He possessed nothing; but she was his home and his hearth; she was the inheritance God had apportioned to him, the only thing in the world that was his.

Therefore he could not leave her behind. She must go with him; she must, she must!

He did not kneel before her. He stood and talked to her with clenched hands and blazing eyes. He did not ask her, he commanded her to go with him, because she was his.

It was no sin to take her away; it was his duty. What would become of her if he deserted her?

Donna Micaela listened to him without moving. She sat silent a long time, even after he had ceased speaking.

"When are you going?" she asked at length.

"I leave Diamante on Saturday."

"And when does the steamer go?"

"It goes on Sunday evening from Messina."

Donna Micaela rose and walked away towards the terrace stairs.

"My father is to go to Catania on Saturday," she said. "I shall ask Don Ferrante to be allowed to go with him." She went down a few steps, as if she did not mean to say anything more. Then she stopped. "If you meet me in Catania, I will go with you whither you will."

She hurried down the steps. Gaetano did not try to detain her. A time would come when she would not run away from him. He knew that she could not help loving him.

Donna Micaela passed the whole of Friday afternoon in the Cathedral. She had come to the Madonna and thrown herself down before her in despair. "Oh, Madonna mia, Madonna mia! Shall I be tomorrow a fugitive wife? Will the world have the right to say all possible evil of me?" Everything seemed equally terrible to her. She was appalled at the thought of fleeing with Gaetano, and she did not know how she could stay with Don Ferrante. She hated the one as much as the other. Neither of them seemed able to offer her anything but unhappiness.

She saw that the Madonna would not help. And now she asked herself if it really would not be a greater misery to go with Gaetano than to remain with Don Ferrante. Was it worth while to ruin herself to be revenged on her husband?

She suffered great anguish. She had been driven on by a devouring restlessness the whole week. Worst of all, she could not sleep. She no longer thought clearly or soundly.

Time and time again she returned to her prayers. But then she thought: "The Madonna cannot help me." And so she stopped.

Then she came to think of the days of her former sorrows, and remembered the little image that once had helped her, when she had been in despair as great as this.

She turned with passionate eagerness to the poor little child. "Help me, help me! Help my old father, and help me myself that I may not be tempted to anger and revenge!"

When she went to bed that night, she was still tormented and distressed. "If I could sleep only one hour," she said, "I should know what I wanted."

Gaetano was to start on his travels early the next morning. She came at last to the decision to speak to him before he left, and tell him that she could not go with him. She could not bear to be considered a fallen woman.

She had hardly decided that before she fell asleep.

She did not wake till the clock struck nine the next morning. And then Gaetano was already gone. She could not tell him that she had changed her mind.

But she did not think of it either. During her sleep something new and strange had come over her. It seemed to her that in the night she had lived in heaven and was filled with bliss.

*W*hat saint is there who does more for man than San Pasquale? Does it not sometimes happen to you to stand and talk in some lonely place in the woods or plains, and either to speak ill of someone or to make plans for something foolish? Now please notice that just as you are talking and talking you hear a rustling near by, and look round in wonder to see if someone has thrown a stone. It is useless to look about long for the thrower of the stone. It comes from San Pasquale. As surely as there is justice in heaven, it was San Pasquale who heard you talking evil, and threw one of his stones in warning.

And anyone who does not like to be disturbed in his evil schemes may not console himself with the thought that San Pasquale's stones will soon come to an end. They will not come to an end at all. There are so many of them that they will hold out till the last day of the world. For when San Pasquale lived here on the earth, do you know by chance what he did, do you know what he thought about more than anything else? San Pasquale gave heed to all the little flint-stones that lay in his path, and gathered them up into his bag. You, signor, you will scarcely stoop to pick up a soldo, but San Pasquale picked up every little flint-stone, and when he died, he took them all with him up to heaven, and there he sits now, and throws them at everybody who thinks of doing anything foolish.

But that is not by any means the only use that San Pasquale is to man. It is he, also, who gives warning if anyone is to be married, or if anyone is to die; and he even gives the sign with something besides stones. Old Mother Saraedda at Randazzo sat by her daughter's sick bed one night and fell asleep. The daughter lay unconscious and was about to die, and no one could summon the priest. How was the mother waked in time? How was she waked, so that she could send her husband to the priest's house? By nothing else than a chair, which began to rock forward and back, and to crack and creak, until she awoke. And it was San Pasquale who did it. Who else but San Pasquale is there to think of such a thing?

There is one thing more to tell about San Pasquale. It was of big Cristoforo from Tre Castagni. He was not a bad man, but he had a bad habit. He could not open his mouth without swearing. He could not say two words without one of them being an oath. And do you think that it did any good for his wife and neighbors to admonish him? But over his bed he had a little picture representing San Pasquale, and the little picture succeeded in helping him. Every night it swung forward and back in its frame, swung fast or slow, as he had sworn that day. And he discovered that he could not sleep a single night until he stopped swearing. In Diamante San Pasquale has a church, which lies outside the Porta Etnea, a little way down the mountain. It is quite small and poor, but the white walls and the red roof stand beautifully embedded in a grove of almond trees.

Therefore, as soon as the almond trees bloom in the spring, San Pasquale's church becomes the most beautiful in Diamante. For the blossoming branches arch over it, thickly covered with white, glistening flowers, like the most gorgeous garment.

San Pasquale's church is very miserable and deserted, because no service can be held there. For when the Garibaldists, who freed Sicily, came to Diamante, they camped in San Pasquale's church and in the Franciscan monastery beside it. And in the church itself they stabled brute beasts, and led such a wild life with women and with gambling that ever since it has been considered unhallowed and unclean, and has never been opened for divine service from that time.

Therefore it is only when the almond trees are in bloom that strangers and fine people pay attention to San Pasquale, For although the whole of the slopes of Etna are white then with almond-blossoms, still the biggest and the most luxuriant trees stand about the old, condemned church.

But the poor people of Diamante come to San Pasquale the whole year round. For although the church is always closed, people go there to get advice from the saint. There is an image of him under a big stone canopy just by the entrance, and people come to ask him about the future. No one can foretell the future better than San Pasquale.

Now it happened that the very morning when Gaetano left Diamante the clouds had come rolling down from Etna, as thick as if they had been dust from innumerable hosts, and they filled the air like dark-winged dragons, and vomited forth rain, and breathed mists and darkness. It grew so thick over Diamante that one could scarcely see across the street. The dampness dripped from everything; the floor was as wet as the roof, the doorposts and balustrades were covered with drops, the fog stood and quivered in the passage-ways and rooms, until one would have thought them full of smoke.

That very morning, at an early hour, before the rain had begun, a rich English lady started in her big traveling-carriage to make the trip round Etna. But when she had driven a few hours a terrible rain began, and everything was wrapped in mist. As she did not wish to miss seeing any of the beautiful district through which she was traveling, she determined to drive to the nearest town and to stay there until the storm was over. That town was Diamante.

The Englishwoman was a Miss Tottenham, and it was she who had moved into the Palazzo Palmeri at Catania. Among all the other things she brought with her in her trunks was the Christ image, upon which Donna Micaela had called the evening before. For that image, which was now both old and mishandled, she always carried with her, in memory of an old friend who had left her her wealth.

It seemed as if San Pasquale had known what a great miracle-worker the image was, for it was as if he wished to greet him. Just as Miss Tottenham's traveling-carriage drove in through Porta Etnea, the bells began to ring on San Pasquale's church.

They rang afterwards all day quite by themselves.

San Pasquale's bells are not much bigger than those that are used on farms to call the work people home; and like them, they are hung under the roof in a little frame, and set in motion by pulling a rope that hangs down by the church wall.

It is not heavy work to make the bells ring, but nevertheless they are not so light that they can swing quite by themselves. Whoever has seen old Fra Felice from the Franciscan monastery put his foot in the loop of the rope and tread up and down to start them going, knows well enough that the bells cannot begin to ring without assistance.

But that was just what they were doing that morning. The rope was fastened to a cleat in the wall, and there was no one touching it. Nor did anyone sit crouching on the roof to set them going. People plainly saw how the bells swung backwards and forwards, and how the tongues hit against the brazen throats. It could not be explained.

When Donna Micaela awoke, the bells were already ringing, and she lay quiet for a long time, and listened, and listened. She had never heard anything more beautiful. She did not know that it was a miracle, but she lay and thought how beautiful it was. She lay and wondered if real bronze bells could sound like that.

No one will ever know what the metal was that rang in San Pasquale's bells that day.

She thought that the bells said to her that now she was to be glad; now she was to live and love; now she was to go to meet something great and beautiful; now she was never again to have regrets and never be sad.

Then her heart began to dance in a kind of stately measure, and she marched solemnly to the sound of bells into a great castle. And to whom could the castle belong, who could be lord of such a beautiful place, if not love?

It can be hidden no longer: when Donna Micaela awoke she felt that she loved Gaetano, and that she desired nothing better than to go with him.

When Donna Micaela drew back the curtain from the window and saw the grey morning, she kissed her hand to it and whispered: "You, who are morning to the day when I am going away, you are the most beautiful morning I have ever seen; and grey as you are, I will caress and kiss you."

But she still liked the bells best.

By that you may know that her love was strong, for to all the others it was torture to hear those bells, that would not stop ringing. No one asked about them during the first half-hour. During the first half-hour people hardly heard any ringing, but during the second and the third!!!

No one need believe that San Pasquale's little bells could not make themselves heard. They are always loud and their clang seemed now to grow and grow. It soon sounded as if the fog were filled with bells; as if the sky hung full of them, although no one could see them for the clouds.

When Donna Elisa first heard the ringing she thought that it was San Giuseppe's little bell, and then that it was the bell of the Cathedral itself. Then she thought she heard the bell of the Dominican monastery chime in, and at last she was certain that all the bells in the town rang and rang all they could, all the bells in the five monasteries and the seven churches. She thought that she recognized them all, until finally she asked, and heard that it was only San Pasquale's little bells that were ringing.

During the first hours, and before people generally knew that the bells were ringing all by themselves, they noticed that the raindrops fell in time to the sound of the bells, and that everyone spoke with a metallic voice. People also noticed that it was impossible to play on mandolin and guitar, because the bells blended with the music and made it ear-splitting; neither could anyone read, because the letters swung to and fro like bell-clappers, and the words acquired a voice, and read themselves out quite audibly.

Soon the people could not bear to see flowers on long stalks, because they thought that they swung to and fro. And they complained that sound came from them, instead of fragrance.

Others insisted that the mist floating through the air moved in time with the sound of the bells, and they said that all the pendulums conformed to it, and that everyone who went by in the rain tried to do likewise.

And that was when the bells had only rung a couple of hours, and when the people still laughed at them.

But at the third hour the ringing seemed to increase even more, and then some stuffed cotton into their ears, while others buried themselves under pillows. But they felt just as distinctly how the air quivered with the strokes, and they thought that they perceived how everything moved in time. Those who fled up to the dark attic found the sound of the bells clear and ringing there, as if they came from the sky; and those who fled down into the cellar heard them as loud and deafening there as if San Pasquale's church stood underground.

Everyone in Diamante began to be terrified except Donna Micaela, whom love protected from fear.

And now people began to think that it must mean something, because it was San Pasquale's bells that rang. Everyone began to ask himself what the saint foretold. Each had his own dread, and believed that San Pasquale gave warning to him of what he least wished. Each had a deed on his conscience to remember, and now thought that San Pasquale was ringing down a punishment for him.

Toward noon, when the bells still rang, everybody was sure that San Pasquale was ringing such a misfortune upon Diamante that they might all expect to die within the year.

Pretty Giannita came terrified and weeping to Donna Micaela, and lamented that it was San Pasquale who was ringing. "God, God, if it had been any other than San Pasquale!"

"He sees that something terrible is coming to us," said Giannita. "The mist does not prevent him from seeing as far as he will. He sees that an enemy's fleet is approaching in the bay! He sees that a cloud of ashes is rising out of Etna which will fall over us and bury us!"

Donna Micaela smiled, and thought that she knew of what San Pasquale was thinking. "He is tolling a passing-bell for the beautiful almond-blossoms, that are destroyed by the rain," she said to Giannita.

She let no one frighten her, for she believed that the bells were ringing for her alone. They rocked her to dream. She sat quite still in the music-room and let joy reign in her. But in the whole world about her was fear and anxiety and restlessness.

No one could sit at his work. No one could think of anything but the great horror that San Pasquale foretold.

People began to give the beggars more gifts than they had ever had; but the beggars did not rejoice, because they did not believe they would survive the morrow. And the priests could not rejoice, although they had so many penitents that they had to sit in the confessional all day long, and although gift upon gift was piled up on the altar of the saint.

Not even Vicenzo da Lozzo, the letter-writer, was glad of the day, although people besieged his desk under the court-house loggia, and were more than willing to pay him a soldo a word, if they only might write a line of farewell on this their last day to their dear ones far away.

It was not possible to keep school that day, for the children cried the whole time. At noon the mothers came, their faces stiff with terror, and took their little ones home with them, so that they might at least be together in misfortune.

The apprentices at the tailors and shoe-makers had a holiday. But the poor boys did not dare to enjoy it; they preferred to sit in their places in the workshops, and wait.

In the afternoon the ringing still continued.

Then the old gatekeeper of the palazzo Geraci, where now no one lives but beggars, and who is himself a beggar, and goes dressed in the most miserable rags, went and put on the light-green velvet livery that he wears only on saints' days and on the king's birthday. And no one could see him sitting in the gateway dressed in that array without being chilled with fear, for people understood that the old man expected that no other than destruction would march in through the gate he was guarding.

It was dreadful how people frightened one another.

Poor Torino, who had once been a man of means, went from house to house and cried that now the time had come when everyone who had cheated and beggared him would get his punishment. He went into all the little shops along the Corso and struck the counter with his hand, saying that now everyone in the town would get his sentence, because all had connived to cheat him.

It was also terrifying to hear of the game of cards at the Café Europa. There the same four had played year after year at the same table, and no one had ever thought that they could do anything else. But now they suddenly let their cards fall, and promised each other that if they survived the horror of this day they would never touch them again.

Donna Elisa's shop was packed with people; to propitiate the saints and to avert the menace, they bought all the sacred things that she had to sell. But Donna Elisa thought only of Gaetano, who was away, and believed that San Pasquale was warning her that he would be lost during the voyage. And she took no pleasure in all the money that she was earning.

When San Pasquale's bells went on ringing the whole afternoon people could hardly hold out.

For now they knew that it was an earthquake which they foretold, and that all Diamante would be wrecked.

In the alleys, where the very houses seemed afraid of earthquakes, and huddled together to support one another, people moved their miserable old furniture out on the street into the rain, and spread tents of bed-quilts over them. And they even carried out their little children in their cradles, and piled up boxes over them.

In spite of the rain, there was such a crowd on the Corso that it was almost impossible to pass through. For everyone was trying to go out through Porta Etnea to see the bells swinging and swinging, and to convince themselves that no one was touching the rope, — that it was firmly tied. And all who came out there fell on their knees in the road, where the water ran in streams, and the mud was bottomless.

The doors to San Pasquale's church were shut, as always, but outside the old grey-brother, Fra Felice, went about with a brass plate, among those who prayed, and received their gifts.

In their turn the frightened people went forward to the image of San Pasquale beneath the stone canopy, and kissed his hand. An old woman came carefully carrying something under a green umbrella. It was a glass with water and oil, in which floated a little wick burning with a faint flame. She placed it in front of the image and knelt before it.

Though many thought that they ought to try to tie up the bells, no one dared to propose it. For no one dared to silence God's voice.

Nor did anyone dare to say that it might be a device of old Fra Felice to collect money. Fra Felice was beloved. It would fare badly with whoever said such things as that.

Donna Micaela also came out to San Pasquale and took her father with her. She walked with her head high and quite without fear. She came to thank him for having rung a great passion into her soul. "My life begins this day," she said to herself.

Don Ferrante did not seem to be afraid either, but he was grim and angry. For everyone had to go in to him in his shop, and tell him what they thought, and hear his opinion, because he was one of the Alagonas, who had governed the town for so many years.

All day terrified, trembling people came into his shop. And they all came up to him and said: "This is a terrible ringing, Don Ferrante. What is to become of us, Don Ferrante?"

Even Ugo Favara, the splenetic advocate, came into the shop, and took a chair, and sat down behind the counter. And Don Ferrante had him sitting there all day, quite livid, quite motionless, suffering the most inconceivable anguish without uttering a word.

Every five minutes Torino-il-Martello came in and struck the counter, saying that the hour had come in which Don Ferrante was to get his punishment.

Don Ferrante was a hard man, but he could no more escape the bells than any other. And the longer he heard them, the more he began to wonder why everybody streamed into his shop. It seemed as if they meant something special. It seemed as if they wished to make him responsible for the ringing, and the evil it portended.

He had not spoken of it to anyone, but his wife must have spread it about. He began to believe that everybody was thinking the same, although they did not dare to say it. He thought that the advocate was sitting and waiting for him to yield. He believed that the whole town came in to see if he would really dare to send his father-in-law away.

Donna Elisa, who had so much to do in her own shop that she could not come herself, sent old Pacifica continually to him to ask what he thought of the bell-ringing. And the priest too came to the shop for a moment and said, like all the others: "Did you ever hear such a terrible ringing, Don Ferrante?"

Don Ferrante would have liked to know if the advocate and Don Matteo and all the others came only to reproach him because he wished to send Cavaliere Palmeri away.

The blood began to throb in his temples. The room swam now and then before his eyes. People came in continually and asked: "Have you ever heard such a terrible ringing?" But one never came and asked, and that was Donna Micaela. She could not come when she felt no fear. She was merely delighted and proud that the passion which was to fill her whole life had come. "My life is to be great and glorious," she said. And she was appalled that till now she had been only a child.

She would travel with the post-carriage that went by Diamante at ten o'clock at night. Towards four, she thought, she must tell her father everything, and begin his packing.

But that did not seem hard to her. Her father would soon come to her in Argentina. She would beg him to be patient for a few months, until they could have a home to offer him. And she was sure that he would be glad to have her leave Don Ferrante.

She moved in a delicious trance. Everything that had seemed dreadful appeared so no longer. There was no shame, no danger; no, none at all.

She only longed to hear the rattling of the post-carriage.

Then she heard many voices on the stairs leading from the courtyard to the second floor. She heard a multitude of heavy feet tramping. She saw people passing through the open portico that ran round the courtyard, and through which one had to go to come into the rooms. She saw that they were carrying something heavy between them, but she could not see what it was, because there was such a crowd.

The pale-faced advocate walked before the others. He came and said to her that Don Ferrante had wished to drive Torino out of his shop; Torino had cut him with his knife. It was nothing dangerous. He was already bandaged and would be well in a fortnight.

Don Ferrante was carried in, and his eyes wandered about the room, not in search of Donna Micaela, but of Cavaliere Palmeri. When he saw him, he let his wife know without a word, only by a few gestures, that her father never would need to leave his house; never, never.

Then she pressed her hands against her eyes. What, what! her father need not go? She was saved. A miracle had come to pass to help her!

Ah, now she must be glad, be content! But she was not. She felt the most terrible pain.

She could not go. Her father was allowed to remain, and so she must be faithful to Don Ferrante. She struggled to understand. It was so. She could not go.

She tried to change it in some way. Perhaps it was a false conclusion. She had been so confused. No, no, it was so, she could not.

Then she became tired unto death. She had traveled and traveled the whole day. She had been so long on the way. And she would never get there. She sank down. A torpor and faintness came over her. There was nothing to do but to rest after the endless journey she had made. But that she could never do. She began to weep because she would never reach her journey's end. Her whole life long she would travel, travel, travel, and never reach the end of her journey.

# VIII

## TWO SONGS

*I*t was the morning after the day when San Pasquale's bells had rung; and Donna Elisa sat in her shop and counted her money. The day before, when everyone had been afraid, there had been an incredible sale in the shop, and the next morning, when she had come down, she had at first been almost frightened. For the whole shop was desolate and empty; the medallions were gone, the wax candles were gone, and so were all the great bunches of rosaries. All Gaetano's beautiful images had been taken down from the shelves and sold, and it was a real grief to Donna Elisa not to see the host of holy men and women about her.

She opened the money-drawer, and it was so full that she could hardly pull it out. And while she counted her money she wept over it as if it had all been false. For what good did it do her to possess all those dirty lire and those big copper coins when she had lost Gaetano!

Alas! she thought that if he had stopped at home one day more he would not have needed to go, for now she was laden down with money.

While she was counting she heard the post-carriage stop outside her door. But she did not even look up; she did not care what happened, since Gaetano was gone. Then the door opened, and the bell rang violently. She only wept and counted. Then someone said: "Donna Elisa, Donna Elisa!" And it was Gaetano!

"But heavens! how can you be at home?" she cried. — "You have sold all your images. I had to come home to carve new ones for you." — "But how did you find out about it?" — "I met the post-carriage at two o'clock in the night. Rosa Alfari was in it, and she told me everything." — "What luck that you went down to the post-carriage! What luck that you happened to think of going down to the post-carriage!" — "Yes; was it not good fortune?" said Gaetano.

In less than an hour Gaetano was again standing in his workshop; and Donna Elisa, who had nothing at all to do in her empty shop, came incessantly to the door to look at him. No, was he really standing there and carving? She could not let five minutes pass without coming to look at him.

But when Donna Micaela heard that he was back she felt no joy, rather anger and despair. For she was afraid that Gaetano would come to tempt her.

She had heard that a rich Englishwoman had come to Diamante the day the bells rang. She was deeply affected when she heard that it was the lady with the Christ image. He had therefore come as soon as she had called on him. The rain and the bell-ringing were his work!

She tried to rejoice her soul with the thought that there had been a miracle for her sake. It would be more to her than all earthly happiness and love to feel that she was surrounded by God's grace. She did not wish anything earthly to come and drag her down from that blessed rapture.

But when she met Gaetano on the street he hardly looked at her; and when she met him at Donna Elisa's he did not take her hand and did not speak to her at all.

For the truth was that, although Gaetano had come home because it had been too hard to go without Donna Micaela, he did not wish to tempt or to persuade her. He saw that she was under the protection of the saints, and she had become so sacred to him that he scarcely dared to dream of her.

He wished to be near her, not in order to love her, but because he believed that her life would blossom with holy deeds. Gaetano longed for miracles, as a gardener longs for the first rose in the spring.

But when weeks went by and Gaetano never tried to approach Donna Micaela, she began to doubt, and to think that he had never loved her. She said to herself that he had won the promise from her to flee with him only in order to show her that the Madonna could work a miracle.

If that were true, she did not know why he had not continued his journey without turning back.

That caused her anxiety. She thought that she could conquer her love better if she knew whether Gaetano loved her. She weighed the pros and cons, and she was more and more sure that he had never loved her.

While Donna Micaela was thinking of this, she had to sit and keep Don Ferrante company. He had lain sick a long time. He had had two strokes of paralysis, and had risen from his sick-bed a broken man. All at once he had become old and dull and afraid, so that he never dared to be alone. He never worked in the shop; he was in every way a changed man.

He had been seized with a great desire to be aristocratic and fashionable. It looked as if poor Don Ferrante's head was turned with pride.

Donna Micaela was very good to him, and sat hour after hour and chatted with him.

"Who could it be," she used to ask, "who once stood in the market-place with plumes on his hat, and braid on his coat, and sword at his side, and who played so that people said that his music was as uplifting as Etna, and as strong as the sea? And who caught sight of a poor signorina dressed in black, who did not dare to show her face to the world, and went forward to her and offered his arm? Who could it be? Could it be Don Ferrante, who stands the whole week in his shop and wears a pointed cap and a short jacket? No; that cannot be possible. No old merchant could have done such a thing."

Don Ferrante laughed. That was just the way he liked to have her talk to him. She would also tell him how it would be when he came to court. The king would say this, and the queen would say that. "The old Alagonas have come up again," they would say at court. And who has brought up the race? People will wonder and wonder. The Don Ferrante, who is a Sicilian prince and Spanish grandee, is that the same man who stood in a shop in Diamante and shouted at the teamsters? No, people will say, it cannot be the same. It is impossible for it to be the same.

Don Ferrante liked that, and wished to hear her talk so day in and day out. He was never tired of listening, and Donna Micaela was very patient with him.

But one day while she was chatting, Donna Elisa came in. "Sister-in-law, if you happen to own the 'Legend of the Holy Virgin of Pompeii,' will you lend it to me?" she asked. — "What, are you going to begin to read?" asked Donna Micaela. — "The saints preserve us! you know very well that I cannot read. Gaetano is asking for it."

Donna Micaela did not own the "Legend of the Holy Virgin at Pompeii." But she did not say so to Donna Elisa; she went to her book-shelf and took a little book, a collection of Sicilian love songs, and gave it to Donna Elisa, who carried the little book over to Gaetano.

But Donna Micaela had no sooner done so before a lively regret seized her. And she asked herself what she had meant by behaving so, — she who had been helped by the little Christ-child?

She blushed with shame as she thought that she had marked one of the little songs, one that ran thus: —

"For one single question's answer longing,
 Night I asked, and asked the daytime's burning;
 Watched the flight of birds, and swift clouds thronging,
 In water strove to read the hot lead's turning;
 Leaves I counted plucked from many flowers,

Lured dark prophets forth, and sought their powers,
Till at last I called on Heaven above me:
'Doth he love me still, as once he loved me?'"

She had hoped to get an answer to it. But it would serve her right if no answer came. It would serve her right if Gaetano despised her and thought her forward.

Yet she had meant no harm. The only thing she had desired had been to find out if Gaetano loved her.

Several weeks again passed and Donna Micaela still sat with Don Ferrante.

But one day Donna Elisa had tempted her out. "Come with me into my garden, sister-in-law, and see my big magnolia tree. You have never seen anything so beautiful."

She had gone with Donna Elisa across the street and had come into her courtyard. And Donna Elisa's magnolia was like the shining sun, so that people were aware of it even before they saw it. At a great distance the fragrance lay and rocked in the air, and there was a murmuring of bees, and a twittering of birds.

When Donna Micaela saw the tree she could hardly breathe. It was very high and broad, with a beautifully even growth, and its large, firm leaves were of a fresh, dark green. But now it was entirely covered with great, bright flowers, that lighted and adorned it so that it looked as if dressed for a feast, and one felt an intoxicating joy streaming forth from the tree. Donna Micaela almost lost consciousness, and a new and irresistible power took possession of her. She drew down one of the stiff branches, and without breaking it spread out the flower that it bore, took a needle and began to prick letters on the flower leaf. "What are you doing, sister-in-law?" asked Donna Elisa. — "Nothing, nothing." — "In my time young girls used to prick love-letters on the magnolia-blossoms." — "Perhaps they do it still." — "Take care; I shall look at what you have written when you are gone." — "But you cannot read." — "I have Gaetano." — "And Luca; you had better ask Luca."

When Donna Micaela came home, she repented of what she had done. Would Donna Elisa really show the flower to Gaetano? No, no; Donna Elisa was too sensible. But if he had seen her from the window of his workshop? Well, he would not answer. She had made herself ridiculous.

No, never, never again would she do such a thing. It was best for her not to know. It was best for her that Gaetano did not ask after her.

Nevertheless she wondered what answer she would get. But none came.

So another week passed. Then it came into Don Ferrante's mind that he would like to go out for a drive in the afternoon.

In the carriage-house of the summer palace there was an ancient state carriage, which was certainly more than a hundred years old. It was very high; it had a small, narrow body, which swung on leather straps between the back wheels, which were as big as the water-wheels of a mill. It was painted white, with gilding; it was lined with red velvet, and had a coat of arms on its doors.

Once it had been a great honor to ride in that carriage; and when the old Alagonas had passed in it along the Corso, people had stood on their thresholds, and crowded to their doors, and hung over balconies to see them. But then it had been drawn by spirited barbs; then the coachman had worn a wig, and the footman gold braid, and it had been driven with embroidered silk reins.

Now Don Ferrante wished to harness his old horses before the gala carriage and have his old shopman take the place of coachman.

When Donna Micaela told him that it could not be, Don Ferrante began to weep. What would people think of him if he did not show himself on the Corso in the afternoon? That was the last thing a man of position denied himself. How could anyone know that he was a nobleman, if he did not drive up and down the street in the carriage of the old Alagonas?

The happiest hour Don Ferrante had enjoyed since his illness was when he drove out for the first time. He sat erect and nodded and waved very graciously to everyone he met. And the people of Diamante bowed, and took off their hats, so that they swept the street. Why should they not give Don Ferrante this pleasure?

Donna Micaela was with him, for Don Ferrante did not dare to drive alone. She had not wished to go, but Don Ferrante had wept, and reminded her that he had married her when she was despised and penniless. She ought not to be ungrateful; she ought not to forget what he had done for her, and ought to come with him. Why did she not wish to drive with him in his carriage? It was the finest old carriage in Sicily.

"Why will you not come with me?" said Don Ferrante. "Remember that I am the only one who loves you. Do you not see that not even your father loves you? You must not be ungrateful."

In this way he had forced Donna Micaela to take her place in the gala carriage.

But it was not at all as she had expected. No one laughed. The women curtsied, and the men bowed as solemnly as if the carriage had been a hundred years younger. And Donna Micaela could not detect a smile on any face.

No one in all Diamante would have wished to laugh; for everyone knew how Don Ferrante treated Donna Micaela. They knew how he loved her, and how he wept if she left him for a single minute. They knew, too, that he tormented her with jealousy, and that he trampled her hats to pieces, if they became her, and never gave her money for new dresses, because no other was to find her beautiful, and love her. But all the time he told her that she was so ugly that no one but he could bear to look at her face. And because everyone in Diamante knew it all, no one laughed. Laugh at her, sitting and chatting with a sick man! They are pious Christians in Diamante, and not barbarians.

So the gala-carriage in its faded glory drove up and down the Corso in Diamante during the hour between five and six. And in Diamante it drove quite alone, for there were no other fine carriages there; but people knew that at that same time all the carriages in Rome drove to Monte Pincio, all those in Naples to the Via Nazionale, and all in Florence to the Cascine, and all in Palermo to La Favorita.

But when the carriage approached the Porta Etnea for the third time, a merry sound of horns was heard from the road outside.

And through the gate swung a big, high coach in the English style.

It was meant to look old-fashioned also. The postilion riding on the off leader had leather trousers, and a wig tied in a pig-tail. The coach was like an old diligence, with the body behind the coach box and seats on the roof.

But everything was new; the horses were magnificent, powerful animals, carriage and harness shone, and the passengers were some young gentlemen and ladies from Catania, who were making an excursion up Etna. And they could not help laughing as they drove by the old gala-carriage. They leaned over from where they sat on the high roof to look at it, and their laughter sounded very loud and echoed between the high, silent houses of Diamante.

Donna Micaela was very unhappy. They were some of her old circle of friends. What would they not say when they came home? "We have seen Micaela Palmeri in Diamante." And they would laugh and talk, laugh and talk.

Her life seemed so squalid. She was nothing but the slave of a fool. Her whole life long she would never do anything but chat with Don Ferrante.

When she came home she was quite exhausted. She was so tired and weak that she could scarcely drag herself up the steps.

And all the time Don Ferrante was rejoicing in his good fortune at having met all those fine people, and having been seen in his state. He told her that now no one would ask whether she was ugly, or whether her father had stolen. Now people knew that she was the wife of a man of rank.

After dinner Donna Micaela sat quite silent, and let her father talk to Don Ferrante. Then a mandolin began to sound quite softly in the street under the window of the summer palace. It was a single mandolin with no accompaniment of guitar or violin.

Nothing could be more light and airy; nothing more captivating and affecting. No one could think that human hands were touching the strings. It was as if bees and crickets and grasshoppers were giving a concert.

"There is someone again who has fallen in love with Giannita," said Don Ferrante. "That is a woman, Giannita. Anyone can see that she is pretty. If I were young I should fall in love with Giannita. She knows how to love."

Donna Micaela started. He was right, she thought. The mandolin-player meant Giannita. That evening Giannita was at home with her mother, but otherwise she always lived at the summer palace. Donna Micaela had arranged it so since Don Ferrante had been ill.

But Donna Micaela liked the mandolin playing, for whomever it might be meant. It came sweet, and soft, and comforting. She went gently into her room to listen better in the dark and loneliness.

A sweet, strong fragrance met her there. What was it? Her hands began to tremble before she found a candle and a match. On her work-table lay a big, widely opened magnolia-blossom.

On one of the flower petals was pricked: "Who loves me?" And now stood under it: "Gaetano."

Beside the flower lay a little white book full of love songs. And there was a mark against one of the little verses: —

"None have known the love that I have brought thee,
Silent, secret, born in midnight's measure.
All my dreams have stolen forth and sought thee;
Miserlike, the while, I watched my treasure:
Tho' the priest shall seek to shrive me, dying,
Silent I, nor needing him to speed me,
Bar the door, fling forth the key, and lying
Thus unshriven, go where death shall lead me."

The mandolin continued to play. There is something of open air and sunlight in a mandolin; something soothing and calming; something of the cheering carelessness of beautiful nature.

# IX

## FLIGHT

*A*t that time the little image from Aracoeli was still in Diamante.

The Englishwoman who owned it had been fascinated by Diamante. She had not been able to bring herself to leave it.

She had hired the whole first floor of the hotel, and had established herself there as in a home. She bought for large sums everything she could find in the way of old pots and old coins. She bought mosaics, and altar-pictures, and holy images. She thought that she would like to make a collection of all the saints of the church.

She heard of Gaetano, and sent him a message to come to her at the hotel.

Gaetano collected what he had carved during the last few days and took them with him to Miss Tottenham. She was much pleased with his little images, and wished to buy them all.

"But the rich Englishwoman's rooms were like the lumber-rooms of a museum. They were filled with every conceivable thing, and there was confusion and disorder everywhere. Here stood half-empty trunks; there hung cloaks and hats; here lay paintings and engravings; there were guide-books, railway time-tables, tea-sets, and alcohol lamps; elsewhere halberds, prayer-books, mandolins, and escutcheons.

And that opened Gaetano's eyes. He flushed suddenly, bit his lips, and began to repack his images.

He had caught sight of an image of the Christchild. It was the outcast, who was standing there in the midst of all the disorder, with his wretched crown on his head and brass shoes on his feet. The color was worn off his face; the rings and ornaments hanging on him were tarnished, and his dress was yellowed with age.

When Gaetano saw that, he would not sell his images to Miss Tottenham; he meant simply to go his way.

When she asked him what was the matter with him he stormed at her, and scolded her.

Did she know that many of the things she had about her were sacred?

Did she know, or did she not know, that that was the holy Christchild himself? And she had let him lose three fingers on one hand, and let the jewels fall out of his crown, and let him lie dirty, and tarnished, and dishonored! And if she had so treated the image of God's own son, how would she let everything else fare? He would not sell anything to her.

When Gaetano burst out at her in that way Miss Tottenham was enraptured, enchanted.

Here was the true faith and the righteous, holy wrath. This young man must become an artist. To England, he should go to England! She wished to send him to the great master, her friend, who was trying to reform art; to him who wished to teach people to make beautiful house-furnishings, beautiful church-fittings, who wished to create a whole beautiful world.

She decided and arranged, and Gaetano let her go on, because he would rather now go away from Diamante.

He saw that he could no longer endure to live there. He believed that it was God leading him out of temptation.

He went away quite unobserved. Donna Micaela scarcely knew anything of it until he was gone. He had not dared to come and bid her good-bye.

# X

## THE SIROCCO

*A*fter that two years passed quietly. The only thing that happened at Diamante and in all Sicily was that the people grew ever poorer and poorer.

Then there came an autumn, and it was about the time when the wine was to be harvested.

At that time songs generally rise full-fledged to the lips; at that time new and beautiful melodies stream from the mandolins.

Then crowds of young people go out to the vineyards, and there is work and laughter all day, dance and laughter all night, and no one knows what sleep is.

Then the bright ocean of air over the mountain is more beautiful than at any other time. Then the air is full of wit; sparkling glances flash through it; it gets warmth not only from the sun, but also from the glowing faces of the young women of Etna.

But that autumn all the vineyards were devastated by the phylloxera. No grape-pickers pushed their way between the vines; no long lines of women carrying heaped-up baskets on their heads wound up to the presses, and at night there was no dancing on the flat roofs.

That autumn no clear, light October air lay over the Etna region. As if it had been in league with the famine, the heavy, weakening wind from the Sahara came over from Africa, and brought with it dust and exhalations that darkened the sky.

Never, as long as that autumn lasted, was there a fresh mountain breeze. The baleful Sirocco blew incessantly.

Sometimes it came dry and heavy with sand, and so hot that they had to shut doors and windows, and keep in their rooms, not to faint away.

But oftener it came warm and damp and enervating. And the people felt no rest; trouble left them neither by day nor by night, and cares piled upon them like snowdrifts on the high mountains.

And the restlessness reached Donna Micaela as she sat and watched with her old husband, Don Ferrante.

During that autumn she never heard anyone laugh, nor heard a song. People crept by one another, so full of anger and despair that they were almost choked. And she said to herself that they were certainly dreaming of an insurrection. She saw that they had to revolt. It would help no one, but they had no other resource.

In the beginning of the autumn, sitting on her balcony, she heard the people talk in the street. They always talked of the famine: We have blight in wheat and wine; there is a crisis in sulfur and oranges; all Sicily's yellow gold has failed. How shall we live?

And Donna Micaela understood that it was terrible. Wheat, wine, oranges, and sulfur, all their yellow gold!

She began to understand, too, that the misery was greater than men could bear long, and she grieved that life should be made so hard. She asked why the people should be forced to bear such enormous taxes. Why should the salt tax exist, so that a poor woman could not go down to the shore and get a pail of salt water, but must buy costly salt in the government shops? Why should there be a tax on palm trees? The peasants, with anger in their hearts, were felling the old trees that had waved so long over the noble isle. And why should a tax be put on windows? What did they want? Was it that the poor should take away their windows, move out of their rooms, and live in cellars?

In the sulfur-mines there were strikes and turbulence, and the government was sending troops to force the people back to work. Donna Micaela wondered if the government did not know that there was no machinery in those mines. Perhaps it had never heard that children dragged the ore up from the deep shafts. It did not know that these children were slaves; it could not imagine that parents had sold them to overseers. Or if the government did know it, why did it wish to help the mine-owners?

At one time she heard of a terrible number of crimes. And she began again with her questions. Why did they let the people become so criminal? And why did they let them be so poor and so ragged? Why must they all be so ragged? She knew that anyone living in Palermo or Catania did not need to ask. But he who lived in Diamante could not help fearing and asking. Why did they let the people be so poor that they died of hunger?

As yet the summer was hardly over; it was no later in the autumn than the end of October, and already Donna Micaela began to see the day when the insurrection would break out. She saw the starved people come rushing along the street. They would plunder the shops and they would plunder the few rich men there were in the town. Outside the summer palace the wild horde would stop, and they would climb up to the balcony and the glass doors. "Bring out the jewels of the old Alagonas; bring out Don Ferrante's millions!" That was their dream, — the summer palace! They believed that it was as full of gold as a fairy palace.

But when they found nothing, they would put a dagger to her throat, to make her give up the treasures that she had never possessed, and she would be killed by the bloodthirsty crowds.

Why could not the great land-owners stop at home? Why must they irritate the poor by living in grand style in Rome and Paris? The people would not be so bitter against them if they stayed at home; they would not swear such a solemn and sacred oath to kill all the rich when the time should come.

Donna Micaela wished that she could have escaped to one of the big towns. But both her father and Don Ferrante fell ill that autumn, and for their sakes she was forced to remain where she was. And she knew that she would be killed as an atonement for the sins of the rich against the poor.

For many years misfortunes had been gathering over Sicily, and now they could no longer be held back. Etna itself began to menace an eruption. At night sulfurous smoke floated red as fire, and rumblings were heard as far away as Diamante. The end of everything was coming. Everything was to be destroyed at once.

Did not the government know of the discontent? Ah, the government had at last heard of it, and it had appointed a committee. It was a great comfort to see the members of the committee come driving one fine day along the Corso in Diamante. If only the people had understood that they wished them well! If the women had not stood in their doorways and spat at the fine gentlemen from the mainland; if the children had not run beside the carriages and cried: "Thief, thief!"

Everything they did only stirred up the revolt, and there was no one who could control the people and quiet them. They trusted no officials. They despised those least who only took bribes. But people said that many belonged to the society of Mafia; they said that their one thought was to extort money and acquire power.

As time went on, several signs showed that something terrible was impending. In the papers they wrote that crowds of working-men were gathering in the larger towns and wandering about the streets. People read also in the papers how the socialist leaders were going through the country, and making seditious speeches. All at once it became clear to Donna Micaela whence all the trouble came. The socialists were inciting the revolt. It was their firebrand speeches that set the blood of the people boiling. How could they let them do it? Who was king in Sicily? Was his name Don Felice, or Umberto?

Donna Micaela felt a horror which she could not shake off. It was as if they had conspired especially against her. And the more she heard of the socialists, the more she feared them.

Giannita tried to calm her. "We have not a single socialist in Diamante," she said. "In Diamante no one is thinking of revolt." Donna Micaela asked her if she did not know what it meant when the old distaff spinners sat in their dark corners, and told of the great brigands and of the famous Palermo fisherman, Giuseppe Alesi, whom they called the Masaniello of Sicily.

If the socialists could once get the revolt started, Diamante would also join in. All Diamante knew already that something dreadful was impending. They had seen the ghost of the big, black monk on the balcony of the Palazzo Geraci; they heard the owls scream through the night, and some declared that the cocks crowed at sunset, and were silent at daybreak.

One day in November Diamante was suddenly filled with terrible people. They were men with the faces of wild beasts, with bushy beards, and with big hands set on enormously long arms. Several of them wore wide, fluttering linen garments, and the people thought that they recognized in them famous bandits and newly freed galley-slaves.

Giannita related that all these wild people lived in the mountain wastes inland and had crossed Simeto and come to Diamante, because a rumor had gone about that revolt had already broken out. But when they had found everything quiet, and the barracks full of soldiers, they had gone away.

Donna Micaela thought incessantly of those people, and expected them to be her murderers. She saw before her their fluttering linen garments and their brute faces. She knew that they were lurking in their mountain holes, and waiting for the day when they should hear shots and the noise of an outbreak in Diamante. Then they would fall upon the town with fire and murder, and march at the head of all the starving people as the generals and leaders in the plundering.

All that autumn Donna Micaela had to nurse both her father and Don Ferrante; for they lay sick month after month. People had told her, however, that their lives were in no danger.

She was very glad to be able to keep Don Ferrante alive, for it was her only hope that at the last the people would spare him, who was of such an old and venerated race.

As she sat by their sick-beds, her thoughts went often in longing to Gaetano, and many were the times when she wished that he were at home. She would not feel such terror and fear of death if he stood once more in his workshop. Then she would have felt nothing but security and peace.

Even now, when he was so far away, it was to him her thoughts turned when fear was driving her mad. Not a single letter had come from him since he had gone away, so that sometimes she believed that he had forgotten her entirely. At other times she was quite sure that he loved her, for she felt herself compelled to think of him, and knew that he was near her in thought, and was calling to her.

That autumn she at last received a letter from Gaetano. Alas, such a letter! Donna Micaela's first thought was to burn it.

She had gone up to the roof-garden in order to be alone when she read the letter. She had once heard Gaetano's declaration of love there. That had not moved her. It had neither warmed her nor frightened her.

But this letter was different. He prayed that she would come to him, be his, give him her life. When she read it she was frightened at herself. She felt how she longed to cry out into the air, "I am coming, I am coming," and set out. It drew her, carried her away.

"Let us be happy!" he wrote. "We are losing time; the years are passing. Let us be happy!"

He described to her how they would live. He told her of other women who had obeyed love and been happy. He wrote as temptingly as convincingly.

But it was not the contents; it was the love that glowed and burned in the letter which overcame her. It rose from the paper like an intoxicating incense, and she felt it penetrate her. It was burning, longing, speaking, in every word.

Now she was no longer a saint to him, as she had been before. It came so unexpectedly, after two years' silence, that she was stunned. And she was troubled because it delighted her.

She had never thought that love was like this. Should she really like it? She found with dismay that she did like it.

And so she punished both herself and him by writing a severe reply. It was moral, moral; it was nothing but moral! She was proud when she had written it. She did not deny that she loved him, but perhaps Gaetano would not be able to find the words of love, they were so buried in admonitions. He could not have found them, for he wrote no more letters.

But now Donna Micaela could no longer think of Gaetano as a shelter and a support. Now he was more dangerous than the men from the mountains.

Every day graver news came to Diamante. Everybody began to get out their weapons. And although it was forbidden, they were carried secretly by everyone.

All travelers left the island, and in their place one regiment after another was sent over from Italy.

The socialists talked and talked. They were possessed by evil spirits; they could not rest until they had brought on the disaster!

At last the ringleaders had decided on the day on which the storm was to break loose. All Sicily, all Italy, was to rise. It was no longer menace; it was reality.

More and more troops came from the mainland. Most of them were Neapolitans, who live in constant feud with the Sicilians. And now the news came that the island had been declared in a state of siege. There were to be no more courts of justice; only court-martials. And the people said that the soldiers would be free to plunder and murder as they pleased.

No one knew what was to happen. Terror seemed to make everyone mad. The peasants raised ramparts in the hills. In Diamante men stood in great groups on the marketplace, stood there day after day, without going to their work. There was something terrible in those groups of men dressed in dark cloaks and slouch hats. They were all probably dreaming of the hour when they should plunder the summer palace.

The nearer the day approached when the insurrection was to break out, the sicker Don Ferrante became; and Donna Micaela began to fear that he would die.

It seemed to her a sign that she was predestined to destruction, that she was also losing Don Ferrante. Who would have any regard for her when he was no longer alive?

She watched over him. She and all the women of the quarter sat in silent prayer about his bed.

One morning, towards six o'clock, Don Ferrante died. And Donna Micaela mourned him, because he had been her only protector, and the only one who could have saved her from destruction; and she wished to honor the dead, as is still the custom in Diamante.

She had them drape the room where the body was lying with black, and close all the shutters, so that the glad sunlight should not enter. She had all the fires put out on the hearths, and sent for a blind singer to come to the palace every day and sing dirges.

She let Giannita care for Cavaliere Palmeri, so that she herself might sit quiet in the death room, among the other women.

It was evening on the day of death before all preparations were completed, and they were waiting only for the White Brotherhood to come and take away the corpse. In the death-chamber there was the silence of the grave. All the women of the quarter sat there motionless with dismal faces.

Donna Micaela sat pale with her great fear, and stared involuntarily at the pall that was spread over the body. It was a pall which belonged to the family; their coat of arms was heavily and gorgeously embroidered on the center, and it had silver fringes and thick tassels. The pall had never been spread over anyone but an Alagona. It seemed to lie there so that Donna Micaela should not for a moment forget that her last support had fallen, and that she was now alone, and without protection from the infuriated people.

Someone came in and announced that old Assunta had come. Old Assunta; what did old Assunta want? Yes, it was she who came to sing the praises of the dead.

Donna Micaela let Assunta come into the room. She appeared just as she looked every day, when she sat and begged on the Cathedral steps; the same patched dress, the same faded head-cloth, and the same crutch.

Little and bent, she limped forward to the coffin. She had a shriveled face, a sunken mouth, and dull eyes. Donna Micaela said to herself that it was incarnate helplessness and feebleness who had come into the room.

The old woman raised her voice and began to speak in the wife's name.

"My lord is dead, and I am alone! He who raised me to his side is dead! Is it not terrible that my home has lost its master? — Why are the shutters of your windows closed? say the passers-by. — I answer, I cannot bear to see the light, because my sorrow is so great; my grief is three-fold. — What, are so many of your race carried away by the White Brethren? — No, none of my race is dead, but I have lost my husband, my husband, my husband!"

Old Assunta needed to say no more. Donna Micaela burst into lamentations. The whole room was filled with the sound of weeping from the sympathetic women; for there is no grief like losing a husband. Those who were widows thought of what they had lost, and those who were not as yet widows thought of the time when they would not be able to go on the street, because no husband would be with them; when they would be left to loneliness, poverty, oblivion; when they would be nothing, mean nothing; when they would be the world's outcast children because they no longer had a husband; because nothing any longer gave them the right to live.

*I*t was late in December, the days between Christmas and the New Year.

There was still the same danger of insurrection, and people still heard terrifying rumors. It was said that Falco Falcone had gathered together a band of brigands in the quarries, and that he was only waiting for the appointed day to break into Diamante and plunder it.

It was also whispered that the people in several of the small mountain towns had risen, torn down the custom's offices at the town-gates, and driven away the officials.

People said too that troops were passing from town to town, arresting all suspicious people, and shooting them down by hundreds.

Everyone said that they must fight. They could not let themselves be murdered by those Italians without trying to make some resistance.

During all this, Donna Micaela sat tied to her father's sick-bed, just as she had sat before by Don Ferrante's. She could not escape from Diamante, and terror so grew within her that she was nothing but one trembling fear.

The last and worst of all the messages of terror that reached her had been about Gaetano.

For when Don Ferrante had been dead a week Gaetano had come home. And that had not caused her dismay; it had only made her glad. She had rejoiced in at last having someone near her who could protect her.

At the same time she decided that she could not receive Gaetano if he came to see her. She felt that she still belonged to the dead. She would rather not see Gaetano until after a year.

But when Gaetaco had been at home a week without coming to the summer palace, she asked Giannita about him. "Where is Gaetano? Has he perhaps gone away again, since no one speaks of him?"

"Alas, Micaela," answered Giannita, "the less people speak of Gaetano, the better for him."

She told Donna Micaela, as if she was telling of a great shame, that Gaetano had become a socialist.

"He has been quite transformed over there, in England," she said. "He no longer worships either God or the saints. He does not kiss the priest's hand when he meets him. He says to everyone that they shall pay no more duties at the town-gates. He encourages the peasants not to pay their rent. He carries weapons. He has come home to start a rebellion, to help the bandits."

She needed to say no more to chill Donna Micaela with a greater terror than she had ever felt before.

It was this that the sultry days of the autumn had portended. It would be he who would shake the bolt from the clouds. Why had she not understood it long ago?

It was a punishment and a revenge. It would be he who would bring the misfortune!

During those last days she had been calmer. She had heard that all the socialists on the island had been put in prison, and all the little insurrection fires lighted in the mountain towns had been quickly choked. It looked almost as if the rebellion would come to nothing!

But now the last Alagona was come, and him the people would follow. Life would enter into those black groups on the marketplace. The men in the linen garments would climb up out of the quarries.

*T*he next evening Gaetano spoke in the marketplace. He had sat by the fountain, and had seen how the people came to get water. For two years he had foregone the pleasure of seeing the slender girls lift the heavy water-jars to their heads and walk away with firm, slow step.

But it was not only the young girls who came to the fountain; there were people of all ages. And when he saw how poor and unhappy most of them were, he began to talk to them of the future.

He promised them better times soon. He said to old Assunta that she hereafter should get her daily bread without needing to ask alms of anyone. And when she said that she did not understand how that could be, he asked her almost with anger if she did not know that now the time had come when no old people and no children should be without care and shelter.

He pointed to the old chair-maker, who was as poor as Assunta, and moreover very sick, and he asked if she believed that the people would endure much longer having no support for the poor, and no hospitals. Could she not understand that it was impossible for such things to continue? Could they not all understand that hereafter the old and the sick should be cared for?

He also saw some children who, as he knew, lived on cresses and sorrel, which they gathered on the river-banks and by the roadside, and he promised that henceforward no one should need to starve. He laid his hand on the children's heads, and swore as solemnly as if he were prince of Diamante, that they should never again want for bread.

They knew nothing in Diamante, he said; they were ignorant; they did not understand that a new and blessed time had come; they believed that this old misery would continue forever.

While he was thus consoling the poor, more and more had gathered about him, and he suddenly sprang up, placed himself on the steps of the fountain, and began to speak.

How could they, he said, be so foolish as to believe that nothing better would come? Should the people, who possessed the whole earth, be content to let their parents starve, and their children grow up to be good-for-nothings and criminals?

Did they not know that there were treasures in the mountains, and in the sea, and in the ground? Had they never heard that the earth was rich? Did they think that it could not feed its children?

They should not murmur among themselves, and say that it was impossible to arrange matters differently. They should not think that there must be rich and poor. Alas, they understood nothing! They did not know their Mother Earth. Did they think that she hated any of them? They had lain down on the ground and heard the earth speak? Perhaps they had seen her make laws? They had heard her pass sentence? She had commanded some to starve, and some to die of luxury?

Why did they not open their ears and listen to the new teachings pouring through the world? Would they not like to have a better life? Did they like their rags? Were they satisfied with sorrel and cresses? Did they not wish to possess a roof over their heads?

And he told them that it made no difference, no difference, if they refused to believe in the new times that were coming. They would come in spite of it. They did not need to lift the sun up from the sea in the morning. The new times would come to them as the sun came, but why would they not be ready to meet them? Why did they shut themselves in, and fear the new light?

He spoke long in the same strain, and more and more of the poor people of Diamante gathered about him.

The longer he continued, the more beautiful became his speech and the clearer grew his voice.

His eyes were full of fire, and to the people looking up at him, he seemed as beautiful as a young prince.

He was one of the race of once powerful lords, who had possessed means to shower happiness and gold on everybody within their wide lands. They believed him when he said that he had happiness to give them. They felt comforted, and rejoiced that their young lord loved them.

When he had finished speaking they began to shout, and call to him that they wished to follow him and do what he commanded.

He had gained ascendancy over them in a moment.

He was so beautiful and so glorious that they could not resist him. And his faith seized and subdued.

That night there was not one poor person in Diamante who did not believe that Gaetano would give him happy days, free from care. That night they called down blessings on him, all those who lived in sheds and out-houses. That night the hungry lay down with the sure belief that the next day tables groaning under many dishes would stand spread for them when they awoke.

For when Gaetano spoke, his power was so great that he could convince an old man that he was young, and a freezing man that he was warm. And people felt that what he promised must come.

He was the prince of the coming times. His hands were generous, and miracles and blessings would stream down over Diamante, now that he had come again.

*T*he next day, towards sunset, Giannita came into the sick-room and whispered to Donna Micaela: "There is an insurrection in Paternó. They have been shooting for several hours, and you can hear them as far away as here. Orders for troops have already gone to Catania. And Gaetano says that it will break out here, too. He says that it will break out in all the towns of Etna at one time."

Donna Micaela made a sign to Giannita to stay with her father, and she herself went across the street and into Donna Elisa's shop.

Donna Elisa sat behind the counter with her frame, but she was not working. The tears fell so heavy and fast that she had ceased to embroider.

"Where is Gaetano?" said Donna Micaela, without any preamble. "I must speak to him."

"God give you strength to talk to him," answered Donna Elisa. "He is in the garden."

She went out across the courtyard and into the walled garden.

In the garden there were many narrow paths winding from terrace to terrace. There was also a number of arbors and grottos and benches. And it was so thick with stiff agaves, and close-growing dwarf palms, and thick-leaved rubber-plants, and rhododendrons, that it was impossible to see two feet in front of one. Donna Micaela walked for a long time on those innumerable paths before she could find Gaetano. The longer she walked, the more impatient she became.

At last she found him at the farther end of the garden. She caught sight of him on the lowest terrace, built out on one of the bastions of the wall of the town. There sat Gaetano at ease, and worked with chisel and hammer on a statuette. When he saw Donna Micaela, he came towards her with outstretched hands.

She hardly gave herself time to greet him. "Is it true," she said, "that you have come home to be our ruin?" He began to laugh. "The syndic has been here," he said. "The priest has been here. Are you coming too?"

It wounded her that he laughed, and that he spoke of the priest and the syndic. It was something different, and more, that she came.

"Tell me," she said, stiffly, "if it is true that we are to have an uprising this evening." — "Oh, no," he answered; "we shall have no uprising."

And he said it in such a voice that it almost made her sorry for him.

"You cause Donna Elisa great grief," she burst out. — "And you too, do I not?" he said, with a slight sneer. "I cause you all sorrow. I am the lost son; I am Judas. I am the angel of justice who is driving you from that paradise where people eat grass."

She answered: "Perhaps we think that what we have is better than being shot by the soldiers." — "Yes, of course; it is better to starve to death. We are used to that." — "Nor is it pleasant to be murdered by bandits." — "But why for Heaven's sake have any bandits, if you do not want to be murdered by them?" — "Yes, I know," she said, more passionately, "that you want all the rich to perish."

He did not answer immediately; he stood and bit his lips, so as not to lose his temper. "Let me talk with you, Donna Micaela!" he said at last. "Let me explain it to you!"

At the same time he put on a patient expression. He talked socialism with her, so clear and simple that a child could have understood.

But she was far from being able to follow it. Perhaps she could have, but she did not wish to. She did not wish just then to hear of socialism.

It had been so wonderful to her to see him. The ground had rocked under her; and something glorious and blessed had passed through and quite overcome her. "God, it is he whom I love!" she said to herself. "It is really he."

Before she had seen him she had known very well what she would say to him. She would have led him back to the faith of his childhood. She would have shown him that those new teachings were detestable and dangerous. But then love came. It made her confused and stupid.

She could not answer him. She only sat and wondered that he could talk.

She wondered if he was much handsomer now than formerly. Formerly she had not been confused at all when she saw him. She had never been attracted to that extent. Or was it that he had become a free, strong man? She was frightened when she felt how he subdued her.

She dared not contradict him. She dared not even speak, for fear of bursting into tears. Had she dared to speak, she would not have talked of public affairs. She would have told him what she had felt the day the bells rang. Or she would have prayed to be allowed to kiss his hand. She would have told him how she had dreamed of him. She would have said that if she had not had him to dream of she could not have borne her life. She would have begged to be allowed to kiss his hand in gratitude, because he had given her life all these years.

If there was to be no uprising, why did he talk socialism? What had socialism to do with them, sitting alone in Donna Elisa's garden? She sat and looked along one of the paths. Luca had put up wooden arches on both sides of it, and up these climbed garlands of light rose-shoots, full of little buds and flowers. One always wondered whither one was coming when one went along that path. And one came to a little weather-beaten cupid. Old Luca understood things better than Gaetano.

While they sat there the sun set, and Etna grew rosy-red. It was as if Etna flushed with anger at what was going on in Donna Elisa's garden. It was at sunset, when Etna glowed red, that she had always thought of Gaetano. It seemed as if they both had been waiting for it. And they had both arranged how it would be when Gaetano came. She had only feared that he would be too fiery, and too passionately wild. And he talked only of those dreadful Socialists, whom she detested and feared.

He talked a long time. She saw Etna grow pale and become bronze-brown, and then the darkness came. She knew that there would be moonlight. There she sat quite still, and hoped for help from the moonlight. She herself could do nothing. She was entirely in his power. But when the moonlight came, it did not help either. He continued to talk of capitalists and working-men.

Then it seemed to her as if there could be but one explanation for all this. He must have ceased to love her.

Suddenly she remembered something. It was a week ago. It was the same day that Gaetano had come home. She had come into Giannita's room, but she had walked so softly that Giannita had not heard her. She had seen Giannita stand as if in ecstasy, with up-stretched arms and up-turned face. And in her hands she held a picture. First she carried it to her lips and kissed it, then she lifted it up over her head and looked up to it in rapture. And the picture had been of Gaetano.

When Donna Micaela had seen that, she had gone away as silently as she had come. She had only thought then that Giannita was to be pitied if she loved Gaetano. But now, when Gaetano only talked socialism, now she remembered it.

Now she began to think that Gaetano also loved Giannita. She remembered that they were friends from childhood. He had perhaps loved her a long time. Perhaps he had come home to marry her. Donna Micaela could say nothing; she had nothing to complain of. It was scarcely a month since she wrote to Gaetano that it was not right of him to love her.

He now leaned towards her, enchained her glance, and actually compelled her to listen to what he was saying.

"You shall understand; you shall see and understand, Donna Micaela! What we need here in the South is a regeneration, a pulling up by the roots, such as Christianity was in its time. Up with the slaves; down with the masters! A plow which turns up new social furrows! We must sow in new earth; the old earth is impoverished. The old surface furrows bear only weak, miserable growth. Let the deep earth come up to the light, and we shall see something different!

"See, Donna Micaela, why does socialism live; why has it not gone under? Because it comes with a new word. 'Think of the earth,' it says, just as Christianity came with the word, 'Think of heaven.' Look about you! Look at the earth; is it not all that we possess? Let us therefore establish ourselves here so that we shall be happy. Why, why, has no one thought of it before? Because we have been so busy with that Hereafter. Let us leave the Hereafter! The earth, the earth, Donna Micaela! Ah, we socialists, we love her! We worship the sacred earth, — the poor, despised mother, who wears mourning because her children yearn for heaven.

"Believe me, Donna Micaela," he said, "it will be accomplished in less than seven years. In the year nineteen hundred it will be ready. Then martyrs will have bled; then apostles will have spoken; then shall crowds upon crowds have been won over! We, the rightful sons of the earth, shall have the victory! And she shall lie before us in all her loveliness; she shall bring us beauty, bring us pleasure, bring us knowledge, bring us health!"

Gaetano's voice began to tremble, and tears quivered in his eyes. He went forward to the edge of the terrace, and he stretched out his arms as if to embrace the moonlit earth. "You are so dazzlingly beautiful," he said, "so dazzlingly beautiful!"

And Donna Micaela for a moment thought she felt his grief over all the sorrow that lay under the surface of beauty. She saw life full of vice and suffering, like a dirty river filled with the stench of uncleanliness, wind through the glistening world of beauty.

"And no one can enjoy you," said Gaetano; "no one can dare to enjoy you. You are untamed, and full of whims and anger. You are uncertainty and peril; you are sorrow and pain; you are want and shame; you are the force that grinds; you are everything terrible that can be named, because the people have not wished to make you better.

"But your day will come," he said, triumphantly. "Some day they will turn to you with all their love; they will not turn to a dream, which gives nothing and is good for nothing."

She interrupted him roughly. She began to fear him more and more.

"So it is true that you have had no success in England?"

"What do you mean?"

"People say that the great master, to whom Miss Tottenham sent you, has said that you —"

"What has he said?"

"That you and your images suited Diamante, but nowhere else."

"Who says such things?"

"People think so, because you are so changed."

"Since I am a socialist."

"Why should you be one if you had been successful?"

"Ah, why — ? You do not know," he continued, with a laugh, "that my master in England himself was a socialist. You do not know that it was he who taught me these opinions —"

He paused, and did not go on with the controversy. He went over to the bench where he had been sitting when she came, and brought back a statuette. He handed it to Donna Micaela. He seemed to wish to say: "See for yourself if you are right."

She took it, and held it up in the moonlight. It was a Mater Dolorosa in black marble. She could see it quite plainly.

She could also recognize it. The image had her own features. It intoxicated her for a moment. In "the next she was filled with horror. He, a socialist; he, an unbeliever; he dared to create a Madonna! And he had given the image her features! He entangled her in his sin!

"I have done it for you, Donna Micaela," he said.

Ah, since it was hers! She threw it out over the balustrade. It struck against the steep mountainside; fell deeper and deeper; broke loose stones, and certainly shattered itself to pieces. At last a splash was heard down in Simeto.

"What right have you to carve Madonnas?" she asked Gaetano.

He stood silent. He had never seen Donna Micaela thus.

In the moment when she rose up before him she had become tall and stately. The beauty that always came and went in her, like an uneasy guest, was enthroned in her face. She looked cold and inflexible; a woman to win and conquer.

"Then you still believe in God, since you carve Madonnas?" she said.

He breathed hurriedly. Now it was he who was paralyzed. He had been a believer himself. He knew how he had wounded her. He saw that he had forfeited her love. He had made a terrible, infinite chasm between them.

He must speak, must win her over to his side.

He began again, but feebly and falteringly.

She listened quietly for a while. Then she interrupted him almost compassionately.

"How did you become so?"

"I thought of Sicily," he said submissively.

"You thought of Sicily," she repeated thoughtfully. "And why did you come home?"

"I came home to cause an insurrection."

It was as if they had spoken of an illness, a chill, that he had contracted, and that could quite easily be cured.

"You came home to be our ruin," she said, sternly.

"As you will; as you will," he said, complying.

"You can call it so. As everything is going now, you are certainly right to call it so. Ah, if they had not given me false information; if I had not come a week too late! Is it not like us Sicilians to let the government anticipate us? When I came the leaders were already arrested, the island garrisoned with forty thousand men. Everything lost!"

It sounded strangely blank when he said that "everything lost." And for that which never could be anything, he had lost happiness. His opinions and principles seemed to him now to be dry cobwebs, which had captured him. He wished to tear himself away to come to her. She was the only reality, the only thing that was his. So he had felt before. It came back now. She was the only thing in the world.

"They are, however, fighting today in Paternó."

"There has been a disagreement by the town-gate," he said. "It is nothing. If I had been able to inflame all Etna, the whole circle of towns round about Etna! Then they would have understood us! they would have listened to us! Now they are shooting down a few hungry peasants to make a few hungry mouths the less. They do not yield an inch to us."

He strove to break through his cobwebs. Could he venture to go up to her, to tell her that all that was of no importance? He did not need to think of politics. He was an artist; he was free! And he wanted to possess her!

Suddenly it seemed as if the air trembled. A shot echoed through the night, then another and another.

She came forward to him and grasped his wrist. "Is that the uprising?" she asked.

Shot upon shot came thundering. Then were heard the cries and din of a crowd rushing down the street.

"It is the uprising; it must be the uprising! Ah, long live socialism!"

He was filled with joy. Entire faith in his belief came back to him. He would win her too. Women have never refused to belong to the victor.

They both hurried without another word through the garden to the door. There Gaetano began to swear and call. He could not get out. There was no key in the lock. He was shut into the garden.

He looked about. There were high walls on three sides, and on the fourth an abyss. There was no way out for him. But from the town came a terrible noise. The people were rushing up and down; there were shots and cries. And they heard them yell: "Long live freedom! Long live socialism! He threw himself against the door, and almost shrieked. He was imprisoned; he could not take part.

Donna Micaela came up to him as quickly as she could. Now, since she had heard him, she no longer thought of keeping him back.

"Wait, wait!" she said. "I took the key."

"You, you!" he said.

"I took it when I came. It occurred to me that I could keep you shut in here if you should want to cause an uprising. I wished to save you."

"What folly!" he said, and snatched the key from her.

While he stood and fumbled to find the keyhole, he still had time to say something.

"Why do you not want to save me now?"

She did not answer.

"Perhaps so that your God may have a chance to destroy me."

She was still silent.

"Do you not dare to save me from His wrath?"

"No, I do not dare," she said quietly.

"You believers are terrible!" he said.

He felt that she threw him aside. It froze him, and took away his courage, that she did not make a single attempt to persuade him to stay.

He turned the key forward and back without being able to open the door, paralyzed by her standing there pale and cold behind him.

Then he suddenly felt her arms about his neck and her lips seeking his.

At the same moment the door flew open and he rushed away. He would not have her kisses, which only consecrated him to death. She was as terrible as a specter to him with her ancient faith. He rushed away like a fugitive.

# XI

## THE FEAST OF SAN SEBASTIANO

When Gaetano rushed away, Donna Micaela stood for a long time in Donna Elisa's garden. She stood there as if turned to stone, and could neither feel nor think.

Then suddenly the thought came that Gaetano and she were not alone in the world. She remembered her father lying sick, whom she had forgotten for so many hours.

She went through the gate of the courtyard out to the Corso, which lay deserted and empty. Tumult and shots were still audible far away, and she said to herself that they must be fighting down by Porta Etnea.

The moon shed its clear light on the façade of the summer-palace, and it amazed her that at such an hour, and on such a night, the balcony doors stood open, and the window shutters were not closed. She was still more surprised that the gate was standing ajar, and that the shop-door was wide open.

As she went in through the gate, she did not see the old gatekeeper, Piero, there. The lanterns in the courtyard were not lighted, and there was not a soul to be seen anywhere.

She went up the steps to the gallery, and her foot struck against something hard. It was a little bronze vase, which belonged in the music-room. A few steps higher up she found a knife. It was a sheath-knife, with a long, daggerlike blade. When she lifted it up a couple of dark drops rolled down from its edge. She knew that it must be blood.

And she understood too that what she had feared all the autumn had now happened. Bandits had been in the summer-palace for plunder. And everyone who could run away had run away; but her father, who could not leave his bed, must be murdered.

She could not tell whether the brigands were not still in the house. But now, in the midst of danger, her fears vanished; and she hurried on, unheeding that she was alone and defenseless.

She went along the gallery into the music-room. Broad rays of moonlight fell upon the floor, and in one of those rays lay a human form stretched motionless.

Donna Micaela bent down over that motionless body. It was Gian-nita. She was murdered; she had a deep, gaping wound in her neck.

Donna Micaela laid the body straight, crossed the hands over the breast, and closed the eyes. In so doing, her hands were wet with the blood; and when she felt that warm, sticky blood, she began to weep. "Alas, my dear, beloved sister," she said aloud, "it is your young life that has ebbed away with this blood. All your life you have loved me, and now you have shed your blood defending my house. Is it to punish my hardness that God has taken you from me? Is it because I did not allow you to love him whom I loved that you have gone from me? Alas, sister, sister, could you not have punished me less severely?"

She bent down and kissed the dead girl's forehead. "You do not believe it," she said. "You know that I have always been faithful to you. You know that I have loved you."

She remembered that the dead was severed from everything earthly, that it was not grief and assurances of friendship she needed. She said a prayer over the body, since the only thing she could do for her sister was to support with pious thoughts the flight of the soul soaring up to God.

Then she went on, no longer afraid of anything that could happen to herself, but in inexpressible terror of what might have happened to her father.

When she had at last passed through the long halls in the state apartment and stood by the door to the sick-room, her hands groped a long time for the latch; and when she had found it, she had not the strength to turn the key.

Then her father called from his room and asked who was there. When she heard his voice and knew that he was alive, everything in her trembled, and burst, and lost its power to serve her. Brain and heart failed her at once, and her muscles could no longer hold her upright. She had still time to think that she had been living in terrible suspense. And with a feeling of relief, she sank down in a long swoon.

Donna Micaela regained consciousness towards morning. In the meantime much had happened. The servants had come out of their hiding places, and had gone for Donna Elisa. She had taken charge of the deserted palace, had summoned the police, and sent a message to the White Brotherhood. And the latter had carried Giannita's body to her mother's house.

When Donna Micaela awoke, she found herself lying on the sofa in a room next her father's. No one was with her, but in her father's room she heard Donna Elisa talking.

"My son and my daughter," said Donna Elisa, sobbing; "I have lost both my son and my daughter."

Donna Micaela tried to raise herself, but she could not. Her body still lay in a stupor, although her soul was awake.

"Cavaliere, Cavaliere," said Donna Elisa, "can you understand? The bandits come here from Etna, creeping down to Diamante. The bandits attack the custom-house and shout: 'Long live Socialism!' They do it only to frighten people away from the streets and to draw the Carabiniere down to Porta Etnea. There is not a single man from Diamante who has anything to do with it. It is the bandits who arrange it all, to be able to plunder Miss Tottenham and Donna Micaela, two women, Cavaliere! What did those officers think at the court-martial? Did they believe that Gaetano was in league with the bandits? Did they not see that he was a nobleman, a true Alagona, an artist? How could they have sentenced him?"

Donna Micaela listened with horror, but she tried to imagine that she was still dreaming. She thought she heard Gaetano ask if she was sacrificing him to God. She thought she answered that she did. Now she was dreaming of how it would be in case he really had been captured. It could be nothing else,

"What a night of misfortune!" said Donna Elisa. "What is flying about in the air, and making people mad and confused? You have seen Gaetano, Cavaliere. He has always been passionate and fiery, but it has not been without intelligence; he has not been without sense and judgment. But tonight he throws himself right into the arms of the troops. You know that he wanted to cause an uprising; you know that he came home for that. And when he hears the shooting, and someone shouting, 'Long live Socialism!' he becomes wild, and beside himself. He says to himself, 'That is the insurrection!' and he rushes down the street to join it. And he shouts the whole time, 'Long live Socialism!' as loud as he can. And so he meets a great crowd of soldiers, a whole host. For they were on their way to Paternó, and heard the shooting as they passed by, and marched in to see what was going on. And Gaetano can no longer recognize a soldier's cap. He thinks that they are the rebels; he thinks that they are angels from heaven, and he rushes in among them and lets them capture him. And they, who have already caught all the bandits sneaking away with their booty, now lay hands on Gaetano too. They go through the town and find everything quiet; but before they leave, they pass sentence on their prisoners. And they condemn Gaetano like the others, condemn him like those who have broken in and murdered women. Have they not lost their senses, Cavaliere?"

Donna Micaela could not hear what her father answered. She wished to ask a thousand questions, but she was still paralyzed and could not move. She wondered if Gaetano had been shot.

"What do they mean by sentencing him to twenty-nine years' imprisonment?" said Donna Elisa. "Do you think that he can live so long, or that anyone who loves him can live so long? He is dead, Cavaliere; as dead for me as Giannita."

Donna Micaela felt as if strong fetters bound her beyond escape. It was worse, she thought, than to be tied to a pillory and whipped.

"All the joy of my old age is taken from me," said Donna Elisa. "Both Giannita and Gaetano! I have always expected them to marry each other. It would have been so suitable, because they were both my children, and loved me. For what shall I live now, when I have no young people about me? I was often poor when Gaetano first came to me, and people said to me that I should have been better off alone. But I answered: 'It makes no difference, none, if only I have young people about me.' And I thought that when he grew up he would find a young wife, and then they would have little children, and I would never need to sit a lonely and useless old woman."

Donna Micaela lay thinking that she could have saved Gaetano, but had not wished to do so. But why had she not wished? It seemed to her quite incomprehensible. She began to count up to herself all her reasons for permitting him to rush to destruction. He was an atheist; a socialist; he wished to cause a revolt. That had outweighed everything else when she opened the garden gate for him. It had crushed her love also. She could not now understand it. It was as if a scale full of feathers had weighed down a scale full of gold.

"My beautiful boy!" said Donna Elisa, "my beautiful boy! He was already a great man over there in England, and he came home to help us poor Sicilians. And now they have sentenced him like a bandit. People say that they were ready to shoot him, as they shot the others. Perhaps it would have been better if they had done so, Cavaliere. It had been better to have laid him in the churchyard than to know that he was in prison. How will he be able to endure all his suffering? He will not be able to bear it; he will fall ill; he will soon be dead."

At these words, Donna Micaela roused herself from her stupor, and got up from the sofa. She staggered across the room and came in to her father and Donna Elisa, as pale as poor murdered Giannita. She was so weak that she did not dare to cross the floor; she stood at the door and leaned against the doorpost.

"It is I," she said; "Donna Elisa, it is I —"

The words would not come to her lips. She wrung her hands in despair that she could not speak.

Donna Elisa was instantly at her side. She put her arm about her to support her, without paying any attention to Donna Micaela's attempt to push her away.

"You must forgive me, Donna Elisa," she said, with an almost inaudible voice. "I did it."

Donna Elisa did not heed much what she was saying. She saw that she had fever, and thought that she was delirious.

Donna Micaela's lips worked; she plainly wished to say something, but only a few words were audible. It was impossible to understand what she meant. "Against him, as against my father," she said, over and over. And then she said something about bringing misfortune on all who loved her.

Donna Elisa had got her down on a chair, and Donna Micaela sat there and kissed her old, wrinkled hands, and asked her to forgive her what she had done.

Yes, of course, of course, Donna Elisa forgave her.

Donna Micaela looked her sharply in the face with great, feverish eyes, and asked if it were true.

It was really true.

Then she laid her head on Donna Elisa's shoulder and sobbed, thanked her, and said that she could not live if she did not obtain her forgiveness. She had sinned against no one so much as against her. Could she forgive her?

"Yes, yes," said Donna Elisa again and again, and thought that the other was out of her head from fever and fright.

"There is something I ought to tell you," said Donna Micaela. "I know it, but you do not know it. You will not forgive me if you hear it."

"Yes, of course I forgive you," said Donna Elisa.

They talked in that way for a long time without understanding each other; but it was good for old Donna Elisa to have someone that night to put to bed, comforted and dosed with strengthening herbs and drops. It was good for her to still have someone to come and lay her head on her shoulder and cry away her grief.

*D*onna Micaela, who had loved Gaetano for nearly three years without a thought that they could ever belong to each other, had accustomed herself to a strange kind of love. It was enough for her to know that Gaetano loved her. When she thought of it, a tender feeling of security and happiness stole through her. "What does it matter; what does it matter?" she said, when she suffered adversity. "Gaetano loves me." He was always with her, cheering and comforting her. He took part in all her thoughts and undertakings. He was the soul of her life.

As soon as Donna Micaela could get his address, she wrote to him. She acknowledged to him that she had firmly believed that he had gone to misfortune. But she had been so much afraid of what he proposed to accomplish in the world that she had not dared to save him.

She also wrote how she detested his teachings. She did not dissemble at all to him. She said that even if he were free she could not be his.

She feared him. He had such power over her that, if they were united, he would make her a socialist and an atheist. Therefore she must always live apart from him, for the salvation of her soul.

But she begged and prayed that in spite of everything he would not cease to love her. He must not; he must not! He might punish her in any way he pleased, if only he did not cease to love her.

He must not do as her father had. He had perhaps reason to close his heart to her now, but he must not. He must be merciful.

If he knew how she loved him! If he knew how she dreamed of him!

She told him that he was nothing less than life itself to her.

"Must I die, Gaetano?" she asked.

"Is it not enough that those opinions and teachings part us? Is it not enough that they have carried you to prison? Will you also cease to love me, because we do not think alike?

"Ah, Gaetano, love me! It leads to nothing; there is no hope in your love, but love me; I die if you do not love me."

Donna Micaela had hardly sent off the letter before she began to wait for the answer. She expected a stormy and angry reply, but she hoped that there would be one single word to show her that he still loved her.

But she waited several weeks without receiving any letter from Gaetano.

It did not help her to stand and wait every morning for the letter-carrier out on the gallery, and almost break his heart because he was always obliged to say that he did not have anything for her.

One day she went herself to the post office, and asked them, with the most beseeching eyes, to give her the letter she was expecting. It must be there, she said. But perhaps they had not been able to read the address; perhaps it had been put into the wrong box? And her soft, imploring eyes so touched the postmaster that she was allowed to look through piles of old, unclaimed letters, and to turn all the drawers in the post office upside down. But it was all in vain.

She wrote new letters to Gaetano; but no answer came.

Then she tried to believe what seemed impossible. She tried to make her soul realize that Gaetano had ceased to love her.

As her conviction increased, she began to shut herself into her room. She was afraid of people, and preferred to sit alone.

Day by day she became more feeble. She walked deeply bent, and even her beautiful eyes seemed to lose their life and light.

After a few weeks she was so weak that she could no longer keep up, but lay all day on her sofa. She was prey to a suffering that gradually deprived her of all vital power. She knew that she was failing, and she was afraid to die. But she could do nothing. There was only one remedy for her, but that never came. While Donna Micaela seemed to be thus quietly gliding out of life, the people of Diamante were preparing to celebrate the feast of San Sebastiano, that comes at the end of January.

It was the greatest festival of Diamante, but in the last few years it had not been kept with customary splendor, because want and gloom had weighed too heavily on their souls.

But this year, just after the revolt had failed, and while Sicily was still filled with troops, and while the beloved heroes of the people languished in prison, they determined to celebrate the festival with all the old-time pomp; for now, they said, was not the time to neglect the saint.

And the pious people of Diamante determined that the festival should be held for a week, and that San Sebastiano should be honored with flags and decorations, and with races and biblical processions, illuminations, and singing contests.

The people bestirred themselves with great haste and eagerness. There was polishing and scrubbing in every house. They brought out the old costumes, and they prepared to receive strangers from all Etna.

The summer-palace was the only house in Diamante where no preparations were made. Donna Elisa was deeply grieved at it, but she could not induce Donna Micaela to have her house decorated. "How can you ask me to trim a house of mourning with flowers and leaves?" she said. "The roses would shed their petals if I tried to use them to mask the misery that reigns here."

But Donna Elisa was very eager for the festival, and expected much good to result from honoring the saint as in the old days. She could talk of nothing but of how the priests had decorated the façade of the Cathedral in the old Sicilian way, with silver flowers and mirrors. And she described the procession: how many riders there were to be, and what high plumes they were to have in their hats, and what long, garlanded staves, with wax candles at the end, they were to carry in their hands.

When the first festival day came, Donna Elisa's house was the most gorgeously decorated. The green, red, and white standard of Italy waved from the roof, and red cloths, fringed with gold, bearing the saint's initials, were spread over the windowsills and balcony railings. Up and down the wall ran garlands of holly, shaped into stars and arches, and round the windows crept wreaths made of the little pink roses from Donna Elisa's garden. Just over the entrance stood the saint's image, framed in lilies, and on the threshold lay cypress-branches. And if one had entered the house, one would have found it as much adorned on the inside as on the outside. From the cellar to the attic it was scoured and covered with flowers, and on the shelves in the shop no saint was too small or insignificant to have an everlasting or a harebell in his hand. Like Donna Elisa, everyone in penniless Diamante had decorated along the whole street. In the street above the house of the little Moor there was such an array of flags that it looked like clothes hung out to dry from the earth to the sky. Every house and every arch carried flags, and across the streets were hung ropes, from which fluttered pennant after pennant.

At every tenth step the people of Diamante had raised triumphal arches over the street. And over every door stood the image of the saint, framed in wreaths of yellow everlastings. The balconies were covered with red quilts and bright-colored tablecloths, and stiff garlands wound up the walls.

There were so many flowers and leaves that no one could understand how they had been able to get them all in January. Everything was crowned and wreathed with flowers. The brooms had crowns of crocuses, and each door-knocker a bunch of hyacinths. In windows stood pictures with monograms, and inscriptions of blood-red anemones.

And between those decorated houses the stream of people rolled as mighty as a rising river. It was not the inhabitants of Diamante alone who were honoring San Sebastiano. From all Etna came yellow carts, beautifully ornamented and painted, drawn by horses in shining harness, and loaded down with people. The sick, the beggars, the blind singers came in great crowds. There were whole trains of pilgrims, unhappy people, who now, after their misfortunes, had someone to pray to.

Such numbers came that the people wondered how they all would ever find room within the town walls. There were people in the streets, people in the windows, people on the balconies. On the high stone steps sat people, and the shops were full of them. The big street-doors were thrown wide, and in the openings chairs were arranged in a half-circle, as in a theater. There the house-owners sat with their guests and looked at the passers-by.

The whole street was filled with an intoxicating noise. It was not only the talking and laughter of the people. There were also organ-grinders standing and turning hand-organs big as pianos. There were street-singers, and there were men and women who declaimed Tasso in cracked, worn-out voices. There were all kinds of criers, the sound of organs streamed from all the churches, and in the square on the summit of the mountain the town band played so that it could be heard over all Diamante.

The joyous noise, and the fragrance of the flowers, and the flapping of the flags outside Donna Micaela's window had power to wake her from her stupor. She rose up, as if life had sent for her. "I will not die," she said to herself. "I will try to live."

She took her father's arm and went out into the street. She hoped that the life there would mount to her head so that she might forget her sorrow. "If I do not succeed," she thought, "if I can find no distraction, I must die."

Now in Diamante there was a poor old stonecutter, who had thought of earning a few soldi during the festival. He had made a couple of small busts out of lava, of San Sebastiano and of Pope Leo XIII. And as he knew that many in Diamante loved Gaetano, and grieved over his fate, he also made a few portraits of him.

Just as Donna Micaela came out into the street she met the man, and he offered her his wretched little images.

"Buy Don Gaetano Alagona, Donna Micaela," said the man; "buy Don Gaetano, whom the government has put in prison because he wished to help Sicily."

Donna Micaela pressed her father's arm hard and went hurriedly on.

In the Café Europa the son of the innkeeper stood and sang canzoni. He had composed a few new ones for the festival, and among others some about Gaetano. For he could not know that people did not care to hear of him.

When Donna Micaela passed by the café and heard the singing, she stopped and listened.

"Alas, Gaetano Alagona!" sang the young man. "Songs are mighty. I shall sing you free with my songs. First I will send you the slender canzone. He shall glide in between your prison-gratings, and break them. Then I will send you the sonnet, that is fair as a woman, and which will corrupt your guards. I will compose a glorious ode to you, which will shake the walls of your prison with its lofty rhythms. But if none of these help you, I will burst out in the glorious epos, that has hosts of words. Oh, Gaetano, mighty as an army it marches on! All the legions of ancient Rome would not have had the strength to stop it!"

Donna Micaela hung convulsively on her father's arm, but she did not speak, and went on.

Then Cavaliere Palmeri began to speak of Gaetano. "I did not know that he was so beloved," he said.

"Nor I," murmured Donna Micaela.

"Today I saw some strangers coming into Donna Elisa's shop, and begging her to be allowed to buy something that he had carved. She had left only a couple of old rosaries, and I saw her break them to pieces and give them out bead by bead."

Donna Micaela looked at her father like a beseeching child. But he did not know whether she wished him to be silent or to go on speaking.

"Donna Elisa's old friends go about in the garden with Luca," he said, "and Luca shows them Gaetano's favorite places and the garden beds that he used to plant. And Pacifica sits in the workshop beside the joiner's-bench, and relates all sorts of things about him, ever since he was — so big."

He could tell no more; the crush and the noise became so great about him that he had to stop.

They meant to go to the Cathedral. On the Cathedral steps sat old Assunta, as usual. She held a rosary in her hands and mumbled the same prayer round the whole rosary. She asked the saint that Gaetano, who had promised to help all the poor, might come back to Diamante.

As Donna Micaela walked by her, she distinctly heard: "San Sebastiano, give us Gaetano! Ah, in your mercy; ah, in our misery, San Sebastiano, give us Gaetano!"

Donna Micaela had meant to go into the church, but she turned on the steps.

"There is such a crowd there," she said, "I do not dare to go in."

She went home again. But while she had been away, Donna Elisa had watched her opportunity. She had hoisted a flag on the roof of the summer-palace; she had spread draperies on the balconies, and as Donna Micaela came home, she was fastening up a garland in the gate-way. For Donna Elisa could not bear to have the summer-palace undecorated. She wished no honor to San Sebastiano omitted at this time. And she feared that the saint would not help Diamante and Gaetano if the palace of the old Alagonas did not honor him.

Donna Micaela was pale as if she had received her death warrant, and bent like an old woman of eighty years.

She murmured to herself: "I make no busts of him; I sing no songs about him; I dare not pray to God for him; I buy none of his beads. How can he believe that I love him? He must love all these others, who worship him, but not me. I do not belong to his world, he can love me no longer."

And when she saw that they wished to adorn her house with flowers, it seemed to her so piteously cruel that she snatched the wreath from Donna Elisa and threw it at her feet, asking if she wished to kill her.

Then she went past her up the stairs to her room. She threw herself on the sofa and buried her face in the cushions.

She now first understood how far apart she and Gaetano were. The idol of the people could not love her.

She felt as if she had prevented him from helping all those poor people.

How he must detest her; how he must hate her!

Then her illness came creeping back over her. That illness which consisted of not being loved! It would kill her. She thought, as she lay there, that it was all over.

While she lay there, suddenly the little Christchild stood before her inward eye. He seemed to have entered the room in all his wretched splendor. She saw him plainly.

Donna Micaela began to call on the Christchild for help. And she was amazed at herself for not having turned before to that good helper. It was probably because the image did not stand in a church, but was carried about as a museum-piece by Miss Tottenham, that she remembered him only in her deepest need.

*I*t was late in the evening of the same day. After dinner Donna Micaela had given all her servants permission to go to the festival, so that she and her father were alone in the big house. But towards ten o'clock her father rose and said he wished to hear the singing-contest in the square. And as Donna Micaela did not dare to sit alone, she was obliged to go with him.

When they came to the square they saw that it was turned into a theater, with lines upon lines of chairs. Every corner was filled with people, and it was with difficulty that they found places.

"Diamante is glorious this evening, Micaela," said Cavaliere Palmeri. The charm of the night seemed to have softened him. He spoke more simply and tenderly to his daughter than he had done for a long time.

Donna Micaela felt instantly that he spoke the truth. She felt as she had done when she first came to Diamante. It was a town of miracles, a town of beauty, a little sanctuary of God.

Directly in front of her stood a high and stately building made of shining diamonds. She had to think for a moment before she could understand what it was.

Yet it was nothing but the front of the Cathedral, covered with flowers of stiff silver and gold paper and with thousands of little mirrors stuck in between the flowers. And in every flower was hung a little lamp with a flame as big as a firefly. It was the most enchanting illumination that Donna Micaela had ever seen.

There was no other light in the marketplace, nor was any needed. That great wall of diamonds shone quite sufficiently. The black Palazzo Geraci was flaming red, as if it had been lighted by a conflagration.

Nothing of the world outside of the square was visible. Everything below it was in the deepest darkness, and that made her think again that she saw the old enchanted Diamante that was not of the earth, but was a holy city on one of the mounts of heaven. The town-hall with its heavy balconies and high steps, the long convent and the Roman gate were again glorious and wonderful. And she could hardly believe it was in that town that she had suffered such terrible pain.

In the midst of the great crowd of people, no chill was felt. The winter night was mild as a spring morning; and Donna Micaela began to feel something of spring in her. It began to stir and tremble in her in a way which was both sweet and terrible. It must feel so in the snow-masses on Etna when the sun melts them into sparkling brooks.

She looked at the people who filled the marketplace, and was amazed at herself that she had been so tortured by them in the forenoon. She was glad that they loved Gaetano. Alas, if he had only continued to love her, she would have been unspeakably proud and happy in their love. Then she could have kissed those old callous hands that made images of him and were clasped in prayers for him.

As she was thinking this, the church-door was thrown open and a big, flat wagon rolled out of the church. Highest on the red-covered wagon stood San Sebastiano by his stake, and below the image sat the four singers, who were to contest.

There was an old blind man from Nicolosi; a cooper from Catania, who was considered to be the best improvisatore in all Sicily; a smith from Termini, and little Gandolfo, who was son to the watchman in the town-hall of Diamante.

Everybody was surprised that Gandolfo dared to appear in such a difficult contest. Did he do it perhaps to please his betrothed, little Rosalia? No one had ever heard that he could improvise. He had never done anything in his whole life but eat mandarins and stare at Etna.

The first thing was to draw lots among the competitors, and the lots fell so that the cooper should come first and Gandolfo last. When it fell so Gandolfo turned pale. It was terrible to come last, when they all were to speak on the same subject.

The cooper elected to speak of San Sebastiano, when he was a soldier of the legion in ancient Rome, and for his faith's sake was bound to a stake and used as a target for his comrades. After him came the blind man, who told how a pious Roman matron found the martyr bleeding and pierced with arrows, and succeeded in bringing him back to life. Then came the smith, who related all the miracles San Sebastiano had worked in Sicily during the pest in the fifteenth century. They were all much applauded. They spoke many strong words of blood and death, and the people rejoiced in them. But everyone from Diamante was anxious for little Gandolfo.

"The smith takes all the words from him. He must fail," they said.

"Ah," said others, "little Rosalia will not take the engagement ribbon out of her hair for that."

Gandolfo shrunk together in his corner of the wagon. He grew smaller and smaller. Those sitting near could hear how his teeth chattered with fright.

When his turn came at last, and he rose and began to improvise, he was very bad. He was worse than anyone had expected. He faltered out a couple of verses, but they were only a repetition of what the others had said.

Then he suddenly stopped and gasped for breath. In that moment the strength of despair came to him. He straightened himself up, and a slight flush rose to his cheeks.

"Oh, signori," said little Gandolfo, "let me speak of that of which I am always thinking! Let me speak of what I always see before me!"

And he began unopposed and with wonderful power to tell what he himself had seen.

He told how he who was son to the watchman of the town-hall had crept through dark attics and had lain hidden in one of the galleries of the court-room the night the court-martial had been held to pass sentence on the insurgents in Diamante.

Then he had seen Don Gaetano Alagona on the bench of the accused with a lot of wild fellows who were worse than brutes.

He told how beautiful Gaetano had been. He had seemed like a god to little Gandolfo beside those terrible people about him. And he described those bandits with their wild-beast faces, their coarse hair, their clumsy limbs. He said that no one could look into their eyes without a quiver of the heart.

Yet, in all his beauty, Don Gaetano was more terrible than those people. Gandolfo did not know how they dared to sit beside him on the bench. Under his frowning brows his eyes flashed at his fellow-prisoners with a look which would have killed their souls, if they like others had possessed such a thing.

"'Who are you,' he seemed to ask, 'who dare to turn to plundering and murder while you call on sacred liberty? Do you know what you have done? Do you know that on account of your devices I am now a prisoner? And it was I who would have saved Sicily!'" And every glance he cast at them was a death warrant.

His eyes fell on all the things that the bandits had stolen and that were now piled up on a table. He recognized them. Could he help knowing the clocks and the silver dishes from the summer palace? could he help knowing the relics and coins that had been stolen from his English patroness? And when he had recognized the things, he turned to his fellow-prisoners with a terrible smile. "'You heroes! you heroes!' said the smile; 'you have stolen from two women!'"

His noble face was constantly changing. Once Gandolfo had seen it contracted by a sudden terror. It was when the man sitting nearest to him stretched out a hand covered with blood. Had he perhaps had a sudden idea of the truth? Did he think that those men had broken into the house where his beloved lived?

Gandolfo told how the officers who were to be the judges had come in, silent and grave, and sat down in their places. But he said when he had seen those noble gentlemen his anxiety had diminished, He had said to himself that they knew that Gaetano was of good birth, and that they would not sentence him. They would not mix him up with the bandits. No one could possibly believe that he had wished to rob two women.

And see, when the judge called up Gaetano Alagona his voice was
without hardness. He spoke to him as to an equal.

"But," said Gandolfo, "when Don Gaetano rose, he stood so that he
could see out over the square. And through the square, through this
same square, where now so many people are sitting in happiness and
pleasure, a funeral procession was passing.

"It was the White Brotherhood carrying the body of the murdered
Giannita to her mother's house. They walked with torches, and the bier,
carried on the bearers' shoulders, was plainly visible. As the procession
passed slowly across the marketplace, one could recognize the pall spread
over the corpse. It was the pall of the Alagonas adorned with a gorgeous
coat of arms and rich silver fringes. When Gaetano saw it, he understood
that the corpse was of the house of Alagona. His face became ashy grey,
and he reeled as if he were going to fall.

"At that moment the judge asked him: 'Do you know the murdered
woman?' And he answered: 'Yes.' Then the judge, who was a merciful
man, continued: 'Was she near to you?' And then Don Gaetano answered: 'I love her.'"

When Gandolfo had come so far in his story, people saw Donna
Micaela suddenly rise, as if she had wished to contradict him, but
Cavaliere Palmeri drew her quickly down beside him.

"Be quiet, be quiet," he said to her.

And she sat quiet with her face hidden in her hands. Now and then
her body rocked and she wailed softly.

Gandolfo told how the judge, when Gaetano had acknowledged that,
had shown him his fellow-prisoners and asked him: "'If you loved that
woman, how can you have anything in common with the men who have
murdered her?'"

Then Don Gaetano had turned towards the bandits. He had raised
his clenched hand and shaken it at them. And he had looked as if he
had longed for a dagger, to be able to strike them down one after another.

"'With those!'" he had shouted. "'Should I have anything in common
with those?'"

And he had certainly meant to say that he had nothing to do with
robbers and murderers. The judge had smiled kindly at him, as if he
had only waited for that answer to set him free.

But then a divine miracle had happened.

And Gandolfo told, how among all the stolen things that lay on the
table, there had also been a little Christ image. It was a yard high, richly
covered with jewels and adorned with a gold crown and gold shoes. Just
at that moment one of the officers bent clown to draw the image to

him; and as he did so, the crown fell to the floor and rolled all the way to Don Gaetano.

Don Gaetano picked up the Christ-crown, held it a moment in his hands and looked at it carefully. It seemed as if he had read something in it.

He did not hold it more than one minute. In the next the guard took it from him.

Donna Micaela looked up almost frightened. The Christ image! He was there already! Should she so soon get an answer to her prayer?

Gandolfo continued: "But when Don Gaetano looked up, everyone trembled as at a miracle, for the man was transformed.

"Ah, signori, he was so white that his face seemed to shine, and his eyes were calm and tender. And there was no more anger in him.

"And he began to pray for his fellow-prisoners; he began to pray for their lives.

"He prayed that they should not kill those poor fellow-creatures. He prayed that the noble judges should do something for them that they might some day live like others. 'We have only this life to live,' he said. 'Our kingdom is only of this world.'

"He began to tell how those men had lived. He spoke as if he could read their souls. He pictured their life, gloomy and unhappy as it had been. He spoke so that several of the judges wept.

"The words came strong and commanding, so that it sounded as if Don Gaetano had been judge and the judges the criminals. 'See,' he said, 'whose fault is it that these poor men have gone to destruction? Is it not you who have the power who ought to have taken care of them?'

"And they were all dismayed at the responsibility he forced upon them.

"But suddenly the judge had interrupted him.

"'Speak in your own defense, Gaetano Alagona,' he said; 'do not speak in that of others!'

"Then Don Gaetano had smiled. 'Signor,' he said, 'I have not much more than you with which to defend myself. But still I have something. I have left my career in England to make a revolt in Sicily. I have brought over weapons. I have made seditious speeches. I have something, although not much.'

"The judge had almost begged him. 'Do not speak so, Don Gaetano,' he had said. 'Think of what you are saying!'

"But he had made confessions that compelled them to sentence him.

"When they told him that he was to sit for twenty-nine years in prison, he had cried out: 'Now may her will be done, who was just carried by. May I be as she wished!'

"And I saw no more of him," said little Gandolfo, "for the guards placed him between them and led him away.

"But I, who heard him pray for those who had murdered his beloved, made a vow that I would do something for him.

"I vowed to recite a beautiful improvisation to San Sebastiano to induce him to help him. But I have not succeeded. I am no improvisatore; I could not."

Here he broke off and threw himself down, weeping aloud before the image. "Forgive me that I could not," he cried, "and help him in spite of it. You know that when they sentenced him I promised to do it for his sake that you might save him. But now I have not been able to speak of you, and you will not help him."

Donna Micaela hardly knew how it happened, but she and little Rosalia, who loved Gandolfo, were beside him at almost the same moment. They drew him to them, and both kissed him, and said that no one had spoken like him; no one, no one. Did he not see that they were weeping? San Sebastiano was pleased with him. Donna Micaela put a ring on the boy's finger and round about him the people were waving many-colored silk handkerchiefs, that glistened like waves of the sea in the strong light from the Cathedral.

"Viva Gaetano! viva Gandolfo!" cried the people.

And flowers and fruits and silk handkerchiefs and jewels came raining down about little Gandolfo. Donna Micaela was crowded away from him almost with violence. But it never occurred to her to be frightened. She stood among the surging people and wept. The tears streamed down her face, and she wept for joy that she could weep. That was the greatest blessing.

She wished to force her way to Gandolfo; she could not thank him enough. He had told her that Gaetano loved her. When he had quoted the words, "Now may her will be done who was just carried by," she had suddenly understood that Gaetano had believed that it was she lying under the pall of the Alagonas.

And of that dead woman he had said: "I love her."

The blood flowed once more in her veins; her heart beat again; her tears fell. "It is life, life," she said to herself, while she let herself be carried to and fro by the crowd. "Life has come again to me. I shall not die."

They all had to come up to little Gandolfo to thank him, because he had given them someone to love, to trust in, to long for in those days of dejection, when everything seemed lost.

# SECOND BOOK

*"Antichrist shall go from land to land and give
bread to the poor"*

# I

## A GREAT MAN'S WIFE

*I*t was in February, and the almond trees were beginning to blossom on the black lava about Diamante.

Cavaliere Palmeri had taken a walk up Etna and had brought home a big almond branch, full of buds and flowers and put it in a vase in the music-room.

Donna Micaela started when she saw it. So they had already come, the almond-blossoms. And for a whole month, for six long weeks, they would be everywhere.

They would stand on the altar in the church; they would lie on the graves, and they would be worn on the breast, on the hat, in the hair. They would blossom over the roads, in the heaps of ruins, on the black lava. And every almond-flower would remind her of the day when the bells rang, when Gaetano was free and happy, and when she dreamed of passing her whole life with him.

It seemed to her as if she never before fully understood what it meant that he was shut in and gone, that she should never see him again.

She had to sit down in order not to fall; her heart seemed to stop, and she shut her eyes.

While she was sitting thus she had a strange experience.

She is all at once at home in the palace in Catania. She is sitting in the lofty hall reading, and she is a happy young girl, Signorina Palmeri. A servant brings in a wandering salesman to her. He is a handsome young fellow with a sprig of almond-blossoms in his buttonhole; on his head he carries a board full of little images of the saints, carved in wood.

She buys some of the images, while the young man's eyes drink in all the works of art in the hall. She asks him if he would like to see their collections. Yes, that he would. And she herself goes with him and shows him.

He is so delighted with what he sees that she thinks that he must be a real artist, and she says to herself that she will not forget him. She asks where his home is. He answers: "In Diamante." — "Is that far away?" — "Four hours in the post-carriage." — "And with the railway?" — "There is no railway to Diamante, signorina." — "You must build one." — "We! we are too poor. Ask the rich men in Catania to build us a railway!"

When he has said that he starts to go, but he turns at the door and comes and gives her his almond-blossoms. It is in gratitude for all the beautiful things she has let him see.

When Donna Micaela opened her eyes she did not know whether she had been dreaming or whether perhaps once some such thing had really happened. Gaetano could really have been some time in the Palazzo Palmeri to sell his images, although she had forgotten it; but now the almond-blossoms had recalled it.

But it was no matter, no matter. The important thing was that the young wood-carver was Gaetano. She felt as if she had been talking to him. She thought she heard the door close behind him.

And it was after that that it occurred to her to build a railway between Catania and Diamante.

Gaetano had surely come to her to ask her to do it. It was a command from him, and she felt that she must obey.

She made no attempt to struggle against it. She was certain that Diamante needed a railway more than anything else. She had once heard Gaetano say that if Diamante only possessed a railway, so that it could easily send away its oranges and its wine and its honey and its almonds, and so that travelers could come there conveniently, it would soon be a rich town.

She was also quite certain that she could succeed with the railway. She must try at all events. It never occurred to her not to. When Gaetano wished it, she must obey.

She began to think how much money she herself could give. It would not go very far. She must get more money. That was the first thing she had to do.

Within the hour she was at Donna Elisa's, and begged her to help her arrange a bazaar. Donna Elisa lifted her eyes from her embroidery. "Why do you want to arrange a bazaar?" — "I mean to collect money for a railway." — "That is like you, Donna Micaela; no one else would have thought of such a thing." — "What, Donna Elisa? What do you mean?" — "Oh, nothing."

And Donna Elisa went on embroidering.

"You will not help me, then, with my bazaar?" — "No, I will not." — "And you will not give a little contribution towards it?" — "One who has so lately lost her husband," answered Donna Elisa, "ought not to trifle."

Donna Micaela saw that Donna Elisa was angry with her for some reason or other, and that she therefore would not help her. But there must be others who would understand; and it was a beautiful plan, which would save Diamante.

But Donna Micaela wandered in vain from door to door. However much she talked and begged, she gained no partisans.

She tried to explain, she used all her eloquence to persuade. No one was interested in her plans.

Wherever she came, people answered her that they were too poor, too poor.

The syndic's wife answered no. Her daughters were not allowed to sell at the bazaar. Don Antonio Greco, who had the marionette theater, would not come with his dolls. The town-band would not play. None of the shop-keepers would give any of their wares. When Donna Micaela was gone they laughed at her.

A railroad, a railroad! She did not know what she was thinking of. There would have to be a company, shares, statutes, concessions. How should a woman manage such things?

While some were content to laugh at Donna Micaela, some were angry with her.

She went to the cellarlike shop near the old Benedictine monastery, where Master Pamphilio related romances of chivalry. She came to ask him if he would come to her bazaar and entertain the public with Charlemagne and his paladins; but as he was in the midst of a story, she had to sit down on a bench and wait.

Then she noticed Donna Concetta, Master Pamphilio's wife, who was sitting on the platform at his feet knitting a stocking. As long as Master Pamphilio was speaking, Donna Concetta's lips moved. She had heard his romances so many times that she knew them by heart, and said the words before they had passed Master Pamphilio's lips. But it was always the same pleasure to her to hear him, and she wept, and she laughed, as she had done when she heard him for the first time.

Master Pamphilio was an old man, who had spoken much in his day, so that his voice sometimes failed him in the big battle-scenes, when he had to speak loud and fast. But Donna Concetta, who knew it all by heart, never took the word from Master Pamphilio. She only made a sign to the audience to wait until his voice came back. But if his memory failed him, Donna Concetta pretended that she had dropped a stitch, raised the stocking to her eyes, and threw him the word behind it, so that no one noticed it. And everyone knew that although Donna

Concetta perhaps could have told the romances better than Master Pamphilio, she would never have been willing to do such a thing, not only because it was not fitting for a woman, but also because it would not give her half so much pleasure as to listen to dear Master Pamphilio.

When Donna Micaela saw Donna Concetta, she fell to dreaming. Oh, to sit so on the platform, where her beloved was speaking; to sit so day in and day out and worship. She knew whom that would have suited.

When Master Pamphilio had finished speaking Donna Micaela went forward and asked him to help her. It was hard for him to say no, on account of the thousand prayers that were written in her eyes. But Donna Concetta came to his rescue. "Master Pamphilio," she said, "tell Donna Micaela of Guglielmo the Wicked." And Master Pamphilio began.

"Donna Micaela," he said, "do you know that once there was a king in Sicily whose name was Guglielmo the Wicked? He was so covetous that he took all his subjects' money. He commanded that everyone possessing gold coins should give them to him. And he was so severe and so cruel that they all had to obey him.

"Well, Donna Micaela, Guglielmo the Wicked wished to know if anyone had gold hidden in his house. Therefore he sent one of his servants along the Corso in Palermo with a beautiful horse. And the man offered the horse for sale, and cried loudly: 'Will be sold for a piece of gold; will be sold for a piece of gold!' But there was no one who could buy the horse.

"Yet it was a very beautiful horse, and a young nobleman, the Duke of Montefiascone, was much taken by him. 'There is no joy for me if I cannot buy the horse,' said he to his steward. 'Signor Duca,' answered his steward, 'I can tell you where you can find a piece of gold. When your noble father died and was carried away by the Capucins, according to the ancient custom I put a piece of gold in his mouth. You can take that, signor.'

"For you must know, Donna Micaela, that in Palermo they do not bury the dead in the ground. They carry them to the monastery of the Capucins, and the monks hang them up in their vaults. Ah, there are so many hanging in those vaults! — so many ladies, dressed in silk and cloth of silver; so many noble gentlemen, with orders on their breasts; and so many priests, with cloak and cap over skeleton and skull.

"The young duke followed his advice. He went to the Capucin monastery, took the piece of gold from his father's mouth and bought the horse with it.

"But you understand that the king had only sent his servant with the horse in order to find out if anyone still had any money. And now the duke was taken before the king. 'How does it happen that you still have gold pieces?' said Guglielmo the Wicked. – 'Sire, it was not mine; it was my father's.' And he told how he had got the piece of gold. 'It is true,' said the king. 'I had forgotten that the dead still had money.' And he sent his servants to the Capucins and had them take all the gold pieces out of the mouths of the dead."

Here old Master Pamphilio, finished his story. And now Donna Concetta turned to Donna Micaela with wrathful eyes. "It is you who are out with the horse," she said.

"Am I? am I?"

"You, you, Donna Micaela! The government will say: 'They are building a railway in Diamante. They must be rich.' And they will increase our taxes. And God knows that we cannot pay the tax with which we are already loaded down, even if we should go and plunder our ancestors."

Donna Micaela tried to calm her.

"They have sent you out to find out if we still have any money. You are spying for the rich; you are in league with the government. Those bloodsuckers in Rome have paid you."

Donna Micaela turned away from her.

"I came to talk to you, Master Pamphilio," she said to the old man.

"But I shall answer you," replied Donna Concetta; "for this is a disagreeable matter, and such things are my affair. I know what is the duty of the wife of a great man, Donna Micaela."

Donna Concetta became silent, for the fine lady gave her a look which was so full of jealous longing that it made her sorry for her. Heavens, yes, there had been a difference in their husbands; Don Ferrante and Master Pamphilio!

# II

## PANEM ET CIRCENSES

*I*n Diamante travelers are often shown two palaces that are falling into ruins without ever having been completed. They have big window-openings without frames, high walls without a roof, and wide doors closed with boards and straw. The two palaces stand opposite each other on the street, both equally unfinished and equally in ruins. There are no scaffoldings about them, and no one can enter them. They seem to be only built for the doves.

Listen to what is told of them.

What is a woman, O signore? Her foot is so little that she goes through the world without leaving a trace behind her. For man she is like his shadow. She has followed him through his whole life without his having noticed her.

Not much can be expected of a woman. She has to sit all day shut in like a prisoner. She cannot even learn to spell a love-letter correctly. She cannot do anything of permanence. When she is dead there is nothing to write on her tombstone. All women are of the same height.

But once a woman came to Diamante who was as much above all other women as the century-old palm is above the grass. She possessed lire by thousands, and could give them away or keep them, as she pleased. She turned aside for no one. She was not afraid of being hated. She was the greatest marvel that had ever been seen.

Of course she was not a Sicilian. She was an Englishwoman. And the first thing she did when she came was to take the whole first floor of the hotel for herself alone. What was that for her? All Diamante would not have been enough for her.

No, all Diamante was not enough for her. But as soon as she had come she began to govern the town like a queen. The syndic had to obey her. Was it not she who made him put stone benches in the square? Was it not at her command that the streets were swept every day?

When she woke in the morning all the young men of Diamante stood waiting outside her door, to be allowed to accompany her on some excursion. They had left shoemaker's awl and stone-cutter's chisel to act as guides to her. Each had sold his mother's silk dress to buy a side-saddle for his donkey, so that *she* might ride on it to the castle or to Tre Castagni. They had divested themselves of house and home in order to buy a horse and carriage to drive her to Randazzo and Nicolosi.

We were all her slaves. The children began to beg in English, and the old blind women at the hotel door, Donna Pepa and Donna Tura, draped themselves in dazzlingly white veils to please her.

Everything moved round her; industries and trades grew up about her. Those who could do nothing else dug in the earth for coins and pottery to offer her. Photographers moved to the town and began to work for her. Coral merchants and hawkers of tortoise-shell grew out of the earth about her. The priests of Santa Agnese dug up the old Dionysius theater, that lay hidden behind their church, for her sake; and everyone who owned a ruined villa unearthed in the darkness of the cellar remains of mosaic floors and invited her by big posters to come and see.

There had been foreigners before in Diamante, but they had come and gone, and no one had enjoyed such power. There was soon not a man in the town who did not put all his trust in the English signorina. She even succeeded in putting a little life into Ugo Favara. You know Ugo Favara, the advocate, who was to have been a great man, but had reverses and came home quite broken. She employed him to take care of her affairs. She needed him, and she took him.

There has never been a woman in Diamante who has done so much business as she. She spread out like green-weed in the spring. One day no one knows that there is any, and the next it is a great clump. Soon it was impossible to go anywhere in Diamante without coming on her traces. She bought country houses and town houses; she bought almond-groves and lava-streams. The best places on Etna to see the view were hers as well as the thirsting earth on the plain. And in town she began to build two big palaces. She was to live in them and rule her kingdom.

We shall never see a woman like her again. She was not content with all that. She wished also to fight the fight with poverty, O signore, with Sicilian poverty! How much she gave out each day, and how much she gave away on feast-days! Wagons, drawn by two pairs of oxen, went down to Catania and came back piled up with all sorts of clothing.

She was determined that they should have whole clothes in the town where she reigned.

But listen to what happened to her; how the struggle with poverty ended and what became of the kingdom and the palace.

She gave a banquet for the poor people of Diamante, and after the banquet an entertainment in the Grecian theater. It was what an old emperor might have done. But who has ever before heard of a woman doing such a thing?

She invited all the poor people. There were the two blind women from the hotel-door, and old Assunta from the Cathedral steps. There was the man from the post-house, who had his chin bound up in a red cloth on account of cancer of the face; and there was the idiot who opens the iron doors of the Grecian theater. All the donkey-boys were there, and the handless brothers, who exploded a bomb in their childhood and lost their fingers; and the man with the wooden leg, and the old chair-maker who had grown too old to work, both were there.

It was strange to see them creep out of their holes, all the poor in Diamante. The old women who sit and spin with distaffs in the dark alleys were there, and the organ-grinder, who has an instrument as big as a church-organ, a wandering young mandolinist from Naples with a body full of all possible deviltries. All those with diseased eyes and all the decrepit; those without a roof over their heads; those who used to collect sorrel by the roadside for dinner; the stone-cutter, who earned one lira a day and had six children to provide for, — they had all been invited and were present at the feast.

It was poverty marshaling its troops for the English signorina. Who has such an army as poverty? But for once the English signorina could conquer it.

She had something to fight with too and to conquer with. She filled the whole square with loaded tables. She had wine-skins arranged along the stone bench that lines the wall of the Cathedral. She had turned the deserted convent into a larder and kitchen. She had all the foreign colony in Diamante dressed in white aprons, to serve the courses. She had all of Diamante who are used to eating their fill, wandering to and fro as spectators.

Ah, spectators, what did she not have for spectators? She had great Etna and the dazzling sun. She had the red peaks of the inland mountains and the old temple of Vulcan, that was now consecrated to San Pasquale. And none of them had ever seen a satisfied Diamante. None of them had ever before happened to think how much more beautiful they themselves would be if the people could look at them without hunger hissing in their ears and trampling on their heels.

But mark one thing! Although that signorina was so wonderful and so great, she was not beautiful. And in spite of all her power, she was neither charming nor attractive. She did not rule with jests, and she did not reward with smiles. She had a heavy, clumsy body, and a heavy, clumsy disposition.

The day she gave food to the poor she became a different person. A chivalrous people live in our noble island. Among all those poor people there was not one who let her feel that she was exercising charity. They worshipped her, but they worshipped her as a woman. They sat down at the table as with an equal. They behaved to her as guests to their hostess. "Today I do you the honor to come to you; tomorrow you do me the honor to come to me. So and not otherwise." She stood on the high steps of the town-hall and looked down at all the tables. And when the old chair-maker, who sat at the head of the table, had got his glass filled, he rose, bowed to her and said: "I drink to your prosperity, signorina."

So did they all. They laid their hands on their hearts and bowed to her. It would have perhaps been good for her if she had met with such chivalry earlier in life. Why had the men in her native land let her forget that women exist to be worshipped?

Here they all looked as if they were burning with a quiet adoration. Thus are women treated in our noble island. What did they not give in return for the food and the wine that she had offered, them? They gave youth and light-heartedness and all the dignity of being worth coveting. They made speeches for her. "Noble-hearted signorina, you who have come to us from over the sea, you who love Sicily," and so on, and so on. She showed that she could blush. She no longer hid her power to smile. When they had finished speaking, the lips of the English signorina began to tremble. She became twenty years younger. It was what she needed.

The donkey-boy was there, who carries the English ladies up to Tre Castagni, and who always falls in love with them before he parts from them. Now his eyes were suddenly opened to the great benefactress. It is not only a slender, delicate body and a soft cheek that are worthy to be adored, but also strength and force. The donkey-boy suddenly dropped knife and fork, leaned his elbows on the table, and sat and looked at her. And all the other donkey-boys did the same. It spread like a contagion. It grew hot with burning glances about the English signorina.

It was not only the poor people who adored her. The advocate, Ugo Favara, came and whispered to her that she had come as a providence to his poor land and to him. "If only I had met such a woman as you before," he said.

Fancy an old bird which has sat in a cage for many years and become rough and lost all the gloss of his feathers. And then someone comes and straightens them out and smooths them back. Think of it, signore!

There was that boy from Naples. He took his mandolin and began to sing his very best. You know how he sings; he pouts with his big mouth and says ugly words. He usually is like a grinning mask. But have you seen the angel in his eyes? An angel which seems to weep over his fall and is filled with a holy frenzy. That evening he was only an angel. He raised his head like one inspired by God, and his drooping body became elastic and full of proud vitality. Color came into his livid cheeks. And he sang; he sang so that the notes seemed to fly like fireflies from his lips and fill the air with joy and dance.

When it grew dark they all went over to the Grecian theater. That was the finishing touch to the entertainment. What did she not have to offer there!

She had the Russian singer and the German varieté artists. She had the English wrestlers and the American magician. But what was that compared to all the rest: the silvery moonlight and the place and its memories? Those poor people seemed to feel like the Greeks and leaders of fashion when they once more took their places on the stone-benches of their own old theater and from between the tottering pillars looked out at the most beautiful panorama.

Those poor people did not stint; they shared all the pleasure they received. They did not spare jubilation; there was no stopping their hand-clapping. The performers left the platform with a wealth of praise.

Someone begged the English signorina to appear. All the adoration was meant for her. She ought to stand face to face with it and feel it. And they told her how intoxicating it was, how elevating, how inflaming.

She liked the proposal. She immediately agreed. She had sung in her youth, and the English never seem to be afraid to sing. She would not have done it if she had not been in a good mood, and she wished to sing for those who loved her.

She came as the last number. Fancy what it was to stand on such an old stage! It was where Antigone had been buried alive and Iphigenia had been sacrificed. The English signorina stepped forward there to receive every conceivable honor.

It stormed to meet her as soon as she showed herself. They seemed to wish to stamp the earth to pieces to honor her.

It was a proud moment. She stood there with Etna as a background and the Mediterranean as wings. Before her on the grass-grown benches was sitting conquered poverty, and she felt that she had all Diamante at her feet.

She chose "Bellini," our own "Bellini." She too wished to be amiable and so she sang "Bellini," who was born here under Etna; "Bellini" whom we know by heart, note for note.

Of course, O signore, of course she could not sing. She had mounted the tribune only to receive homage. She had come in order to let the love of the people find an outlet. And now she sang false and feebly. And the people knew every note.

It was that mandolinista from Naples. He was the first to grimace and to take a note as false as that of the English signorina. Then it was the man with the cancer, who laughed till he laughed his neckcloth off. Then it was the donkey-boy, who began to clap his hands.

Then they all began. It was madness, but that they did not understand. It is not in the land of the old Greeks that people can bear barbarians who sing false. Donna Pepa and Donna Tura laughed as they had never done before in their lives. "Not one true note! By the Madonna and San Pasquale, not one true note!"

They had eaten their fill for once in their lives. It was natural that intoxication and madness should take hold of them. And why should they not laugh? She had not given them food in order to torture their ears with files and saws. Why should they not defend themselves by laughing? Why should they not mimic and hiss and scream? Why should they not lean backward and split their sides with laughter? They were not the English signorina's slaves, I suppose.

It was a terrible blow to her. It was too great a blow for her to understand. Were they hissing her? It must be something happening among them; something that she could not see. She sang the aria to its end. She was convinced that the laughter was for something with which she had nothing to do.

When she had finished a sort of storm of applause roared over her. At last she understood. Torches and the moonlight made the night so bright that she could see the rows of people twisting with laughter. She heard the scoffs and the jests now, when she was not singing. They were for her. Then she fled from the stage. It seemed to her that Etna itself heaved with laughter, and that the sea sparkled with merriment.

But it grew worse and worse. They had had such a good time, those poor people; they had never had such a good time before, and they wished to hear her once again. They called for her; they cried: "Bravo! Bis! Da capo!" They could not lose such a pleasure. She, she was almost unconscious. There was a storm about her. They screamed; they roared to get her in. She saw them lift their arms and threaten her to get her in. All at once it was all turned into an old circus. She had to go in to be devoured by monsters.

It went on; it went on; it became wilder and wilder. The other performers were frightened and begged her to yield. And she herself was frightened. It looked as if they would have killed her if she did not do what they wished.

She dragged herself on the stage and stood face to face with the crowd. There was no pity. She sang because they all wished to be amused. That was the worst. She sang because she was afraid of them and did not dare not to. She was a foreigner and alone, and she had no one to protect her, and she was afraid. And they laughed and laughed.

Screams and cries, crowing and whistling accompanied the whole aria. No one had mercy on her. For the first time in her life she felt the need of mercy.

Well, the next day she resolved to depart. She could not endure Diamante any longer. But when she told the advocate, Favara, he implored her to stay for his sake and made her an offer of marriage.

He had chosen his time well. She said yes, and was married to him. But after that time she built no more on her palaces; she made no struggle against poverty; she cared nothing to be queen in Diamante. Would you believe it? She never showed herself on the street; she lived indoors like a Sicilian.

Her little house stood hidden away behind a big building, and of herself no one knew anything. They only knew that she was quite changed. No one knew whether she was happy or unhappy; whether she shut herself in because she hated the people, or because she wished to be as a Sicilian wife ought to be.

Does it not always end so with a woman? When they build their palaces they are never finished. Women can do nothing that has permanence.

# III

## THE OUTCAST

When Donna Micaela heard how the poor people had hooted Miss Tottenham out, she hurried to the hotel to express her condolence. She wished to beg her not to judge those poor creatures by what they had done when they had been out of their heads with pleasure and wine. She would beg her not to take her hand from Diamante. She herself did not care very much for Miss Tottenham, but for the sake of the poor — She would say anything to pacify her.

When she came to the hotel Etna, she saw the whole street filled with baggage-wagons. So there was no hope. The great benefactress was going away.

Outside the hotel there was much sorrow and despair. The two old blind women, Donna Pepa and Donna Tura, who had always sat in the hotel courtyard, were now shut out, and they were kneeling before the door. The young donkey-driver, who loved all young English ladies, stood with his face pressed against the wall and wept.

Inside the hotel the landlord walked up and down the long corridor, raging at Providence for sending him this misfortune. "Signor Dio," he mumbled, "I am beggared. If you let this happen, I will take my wife by the hand and my children in my arms and throw myself with them down into Etna."

The landlady was very pale and humble. She scarcely dared to lift her eyes from the ground. She would have liked to creep about on her knees to prevail upon the rich signorina to remain.

"Do you dare to speak to her, Donna Micaela?" she said. "May God help you to speak to her! Alas! tell her that the Neapolitan boy, who was the cause of the whole misfortune, has been turned out of the town. Tell her that they all wish to make amends. Speak to her, signora!"

The landlady took Donna Micaela to the Englishwoman's drawing room and went in with her card. She came back immediately and asked her to wait a few minutes. Signorina Tottenham was having a business talk with Signor Favara.

It was the very moment when the advocate Favara asked Miss Tottenham's hand in marriage; and while Donna Micaela waited she heard him say quite loud: "You must not go away, signorina! What will become of me if you go away? I love you; I cannot let you go. I should not have dared to speak if you had not threatened to go away. But now —"

He lowered his voice again, but Donna Micaela would hear no more and went away. She saw that she was superfluous. If Signor Favara could not succeed in keeping the great benefactress, no one could.

When she went out again through the gateway the landlord was standing there quarreling with the old Franciscan, Fra Felice. He was so irritated that he not only quarreled with Fra Felice, he also drove him from his house.

"Fra Felice," he cried, "you come to make more trouble with our great benefactress. You will only make her more angry. Go away, I tell you! You wolf, you man-eater, go away!"

Fra Felice was quite as enraged as the landlord, and tried to force his way past him. But then the latter took him by the arm, and without further notice marched him down the steps.

Fra Felice was a man who had received a great gift from his Creator. In Sicily, where everybody plays in the lottery, there are people who have the power to foretell what numbers will win at the next drawing. He who has such second sight is called "polacco," and is most often found in some old begging monk. Fra Felice was such a monk. He was the greatest polacco in the neighborhood of Etna.

As everyone wished him to tell them a winning tern or quartern, he was always treated with great consideration. He was not used to be taken by the arm and be thrown into the street, Fra Felice.

He was nearly eighty years old and quite dried-up and infirm. As he staggered away between the wagons, he stumbled, trod on his cloak, and almost fell. But none of the porters and drivers that stood by the door talking and lamenting had time that day to think of Fra Felice.

The old man tottered along in his heavy homespun cloak. He was so thin and dry that there seemed to be more stiffness in the cloak than in the monk. It seemed to be the old cloak that held him up.

Donna Micaela caught up with him and gently drew the old man's arm through her own. She could not bear to see how he struck against the lamp-posts and fell over steps. But Fra Felice never noticed that she was looking after him. He walked and mumbled and cursed, and did not know but that he was as much alone as if he sat in his cell.

Donna Micaela wondered why Fra Felice was so angry with Miss Tottenham. Had she been out to his monastery and taken down frescos from the walls, or what had she done?

Fra Felice had lived for sixty years in the big Franciscan monastery outside the Porta Etnea, wall to wall with the old church San Pasquale.

Fra Felice had been monk there for thirty years, when the monastery was given up and sold to a layman. The other monks moved away, but Fra Felice remained because he could not understand what selling the house of San Francisco could mean.

If laymen were to come there, it seemed to Fra Felice almost more essential that at least one monk should remain. Who else would attend to the bell-ringing, or prepare medicines for the peasant women, or give bread to the poor of the monastery? And Fra Felice chose a cell in a retired corner of the monastery, and continued to go in and out as he had always done.

The merchant who owned the monastery never visited it. He did not care about the old building; he only wanted the vineyards belonging to it. So Fra Felice still reigned in the old monastery, and fastened up the fallen cornices and whitewashed the walls. As many poor people as had received food at the monastery in former days, still received it. For his gift of prophecy Fra Felice got such large alms as he wandered through the towns of Etna that he could have been a rich man; but every bit of it went to the monastery.

Fra Felice had suffered an even greater grief than for the monastery on account of the monastery church. It had been desecrated during war, with bloody fights and other atrocities, so that mass could never be held there. But that he could not understand either. The church, where he had made his vows, was always holy to Fra Felice.

It was his greatest sorrow that his church had fallen entirely into ruin. He had looked on when Englishmen had come and bought pulpit and lectern and choir chairs. He had not been able to prevent collectors from Palermo coming and taking the chandeliers and pictures and brass hooks. However much he had wished it, he had not been able to do anything to save his church. But he hated those church-pillagers; and when Donna Micaela saw him so angry, she thought that Miss Tottenham had wished to take some of his treasures from him.

But the fact was that now, when Fra Felice's church was emptied, and no one came anymore to plunder there, he had begun to think of doing something to embellish it once more, and he had had his eye on the collection of images of the saints in the possession of the rich English lady. At her entertainment, when she had been kind and gentle towards everyone, he had dared to ask her for her beautiful Madonna, who had a dress of velvet and eyes like the sky. And his request had been granted

That morning Fra Felice had swept and dusted the church, and put flowers on the altar, before he went to fetch the image. But when he came to the hotel, the Englishwoman had changed her mind; she had not been at all willing to give him the valuable Madonna. In its stead she had given him a little ragged, dirty image of the Christchild, which she thought she could spare without regret.

Ah, what joy and expectation old Fra Felice had felt, and then had been so disappointed! He could not be satisfied; he came back time after time to beg for the other image. It was such a valuable image that he could not have bought it with all that he begged in a whole year. At last the great benefactress had dismissed him; and it was then that Donna Micaela had found him.

As they went along the street, she began to talk to the old man and won his story from him. He had the image with him, and right in the street he stopped, showed it to her, and asked her if she had ever seen a more miserable object.

Donna Micaela looked at the image for a moment with stupefaction. Then she smiled and said: "Lend me the image for a few days, Fra Felice!"

"You can take it and keep it," said the old man. "May it never come before my eyes again!"

Donna Micaela took the image home and worked on it for two days. When she then sent it to Fra Felice it shone with newly polished shoes; it had a fresh, clean dress; it was painted, and in its crown shone bright stones of many colors.

He was so beautiful, the outcast, that Fra Felice placed him on the empty altar in his church.

*I*t was very early one morning. The sun had not risen, and the broad sea was scarcely visible. It was really very early. The cats were still roaming about the roofs; no smoke rose from the chimneys; and the mists lay and rolled about in the low valley round the steep Monte Chiaro.

Old Fra Felice came running towards the town. He ran so fast that he thought he felt the mountain tremble beneath him. He ran so fast that the blades of grass by the roadside had no time to sprinkle his cloak with dew; so fast that the scorpions had no time to lift their tails and sting him.

As the old man ran, his cloak flapped unfastened about him, and his rope swung unknotted behind. His wide sleeves waved like wings, and his heavy hood pounded up and down on his back, as if it wished to urge him on.

The man in the custom-office, who was still asleep, woke and rubbed his eyes as Fra Felice rushed by, but he had no time to recognize him. The pavements were slippery with dampness; beggars lay and slept by the high stone steps with their legs heedlessly stretched out into the street; exhausted domino-players were going home from the Café reeling with sleep. But Fra Felice hastened onward regardless of all obstructions.

Houses and gateways, squares and arched-over alleys disappeared behind old Fra Felice. He ran halfway up the Corso before he stopped.

He stopped in front of a big house with many heavy balconies. He seized the door-knocker and pounded until a servant awoke. He would not be quiet till the servant called up a maid, and the maid waked the signora.

"Donna Micaela, Fra Felice is downstairs. He insists on speaking to you."

When Donna Micaela at last came down to Fra Felice, he was still panting and breathless, but there was a fire in his eyes, and little pale roses in his cheeks.

It was the image, the image. When Fra Felice had rung the four-o'clock matins that morning he had gone into the church to look at him.

Then he had discovered that big stones had loosened from the dome just over the image. They had fallen on the altar and broken it to pieces, but the image had stood untouched. And none of the plaster and dust that had tumbled down had fallen on the image; it was quite uninjured.

Fra Felice took Donna Micaela's hand and told her that she must go with him to the church and see the miracle. She should see it before anyone, because she had taken care of the image.

And Donna Micaela went with him through the grey, chilly morning to his monastery, while her heart throbbed with eagerness and expectation.

When she arrived and saw that Fra Felice had told the truth, she said to him that she had recognized the image as soon as she had caught sight of it, and that she knew that it could work miracles. "He is the greatest and gentlest of miracle-workers," she said.

Fra Felice went up to the image and looked into its eyes. For there is a great difference in images, and the wisdom of an old monk is needed to understand which has power and which has not. Now Fra Felice saw that this image's eyes were deep and glowing, as if they had life; and that on its lips hovered a mysterious smile.

Then old Fra Felice fell on his knees and stretched his clasped hands towards the image, and his old shriveled face was lighted by a great joy.

It seemed to Fra Felice all at once as if the walls of his church were covered with pictures and purple hangings; candles shone on the altar; song sounded from the gallery; and the whole floor was covered with kneeling, praying people.

All imaginary glory would fall to the lot of his poor old church, now that it possessed one of the great miracle-working images.

# IV

## THE OLD MARTYRDOM

*F*rom the summer-palace in Diamante many letters were sent during that time to Gaetano Alagona, who was in prison in Como. But the letter-carrier never had a letter in his bag from Gaetano addressed to the summer-palace.

For Gaetano had gone into his life-long imprisonment as if it had been a grave. The only thing he asked or desired was that it should give him the grave's forgetfulness and peace.

He felt as if he were dead; and he said to himself that he did not wish to hear the laments and wails of the survivors. Nor did he wish to be deceived with hopes, or be tempted by tender words to long for family and friends. Nor did he wish to hear anything of what was happening in the world, when he had no power to take part and to lead.

He found work in the prison, and carved beautiful works of art, as he had always done. But he never would receive a letter, nor a visitor. He thought that in that way he could cease to feel the bitterness of his misfortunes. He believed that he would be able to teach himself to live a whole life within four narrow walls.

And for that reason Donna Micaela never had a word of answer from him.

Finally she wrote to the director of the prison and asked if Gaetano was still alive. He answered that the prisoner she asked about never read a letter. He had asked to be spared all communications from the outside world.

So she wrote no more. Instead she continued to work for her railway. She hardly dared to speak of it in Diamante, but nevertheless she thought of nothing else. She herself sewed and embroidered, and she had all her servants make little cheap things that she could sell at her bazaar. In the shop she looked up old wares for the tombola. She had Piero, the gatekeeper, prepare colored lanterns; she persuaded her father to paint signs and placards; and she had her maid, Lucia, who was from Capri, arrange coral necklaces and shell boxes.

She was not at all sure that even one person would come to her entertainment. Everyone was against her; no one would help her. They did not even like her to show herself on the streets or to talk business. It was not fitting for a well-born lady.

Old Fra Felice tried to assist her, for he loved her because she had helped him with the image.

One day, when Donna Micaela was lamenting that she could not persuade anyone that the people ought to build the railway, he lifted his cap from his head and pointed to his bald temples.

"Look at me, Donna Micaela," he said. "So bald will that railway make your head if you go on as you have begun."

"What do you mean, Fra Felice?"

"Donna Micaela," said the old man, "would it not be folly to start on a dangerous undertaking without having a friend and helper?"

"I have tried enough to find friends, Fra Felice."

"Yes, men!" said the old man. "But how do men help? If anyone is going fishing, Donna Micaela, he knows that he must call on San Pietro; if anyone wishes to buy a horse, he can ask help of San Antonio Abbate. But if I want to pray for your railway, I do not know to whom I shall turn."

Fra Felice meant that the trouble was that she had chosen no patron saint for her railway. He wished her to choose the crowned child that stood out in his old church as its first friend and promoter. He told her that if she only did that she would certainly be helped.

She was so touched that anyone was willing to stand by her that she instantly promised to pray for her railway to the child at San Pasquale.

Fra Felice got a big collection-box and painted on it in bright, distinct letters: "Gifts for the Etna Railway," and he hung it in his church beside the altar.

It was not more than a day after that that Don Antonio Greco's wife, Donna Emilia, came out to the old, deserted church to consult San Pasquale, who is the wisest of all the saints.

During the autumn Don Antonio's theater had begun to fare ill, as was to be expected when no one had any money.

Don Antonio thought to run the theater with less expense than before. He had cut off a couple of lamps and did not have such big and gorgeously painted play-bills.

But that had been great folly. It is not at the moment when people are losing their desire to go to the theater that it will answer to shorten the princesses' silk trains and economize on the gilding of the king's crowns.

Perhaps it is not so dangerous at another theater, but at a marionette theater it is a risk to make any changes, because it is chiefly half-grown boys who go to the marionette theater. Big people can understand that sometimes it is necessary to economize, but children always wish to have things in the same way.

Fewer and fewer spectators carne to Don Antonio, and he went on economizing and saving. Then it occurred to him that he could dispense with the two blind violin-players, Father Elia and Brother Tommaso, who also used to play during the interludes and in the battle-scenes.

Those blind men, who earned so much by singing in houses of mourning, and who took in vast sums on feast-days, were expensive. Don Antonio dismissed them and got a hand-organ.

That caused his ruin. All the apprentices and shop-boys in Diamante ceased to go to the theater. They would not sit and listen to a hand-organ. They promised one another not to go to the theater till Don Antonio had taken back the fiddlers, and they kept their promise. Don Antonio's dolls had to perform to empty walls.

The young boys who otherwise would rather go without their supper than the theater, stayed away night after night. They were convinced that they could force Don Antonio to arrange everything as before.

But Don Antonio comes of a family of artists. His father and his brother have marionette theaters; his brothers-in-law, all his relations are of the profession. And Don Antonio understands his art. He can change his voice indefinitely; he can maneuver at the same time a whole army of dolls; and he knows by heart the whole cycle of plays founded on the chronicles of Charlemagne.

And now Don Antonio's artistic feelings were hurt. He would not be forced to take back the blind men. He wished to have the people come to his theater for his sake, and not for that of the musicians.

He changed his tactics and began to play big dramas with elaborate mountings. But it was futile.

There is a play called "The Death of the Paladin," which treats of Roland's fight at Ronceval. It requires so much machinery that a puppet theater has to be kept shut for two days for it to be set up. It is so dear to the public that it is generally played for double price and to full houses for a whole month. Don Antonio now had that play mounted, but he did not need to play it; he had no spectators.

After that his spirit was broken. He tried to get Father Elia and Brother Tommaso back, but they now knew what their value was to him.

They demanded such a price that it would have been ruin to pay them. It was impossible to come to any agreement.

In the small rooms back of the marionette theater they lived as in a besieged fortress. They had nothing else to do but to starve. Donna Emilia and Don Antonio were both gay young people, but now they never laughed. They were in great want, but Don Antonio was a proud man, and he could not bear to think that his art no longer had the power to draw.

So, as I said, Donna Emilia went down to the church of San Pasquale to ask the saint for good advice. It had been her intention to repeat nine prayers to the great stone-image standing outside of the church, and then to go; but before she had begun to pray she had noticed that the church-door stood open. "Why is San Pasquale's church-door open?" said Donna Emilia. "That has never happened in my time," — and she went into the church.

The only thing to be seen there was Fra Felice's beloved image and the big collection-box. The image looked so beautiful in his crown and his rings that Donna Emilia was tempted forward to him, but when she came near enough to look into his eyes, he seemed to her so tender and so cheering that she knelt down before him and prayed. She promised that if he would help her and Don Antonio in their need, she would put the receipts of a whole evening in the big box that hung beside him.

After her prayers were over, Donna Emilia concealed herself behind the church-door, and tried to catch what the passers-by were saying. For if the image was willing to help her, he would let her hear a word which would tell her what to do.

She had not stood there two minutes before old Assunta of the Cathedral steps passed by with Donna Pepa and Donna Tura. And she heard Assunta say in her solemn voice: "That was the year when I heard 'The Old Martyrdom' for the first time." Donna Emilia heard quite distinctly. Assunta really said "The Old Martyrdom."

Donna Emilia thought that she would never reach her home. It was as if her legs could not carry her fast enough, and the distance increased as she ran. When she finally saw the corner of the theater with the red lanterns under the roof and the big illustrated play-bills, she felt as if she had gone many miles.

When she came in to Don Antonio, he sat with his big head leaning on his hand and stared at the table. It was terrible to see Don Antonio. In those last weeks he had begun to lose his hair; on the very top of his head it was so thin that the skin shone through. Was it strange, when he was in such trouble? While she had been away he had taken all his puppets out and inspected them. He did that now every day. He used to sit and look at the puppet that played Armida. Was she no longer beautiful and beguiling? he would ask. And he tried to polish up Roland's sword and Charlemagne's crown. Donna Emilia saw that he had gilded the emperor's crown again; it was for at least the fifth time. But then he had stopped in the midst of his work and had sat down to brood. He had noticed it himself. It was not gilding that was lacking; it was an idea.

As Donna Emilia came into the room, she stretched out her hands to her husband.

"Look at me, Don Antonio Greco," she said. "I bear in my hands golden bowls full of ripe figs!"

And she told how she had prayed, and what she had vowed, and what she had been advised.

When she said that to Don Antonio, he sprang up. His arms fell stiffly beside his body, and his hair raised itself from his head. He was seized with an unspeakable terror. "'The Old Martyrdom'!" he screamed, "'The Old Martyrdom'!"

For "The Old Martyrdom" is a miracle-play, which in its time was given in all Sicily. It drove out all other oratorios and mysteries, and was played every year in every town for two centuries. It was the greatest day of the year, when "The Old Martyrdom" was performed. But now it is never played; now it only lives in the people's memory as a legend.

In the old days it was also played in the marionette theaters. But now it has come to be considered old-fashioned and out-of-date. It has probably not been played for thirty years.

Don Antonio began to roar and scream at Donna Emilia, because she tortured him with such folly. He struggled with her as with a demon, who had come to seize him. It was amazing; it was heartrending, he said. How could she get hold of such a word? But Donna Emilia stood quiet and let him rave. She only said that what she had heard was God's will.

Soon Don Antonio began to be uncertain. The great idea gradually took possession of him. Nothing had ever been so loved and played in Sicily, and did not the same people still live on the noble isle? Did they not love the same earth, the same mountains, the same skies as their forefathers had loved? Why should they not also love "The Old Martyrdom?"

He resisted as long as he could. He said to Donna Emilia that it would cost too much. Where could he get apostles with long hair and beards? He had no table for the Last Supper; he had none of the machinery required for the entry, and carrying of the cross.

But Donna Emilia saw that he was going to give in, and before night he actually went to Fra Felice and renewed her vow to put the receipts of one evening in the box of the little image, if it proved to be good advice.

Fra Felice told Donna Micaela about the vow, and she was glad, and at the same time anxious how it would turn out.

Through all the town it was known that Don Antonio was mounting "The Old Martyrdom," and everyone laughed at him. Don Antonio had lost his mind.

The people would have liked well enough to see "The Old Martyrdom," if they could have seen it as it was played in former days. They would have liked to see it given as in Aci, where the noblemen of the town played the kings and the servants, and the artisans took the parts of the Jews and the apostles; and where so many scenes from the Old Testament were added that the spectacle lasted the whole day.

They would have also liked to see those wonderful days in Castelbuoco, when the whole town was transformed into Jerusalem. There the mystery was given so that Jesus came riding to the town, and was met with palms at the town-gate. There the church represented the temple at Jerusalem and the town-hall Pilate's palace. There Peter warmed himself at a fire in the priest's courtyard; the crucifixion took place on a mountain above the town; and Mary looked for the body of her son in the grottoes of the syndic's garden.

When the people had such things in their memory how could they be content to see the great mystery in Don Antonio's theater?

But in spite of everything, Don Antonio worked with the greatest eagerness to prepare the actors and to arrange the elaborate machinery.

And behold, in a few days came Master Battista, who painted placards, and presented him with a play-bill. He had been glad to hear that Don Antonio was going to play "The Old Martyrdom;" he had seen it in his youth, and had great pleasure in it.

So there now stood in large letters on the corner of the theater: "'The Old Martyrdom' or 'The Resurrected Adam,' tragedy in three acts by Cavaliere Filippo Orioles."

Don Antonio wondered and wondered what the people's mood would be. The donkey-boys and apprentices who passed by his theater read the notice with scoffs and derision. It looked very black for Don Antonio, but in spite of it he went on faithfully with his work.

When the appointed evening came, and the "Martyrdom" was to be played, no one was more anxious than Donna Micaela. "Is the little image going to help me?" she asked herself incessantly.

She sent out her maid, Lucia, to look about. Were there any groups of boys in front of the theater? Did it look as if there were going to be a crowd? Lucia might go to Donna Emilia, sitting in the ticket-office, and ask her if it looked hopeful.

But when Lucia came back she had not the slightest hope to offer. There was no crowd outside the theater. The boys had resolved to crush Don Antonio.

Towards eight o'clock Donna Micaela could no longer endure sitting at home and waiting. She persuaded her father to go with her to the theater. She knew well that a signora had never set her foot in Don Antonio's theater, but she needed to see how it was going to be. It would be such a dizzily great success for her railway if Don Antonio succeeded.

When Donna Micaela came to the theater it was a few minutes before eight, and Donna Emilia had not sold a ticket.

But she was not depressed; "Go in, Donna Micaela!" she said; "we shall play at any rate, it is so beautiful. Don Antonio will play it for you and your father and me. It is the most beautiful thing he has ever performed."

Donna Micaela came into the little hall. It was hung with black, as the big theaters always were in the old days when "The Old Martyrdom" was given. There were dark, silver-fringed curtains on the stage, and the little benches were covered with black.

Immediately after Donna Micaela came in, Don Antonio's bushy eyebrows appeared in a little hole in the curtain. "Donna Micaela," he cried, as Donna Emilia had done, "we shall play at any rate. It is so beautiful, it needs no spectators."

Just then came Donna Emilia herself, and opened the door, and curtsying, held it back. It was the priest, Don Matteo, who entered.

"What do you say to me, Donna Micaela?" he said, laughing. "But you understand; it is 'The Old Martyrdom.' I saw it in my youth at the big opera in Palermo; and I believe that it was that old play that made me become a priest."

The next time the door opened it was Father Elia and Brother Tommaso, who came with their violins under their arms and felt their way to their usual places, as quietly as if they had never had any disagreement with Don Antonio.

The door opened again. It was an old woman from the alley above the house of the little Moor. She was dressed in black, and made the sign of the cross as she came in.

After her came four, five other old women; and Donna Micaela looked at them almost resentfully, as they gradually filled the theater. She knew that Don Antonio would not be satisfied till he had his own public back again, — till he had his self-willed, beloved boys to play for.

Suddenly she heard a hurricane or thunder. The doors flew open, — all at the same time! It was the boys. They threw themselves down in their usual places, as if they had come back to their home.

They looked at one another, a little ashamed. But it had been impossible for them to see one old woman after another go into their theater to see what was being played for them. It had been quite impossible to see the whole street full of old distaff-spinners in slow procession toward the theater, and so they had rushed in.

But hardly had the gay young people reached their places before they noticed that they had come under a severe master. Ah, "The Old Martyrdom," "The Old Martyrdom!"

It was not given as in Aci and in Castelbuoco; it was not played as at the opera in Palermo; it was only played with miserable marionettes with immovable faces and stiff bodies; but the old play had not lost its power.

Donna Micaela noticed it already in the second act during the Last Supper. The boys began to hate Judas. They shouted threats and insults at him.

As the story of the Passion went on, they laid aside their hats and clasped their hands. They sat quite still, with their beautiful brown eyes turned towards the stage. Now and then a few tears dropped. Now and then a fist was clenched in indignation.

Don Antonio spoke with tears in his voice; Donna Emilia was on her knees at the entrance. Don Matteo looked with a gentle smile at the little puppets and remembered the wonderful spectacle in Palermo that had made him a priest.

But when Jesus was cast into prison and tortured, the young people were ashamed of themselves. They too had hated and persecuted. They were like those pharisees, like those Romans. It was a shame to think of it. Could Don Antonio forgive them?

# V

## THE LADY WITH THE IRON RING

Donna Micaela often thought of a poor little dressmaker whom she had seen in her youth in Catania. She dwelt in the house next to the Palazzo Palmeri, sitting always in the gateway with her work, so that Donna Micaela had seen her a thousand times. She always sat and sang, and she had certainly only known a single canzone. Always, always she sang the same song.

"I have cut a curl from my black hair," she had sung. "I have unfastened my black, shining braids, and cut a curl from my hair. I have done it to gladden my friend, who is in trouble. Alas, my beloved is sitting in prison; my beloved will never again twine my hair about his fingers. I have sent him a lock of my hair to remind him of the silken chains that never more will bind him."

Donna Micaela remembered the song well. It seemed as if it had sounded through all her childhood to warn her of the suffering that awaited her.

Donna Micaela often sat at that time on the stone steps of the church of San Pasquale. She saw wonderful events take place far off on that Etna so rich in legends.

Over the black lava glided a railway train on newly laid shining rails. It was a festival train; flags waved along the road; there were wreaths on the carriages; the seats were covered with purple cushions. At the stations the people stood and shouted: "Long live the king! long live the queen! long live the new railway!"

She heard it so well; she herself was on the train. Ah, how honored, how honored she was! She was summoned before the king and queen; and they thanked her for the new railway. "Ask a favor of us, princess!"

said the king, giving her the title that the ladies of the race of Alagona had formerly borne.

"Sire," she answered, as people answer in stories, "give freedom to the last Alagona!"

And it was granted to her. The king could not say no to a prayer from her who had built that fine railway, which was to give riches to all Etna.

*W*hen Donna Micaela lifted her arm so that her dress-sleeve slid up, one saw that she wore as a bracelet a ring of rusty iron. She had found it in the street, forced it over her hand, and now she always wore it. Whenever she happened to see or touch it, she grew pale, and her eyes no longer saw anything of the world about her. She saw a prison like that of Foscari in the doge's palace in Venice. It was a dark, narrow, cellarlike hole; light filtered in through a grated aperture; and from the wall hung a great bunch of chains, which wound like serpents round the prisoner's legs and arms and neck.

May the saint work a miracle! May the people work! May she herself soon have such praise that she can beg freedom for her prisoner! He will die if she does not hurry. May the iron ring eat incessantly into her arm, so that she shall not forget him for a second.

# VI

## FRA FELICE'S LEGACY

*W*hen Donna Emilia opened the ticket-office to sell tickets for the second performance of "The Old Martyrdom," the people stood in line to get places; the second evening the theater was so overcrowded that people fainted in the crush, and the third evening people came from both Adernó and Paternó to see the beloved tragedy. Don Antonio foresaw that he would be able to play it a whole month for double price, and with two performances every evening.

How happy they were, he and Donna Emilia, and with what joy and gratitude they laid twenty-five lire in the collection-box of the little image!

In Diamante the incident caused great surprise, and many came to Donna Elisa to find out if she believed that the saint wished them to support Donna Micaela.

"Have you heard, Donna Elisa," they said, "that Don Antonio Greco has been helped by the Christchild in San Pasquale, because he promised to give the receipts of one evening to Donna Micaela's railway?"

But when they asked Donna Elisa about it, she shut her mouth and looked as if she could not think of anything but her embroidery.

Fra Felice himself came in and told her of the two miracles the image had already worked.

"Signorina Tottenham was very stupid to let the image go, if it is such a miracle-worker," said Donna Elisa.

So they all thought. Signorina Tottenham had owned the image many years, and she had not noticed anything. It probably could not work miracles; it was only a coincidence.

It was unfortunate that Donna Elisa would not believe. She was the only one of the old Alagonas left in Diamante, and the people followed her, more than they themselves knew. If Donna Elisa had believed, the whole town would have helped Donna Micaela.

But Donna Elisa could not believe that God and the saints wished to aid her sister-in-law.

She had watched her since the festival of San Sebastiano. Whenever anyone spoke of Gaetano, she turned pale, and looked very troubled. Her features became like those of a sinful man, when he is racked with the pangs of conscience.

Donna Elisa sat and thought of it one morning, and it was so engrossing that she let her needle rest. "Donna Micaela is no Etna woman," she said to herself. "She is on the side of the government; she is glad that Gaetano is in prison."

Out in the street at that same moment people came carrying a great stretcher. On it lay heaped up a mass of church ornaments; chandeliers and shrines and reliquaries. Donna Elisa looked up for a moment, then returned to her thoughts.

"She would not let me adorn the house of the Alagonas on the festival of San Sebastiano," she thought. "She did not wish the saint to help Gaetano."

Two men came by dragging a rattling dray on which lay a mountain of red hangings, richly embroidered stoles, and altar pictures in broad, gilded frames.

Donna Elisa struck out with her hand as if to push away all doubts. It could not be an actual miracle which had happened. The saint must know that Diamante could not afford to build a railway.

People now came past driving a yellow cart, packed full of music-stands, prayer-books, praying-desks and confessionals.

Donna Elisa woke up. She looked out between the rosaries that hung in garlands over the windowpanes. That was the third load of church furnishings that had passed. Was Diamante being plundered? Had the Saracens come to the town?

She went to the door to see better. Again came a stretcher, and on it lay mourning-wreaths of tin, tablets with long inscriptions, and coats of arms, such as are hung up in churches in memory of the dead.

Donna Elisa asked the bearers, and learned what was happening. They were clearing out the church of Santa Lucia in Gesù. The syndic and the town council had ordered it turned into a theater. After the uprising there had been a new syndic in Diamante. He was a young man from Rome, who did not know the town, but nevertheless wished to do something for it. He had proposed to the town-council that Diamante should have a theater like Taormina and other towns. They could quite easily fit up one of the churches as a play-house. They certainly had more than enough, with five town churches and seven monastery churches; they could easily spare one of them.

There was for instance the Jesuits' church, Santa Lucia in Gesù. The monastery surrounding it was already changed to a barracks, and the church was practically deserted. It would make an excellent theater.

That was what the new syndic had proposed, and the town-council had agreed to it.

When Donna Elisa heard what was going on she threw on her mantilla and veil, and hurried to the Lucia church, with the same haste with which one hurries to the house where one knows that someone is dying.

"What will become of the blind?" thought Donna Elisa. "How can they live without Santa Lucia in Gesù?"

When Donna Elisa reached the silent little square, round which the Jesuits' long, ugly monastery is built, she saw on the broad stone steps that extend the whole length of the church front, a row of ragged children and rough-haired dogs. All of them were leaders of the blind, and they cried and whined as loud as they could.

"What is the matter with you all?" asked Donna Elisa. "They want to take our church away from us," wailed the children. And thereupon all the dogs howled more piteously than ever, for the dogs of the blind are almost human.

At the church-door Donna Elisa met Master Pamphilio's wife, Donna Concetta. "Ah, Donna Elisa," she said, "never in all your life have you seen anything so terrible. You had better not go in."

But Donna Elisa went on.

In the church at first she saw nothing but a white cloud of dust. But hammer-strokes thundered through the cloud, for some workmen were busy breaking away a big stone knight, lying in a window niche.

"Lord God!" said Donna Elisa, and clasped her hands together; "they are tearing down Sor Arrigo!" And she thought how tranquilly he had lain in his niche. Every time she had seen him she had wished that she might be as remote from disturbance and change as old Sor Arrigo.

In the church of Lucia there was still another big monument. It represented an old Jesuit, lying on a black marble sarcophagus with a scourge in his hand and his cap drawn far down over his forehead. He was called Father Succi, and the people used to frighten their children with him in Diamante.

"Would they also dare to touch Father Succi?" thought Donna Elisa. She felt her way through the plaster dust to the choir, where the sarcophagus stood, in order to see if they had dared to move the old Jesuit.

Father Succi still lay on his stone bed. He lay there dark and hard, as he had been in life; and one could almost believe that he was still alive. Had there been doctors and tables with medicine-bottles and burning candles beside the bed, one would have believed that Father Succi lay sick in the choir of his church, waiting for his last hour.

The blind sat round about him, like members of the family who gather round a dying man, and rocked their bodies in silent grief. There were both the women from the hotel courtyard, Donna Pepa and Donna Tura; there was old Mother Saraedda, who ate the bread of charity at the house of the Syndic Voltaro; there were blind beggars, blind singers, blind of all ages and conditions. All the blind of Diamante were there, and in Diamante there is an incredible number who no longer see the light of the sun.

They all sat silent most of the time, but every now and then one of them burst into a wail. Sometimes one of them felt his way forward to the monk, Father Succi, and threw himself weeping aloud across him.

It made it all the more like a deathbed that the priest and Father Rossi from the Franciscan monastery were there and were trying to comfort the despairing people.

Donna Elisa was much moved. Ah, so often she had seen those people happy in her garden, and now to meet them in such misery! They had won pleasant tears from her when they had sung mourning-songs over her husband, Signor Antonelli, and over her brother, Don Ferrante. She could not bear to see them in such need.

Old Mother Saraedda began to speak to Donna Elisa.

"I knew nothing when I came, Donna Elisa," said the old woman. "I left my dog outside on the steps and went in through the church door. Then I stretched out my arm to push aside the curtain over the door, but the curtain was gone. I put my foot down as if there were a step to mount before the threshold, but there was no step. I stretched out my hand to take the holy water; I curtsied as I went by the high altar; and I listened for the little bell that always rings when Father Rossi comes to the mass. Donna Elisa, there was no holy water, no altar, no bell; there was nothing!"

"Poor thing, poor thing," said Donna Elisa.

"Then I hear how they are hammering and pounding up in a window. 'What are you doing with Sor Arrigo?' I cry, for I hear instantly that it is in Sor Arrigo's window.

"'We are going to carry him away,' they answer me.

"Just then the priest, Don Matteo, comes to me, takes me by the hand, and explains everything. And I am almost angry with the priest when he says that it is for a theater. They want our church for a theater!

"'Where is Father Succi?' I say instantly. 'Is Father Succi still here?' And he leads me to Father Succi. He has to lead me, for I cannot find my way. Since they have taken away all the chairs and praying-desks and carpets and platforms and folding steps, I cannot find my way. Before, I found my way about here as well as you."

"The priest will find you another church," said Donna Elisa. "Donna Elisa," said the old woman, "what are you saying? You might as well say that the priest can give us sight. Can Don Matteo give us a church where we see, as we saw in this? None of us needed a guide here. There, Donna Elisa, stood an altar; the flowers on it were red as Etna at sunset, and we saw it. We counted sixteen wax-lights over the high altar on Sundays, and thirty on festival days. We could see when Father Rossi held the mass here. What shall we do in another church, Donna Elisa? There we shall not be able to see anything. They have extinguished the light of our eyes anew."

Donna Elisa's heart grew as warm as if molten lava had run over it. It was certainly a great wrong they were doing to those blind unfortunates.

So Donna Elisa went over to Don Matteo.

"Your Reverence," she said, "have you spoken to the syndic?"

"Alas, alas, Donna Elisa," said Don Matteo, "it is better for you to try to talk to him than for me."

"Your Reverence, the syndic is a stranger; perhaps he has not heard of the blind."

"Signor Voltaro has been to him; Father Rossi has been to him; and I too, I too. He answers nothing but that he cannot change what is decided in the town Junta. We all know, Donna Elisa, that the town Junta cannot take back anything. If it has decided that your cat shall hold mass in the Cathedral, it cannot change it."

Suddenly there was a movement in the church. A large blind man came in. "Father Elia!" the people whispered, "Father Elia!"

Father Elia was the head man of the company of blind singers, who always collected there. He had long white hair and beard, and was beautiful as one of the holy patriarchs.

He, like all the others, went forward to Father Succi. He sat down beside him, and leaned his head against the coffin.

Donna Elisa went up to Father Elia and spoke to him. "Father Elia," she said, "*you* ought to go to the syndic."

The old man recognized Donna Elisa's voice, and he answered her, in his thick, old-man's tones: —

"Do you suppose that I have waited to have you say that to me? Don't you know that my first thought was to go to the syndic?"

He spoke with such a hard and distinct voice that the workmen stopped hammering and listened, thinking someone had begun to preach.

"I told him that we blind singers are a company, and that the Jesuits opened their church for us more than three hundred years ago, and gave us the right to gather here to select new members and try new songs.

"And I said to him that there are thirty of us in the company; and that the holy Lucia is our patroness; and that we never sing in the streets, only in courts and in rooms; and that we sing legends of the saints and mourning-songs, but never a wanton song; and that the Jesuit, Father Succi, opened the church for us, because the blind are Our Lord's singers.

"I told him that some of us are *recitatori,* who can sing the old songs, but others are *trovatori,* who compose new ones. I said to him that we give pleasure to many on the noble isle. I asked him why he wished to deprive us of life. For the homeless cannot live.

"I said to him that we wander from town to town through all Etna, but the church of Lucia is our home, and mass is held here for us every morning. Why should he refuse us the comfort of God's word?

"I told him that the Jesuits once changed their attitude towards us and wished to drive us away from their church, but they did not succeed. We received a letter from the Viceroy that we might hold our meetings in perpetuity in Santa Lucia in Gesù. And I showed him the letter."

"What did he answer?"

"He laughed at me."

"Can none of the other gentlemen help you?"

"I have been to them, Donna Elisa. All the morning I have been sent from Herod to Pilatus."

"Father Elia," said Donna Elisa with lowered voice, "have you forgotten to call on the saints?"

"I have called on both the black Madonna and San Sebastiano and Santa Lucia. I have prayed to as many as I could name."

"Do you think, Father Elia," said Donna Elisa, and lowered her voice still more, "that Don Antonio Greco was helped, because he promised money to Donna Micaela's railway?"

"I have no money to give," said the old man, disconsolately.

"Still, you ought to think of it, Father Elia," said Donna Elisa, "since you are in such straits. You ought to try if, by promising the Christ-image that you yourself and all who belong to your company will speak and sing of the railway, and persuade people to give contributions to it, you may keep your church. We do not know if it can help, but one ought to try every possible thing, Father Elia. It costs nothing to promise."

"I will promise anything for your sake," said the old man.

He laid his old blind head again against the black coffin, and Donna Elisa understood that he had given the promise in his desire to be left in peace with his sorrow.

"Shall I present your vow to the Christ-image?" she said.

"Do as you will, Donna Elisa," said the old man.

*T*hat same day old Fra Felice had risen at five o'clock in the morning and begun to sweep out his church. He felt quite active and well; but while he was working it seemed as if San Pasquale, sitting with his bag of stones outside the church-door, had something to say to him. He went out, but there was nothing the matter with San Pasquale; quite the contrary. Just then the sun glided up from behind Etna, and down the dark mountain-sides the rays came hurrying, many-colored as harp-strings. When the rays reached Fra Felice's old church they turned it rosy red; rosy red were also the old barbaric pillars that held up the canopy over the image, and San Pasquale with his bag of stones, and Fra Felice himself. "We look like young boys," thought the old man; "we have still long years to live."

But as he was going back into the church, he felt a sharp pressure at his heart, and it came into his mind that San Pasquale had called him out to say farewell. At the same time his legs became so heavy that he could hardly move them. He felt no pain, but a weariness which could mean nothing but death. He was scarcely able to put his broom away behind the door of the sacristy; then he dragged himself up the choir, lay down on the platform in front of the high altar, and wrapped his cloak about him.

The Christ-image seemed to nod to him and say:

"Now I need you, Fra Felice."

He lay and nodded back: "I am ready; I shall not fail you."

It was only to lie and wait; and it was beautiful, Fra Felice thought. He had never before in all his life had time to feel how tired he was. Now at last he might rest. The image would keep up the church and the monastery without him.

He lay and smiled at the thought that old San Pasquale had called him out to say good-morning to him.

Fra Felice lay thus till late in the day, and dozed most of the time. No one was with him, and a feeling came over him that it would not do to creep in this way out of life. It was as if he had cheated somebody of something. That woke him time after time. He ought of course to get the priests, but he had no one to send for them.

While he lay there he thought that he shrank together more and more. Every time he awoke he thought that he had grown smaller. He felt as if he were quite disappearing. Now he could certainly wind his cloak four times about him.

He would have died quite by himself if Donna Elisa had not come to ask help for the blind of the little image. She was in a strange mood when she came, for she wished of course to get help for the blind, but yet she did not wish Donna Micaela's plans to be promoted.

When she came into the church she saw Fra Felice lying on the platform under the altar, and she went forward and knelt beside him.

Fra Felice turned his eyes towards her and smiled quietly. "I am going to die," he said, hoarsely; but he corrected himself and said: "I am permitted to die."

Donna Elisa asked what the matter was, and said that she would fetch help.

"Sit down here," he said, and made a feeble attempt to wipe away the dust on the platform with his sleeve.

Donna Elisa said that she wished to fetch the priests and sisters of charity.

He seized her skirt and held her back.

"I want to speak to you first, Donna Elisa."

It was hard for him to talk, and he breathed heavily after each word. Donna Elisa sat down beside him and waited.

He lay for a while and panted; then a flush rose to his cheeks; his eyes began to shine, and he spoke with ease and eagerness.

"Donna Elisa," said Fra Felice, "I have a legacy to give away. It has troubled me all day. I do not know to whom I shall give it."

"Fra Felice," said Donna Elisa, "do not concern yourself with such a thing. There is no one who does not need a good gift."

But now when Fra Felice's strength had returned, he wished, before he made up his mind about the legacy, to tell Donna Elisa how good God had been to him.

"Has not God been great in his grace to make me a polacco?" he said.

"Yes, it is a great gift," said Donna Elisa.

"Only to be a little, little *polacco* is a great gift," said Fra Felice; "it is especially useful since the monastery has been given up, and when my comrades are gone or dead. It means having a bag full of bread before one even stretches out one's hand to beg. It means always seeing bright faces, and being greeted with deep reverences. I know no greater gift for a poor monk, Donna Elisa."

Donna Elisa thought how revered and loved Fra Felice had been, because he had been able to predict what numbers would come out in the lottery. And she could not help agreeing with him.

"If I came wandering along the road in the heat," said Fra Felice, "the shepherd came to me and went with me a long way, and held his umbrella over me as shelter against the sun. And when I came to the laborers in the cool stone-quarries, they shared their bread and their bean-soup with me. I have never been afraid of brigands nor of *carabinieri*. The official at the custom-house has shut his eyes when I went by with my bag. It has been a good gift, Donna Elisa."

"True, true," said Donna Elisa.

"It has not been an arduous profession," said Fra Felice. "They spoke to me, and I answered them; that was all. They knew that every word has its number, and they noticed what I said and played accordingly. I never knew how it happened, Donna Elisa; it was a gift from God."

"You will be a great loss to the poor people, Fra Felice," said Donna Elisa.

Fra Felice smiled. "They care nothing for me on Sunday and Monday, when there has just been a drawing," he said. "But they come on Thursday and Friday and on Saturday morning, because there is a drawing every Saturday."

Donna Elisa began to be anxious, because the dying man thought of nothing but that. Suddenly there flashed across her memory thoughts of one and another who had lost in the lottery, and she remembered several who had played away all their prosperity. She wished to turn his thoughts from that sinful lottery business.

"You said that you wished to speak of your will, Fra Felice."

"But it is because I have so many friends that it is hard for me to know to whom I shall give the legacy. Shall I give it to those who have baked sweet cakes for me, or to those who have offered me artichokes, browned in sweet oil? Or shall I bequeath it to the sisters of charity who nursed me when I was ill?"

"Have you much to give away, Fra Felice?"

"It will do, Donna Elisa. It will do."

Fra Felice seemed to be worse again; he lay silent with panting breast.

"I had also wished to give it to all poor, homeless monks, who had lost their monasteries," he whispered.

And then after thinking for a while: "I should also have liked to give it to the good old man in Rome. He, you know, who watches over us all."

"Are you so rich, Fra Felice?" said Donna Elisa.

"I have enough, Donna Elisa; I have enough."

He closed his eyes, and rested for a while; then he said: —

"I want to give it to everybody, Donna Elisa."

He acquired new strength at the thought; a slight flush was again visible in his cheeks, and he raised himself on his elbow.

"See here, Donna Elisa," he said, while he thrust his hand into his cloak and drew out a sealed envelope, which he handed to her, "you shall go and give this to the syndic, to the syndic of Diamante.

"Here, Donna Elisa," said Fra Felice, "here are the five numbers that win next Saturday. They have been revealed to me, and I have written them down. And the syndic shall take these numbers and have them fastened up on the Roman Gate, where everything of importance is published. And he shall let the people know that it is my testament. I bequeath it to the people. Five winning numbers, a whole quintern, Donna Elisa!"

Donna Elisa took the envelope and promised to give it to the syndic. She could do nothing else, for poor Fra Felice had not many minutes left to live.

"When Saturday comes," said Fra Felice, "there will be many who will think of Fra Felice. 'Can old Fra Felice have deceived us?' they will ask themselves. 'Can it be possible for us to win the whole quintern?'

"On Saturday evening there is a drawing on the balcony of the town-hall in Catania, Donna Elisa. Then they carry out the lottery-wheel and table, and the managers of the lottery are there, and the pretty little poor-house child. And one number after another is put into the lucky wheel until they are all there, the whole hundred.

"All the people stand below and tremble in expectation, as the sea trembles before the storm-wind.

"Everybody from Diamante will be there, and they will stand quite pale and hardly daring to look one another in the face. Before, they have believed, but not now. Now they think that old Fra Felice has deceived them. No one dares to cherish the smallest hope.

"Then the first number is drawn, and I was right. Ah, Donna Elisa, they will be so astonished they will scarcely be able to rejoice. For they have all expected disappointment. When the second number comes out, there is the silence of death. Then comes the third. The lottery managers will be astonished that everything is so quiet. 'Today they are not winning anything,' they will say. 'Today the state has all the prizes.' Then comes the fourth number. The poor-house child takes the roll from the wheel; and the marker opens the roll, and shows the number. Down among the people it is almost terrible; no one is able to say a word for joy. Then the last number comes. Donna Elisa, the people scream, they cry, they fall into one another's arms and sob. They are rich. All Diamante is rich —"

Donna Elisa had kept her arm under Fra Felice's head and supported him while he had panted out all this. Suddenly his head fell heavily back. Old Fra Felice was dead.

While Donna Elisa was with old Fra Felice, many people in Diamante had begun to trouble themselves about the blind. Not the men; most of the men were in the fields at work; but the women. They had come in crowds to Santa Lucia to console the blind, and finally, when about four hundred women had gathered together, it occurred to them to go and speak to the syndic.

They had gone up to the square and called for the syndic. He had come out on the balcony of the town-hall, and they had prayed for the blind. The syndic was a kind and handsome man. He had answered them pleasantly, but had not been willing to yield. He could not repeal what had been decided in the town Junta. But the women were determined that it should be repealed, and they remained in the square. The syndic went into the town-hall again, but they stayed in the square and called and prayed. They did not intend to go away till he yielded.

While this was going on, Donna Elisa came to give the syndic Fra Felice's testament. She was grieved unto death at all the misery, but at the same time she felt a bitter satisfaction, because she had received no help from the Christchild. She had always believed that the saints did not wish to help Donna Micaela.

It was a fine gift she had received in San Pasquale's church. Not only could it not help the blind, but it was in a fair way to ruin the whole town. Now what little the people still possessed would go to the lottery collector. There would be a borrowing and a pawning.

The syndic admitted Donna Elisa immediately, and was as calm and polite as always, although the women were calling in the square, the blind were bemoaning themselves in the waiting-room, and people had run in and out of his room all day.

"How can I be at your service, Signora Antonelli?" he said. Donna Elisa first looked about and wondered to whom he was speaking. Then she told about the testament.

The syndic was neither frightened nor surprised. "That is very interesting," he said, and stretched out his hand for the paper.

But Donna Elisa held the envelope fast and asked: "Signor Sindaco, what do you intend to do with it? Do you intend to fasten it to the Roman Gate?"

"Yes; what else can I do, signora? It is a dead man's last wish."

Donna Elisa would have liked to tell him what a terrible testament it was, but she checked herself to speak of the blind.

"Padre Succi, who directed that the blind should always be allowed in his church, is also a dead man," she interposed.

"Signora Antonelli, are you beginning with that too?" said the syndic, quite kindly. "It was a mistake; but why did no one tell me that the blind frequent the church of Lucia? Now, since it is decided, I cannot annul the decision; I cannot."

"But their rights and patents, Signor Sindaco?"

"Their rights are worth nothing. They have to do with the Jesuits' monastery, but there is no longer such a monastery. And tell me, Signora Antonelli, what will become of me if I yield?"

"The people will love you as a good man."

"Signora, people will believe that I am a weak man, and every day I shall have four hundred laborers' wives outside the town-hall, begging now for one thing, now for another. It is only to hold out for one day. Tomorrow it will be forgotten."

"Tomorrow!" said Donna Elisa; "we shall never forget it."

The syndic smiled, and Donna Elisa saw that he thought that he knew the people of Diamante much better than she.

"You think that their hearts are in it?" he said.

"I think so, Signor Sindaco."

Then the syndic laughed softly. "Give me that envelope, Signora."

He took it and went out on the balcony.

He began to speak to the women. "I wish to tell you," he said, "that I have just now heard that old Fra Felice is dead, and that he has left a legacy to you all. He has written down five numbers that are supposed to win in the lottery next Saturday, and he bequeaths them to you. No one has seen them yet. They are lying here in this envelope, and it is unopened."

He was silent a moment to let the women have time to think over what he had said.

Instantly they began to cry: "The numbers, the numbers!"

The syndic signed to them to be silent.

"You must remember," he said, "that it was impossible for Fra Felice to know what numbers will be drawn next Saturday. If you play on these numbers, you may all lose. And we cannot afford to be poorer than we are already here in Diamante. I ask you therefore to let me destroy the testament without anyone seeing it."

"The numbers," cried the women, "give us the numbers!"

"If I am permitted to destroy the testament," said the syndic, "I promise you that the blind shall have their church again."

There was silence in the square. Donna Elisa rose from her seat in the hall of the courthouse and seized the back of her chair with both hands.

"I leave it to you to choose between the church and the numbers," said the syndic.

"God in heaven!" sighed Donna Elisa, "is he a devil to tempt poor people in such a way?"

"We have been poor before," cried one of the women, "we can still be poor."

"We will not choose Barabbas instead of Christ," cried another.

The syndic took a match-box from his pocket, lighted a match, and brought it slowly up to the testament.

The women stood quiet and let Fra Felice's five numbers be destroyed. The blind people's church was saved.

"It is a miracle," whispered old Donna Elisa; "they all believe in Fra Felice, and they let his numbers burn. It is a miracle."

*L*ater in the afternoon Donna Elisa again sat in her shop with her embroidery frame. She looked old as she sat there, and there was something shaken and broken about her. It was not the usual Donna Elisa; it was a poor, elderly, forsaken woman.

She drew the needle slowly through the cloth, and when she wished to take another stitch she was uncertain and at a loss. It was hard for her to keep the tears from falling on her embroidery and spoiling it.

Donna Elisa was in such great grief for today she had lost Gaetano forever. There was no more hope of getting him back.

The saints had gone over to the side of the opponent, and worked miracles in order to help Donna Micaela. No one could doubt that a miracle had happened. The poor women of Diamante would never have been able to stand still while Fra Felice's numbers burned if they had not been bound by a miracle.

It made a poor soul so old and cross to have the good saints help Donna Micaela, who did not like Gaetano.

The door-bell jingled violently, and Donna Elisa rose from old habit. It was Donna Micaela. She was joyful, and came toward Donna Elisa with outstretched hands. But Donna Elisa turned away, and could not press her hand.

Donna Micaela was in raptures. "Ah, Donna Elisa, you have helped my railway. What can I say? How shall I thank you?"

"Never mind about thanking me, sister-in-law!"

"Donna Elisa!"

"If the saints wish to give us a railway, it must be because Diamante needs it, and not because they love you."

Donna Micaela shrank back. At last she thought she understood why Donna Elisa was angry with her. "If Gaetano were at home," she said. She stood and pressed her hand to her heart and moaned. "If Gaetano were at home he would not allow you to be so cruel to me."

"Gaetano? — would not Gaetano?"

"No, he would not. Even if you are angry with me because I loved him while my husband was alive, you would not dare to upbraid me for it if he were at home."

Donna Elisa lifted her eyebrows a little. "You think that he could prevail upon me to be silent about such a thing," she said, and her voice was very strange.

"But, Donna Elisa," Donna Micaela whispered in her ear, "it is impossible, quite impossible not to love him. He is beautiful; don't you know it? And he subjugates me, and I am afraid of him. You must let me love him."

"Must I?" Donna Elisa kept her eyes down and spoke quite shortly and harshly.

Donna Micaela was beside herself, "It is I whom he loves," she said. "It is not Giannita, but me, and you ought to consider me as a daughter; you ought to help me; you ought to be kind to me. And instead you stand against me; you are cruel to me. You do not let me come to you and talk of him. However much I long, and however much I work, I may not tell you of it."

Donna Elisa could hold out no longer. Donna Micaela was nothing but a child, young and foolish and quivering like a bird's heart, — just one to be taken care of. She had to throw her arms about her.

"I never knew it, you poor, foolish child," she said.

# VII

## AFTER THE MIRACLE

*T*he blind singers had a meeting in the church of Lucia. Highest up in the choir behind the altar sat thirty old, blind, men on the carved chairs of the Jesuit fathers. They were poor, most of them; most of them had a beggar's wallet and a crutch beside them.

They were all very earnest and solemn; they knew what it meant to be members of that holy band of singers, of that glorious old Academy.

Now and then below in the church a subdued noise was audible. The blind men's guides were sitting there, children, dogs, and old women, waiting. Sometimes the children began to romp with one another and with the dogs, but it was instantly suppressed and silenced.

Those of the blind who were *trovatori* stood up one after another and spoke new verses.

"You people who live on holy Etna," one of them recited, "men who live on the mountain of wonders, rise up, give your mistress a new glory! She longs for two ribbons to heighten her beauty, two long, narrow bands of steel to fasten her mantle. Give them to your mistress, and she will reward you with riches; she will give gold for steel. Countless are the treasures that she in her might will give them who assist her."

"A gentle worker of miracles has come among us," said another. "He stands poor and unnoticed in the bare old church, and his crown is of tin, and his diamonds of glass. 'Make no sacrifices to me, O ye poor,' he says; 'build me no temple, all ye who suffer. I will work for your happiness. If prosperity shines from your houses, I shall shine with precious stones; if want flees from the land, my feet will be clothed in golden shoes embroidered with pearls.'"

As each new verse was recited, it was accepted or rejected. The blind men judged with great severity.

The next day they wandered out over Etna, and sang the railway into the people's hearts.

*A*fter the miracle of Fra Felice's legacy, people began to give contributions to the railway. Donna Micaela soon had collected about a hundred lire. Then she and Donna Elisa made the journey to Messina to look at the steam-tram that runs between Messina and Pharo. They had no greater ambition; they would be satisfied with a steam-tram.

"Why does a railway need to be so expensive?" said Donna Elisa. "It is just an ordinary road, although people do lay down two steel rails on it. It is the engineer and the fine gentlemen who make a railway expensive. Don't trouble yourself about engineers, Micaela! Let our good road-builders, Giovanni and Carmelo, build your railway."

They carefully inspected the steam-tramway to Pharo and brought back all the knowledge they could. They measured how wide it ought to be between the rails, and Donna Micaela drew on a piece of paper the way the rails ran by one another at the stations. It was not so difficult; they were sure they would come out well.

That day there seemed to be no difficulties. It was as easy to build a station as an ordinary house, they said. Besides, more than two stations were not needed; a little sentry-box was sufficient at most of the stop-ping-places.

If they could only avoid forming a company, taking fine gentlemen into their service, and doing things that cost money, their plan of the railway would be realized. It would not cost so much. The ground they could certainly get free. The noble gentlemen who owned the land on Etna would of course understand how much use of the railway they would have, and would let it pass free of charge over their ground.

They did not trouble themselves to stake out the line beforehand. They were going to begin at Diamante and gradually build their way to Catania. They only needed to begin and lay a little piece every day. It was not so difficult.

After that journey they began the attempt to build the road at their own risk. Don Ferrante had not left a large inheritance to Donna Micaela, but one good thing that he had bequeathed her was a long stretch of lava-covered waste land off on Etna. Here Giovanni and Carmelo began to break ground for the new railway.

When the work began, the builders of the railway possessed only one hundred lire. It was the miracle of the legacy that had filled them with holy frenzy.

What a railway it would be, what a railway!

The blind singers were the share-collectors, the Christ-image gave the concession, and the old shop woman, Donna Elisa, was the engineer.

# VIII

## A JETTATORE

*I*n Catania there was once a man with "the evil eye," a *jettatore*. He was almost the most terrible *jettatore* who had ever lived in Sicily. As soon as he showed himself on the street people hastened to bend their fingers to the protecting sign. Often it did not help at all; whoever met him could prepare himself for a miserable day; he would find his dinner burned, and the beautiful old jelly-bowl broken. He would hear that his banker had suspended payments, and that the little note that he had written to his friend's wife had come into the wrong hands.

Most often a *jettatore* is a tall, thin man, with pale, shy eyes and a long nose, which overhangs and *hacks* his upper lip. God has set the mark of a parrot's beak upon the *jettatore*. Yet all things are variable; nothing is absolutely constant. This *jettatore* was a little fellow with a nose like a San Michele.

Thereby he did much more harm than an ordinary *jettatore*. How much oftener is one pricked by a rose than burned by a nettle!

A *jettatore* ought never to grow up. He is well off only when he is a child. Then he still has his little mamma, and she never sees the evil eye; she never understands why she sticks the needle into her finger every time he comes to her work-table. She will never be afraid to kiss him. Although she has sickness constantly in the house, and the servants leave, and her friends draw away, she never notices anything.

But after the *jettatore* has come out into the world, he often has a hard time enough. Everyone must first of all think of himself; no one can ruin his life by being kind to a *jettatore*.

There are several priests who are *jettatori*. There is nothing strange in that; the wolf is happy if he can tear to pieces many sheep. They could not very well do more harm than by being priests. One need only ask what happens to the children whom he baptizes, and the couples whom he marries.

The *jettatore* in question was an engineer and wished to build railways. He had also a position in one of the state railway buildings. The state could not know that he was a *jettatore*. Ah, but what misery, what misery! As soon as he obtained a place on the railway a number of accidents occurred. When they tunneled through a hill, one cave-in after another; when they tried to lay a bridge, breach upon breach; when they exploded a blast, the workmen were killed by the flying fragments.

The only one who was never injured was the engineer, the *jettatore*.

The poor fellows working under him! They counted their fingers and limbs every evening. "Tomorrow perhaps we will have lost you," they said.

They informed the chief engineer; they informed the minister. Neither of them would listen to the complaint. They were too sensible and too learned to believe in the evil eye. The workmen ought to mind better what they were about. It was their own fault that they met with accidents.

And the gravel-cars tipped over; the locomotive exploded.

One morning there was a rumor that the engineer was gone. He had disappeared; no one knew what had become of him. Had someone perhaps stabbed him? Oh, no; oh, no! would anyone have dared to kill a *jettatore?*

But he was really gone; no one ever saw him again.

It was a few years later that Donna Micaela began to think of building her railway. And in order to get money for it, she wished to hold a bazaar in the great Franciscan monastery outside Diamante.

There was a cloister garden there, surrounded by splendid old pillars. Donna Micaela arranged little booths, little lotteries, and little places of diversion under the arcades. She hung festoons of Venetian lanterns from pillar to pillar. She piled up great kegs of Etna wine around the cloister fountain.

While Donna Micaela worked there she often conversed with little Gandolfo, who had been made watchman at the monastery since Fra Felice's death.

One day she made Gandolfo show her the whole monastery. She went through it all from attic to cellar, and when she saw those countless little cells with their grated windows and whitewashed walls and hard wooden seats, she had an idea.

She asked Gandolfo to shut her in in one of the cells and to leave her there for the space of five minutes.

"Now I am a prisoner," she said, when she was left alone. She tried the door; she tried the window. She was securely shut in.

So that was what it was to be a prisoner! Four empty walls about one, the silence of the grave, and the chill.

"Now I can feel as a prisoner feels," she thought.

Then she forgot everything else in the thought that possibly Gandolfo might not come to let her out. He could be called away; he could be taken suddenly ill; he could fall and kill himself in some of the dark passage-ways. Many things could happen to prevent him from coming.

No one knew where she was; no one would think of looking for her in that out-of-the-way cell. If she were left there for even an hour she would go mad with terror.

She saw before her starvation, slow starvation. She struggled through interminable hours of anguish. Ah, how she would listen for a step; how she would call!

She would shake the door; she would scrape the masonry of the walls with her nails; she would bite the grating with her teeth.

When they finally found her she would be lying dead on the floor, and they would find everywhere traces of how she had tried to break her way out.

Why did not Gandolfo come? Now she must have been there a quarter of an hour, a half-hour. Why did he not come?

She was sure that she had been shut in a whole hour when Gandolfo came. Where had he been such a long time?

He had not been long at all. He had only been away five minutes.

"God! God! so that is being a prisoner; that is Gaetano's life!" She burst into tears when she saw the open sky once more above her.

A while later, as they stood out on an open *loggia,* Gandolfo showed her a couple of windows with shutters and green shades.

"Does anyone live there?" she asked.

"Yes, Donna Micaela, someone does."

Gandolfo told her that a man lived there who never went out except at night, — a man who never spoke to anyone."

"Is he crazy?" asked Donna Micaela.

"No, no; he is as much in his right mind as you or I. But people say that he has to conceal himself. He is afraid of the government."

Donna Micaela was much interested in the man. "What is his name?" she said.

"I call him Signor Alfredo."

"How does he get any food?" she asked.

"I prepare it for him," said Gandolfo.

"And clothes?"

"I get them for him. I bring him books and newspapers, too."

Donna Micaela was silent for a while. "Gandolfo," she said, and gave him a rose which she held in her hand, "lay this on the tray the next time you take food to your poor prisoner."

After that Donna Micaela sent some little thing almost every day to the man in the monastery. It might be a flower, a book or some fruit. It was her greatest pleasure. She amused herself with her fancies. She almost succeeded in imagining that she was sending all these things to Gaetano.

When the day for the bazaar came, Donna Micaela was in the cloister early in the morning. "Gandolfo," she said, "you must go up to your prisoner and ask him if he will come to the entertainment this evening."

Gandolfo soon came back with the answer. "He thanks you very much, Donna Micaela," said the boy. "He will come."

She was surprised, for she had not believed that he would venture out. She had only wished to show him a kindness.

Something made Donna Micaela look up. She was standing in the cloister garden, and a window was thrown open in one of the buildings above her. Donna Micaela saw a middle-aged man of an attractive appearance standing up there and looking down at her.

"There he is, Donna Micaela," said Gandolfo.

She was happy. She felt as if she had redeemed and saved the man. And it was more than that. People who have no imagination will not understand it. But Donna Micaela trembled and longed all day; she considered how she would be dressed. It was as if she had expected Gaetano.

Donna Micaela soon had something else to do than to dream; the livelong day a succession of calamities streamed over her.

The first was a communication from the old Etna brigand, Falco Falcone: —

DEAR FRIEND, DONNA MICAELA, —

As I have heard that you intend to build a railway along Etna, I wish to tell you that with my consent it will never be. I tell you this now so that you need not waste anymore money and trouble on the matter.

Enlightened and most nobly born signora, I remain

Your humble servant,

FALCO FALCONE

Passafiero, my sister's son, has written this letter.

Donna Micaela flung the dirty letter away. It seemed to her as if it were the death sentence of the railway, but today she would not think of it. Now she had her *bazaar.*

The moment after, her road-builders, Giovanni and Carmelo, appeared. They wished to counsel her to get an engineer. She probably did not know what kind of ground there was on Etna. There was, first, lava; then there was ashes; and then lava again. Should the road be laid on the top layer of lava, or on the bed of ashes, or should they dig down still deeper? About how firm a foundation did a railway need? They could not go ahead without a man who understood that.

Donna Micaela dismissed them. Tomorrow, tomorrow; she had no time to think of it today.

Immediately after, Donna Elisa came with a still worse piece of news.

There was a quarter in Diamante where a poverty-stricken and wild people lived. Those poor souls had been frightened when they heard of the railway. "There will be an eruption of Etna and an earthquake," they had said. Great Etna will endure no fetters. It will shake off the whole railway. And people said now that they ought to go out and tear up the track as soon as a rail was laid on it.

A day of misfortune, a day of misfortune! Donna Micaela felt farther from her object than ever.

"What is the good of our collecting money at our bazaar?" she said despondingly.

The day promised ill for her bazaar. In the afternoon it began to rain. It had not rained so in Diamante since the day when the clocks rang. The clouds sank to the very house-roofs, and the water poured down from them. People were wet to the skin before they had been two minutes in the street. Towards six o'clock, when Donna Micaela's bazaar was to open, it was raining its very hardest. When she came out to the monastery, there was no one there but those who were to help in serving and selling.

She felt ready to cry. Such an unlucky day! What had dragged down all these adversities upon her?

Donna Micaela's glance fell on a strange man who was leaning against a pillar, watching her. Now all at once she recognized him. He was the *jettatore* — the *jettatore* from Catania, whom people had taught her to fear as a child.

Donna Micaela went quickly over to him. "Come with me, signor," she said, and went before him. She wished to go so far away that no one should hear them, and then she wished to beg of him never to come before her eyes again. She could do no less. He must not ruin her whole life.

She did not think in what direction she went. Suddenly she was at the door of the monastery church and turned in there.

Within, it was almost dark. Only by the Christ-image a little oil lamp was burning.

When Donna Micaela saw the Christ-image she was startled. Just then she had not wished to see him.

He reminded her of the time when his crown had rolled to Gaetano's feet, when he had been so angry with the brigands. Perhaps the Christ-image did not wish her to drive away the *jettatore*.

She had good reason to fear the *jettatore*. It was wrong of him to come to her entertainment; she must somehow be rid of him.

Donna Micaela had gone on through the whole church, and now stood and looked at the Christ-image. She could not say a word to the man who followed her.

She remembered what sympathy she had lately felt for him, because a prisoner, like Gaetano. She had been so happy that she had tempted him out to life. What did she now wish to do? Did she wish to send him back to captivity?

She remembered both her father and Gaetano. Should this man be the third that she —

She stood silent and struggled with herself. At last the *jettatore* spoke: —

"Well, signora, is it not true that now you have had enough of me?"

Donna Micaela made a negative gesture.

"Do you not desire me to return to my cell?"

"I do not understand you, signor."

"Yes, yes, you understand. Something terrible has happened to you today. You do not look as you did this morning."

"I am very tired," said Donna Micaela, evasively.

The man came close up to her as if to force out the truth. Questions and answers flew short and panting between them.

"Do you not see that all your festival is likely to be a failure?" — "I must arrange it again tomorrow." — "Have you not recognized me?" — "Yes, I have seen you before in Catania." — "And you are not afraid of the *jettatore*?" — "Yes, formerly, as a child." — "But now, now are you not afraid?" She avoided answering him. "Are you yourself afraid?" she said. "Speak the truth!" he said, impatiently. "What did you wish to say to me when you brought me here?"

She looked anxiously about her. She had to say something; she must have something to answer him. Then a thought occurred to her which seemed to her quite terrible. She looked at the Christ-image. "Do you require it?" she seemed to ask him. "Shall I do it for this strange man? But it is throwing away my only hope."

"I hardly know whether I dare to speak of what I wish of you," she said. "No, you see; you do not dare." — "I intend to build a railway; you know that?" — "Yes, I know." — "I want you to help me." — "I?"

Now that she had made a beginning, it was easier for her to continue. She was surprised that her words sounded so natural.

"I know that you are a railroad builder. Yes, you understand of course that with my railroad no pay is given. But it would be better for you to help me work than to sit shut in here. You are making no use of your time."

He looked at her almost sternly. "Do you know what you are saying?" — "It is of course a presumptuous request." — "Just so, yes, a presumptuous request."

Thereupon the poor man began to try to terrify her.

"It will go with your railway as with your festival." Donna Micaela thought so too, but now she thought that she had closed all ways of escape for herself; now she must go on being good. "My festival will soon be in full swing," she said calmly.

"Listen to me, Donna Micaela," said the man. "The last thing a man ceases to believe good of is himself. No one can cease to have hope for himself."

"No; why should he?"

He made a movement as if he were impatient with her confidence.

"When I first began to think about the thing," he said, "I was easily consoled. 'There have been a few unfortunate occurrences,' I said to myself, 'so you have the reputation, and it has become a belief. It is the belief that has made the trouble. People have met you, and people have believed that they would come to grief, and come to grief they did. It is a misfortune worse than death to be considered a *jettatore*, but you need not yourself believe it.'"

"It is so absurd," said Donna Micaela.

"Yes, of course, whence should my eyes have got the power to bring misfortune? And when I thought of it I determined to make a trial. I traveled to a place where no one knew me. The next day I read in the paper that the train on which I had traveled had run over a flagman. When I had been one day in the hotel, I saw the landlord in despair, and all the guests leaving. What had happened? I asked. 'One of our servants has been taken with smallpox.' Ah, what a wretched business!

"Well, Donna Micaela, I shut myself in and drew back from all intercourse with people. When a year had passed I had found peace. I asked myself why I was shut in so. 'You are a harmless man,' I said; 'you wish to hurt no one. Why do you live as miserably as a criminal?' I had just meant to go back to life again, when I met Fra Felice in one of the passages. 'Fra Felice, where is the cat?' — 'The cat, signor?' — 'Yes, the monastery cat, that used to come and get milk from me; where is he now?' — 'He was caught in a rat-trap.' — 'What do you say, Fra Felice?' — 'He got his paw in a steel trap and he could not get loose. He dragged himself to one of the garrets and died of starvation.' What do you say to that, Donna Micaela?"

"Was it supposed to be your fault that the cat died?"

"I am a *jettatore.*"

She shrugged her shoulders. "Ah, what folly!"

"When some time had passed, again the desire to live awoke within me. Then Gandolfo knocked on my door, and invited me to your festival. Why should I not go? It is impossible to believe that one brings misfortune only by showing one's self. It was a festival in itself, Donna Micaela, only to get ready and to take out one's black clothes, brush them, and put them on. But when I came down to the scene of the festival, it was deserted; the rain streamed in torrents; your Venetian lanterns were filled with water. And you yourself looked as if you had suffered all life's misfortunes in a single day. When you looked at me you became ashy grey with terror. I asked someone: 'What was Signora Alagona's maiden name?' — 'Palmeri.' — 'Ah, Palmeri; so she is from Catania. She has recognized the *jettatore*.'"

"Yes, it is true; I recognized you."

"You have been very friendly, very kind, and I am distressed to have spoiled your festival. But now I promise you that I shall keep away both from your entertainment and your railway."

"Why should you keep away?"

"I am a *jettatore*."

"I do not believe it. I cannot believe it."

"I do not believe it either. Yes, yes, I believe. Do you see, people say that no one can have power over a *jettatore* who is not as great in evil as he. Once, they say, a *jettatore* looked at himself in the glass, and then fell down and died. Well, I never look at myself in the glass. Therefore I believe it."

"I do not believe it. I think I almost believed it when I saw you out there. Now I do not believe it."

"Perhaps you will let me work on your railway?"

"Yes, yes, if you only will."

He came again close up to her, and they exchanged a few short sentences. "Come forward to the light; I wish to see your face!" — "You think that I am dissembling." — "I think that you are polite." — "Why should I be polite to you?" — "That railway means something to you?" — "It means life and happiness to me." — "How is that?" — "It will win one who is dear to me." — "Very dear?"

She did not reply, but he read the answer in her face.

He bent his knee to her, and sank his head so low that he could kiss the hem of her dress. "You are good; you are very good. I shall never forget it. If I were not who I am, how I would serve you!"

"You *shall* serve me," she said. And she was so moved by his misfortunes that she felt no more fear of his injuring her.

He sprang up. "I will tell you something. You cannot go across the floor without stumbling if I look at you."

"Oh!" she said.

"Try!"

And she tried. She was very much frightened, and had never felt so unsteady as when she took her first step. Then she thought: "If it were for Gaetano's sake, I could do it." And then it was easy.

She walked to and fro on the church floor. "Shall I do it again?" He nodded.

As she was walking, the thought flashed through her brain: "The Christchild has taken the curse from him, because he is to help me." She turned suddenly and came back to him.

"Do you know, do you know? you are no *jettatore!*"

"Am I not?"

"No, no!" She took him by the shoulders and shook him. "Do you not see? do you not understand? It is taken from you."

Little Gandolfo's voice was heard in the path outside the church. "Donna Micaela, Donna Micaela, where are you? There are so many people, Donna Micaela. Do you hear; do you hear?"

"Is it no longer raining?" said the *jettatore,* in an uncertain voice.

"It is not raining; how could it be raining? The Christ-image has taken the curse from you because you are going to work for his railway."

The man reeled and grasped at the air with his hands. "It is gone. Yes, I think it is gone. Just now it was there. But now —"

He wished again to fall on his knees before Donna Micaela.

"Not to me," she said; "to him, to him." She pointed to the Christ-image.

But nevertheless he fell down before her. He kissed her hands, and with a voice broken by sobs he told her how everyone had hated and persecuted him, and how much misery life had brought him hitherto.

The next day the *jettatore* went out on Etna and staked out the road. And he was no more dangerous than anyone else.

# IX

## PALAZZO GERACI AND PALAZZO CORVAJA

At the time when the Normans ruled in Sicily, long before the family of Alagona had come to the island, the two magnificent buildings, Palazzo Geraci and Palazzo Corvaja, were built in Diamante.

The noble Barons Geraci placed their house in the square, high up on the summit of Monte Chiaro. The Barons Corvaja, on the other hand, built their home far down the mountain and surrounded it with gardens.

The black-marble walls of Palazzo Geraci were built round a square courtyard, full of charm and beauty. A long flight of steps, passing under an arch adorned with an escutcheon, led to the second story. Not entirely round the courtyard, but here and there in the most unexpected places, the walls opened into little pillared loggias. The walls were covered with bas-reliefs, with speckled slabs of Sicilian marble and with the coats of arms of the Geraci barons. There were windows also, very small, but with exquisitely carved frames; some round, with panes so small that they could be covered with a grape leaf; some oblong, and so narrow that they let in no more light than a slit in a curtain.

The Barons Corvaja did not try to adorn the courtyard of their palace, but on the lower floor of the house they fitted up a magnificent hall. In the floor was built a basin for gold-fish; in niches in the walls fountains covered with mosaic, in which clear water spouted into gigantic shells. Over it all, a Moorish vaulted roof, supported on slender pillars, with twining vines in mosaic. It was a hall whose equal is only to be seen in the Moorish palace in Palermo.

There was much rivalry and emulation during all the time of building. When Palazzo Geraci put forth a balcony, Palazzo Corvaja acquired its high Gothic bay-windows; when the roof of Palazzo Geraci was adorned with richly carved battlements, a frieze of black marble, inlaid with white a yard wide, appeared on Palazzo Corvaja. The Geraci house was crowned by a high tower; the Corvaja had a roof garden, with antique pots along the railing.

When the palaces were finished the rivalry began between the families who had built them. The houses seemed to breed hostility and strife for all who lived in them. A Baron Geraci could never agree with a Baron Corvaja. When Geraci fought for Anjou, Corvaja fought for Manfred. If Geraci changed sides, and supported Aragoni, Corvaja went to Naples, and fought for Robert and Joanna.

But that was not all. It was an understood thing that when Geraci found a son-in-law, Corvaja had to increase his power by a rich marriage. Neither of the families could rest. They had to vie with each other while eating, while amusing themselves, while working. The Geraci came to the court of the Bourbons in Naples, not out of desire of distinction, but because the Corvaja were there. The Corvaja on the other hand had to grow grapes and mine sulfur, because the Geraci were interested in agriculture and the working of mines. When a Geraci received an inheritance some old relative of the Corvaja had to lie down and die, so that the honor of the family should not be hazarded.

Palazzo Geraci was always kept busy counting its servants, in order not to let Palazzo Corvaja lead. But not only the servants, but the braid on the caps, the harnesses and the horses. The pheasant feather on the heads of the Corvaja leaders must not be an inch higher than that on the Geraci. Their goats must increase in the same proportion, and the Geraci's oxen must have just as long horns as the Corvaja's.

In our time one might have expected an end to the enmity between the two palaces. In our time there are just as few Corvaja in the one palace as there are Geraci in the other.

The Geraci courtyard is now a dirty hole, which contains donkey-stalls and pigsties and chicken houses. On the high steps rags are dried and the bas-reliefs are broken and moldy. In one of the passage-ways a trade in vegetables is carried on, and in the other shoes are made. The gatekeeper looks like the most ragged of beggars, and from cellar to attic live none but poor and penniless people.

It is no better in Palazzo Corvaja. There is not a vestige of the mosaic left in the big hall; only bare, empty arches. No beggars live there, because the palace is principally in ruins. It no longer raises its beautiful façade with the carved windows to the bright Sicilian sky.

But the enmity between Geraci and Corvaja is not over. In the old days it was not only the noble families themselves who competed with one another; it was also their neighbors and dependents. All Diamante is to this day divided into Geraci and Corvaja. There is still a high, loopholed wall running across the town, dividing the part of Diamante which stands by the Geraci from that which has declared itself for the Corvaja.

Even in our day no one from Geraci will marry a girl from Corvaja. And a shepherd from Corvaja cannot let his sheep drink from a Geraci fountain. They have not even the same saints. San Pasquale is worshipped in Geraci, and the black Madonna is Corvaja's patron saint.

A man from Geraci can never believe but that all Corvaja is full of magicians, witches, and werewolves. A man from Corvaja will risk his salvation that in Geraci there are none but rogues and pick-pockets.

Donna Micaela lived in the Geraci district, and soon all that part of the town were partisans of her railway. But then Corvaja could do no less than to oppose her.

The inhabitants of Corvaja specially disliked two things. They were jealous of the reputation of the black Madonna, and therefore did not like to have another miracle-working image come to Diamante. That was one thing. The other was that they feared that Mongibello would bury all Diamante in ashes and fire if anyone tried to encircle it with a railway.

A few days after the bazaar Palazzo Corvaja began to show itself hostile. Donna Micaela one day found on the roof-garden a lemon, which was so thickly set with pins that it looked like a steel ball.

It was Palazzo Corvaja, that was trying to bewitch as many pains into her head as there were pins in the lemon.

Then Corvaja waited a few days to see what effect the lemon would have. But when Donna Micaela's people continued to work on Etna and stake out the line, they came one night and pulled everything up. And when the stakes were set up again the next day, they broke the windows in the church of San Pasquale and threw stones at the Christ-image.

*T*here was a long and narrow little square on the south side of Monte Chiaro. On both the long sides stood dark, high buildings. On one of the short sides was an abyss; on the other rose the steep mountain. The mountain wall was arranged in terraces, but the steps were crumbled and the marble railings broken. On the broadest of the terraces rose the stately ruins of Palazzo Corvaja.

The chief ornament of the square was a beautiful, oblong water-basin which stood quite under the terraces, close to the mountain wall. It stood there white as snow, covered with carvings, and full of clear, cold water. It was the best preserved of all the former glories of the Corvaja.

One beautiful and peaceful evening two ladies dressed in black came walking into the little square. For the moment it was almost empty. The two ladies looked about them, and when they saw no one they sat down on the bench by the fountain, and waited.

Soon several inquisitive children came forward and looked at them, and the older of the two began to talk to the children. She began to tell them stories: "It is said," and "It is told," and "Once upon a time," she said.

Then the children were told of the Christchild who turned himself into roses and lilies when the Madonna met one of Herod's soldiers, who had been commanded to kill all children. And they were told the legend of how the Christchild once had sat and shaped birds out of clay, and how he clapped his hands and gave the clay pigeons wings with which to fly away when a naughty boy wished to break them to pieces.

While the old lady was talking, many children gathered about her, and also big people. It was a Saturday evening, so that the laborers were coming home from their work in the fields. Most of them came up to the Corvaja fountain for water. When they heard that someone was telling legends they stopped to listen. Both the ladies were soon surrounded by a close, dark wall of heavy, black cloaks and slouch hats.

Suddenly the old lady said to the children: "Do you like the Christchild?" "Yes, yes," they said, and their big, dark eyes sparkled. — "Perhaps you would like to see him?" — "Yes, we should indeed."

The lady threw back her mantilla and showed the children a little Christ-image in a jeweled dress, and with a gold crown on his head and gold shoes on his feet. "Here he is," she said. "I have brought him with me to show you."

The children were in raptures. First they clasped their hands at the sight of the image's grave face, then they began to throw kisses to it.

"He is beautiful, is he not?" said the lady.

"Let us have him! Let us have him!" cried the children.

But now a big, rough workman, a dark man with a bushy, black beard, pushed forward. He wished to snatch away the image. The old lady had barely time to thrust it behind her back.

"Give it here, Donna Elisa, give it here!" said the man.

Poor Donna Elisa cast one glance at Donna Micaela, who had sat silent and displeased the whole time by her side. Donna Micaela had been persuaded with difficulty to go to Corvaja and show the image to the people there. "The image helps us when it wills," she said. "We shall not force miracles."

But Donna Elisa had been determined to go, and she had said that the image was only waiting to be taken to the faithless wretches in Corvaja. After everything that he had done, they might have enough faith in him to believe that he could win them over also.

Now she, Donna Elisa, stood there with the man over her, and she did not know how she could prevent him from snatching the image away.

"Give it to me amicably, Donna Elisa," said the man, "otherwise, by God, I will take it in spite of you. I will hack it to small pieces, to small, small pieces. You shall see how much there will be left of your wooden doll. You shall see if it can withstand the black Madonna."

Donna Elisa pressed against the mountain wall; she saw no escape. She could not run, and she could not struggle. "Micaela!" she wailed, "Micaela!"

Donna Micaela was very pale. She held her hands against her heart, as she always did when anything agitated her. It was terrible to her to stand opposed to those dark men. These were they of the slouch hats and short cloaks of whom she had always been afraid.

But now, when Donna Elisa appealed to her, she turned quickly, seized the image and held it out to the man.

"See here, take it!" she said defiantly. And she took a step towards him. "Take it, and do with it what you can!"

She held the image on her outstretched arms, and came nearer and nearer to the dark workman.

He turned towards his comrades. "She does not believe that I can do anything to the doll," he said, and laughed at her. And the whole group of workmen slapped themselves on the knee and laughed.

But he did not take the image; he grasped instead the big pick-axe, which he held in his hand. He drew back a few steps, lifted the pick over his head, and stiffened his whole body for a blow which was to crush at once the entire hated wooden doll.

Donna Micaela shook her head warningly. "You cannot do it," she said, and she did not draw the image back.

He saw that nevertheless she was afraid, and he enjoyed frightening her. He stood longer than was necessary with uplifted pick.

"Piero!" came a cry shrill and wailing.

"Piero! Piero!"

The man dropped his pick without striking. He looked terrified.

"God! it is Marcia calling!" he said.

At the same moment a crowd of people came tumbling out of a little cottage which was built among the ruins of the old Palazzo Corvaja. There were about a dozen women and a carabiniere, who were fighting. The carabiniere held a child in his arms, and the women were trying to drag the child away from him. But the policeman, who was a tall, strong fellow, freed himself from them, lifted the child to his shoulder, and ran down the terrace steps.

The dark Piero had looked on without making a movement. When the carabiniere freed himself, he bent down to Donna Micaela and said eagerly: "If *the little one* can prevent that, all Corvaja shall be his friend."

Now the carabiniere was down in the square. Piero made a sign with his hand. Instantly all his comrades closed in a ring round the fugitive. He turned squarely round. Everywhere a close ring of men threatened him with picks and shovels.

All at once there was terrible confusion. The women who had been struggling with the carabiniere came rushing down with loud cries. The little girl, whom he held in his arms, screamed as loud as she could and tried to tear herself away. People came running from all sides. There were questionings and wonderings.

"Let us go now," said Donna Elisa to Donna Micaela. "Now no one is thinking of us."

But Donna Micaela had caught sight of one of the women. She screamed least, but it was instantly apparent that it was she whom the matter concerned. She looked as if she was about to lose her life's happiness.

She was a woman who had been very beautiful, although all freshness now was gone from her, for she was no longer young. But hers was still an impressive and large-souled face. "Here dwells a soul which can love and suffer," said the face. Donna Micaela felt drawn to that poor woman as to a sister.

"No, it is not the time to go yet," she said to Donna Elisa.

The carabiniere asked and asked if they would not let him come out. No, no, no! Not until he let the child go!

It was the child of Piero and his wife, Marcia. But they were not the child's real parents. The trouble arose from that.

The carabiniere tried to win the people over to his side. He tried to convince, not Piero nor Marcia, but the others. "Ninetta is the child's mother," he said; "you all know that. She has not been able to have the child with her while she was unmarried; but now she is married, and wishes to have her child back. And now Marcia refuses to give her the boy. It is hard on Ninetta, who has not been able to have her child with her for eight years. Marcia will not give him up. She drives Ninetta away when she comes and begs for her child. Finally Ninetta had to complain to the syndic. And the syndic has told us to get her the child. It is Ninetta's own child," he said appealingly.

But it had no great effect on the men of Corvaja.

"Ninetta is a Geraci," burst out Piero, and the circle stood fast round the carabiniere.

"When we came here to fetch the child," said the latter, "we did not find him. Marcia was dressed in black, and her rooms were draped with black, and a lot of women sat and mourned with her. And she showed us the certificate of the child's death. Then we went and told Ninetta that her child was in the churchyard.

"Well, well, a while afterwards I went on guard here in the square. I watched the children playing there. Who was strongest, and who shouted the loudest, if not one of the girls? 'What is your name?' I asked her. 'Francesco,' she answered instantly.

"It occurred to me that that girl, Francesco, might be Ninetta's boy, and I stood quiet and waited. Just now I saw Francesco go into Marcia's house. I followed, and there sat the girl Francesco and ate supper with Marcia. She and all the mourners began to scream when I appeared.

Then I seized Signorina Francesco and ran. For the child is not Marcia's. Remember that, signori! He is Ninetta's. Marcia has no right to him."

Then at last Marcia began to speak. She spoke in a deep voice which compelled everyone to listen, and she made only a few, but noble gestures. Had she no right to the child? But who had given him food and clothing? He had been dead a thousand times over if she had not been there. Ninetta had left him with La Felucca. They knew La Felucca. To leave one's child to her was the same as saying to it: "You shall die." And, moreover, right? right? What did that mean? The one whom the boy loved had a right to him. The one who loved the boy had a right to him. Piero and she loved the boy like their own son. They could not be parted from him.

The wife was desperate, the husband perhaps even more so. He threatened the carabiniere whenever he made a movement. Yet the carabiniere seemed to see that the victory would be his. The people had laughed when he spoke of "Signorina Francesco." "Cut me down, if you will," he said to Piero. "Does it help you? Will you retain the child for that? He is not yours. He is Ninetta's."

Piero turned to Donna Micaela. "Pray to him to help me." He pointed to the image.

Donna Micaela instantly went forward to Marcia. She was shy and trembled for what she was venturing, but it was not the time for her to hold back. "Marcia," she whispered, "confess! Confess, — if you dare!" The startled woman looked at her. "I see it so well," whispered Donna Micaela; "you are as alike as two berries. But I will say nothing if you do not wish it." "He will kill me," said Marcia. "I know one who will not let him kill you," said Donna Micaela. "Otherwise they will take your child from you," she added.

All were silent, with eyes fixed on the two women. They saw how Marcia struggled with herself. The features of her strong face were distorted. Her lips moved. "The child is mine," she said, but in so low a voice that no one heard it. She said it again, and now it came in a piercing scream: "The child is mine!"

"What will you do to me when I confess it?" she said to the man. "The child is mine, but not yours. He was born in the year when you were at work in Messina. I put him with La Felucca, and Ninetta's boy was there too. One day when I came to La Felucca she said, 'Ninetta's boy is dead.'

At first I only thought: 'God! if it had been mine!' Then I said to La Felucca: 'Let my boy be dead, and let Ninetta's live.' I gave La Felucca my silver comb, and she agreed. When you came home from Messina I said to you: 'Let us take a foster child. We have never been on good terms. Let us try what adopting a child will do.' You liked the proposal, and I adopted my own child. You have been happy with him, and we have lived as if in paradise."

Before she finished speaking the carabiniere put the child down on the ground. The dark men silently opened their ranks for him, and he went his way. A shiver went through Donna Micaela when she saw the carabiniere go. He should have stayed to protect the poor woman. His going seemed to mean: "That woman is beyond the pale of the law; I cannot protect her." Every man and woman standing there felt the same: "She is outside of the law."

One after another went their way.

Piero, the husband, stood motionless without looking up. Something fierce and dreadful was gathering in him. Rage and suffering were gathering within him. Something terrible would happen as soon as he and Marcia were alone.

The woman made no effort to escape. She stood still, paralyzed by the certainty that her fate was sealed, and that nothing could change it. She neither prayed nor fled. She shrank together like a dog before an angry master. The Sicilian women know what awaits them when they have wounded their husbands' honor.

The only one who tried to defend her was Donna Micaela. Never would she have begged Marcia to confess, she said to Piero, if she had known what he was. She had thought that he was a generous man. Such a one would have said: "You have done wrong; but the fact that you confess your sin publicly, and expose yourself to my anger to save the child, atones for everything. It is punishment enough. A generous man would have taken the child on one arm, put the other round his wife's waist, and have gone happy to his home. A signor would have acted so. But he was no signor; he was a bloodhound.

She talked in vain; the man did not hear her; the woman did not hear her. Her words seemed to be thrown back from an impenetrable wall.

Just then the child came to the father, and tried to take his hand. Furious, he looked at the boy. As the latter was dressed in girl's clothes, his hair smoothly combed and drawn back by the ears, he saw instantly the likeness to Marcia, which he had not noticed before. He kicked Marcia's son away.

There was a terrible tension in the square. The neighbors continued to go quietly and slowly away. Many went unwillingly and with hesitation, but still they went. The husband seemed only to be waiting for the last to go.

Donna Micaela ceased speaking; she took the image instead and laid it in Marcia's arms. "Take him, my sister Marcia, and may he protect you!" she said.

The man saw it, and his rage increased. It seemed as if he could no longer contain himself till he was alone. He crouched like a wild beast ready to spring.

But the image did not rest in vain in the woman's arms. The outcast moved her to an act of the greatest love.

"What will Christ in Paradise say to me, who have first deceived my husband, and then made him a murderer?" she thought. And she remembered how she had loved big Piero in the days of her happy youth. She had not then thought of bringing such misery upon him.

"No, Piero, no, do not kill me!" she said eagerly. "They will send you to the galleys. You shall be relieved of seeing me again without that."

She ran towards the other side of the square, where the ground fell away into an abyss. Everyone understood her intention. Her face bore witness for her.

Several hurried after her, but she had a good start. Then the image, which she still carried, slipped from her arms and lay at her feet. She stumbled over it, fell, and was overtaken.

She struggled to get away, but a couple of men held her fast. "Ah, let me do it!" she cried; "it is better for him!"

Her husband came up to her also. He had caught up her child and placed him on his arm. He was much moved.

"See, Marcia, let it be as it is," he said. He was embarrassed, but his dark, deep-set eyes shone with happiness and said more than his words. "Perhaps, according to old custom, it ought to be so, but I do not care for that. Look, come now! It would be a pity for such a woman as you, Marcia."

He put his arm about Marcia's waist, and went towards his house in the ruins of Palazzo Corvaja.

It was like a triumphal entry of one of the former barons. The people of Corvaja stood on both sides of the way and bowed to him and Marcia.

As they went past Donna Micaela, they both stopped, bowed deep to her, and kissed the image which someone had given back to her. But Donna Micaela kissed Marcia. "Pray for me in your happiness, sister Marcia!" she said.

# X

## FALCO FALCONE

*T*he blind singers have week after week sung of Diamante's railway, and the big collection-box in the church of San Pasquale has been filled every evening with gifts. Signor Alfredo measures and sets stakes on the slopes of Etna, and the distaff-spinners in the dark alleys tell stories of the wonderful miracles that have been performed by the little Christ-image in the despised church. From the rich and powerful men who own the land on Etna comes letter after letter promising to give ground to the blessed undertaking.

During these last weeks everyone comes with gifts. Some give building stone for the stations, some give powder to blast the lava blocks, some give food to the workmen. The poor people of Diamante, who have nothing, come in the night after their work. They come with shovels and wheelbarrows and creep out on Etna, dig the ground, and ballast the road. When Signor Alfredo and his people come in the morning they believe that the Etna goblins have broken out from their lava streams and helped on the work.

All the while people have been questioning and asking: "Where is the king of Etna, Falco Falcone? Where is the mighty Falco who has held sway on the slopes of Etna for five and twenty years? He wrote to Don Ferrante's widow that she would not be allowed to construct the railway. What did he mean by his threat? Why does he sit still when people are braving his interdiction? Why does he not shoot down the people of Corvaja when they come creeping through the night with wheelbarrows and pickaxes? Why does he not drag the blind singers down into the quarry and whip them? Why does he not have Donna Micaela carried off from the summer-palace, in order to be able to demand a cessation in the building of the railway as a ransom for her life?"

Donna Micaela says to herself: "Has Falco Falcone forgotten his promise, or is he waiting to strike till he can strike harder?"

Everybody asks in the same way: "When is Etna's cloud of ashes to fall on the railway? When will Mongibello cataracts tear it away? When will the mighty Falco Falcone be ready to destroy it?"

While everyone is waiting for Falco to destroy the railway, they talk a great deal about him, especially the workmen under Signor Alfredo.

Opposite the entrance to the church of San Pasquale, people say, stands a little house on a bare crag. The house is narrow, and so high that it looks like a chimney left standing on a burned building site. It is so small that there is no room for the stairs inside the house; they wind up outside the walls. Here and there hang balconies and other projections that are arranged with no more symmetry than a bird's nest on a tree-trunk.

In that house Falco Falcone was born, and his parents were only poor working-people. In that miserable hut Falco learned arrogance.

Falco's mother was an unfortunate woman, who during the first years of her marriage brought only daughters into the world. Her husband and all her neighbors despised her.

The woman longed continually for a son. When she was expecting her fifth child she strewed salt every day on the threshold and sat and watched who should first cross it. Would it be a man or a woman? Should she bear a son or a daughter?

Every day she sat and counted. She counted the letters in the month when her child was to be born. She counted the letters in her husband's name and in her own. She added and subtracted. It was an even number; therefore she would bear a son. The next day she made the calculation over again. "Perhaps I counted wrong yesterday," she said.

When Falco was born his mother was much honored, and she loved him on account of it more than all her other children. When the father came in to see the child he snatched off his cap and made a low bow. Over the house-door they set a hat as a token of honor, and they poured the child's bath water over the threshold, and let it run out into the street. When Falco was carried to the church he was laid on his god-mother's right arm; when the neighbors' wives came to look after his mother they curtsied to the child sleeping in his cradle.

He was also bigger and stronger than children generally are. Falco had thick hair when he was born, and when he was a week old he already had a tooth. When his mother laid him to her breast he was so wild that she laughed and said: "I think that I have brought a hero into the world."

She was always expecting great achievements from Falco, and she put pride into him. But who else hoped anything of him? Falco could not even learn to read. His mother tried to take a book and teach him the letters. She pointed to A, that is the big hat; she pointed to B, that is the spectacles; she pointed to C, that is the snake. That he could learn. Then his mother said: "If you put the spectacles and the big hat together, it makes Ba." That he could not learn. He became angry and struck her, and she let him alone. "You will be a great man yet," she said.

Falco was dull and bad-tempered in his childhood and youth. As a child, he would not play; as a youth, he would not dance. He had no sweetheart, but he liked to go where fighting was to be expected.

Falco had two brothers who were like other people, and who were much more esteemed than he. Falco was wounded to see himself eclipsed by his brothers, but he was too proud to show it. His mother was always on his side. After his father's death she had him sit at the head of the table, and she never allowed anyone to jest with him. "My oldest son is the best of you all," she said.

When the people remember it all they say: "Falco is proud. He will make it a point of honor to destroy the railway."

And they have hardly terrified themselves with one story before they remember another about him.

For thirty long years, people say, Falco lived like any other poor person on Etna. On Monday he went away to his work in the fields with his brothers. He had bread in his sack for the whole week, and he made soup of beans and rice like everyone else. And he was glad on Saturday evening to be able to return to his home. He was glad to find the table spread, with wine and macaroni, and the bed made up with soft pillows.

It was just such a Saturday evening. Falco and Falco's brothers were on their way home; Falco, as usual, a little behind the others, for he had a heavy and slow way of walking. But look, when the brothers reached home, no supper was waiting, the beds were not made, and the dust lay thick on the threshold. What, were all in the house dead? Then they saw their mother sitting on the floor in a dark corner of the cottage. Her hair was drawn down over her face, and she sat and traced patterns with her finger on the earth floor. "What is the matter?" said the brothers. She did not look up; she spoke as if she had spoken to the earth. "We are beggared, beggared." "Do they want to take our house from us?" cried the brothers. "They wish to take away our honor and our daily bread."

Then she told: "Your eldest sister has had employment with Baker Gasparo, and it has been good employment. Signor Gasparo gave Pepa all the bread left over in the shop, and she brought it to me. There has been so much that there was enough for us all. I have been happy ever since Pepa found that employment. It will give me an old age free from care, I thought. But last Monday Pepa came home to me and wept; Signora Gasparo had turned her away."

"What had Pepa done?" asked Nino, who was next younger to Falco.

"Signora Gasparo accused Pepa of stealing bread. I went to Signora Gasparo and asked her to take Pepa back. 'No,' she said, 'the girl is not honest.' 'Pepa had the bread from Signor Gasparo,' I said; 'ask him.' 'I cannot ask him,' said the signora; 'he is away, and comes home next month.' 'Signora,' I said, 'we are so poor. Let Pepa come back to her place.' 'No,' she said; 'I myself will leave Signor Gasparo if he takes that girl back.' 'Take care,' I said then; 'if you take bread from me, I will take life from you.' Then she was frightened and called others in, so that I had to go."

"What is to be done about it?" said Nino. "Pepa must find some other work."

"Nino," said Mother Zia, "you do not know what that woman has said to the neighbors about Pepa and Signor Gasparo."

"Who can prevent women from talking?" said Nino.

"If Pepa has nothing else to do, now she might at least have cooked dinner for us," said Turiddo.

"Signora Gasparo has said that her husband let Pepa steal bread that she should —"

"Mother," interrupted Nino, red as fire, "I do not intend to have myself put in the galleys for Pepa's sake."

"The galleys do not eat Christians," said Mother Zia.

"Nino," said Pietro, "we had better go to the town to get some food."

As they said it they heard someone laugh behind them. It was Falco who laughed.

A while later Falco entered Signora Gasparo's shop and asked for bread. The poor woman was frightened when Pepa's brother came into the shop.

But she thought: "He has just come from his work. He has not been home yet. He knows nothing."

"Beppo," she said to him, for Falco's name was not then Falco, "is the harvest a good one?" And she was prepared not to have him answer.

Falco was more talkative than usual, and immediately told her how many grapes had already been put through the press. "Do you know," he continued, "that a farmer was murdered yesterday." — "Alas, yes, poor Signor Riego; I heard so." And she asked how it had happened.

"It was Salvatore who did it. But it is too dreadful for a signora to hear!" — "Oh, no, what is done can be and is told."

"Salvatore went up to him in this way, signora." And Falco drew his knife and laid his hand on the woman's head. "Then he cut him across the throat from ear to ear."

As Falco spoke, he suited the action to the word. The woman did not even have time to scream. It was the work of a master.

After that, Falco was sent to the galleys, where he remained five years.

When the people tell of that, their terror increases. "Falco is brave," they say. "Nothing in the world can frighten him away from his purpose."

That immediately made them think of another story.

Falco was taken to the galleys in August, where he became acquainted with Biagio, who afterwards followed him through his whole life. One day he and Biagio and a third prisoner were ordered to go to work in the fields. One of the overseers wished to construct a garden around his house. They dug there quietly, but their eyes began to wander and wander. They were outside the walls; they saw the plain and the mountains; they even saw up to Etna. "It is the time," whispered Falco to Biagio. "I will rather die than go back to prison," said Biagio. Then they whispered to the other prisoner that he must stand by them. He did not wish to do so, because his time of punishment was soon up. "Else we will kill you," they said, and then he agreed.

The guard stood over, them with his loaded rifle in his hand. On account of their fetters, Falco and Biagio hopped with feet together over to the guard. They swung their shovels over him, and before he had time to think of shooting he was thrown down, bound, and had a clump of earth in his mouth. Thereupon the prisoners pried open their chains with the shovels, so that they could take a step, and crept away over the plain to the hills.

When night came Falco and Biagio abandoned the prisoner whom they had taken with them. He was old and feeble, so that he would have hindered their flight. The next day he was seized by the carabinieri, and shot.

They shudder when they think of it. "Falco is merciless," they say. They know that he will not spare the railway.

Story after story comes to frighten the poor people working on the railway on the slopes of Etna.

They tell of all the sixteen murders that Falco has committed. They tell of his attacks and plunderings.

There is one story more terrifying than all the others together.

When Falco escaped from the galleys he lived in the woods and caves, and in the big quarry near Diamante. He soon gathered a band about him, and became a wonderful and famous brigand hero.

All his family were held in much greater consideration than before. They were respected, as the mighty are respected. They scarcely needed to work, for Falco loved his relations and was generous to them. But he was not lenient towards them; he was very stern.

Mother Zia was dead, and Nino was married and lived in his father's cottage. It happened one day that Nino needed money, and he knew no better way than to go to the priest, — not Don Matteo, but to old Don Giovanni. "Your Reverence," said Nino to him, "my brother asks you for five hundred lire." "Where shall I find five hundred lire?" said Don Giovanni. "My brother needs them; he must have them," said Nino.

Then old Don Giovanni promised to give the money, if he only were given time to collect it. Nino was hardly willing to agree to that. "You can scarcely expect me to take five hundred lire from my snuff-box," said Don Giovanni. And Nino granted him three days' respite. "But beware of meeting my brother during that time," he said.

The next day Don Giovanni rode to Nicolosi to try to claim a payment. Who should he meet on the way but Falco and two of his band. Don Giovanni threw himself from his donkey and fell on his knees before Falco. "What does this mean, Don Giovanni?" — "As yet I have no money for you, Falco, but I will try to get it. Have mercy upon me!"

Falco asked, and Don Giovanni told the whole story. "Your Reverence," said Falco, "he has been deceiving you." He begged Don Giovanni to go with him to Diamante. When they came to the old house Don Giovanni rode in behind the wall of San Pasquale, and Falco called Nino out. Nino came out on one of the balconies. "Eh, Nino!" said Falco, and laughed. "You have cheated the priest out of money?" "Do you know it already?" said Nino. "I was just going to tell it to you."

Now Falco became sterner. "Nino," he said, "the priest is my friend, and he believes that I have wished to rob him. You have done very wrong." He suddenly put his gun to his shoulder and shot Nino down, and when he had done so he turned to Don Giovanni, who had almost fallen from his donkey with terror. "You see now, your Reverence, that I had no part in Nino's designs on you!"

And that happened twenty years ago, when Falco had not been a brigand for more than five years.

"Will Falco spare the railway," people say, as they tell it, "when he did not spare his own brother?"

There was yet more.

After Nino's murder there was a vendetta over Falco. Nino's wife was so terrified when she found her husband dead that half her body became paralyzed, and she could no longer walk. But she took her place at the window in the old cottage. There she has sat for twenty years with a gun beside her, and waited for Falco. And of her the great brigand has been afraid. For twenty years he has not gone past the home of his ancestors.

The woman has not deserted her post. No one ever goes to the church of San Pasquale without seeing her revengeful eyes shining behind the panes. Who has ever seen her sleep? Who has seen her work? She could do nothing but await her husband's murderer.

When people hear that, they are even more afraid. Falco has luck on his side, they think. The woman who wishes to kill him cannot move from her place. He has luck on his side. He will also succeed in destroying the railway. Fortune has never failed Falco. The carabinieri have hunted, but have never been able to catch him. The carabinieri have feared Falco more than Falco has feared the carabinieri.

People tell a story of a young carabiniere lieutenant who once pursued Falco. He had arranged a line of beaters and hunted Falco from one thicket to another. At last the officer was certain that he had Falco shut in in a grove. A guard was stationed round the wood, and the officer searched the covert, gun in hand. But however much he searched, he saw no Falco. He came out, and met a peasant. "Have you seen Falco Falcone?" – "Yes, signor; he just went by me, and he asked me to greet you." – *"Diavolo!"* – "He saw you in the thicket, and he was just going to shoot you, but he did not do so, because he thought that perhaps it was your duty to prosecute him." – *"Diavolo! Diavolo!"* – "But if you try another time –" – *"Diavolo! Diavolo! Diavolo!"*

Do you think that lieutenant came back? Do you not think that he instantly sought out a district where he did not need to hunt brigands?

And the workmen on Etna asked themselves: "Who will protect us against Falco? He is terrible. Even the soldiers tremble before him."

They remember that Falco Falcone is now an old man. He no longer plunders post-wagons; he does not carry off land-owners. He sits quiet generally in the quarry near Diamante, and instead of robbing money and estates, he takes money and estates under his protection.

He takes tribute from the great landed proprietors and guards their estates from other thieves, and it has become calm and peaceful on Etna, for he allows no one to injure those who have paid a tax to him.

But that is not reassuring. Since Falco has become friends with the great, he can all the more easily destroy the railway.

And they remember the story of Niccola Galli, who is overseer on the estate of the Marquis di San Stefano on the southern side of Etna. Once his workmen struck in the middle of the harvest time. Niccola Galli was in despair. The wheat stood ripe, and he could not get it reaped.

His workmen would not work; they lay down to sleep at the edge of a ditch.

Niccola placed himself on a donkey and rode down to Catania to ask his lord for advice. On the way he met two men with guns on their shoulders. "Whither are you riding, Niccola?"

Before Niccola had time to say many words they took his donkey by the bit and turned him round. "You must not ride to the Marquis, Niccola?" — "Must I not?" — "No; you must ride home."

As they went along, Niccola sat and shook on his donkey. When they were again at home the men said: "Now show us the way to the fields!" And they went out to the laborers. "Work, you scoundrels! The marquis has paid his tribute to Falco Falcone. You can strike in other places, but not here." That field was reaped as never before. Falco stood on one side of it and Biagio on the other. The grain is soon harvested with such overseers.

When the people remember that, their terror does not decrease. "Falco keeps his word," they say. "He will do what he has threatened to do."

No one has been a robber chief as long as Falco. All the other famous heroes are dead or captives. He alone keeps himself alive and in his profession by incredible good fortune and skill.

Gradually he has collected about him all his family. His brothers-in-law and nephews are all with him. Most of them have been sent to the galleys, but not one of them thinks whether he suffers in prison; he only asks if Falco is satisfied with him.

In the newspapers there are often accounts of Falco's deeds. Englishmen thrust a note of ten lire into their guide's hand if he will show them the way to Falco's quarry. The carabinieri no longer shoot at him, because he is the last great brigand.

He so little fears to be captured that he often comes down to Messina or Palermo. He has even crossed the sound and been in Italy. He went to Naples when Guglielmo and Umberto were there to christen a battle-ship. He traveled to Rome when Umberto and Margherita celebrated their silver wedding.

The people think of it all, and tremble. "Falco is loved and admired," the workmen say. "The people worship Falco. He can do what he will."

They know too that when Falco saw Queen Margherita's silver wedding, it pleased him so much that he said: "When I have lived on Etna for five and twenty years, I shall celebrate my silver wedding with Mongibello."

People laughed at that and said that it was a good idea of Falco's. For he had never had a sweetheart, but Mongibello with its caves and forests and craters and ice-fields had served and protected him like a wife. To no one in the world did Falco owe such gratitude as to Mongibello.

People ask when Falco and Mongibello are going to celebrate their silver wedding. And people answer that it will be this spring. Then the workmen think: *"He is coming to destroy our railway on the day of Mongibello."*

They are filled with doubt and terror. They soon will not dare to work anymore. The nearer the time approaches when Falco is to celebrate his union with Mongibello, the more there are who leave Signor Alfredo. Soon he is practically alone at the work.

*T*here are not many people in Diamante who have seen the big quarry on Etna. They have learned to avoid it because Falco Falcone lives there. They have been careful to keep out of range of his gun.

They have not seen the great hole in Mongibello's side from which their ancestors, the Greeks, took stone in remote times. They have not seen the beautifully colored walls, and the mighty rocks that look like ruined pillars. Perhaps they do not know that on the bottom of the quarry grow more magnificent flowers than in a conservatory. There it is no longer Sicily; it is India.

In the quarry are mandarin trees, so yellow with fruit that they look like gigantic sun-flowers; the camellias are as big as tambourines; and on the ground between the trees lie masses of magnificent figs and downy peaches embedded in fallen rose-leaves.

One evening Falco is sitting alone in the quarry. Falco is busy making a wreath, and he has beside him a mass of flowers. The string he is using is as thick as a rope; he holds his foot on the ball so that it shall not roll away from him. He wears spectacles, which continually slip too far down his hooked nose.

Falco is swearing horribly, for his hands are stiff and callous from incessantly handling a gun, and cannot readily hold flowers. The fingers squeeze them together like steel tongs. Falco swears because the lilies and anemones fall into little pieces if he merely looks at them.

Falco sits in his leather breeches and in the long, buttoned-up coat, buried in flowers like a saint on a feast-day. Biagio and his nephew, Passafiore, have gathered them for him. They have piled up in front of him an Etna of the most beautiful flowers of the quarry. Falco can choose among lilies and cactus-flowers and roses and pelargoniums. He roars at the flowers that he will trample them to dust under his leather sandals if they do not submit themselves to his will.

Never before has Falco Falcone had to do with flowers. In the whole course of his life he has never tied a nosegay for a girl, or plucked a rose for his buttonhole. He has never even laid a wreath on his mother's grave.

Therefore the delicate flowers rebel against him. The flower sprays are entangled in his hair and in his hat, and the petals have caught in his bushy beard. He shakes his head violently, and the scar in his cheek glows red as fire as it used to do in the old days, when he fought with the carabinieri.

Still the wreath grows, and thick as a tree-trunk it winds round Falco's feet and legs. Falco swears at it as if it were the steel fetters that once dragged between his ankles. He complains more, when he tears himself on a thorn or burns himself on a nettle, than he did when the whip of the galley guard lashed his back.

Biagio and Passafiore, his nephew, do not dare to show themselves; they lie concealed in a cave till everything is ready. They laugh at Falco with all their might, for such wailings as Falco's have not sounded in the quarry since unhappy prisoners of war were kept at work there.

Biagio looks up to great Etna, which is blushing in the light of the setting sun. "Look at Mon-gibello," he says to Passafiore; "see how it blushes. It must guess what Falco is busy with down in the quarry." And Passafiore answers: "Mongibello has probably never thought that it would ever have anything on its head but ashes and snow."

But suddenly Biagio stopped laughing. "It is not well, Passafiore," he said. "Falco has become too proud. I am afraid that the great Mongibello is going to make a fool of him."

The two bandits look one another in the eyes questioningly. "It is well if it is only pride," says Passafiore.

But now they look away at the same moment, and dare say no more. The same thought, the same dread has seized them both. Falco is going mad. He is already mad at times. It is always so with great brigand chiefs; they cannot bear their glory and their greatness; they all go mad.

Passafiore and Biagio have seen it for a long time, but they have borne it in silence, and each has hoped that the other has seen nothing. Now they understand that they both know it. They press each other's hands without a word. There is still something so great in Falco. Both of them, Passafiore and Biagio, will take care that no one shall perceive that he is no longer the man he was.

Finally Falco has his wreath ready; he hangs it on the barrel of his gun and comes out to the others. All three climb out of the quarry, and at the nearest farmhouse they take horses in order to come quickly to the top of Mongibello.

They ride at full gallop so that they have no chance to talk, but as they pass the different farms' they can see the people dancing on the flat roofs. And from the sheds, where the laborers sleep at night, they hear talk and laughter. There happy, peaceful people are sitting, guessing conundrums and matching verses. Falco storms by, such things are not for him. Falco is a great man.

They gallop towards the summit. At first they ride between almond trees and cactus, then under plane trees and stone-pines, then under oaks and chestnut trees.

The night is dark; they see nothing of the beauty of Mongibello. They do not see the vine-encircled Monte Rosso; they do not see the two hundred craters that stand in a circle round Etna's lofty peak like towers round a town; they do not see the endless stretches of thick forest.

In Casa del Bosco, where the road ends, they dismount. Biagio and Passafiore take the wreath and carry it between them. As they walk along, Falco begins to talk. He likes to talk since he has grown old.

Falco says that the mountain is like the twenty-five years of his life that he has passed there. The years that founded his greatness had blossomed with deeds. To be with him then had been like going through an endless arbor, where lemons and grapes hung down overhead. Then his deeds had been as numerous as the orange trees round Etna's base. When he had come higher the deeds had been less frequent, but those he had executed had been mighty as the oaks and chestnut trees on the rising mountain. Now that he was at the summit of greatness, he scorned to act. His life was as bald as the mountain top; he was content to see the world at his feet. But people ought to understand that, if he should now undertake anything, nothing could resist him. He was terrible, like the fire-spouting summit.

Falco walks before and talks; Passafiore and Biagio follow him in silent terror. Dimly they see the mighty slopes of Mongibello with their towns and fields and forests spread out beneath them. And Falco thinks that he is as mighty as all that!

As they struggle upwards they are beset with a growing feeling of dread. The gaping fissures in the ground; the sulfur smoke from the crater, which rolls down the mountain, too heavy to rise into the air; the explosions inside the mountain; the incessant, gently rumbling earthquake; the slippery, rough ice-fields crossed by gushing brooks; the extreme cold, the biting wind, – make the walk hideous. And Falco says that it is like him! How can he have such things in his soul? Is it filled with a cold and a horror to be compared to Etna's?"

They stumble over blocks of ice, and they struggle forward through snow lying sometimes a yard deep. The mountain blast almost throws them down. They have to wade through slush and water, for through the day the sun has melted a mass of snow. And while they grow stiff with cold, the ground shakes under them with the everlasting fire.

They remember that Lucifer and all the damned are lying under them. They shudder because Falco has brought them to the gates of Hell.

But nevertheless beyond the ice-field they reach the steep cone of ashes on the very summit of the mountain. Here they drag themselves up, walking on sliding ashes and pumice-stone. When they are halfway up the cone Falco takes the wreath, and motions to the others to wait. He alone will scale the summit.

The day is just breaking, and as Falco reaches the top the sun is visible. The glorious morning light streams over Mongibello and over the old Etna brigand on its summit. The shadow of Etna is thrown over the whole of Sicily, and it looks as if Falco, standing up there, reached from sea to sea, across the island.

Falco stands and gazes about him. He looks across to Italy; he fancies he sees Naples and Rome. He lets his glance pass over the sea to the land of the Turk to the east and the land of the Saracen to the south. He feels as if it all lay at his feet and acknowledged *his* greatness.

Then Falco lays the wreath on the summit of Mongibello.

When he comes down to his comrades he solemnly presses their hands. As he leaves the cone they see that he picks up a piece of pumice-stone, and puts it in his pocket. Falco takes with him a souvenir of the most beautiful hour of his life. He has never before felt himself so great as on the top of Mongibello.

On that day of happiness Falco will do no work. The next day, he says, he will begin the undertaking of freeing Mongibello from the railway.

*T*here is a lonely farmhouse on the road between Paternó and Adernó. It is quite large, and it is owned by a widow, Donna Silvia, who has many strong sons. They are bold people who dare to live alone the whole year in the country.

It is the day following the one when Falco crowned Mongibello. Donna Silvia is sitting on the grass-plot with her distaff; she is alone; there is no one else at home on the farm. A beggar comes softly creeping in through the gate.

He is an old man with a long, hooked nose which hangs down over his upper lip, a bushy beard, pale eyes with red eyelids. They are the ugliest eyes imaginable; the whites are yellowish, and they squint. The beggar is tall and very thin; he moves his body when he walks, so that it looks as if he wriggled forward. He walks so softly that Donna Silvia does not hear him. The first thing she notices is his shadow, which, slender as a snake, bends down towards her.

She looks up when she sees the shadow. Then the beggar bows to her and asks for a dish of macaroni.

"I have macaroni on the fire," says Donna Silvia. "Sit down and wait; you shall have your fill."

The beggar sits down beside Donna Silvia, and after a while they begin to chat. They soon talk of Falco.

"Is it true that you let your sons work on Donna Micaela's railway?" says the beggar.

Donna Silvia bites her lips together, and nods an assent.

"You are a brave woman, Donna Silvia. Falco might be revenged on you."

"Then he can take revenge," says Donna Silvia. "But I will not obey one who has killed my father. He forced him to escape from prison in Augusta, and my father was captured and shot."

And so saying she rises and goes in to get the food.

As she stands in the kitchen she sees the beggar through the window, sitting and rocking on the stone-bench. He is not quiet for a moment. And in front of him writhes his shadow, slender and lithe as a snake.

Donna Silvia remembers what she had once heard Caterina, who had been married to Falco's brother, Nino, say. "How will you recognize Falco after twenty years?" people had asked her. "Should I not recognize the man with the snake-shadow?" she answered. "He will never lose it, long as he may live."

Donna Silvia presses her hand on her heart.

There in her yard Falco Falcone is sitting. He has come to be revenged because her sons work on the railway. Will he set fire to the house, or will he murder her?

Donna Silvia is shaking in every limb as she serves up her macaroni.

Falco begins to find the time long as he sits on the stone-bench. A little dog comes up to him and rubs against him. Falco feels in his pocket for a piece of bread, but he finds only a stone, which he throws to the dog.

The dog runs after the stone and brings it back to Falco. Falco throws it again. The dog takes the stone again, but now he runs away with it.

Falco remembers that it is the stone he picked up on Mongibello, and goes after the dog to get it back. He whistles to the dog, and it comes to him instantly. "Drop the stone!" The dog puts its head on one side and will not drop it. "Ah, give me the stone, rascal!" The dog shuts its mouth. It has no stone. "Let me see; let me see!" says Falco. He bends the dog's head back and forces it to open its mouth. The stone lies far in under the gums, and Falco tries to force it out. Then the dog bites him, till the blood flows.

Falco is terrified. He goes in to Donna Silvia. "I hope your dog is healthy," he says.

"My dog? I have no dog. It is dead." — "But the one running outside?" — "I do not know which one you mean," she says.

Falco says nothing more, nor does he do Donna Silvia any harm. He simply goes his way, frightened; he thinks that the dog is mad, and he fears hydrophobia.

One evening Donna Micaela sits alone in the music-room. She has put out the lamp and opened the balcony doors. She likes to listen to the street in the evening and at night. No more smiths and stone-cutters and criers are heard. There is song, laughter, whispering, and mandolins.

Suddenly she sees a dark hand laid on the balcony railing. The hand drags up after it an arm and a head; within a moment a whole human being swings himself into the balcony. She sees him plainly, for the street-lamps are still burning. He is a small, broad-shouldered, bearded fellow, dressed like a shepherd, with leather sandals, a slouch hat, and an umbrella tied to his back. As soon as he is on his feet he snatches his gun from his shoulder and comes into the room with it in his hands.

She sits still without giving a sign of life. There is no time either to summon help or to escape. She hopes that the man will take what he wishes to take, and go away without noticing her, sitting back in the dark room.

The man puts his gun down between his legs, and she hears him scratching with a match. She shuts her eyes. He will believe that she is asleep.

When the robber gets the match lighted, he sees her instantly. He coughs to wake her. As she remains motionless, he creeps over to her and carefully stretches out a finger towards her arm. "Do not touch me! do not touch me!" she screams, and can no longer sit still. The man draws back instantly. "Dear Donna Micaela, I only wanted to wake you."

There she sits and shakes with terror, and he hears how she is sobbing. "Dear signora, dear signora!" he says. "Light a candle that I can see where you are," she cries. He scratches a new match, lifts the shade and chimney off the lamp, and lights it as neatly as a servant. He places himself again by the door, as far from her as possible. Suddenly he goes out on the balcony with his gun. "Now the signora cannot be afraid any longer."

But when she does not cease weeping he says: "Signora, I am Passafiore; I come with a message to you from Falco. He no longer wishes to destroy your railway."

"Have you come to jest with me?" she says.

Then the man answers, almost weeping: "Would God that it were a jest! God! that Falco were the man he has been!"

He tells her how Falco went up Mongibello and crowned its top. But the mountain had not liked it; it had now overthrown Falco. A single little piece of pumice-stone from Mongibello had been enough to overthrow him.

"It is all over with Falco," says Passanore. "He goes about in the quarry, and waits to fall ill. For a week he has neither slept nor eaten. He is not sick yet, but the wound in his hand does not heal either. He thinks that he has the poison in his body. 'Soon I shall be a mad dog,' he says. No wine nor food tempt him. He takes no pleasure in my praising his deeds. 'What is that to talk about?' he says. 'I shall end my life like a mad dog.'"

Donna Micaela looked sharply at Passafiore. "What do you wish me to do about it? You cannot mean that I am to go down into the quarry to Falco Falcone?"

Passafiore looks down and dares not answer anything.

She explains to him what that same Falco has made her suffer. He has frightened away her workmen. He has set himself against her dearest wish.

All of a sudden Passafiore falls on his knees. He dares not go a step nearer to her than he is, but he falls on his knees.

He implores her to understand the importance of it. She does not know, she does not understand who Falco is. Falco is a great man. Ever since Passafiore was a little child he has heard of him. All his life long he has longed to come out to the quarry and live with him. All his cousins went to Falco; his whole race were with him. But the priest had set his heart that Passafiore should not go. He apprenticed him to a tailor; only think, to a tailor! He talked to him, and said that he should not go. It was such a terrible sin to live like Falco. Passafiore had also struggled against it for many years for Don Matteo's sake. But at last he had not been able to resist; he had gone to the quarry. And now he has not been with Falco more than a year before the latter is quite destroyed. It is as if the sun had gone out in the sky. His whole life is ruined.

Passafiore looks at Donna Micaela. He sees that she is listening to him, and understands him.

He reminds Donna Micaela that she had helped a *jettatore* and an adulteress. Why should she be hard to a brigand? The Christ-image in San Pasquale gave her everything she asked for. He was sure that she prayed to the Christchild to protect the railway from Falco. And he had obeyed her; he had made Mongibello's pumice-stone break Falco's might. But now, would she not be gracious, and help them, that Falco might get his health again, and be an honor to the land, as he had been before?

Passafiore succeeds in moving Donna Micaela. All at once she understands how it is with the old brigand in the dark caves of the quarry. She sees him there, waiting for madness. She thinks how proud he has been, and how broken and crushed he now is. No, no; no one ought to suffer so. It is too much, too much.

"Passafiore," she exclaims, "tell me what you wish. I will do whatever I can. I am no longer afraid. No, I am not at all afraid."

"Donna Micaela, we have begged Falco to go to the Christchild and ask for grace. But Falco will not believe in the image. He will not do anything but sit still and wait for the disaster. But today, when I implored him to go and pray, he said: 'You know who sits and waits for me in the old house opposite the church. Go to her, and ask her if she will give me the privilege to go by her into the church. If she gives her permission, then I shall believe in the image, and say my prayers to him.'"

"Well?" questions Donna Micaela.

"I have been to old Caterina, and she has given her permission. 'He shall be allowed to go into San Pasquale without my killing him,' she said."

Passafiore is still on his knees.

"Has Falco already been to the church?" asks Donna Micaela.

Passafiore moves somewhat nearer. He wrings his hands in despair. "Donna Micaela, Falco is very ill. It is not alone that about the dog; he was ill before." And Passafiore struggles with himself before he can say it out. At last he acknowledges that although Falco is a very great man, he sometimes has attacks of madness. He had not spoken of old Caterina alone; he had said: "If Caterina will let me go into the church, and if Donna Micaela Alagona comes down into the quarry and gives me her hand, and leads me to the church, I will go to the image." And from that no one had been able to move him. Donna Micaela, who was greatest and holiest of women, must come to him, or he would not go.

When Passafiore has finished, he remains kneeling with bowed head. He dares not look up.

But Donna Micaela does not hesitate a second, since there has been question of the Christ-image. She seems not to think of Falco's being already mad. She does not say a word of her terror. Her faith in the image is such that she answers softly, like a subdued and obedient child: —

"Passafiore, I will go with you."

She follows him as if walking in her sleep. She does not hesitate to go with him up Etna. She does not hesitate to climb down the steep cliffs into the quarry. She comes, pale as death, but with shining eyes, to the old brigand in his hole in the cliff and gives him her hand. He rises up, ghastly pale as she, and follows her. They do not seem like human beings, but like specters. They move on towards their goal in absolute silence. Their own identity is dead, but a mightier spirit guides and leads them.

Even the day after it seems like a fairy tale to Donna Micaela that she has done such a thing. She is sure that her own compassion, or pity, or love could never have made her go down into the brigands' cave at night if a strange power had not led her.

While Donna Micaela is in the robber's cave, old Caterina sits at her window, and waits for Falco. She has consented, almost without their needing to ask her.

"He shall go in peace to the church," she says. "I have waited for him twenty years, but he shall go to the church."

Soon Falco comes by, walking with Donna Micaela's hand in his. Passafiore and Biagio follow him. Falco is bent; it is plain that he is old and feeble. He alone goes into the church; the others remain outside.

Old Caterina has seen him very plainly, but she has not moved. She sits silent all the time Falco is inside the church. Her niece, who lives with her, believes that she is praying and thanking God because she has been able to conquer her thirst for revenge.

At last Caterina asks her to open a window. "I wish to see if he still has his snake shadow," she says.

But she is gentle and friendly. "Take the gun, if you wish," she says. And her niece moves the gun over to the other side of the table.

At last Falco comes from the church. The moonlight falls on his face, and Caterina sees that he is unlike the Falco she remembered. The terrible moroseness and arrogance are no longer visible in his face. He comes bent and broken; he almost inspires her with pity.

"*He* helps me," he says aloud to Passafiore and Biagio. "He has promised to help me."

The brigands wish to go, but Falco is so happy that he must first tell them of his joy.

"I feel no buzzing in my head; there is no burning, no uneasiness. He is helping me."

His comrades take him by the hand to lead him away.

Falco goes a few steps, then stops again. He straightens himself up, and at the same time moves his body so that the snake shadow writhes and twists on the wall.

"I shall be quite well, quite well," he says. The men drag him away, but it is too late. Caterina's eyes have fallen on the snake shadow. She can control herself no longer; she throws herself across the table, takes the gun, shoots and kills Falco. She had not intended to do it, but when she saw him it was impossible for her to let him go. She had cherished the thought of revenge for twenty years. It took the upper hand over her. "Caterina, Caterina," screams her niece. "He only asked me to be allowed to go in peace *into* the church," answers the old woman.

Old Biagio lays Falco's body straight, and says with a grim look: −

"He would be quite well; quite well."

# XI

## VICTORY

*F*ar back in ancient days the great philosopher Empedokles lived in Sicily. He was the most beautiful and the most perfect of men; so wonderful and so wise that the people regarded him as an incarnate god.

Empedokles owned a country-place on Etna, and one evening he prepared a feast there for his friends. During the repast he spoke such words that they cried out to him: "Thou art a god, Empedokles; thou art a god!"

During the night Empedokles thought: "You have risen as high as you can rise on earth. Now die, before adversity and feebleness take hold of you." And he wandered up to the summit of Etna and threw himself into the burning crater. "When no one can find my body," he thought, "the people will say that I have been taken up alive to the gods."

The next morning his friends searched for him through the villa and on the mountain. They too came up to the crater, and there they found by the crater's mouth Empedokles' sandal. They understood that Empedokles had sought death in the crater in order to be counted among the immortals.

He would have succeeded had not the mountain cast up his shoe.

But on account of that story Empedokles' name has never been forgotten, and many have wondered where his villa could have been situated. Antiquaries and treasure-seekers have looked for it; for the villa of the wonderful Empedokles was naturally filled with marble statues, bronzes, and mosaics.

Donna Micaela's father, Cavaliere Palmeri, had set his heart on solving the problem of the villa. Every morning he mounted his pony, Domenico, and rode away to search for it. He was armed as an investigator, with a scraper in his belt, a spade at his side, and a big knapsack on his back.

Every evening, when Cavaliere Palmeri came home, he told Donna Micaela about Domenico. During the years that they had ridden about on Etna, Domenico had become an antiquary. Domenico turned from the road as soon as he caught sight of a ruin. He stamped on the ground in places where excavations should be made. He snorted scornfully and turned away his head if anyone showed him a counterfeit piece of old money.

Donna Micaela listened with great patience and interest. She was sure that in case that villa finally did let itself be found Domenico would get all the glory of the discovery.

Cavaliere Palmeri never asked his daughter about her undertaking. He never showed any interest in the railway. It seemed almost as if he were ignorant that she was working for it.

It was not singular however; he never showed interest in anything that concerned his daughter.

One day, as they both sat at the dining-table, Donna Micaela all at once began to talk of the railway.

She had won a victory, she said; she had finally won a victory.

He must hear what news she had received that day. It was not merely to be a railway between Catania and Diamante, as she first had thought; it was to be a railway round the whole of Etna.

By Falco's death she had not only been rid of Falco himself, but now the people believed also that the great Mongibello and all the saints were on her side. And so there had arisen an agitation of the people to make the railway an actuality. Contributions were signed in all the towns of Etna. A company was formed. Today the concession had come; tomorrow the work was to begin in earnest.

Donna Micaela was excited; she could not eat. Her heart swelled with joy and thankfulness. She could not help talking of the tremendous enthusiasm that had seized the people. She spoke with tears in her eyes of the Christchild in the church of San Pasquale.

It was touching to see how her face shone with hope. It was as if she had, besides the happiness of which she was speaking, a whole world of bliss in expectation.

That evening she felt that Providence had guided her well and happily. She perceived that Gaetano's imprisonment had been the work of God to lead him back to faith. He would be set free by the miracles of the little image, and that would convert him so that he would become a believer as before. And she might be his. How good God was!

And while this great bliss stirred within her, her father sat opposite her quite cold and indifferent.

"It was very extraordinary," was all he said.

"You will come tomorrow to the ceremony of the laying of the foundations?"

"I do not know; I have my investigations."

Donna Micaela began to crumble her bread rather hastily. Her patience was exhausted. She had not asked him to share her sorrows, but her joys; he must share her joys!

All at once the shackles of submission and fear, which had bound her ever since the time of his imprisonment, broke.

"You who ride so much about Etna," she said with a very quiet voice, "must have also come to Gela?"

The cavaliere looked up and seemed to search his memory. "Gela, Gela?"

"Gela is a village of a hundred houses, which is situated on the southern side of Monte Chiaro, quite at its foot," continued Donna Micaela, with the most innocent expression. "It is squeezed in between Simeto and the mountain, and a branch of the river generally flows through the principal street of Gela so that it is very unusual to be able to pass dry-shod through the village. The roof of the church fell in during the last earthquake, and it has never been mended, for Gela is quite destitute. Have you really never heard of Gela?"

Cavaliere Palmeri answered with inexpressible solemnity: "My investigations have taken me up the mountain. I have not thought of looking for the great philosopher's villa in Gela."

"But Gela is an interesting town," said Donna Micaela, obstinately. "They have no separate outhouses there. The pigs live on the lower floor, the people one flight up. There is an endless number of pigs in Gela. They thrive better than the people, for the people are almost always sick. Fever is always raging there; malaria never leaves it. It is so damp that the cellars are always under water, and it is wrapped in swamp mists every night. In Gela there are no shops and no police, nor post office, nor doctor, nor apothecary. Six hundred people are living there forgotten and brutalized. You have never heard of Gela?" She looked honestly surprised.

Cavaliere Palmeri shook his head. "Of course I have heard the name —"

Donna Micaela cast a questioning glance on her father. She then bent quickly forward towards him, and drew out of his breast-pocket a small, bent knife, such a knife as is used to prune grape-vines.

"Poor Empedokles," she said, and all at once her whole face sparkled with fun. "You may believe you have mounted to the gods, but Etna always throws up your shoe."

Cavaliere Palmeri sank back as if shot.

"Micaela!" he said, feebly fencing like someone who does not know how he shall defend himself.

But she was instantly as serious and innocent as before. "I have been told," she said, "that Gela a few years ago was on the way to ruin. All the people there grow grapes, and when the phylloxera came and destroyed their vineyards, they almost starved to death. The Agricultural Society sent them some of those American plants that are not affected by the phylloxera. The people of Gela set them out, but all the plants died. How could the people of Gela know how to tend American vines? Well, someone came and taught them."

"Micaela!" — it came almost like a wail. Donna Micaela thought that her father already looked like a conquered man, but she continued as if she had noticed nothing.

"*Someone came,*" she said with strong emphasis, "and he had had new vines sent out. He began to plant them in their vineyards. They laughed at him; they said that he was mad. But look, his vines grew and lived; they did not die. And he has saved Gela."

"I do not think that your story is entertaining, Micaela," said Cavaliere Palmeri with an attempt to interrupt her.

"It is quite as entertaining as your investigations," she said, calmly. "But I will tell you something. One day I went into your room to get a book on antiquities. Then I found that all your bookshelves were full of pamphlets about the phylloxera, about the cultivation of grapes, about wine-making."

The cavaliere twisted on his chair like a worm. "Be silent; be silent!" he said feebly. He was more embarrassed than when he was accused of theft.

Now all the suppressed fun shone once more in her eyes.

"I sometimes looked at the letters you sent off," she continued. "I wished to see with what learned men you corresponded. It surprised me that the letters were always addressed to presidents and secretaries of Agricultural Societies."

Cavaliere Palmeri was unable to utter a word. Donna Micaela enjoyed his helplessness more than can be described.

She looked him steadily in the eyes. "I do not believe that Domenico has yet learned to recognize a ruin," she said with emphasis. "The dirty children of Gela play with him every day, and feed him with watercresses. Domenico seems to be a god in Gela, to say nothing of his —"

Cavaliere Palmeri seemed to have an idea.

"Your railway," he said; "what did you say about your railway? Perhaps I really can come tomorrow."

Donna Micaela did not listen to him. She took up her pocketbook.

"I have here a counterfeit old coin," she said, — "a 'Demarata' of nickel. I bought it to show Domenico. He is going to snort."

"Listen, child!"

She did not answer his attempts to make amends. Now the power was hers. It would take more than that to pacify her.

"Once I opened your knapsack to look at your antiquities. The only thing there was an old grapevine."

She was full of sparkling gayety.

"Child, child!"

"What is it to be called? It does not seem to be investigating. Is it perhaps charity; is it perhaps atonement —"

Cavaliere Palmeri struck with his clenched fist on the table so that the glasses and plates rang. It was unbearable. A dignified and solemn old gentleman could not endure such mockery. "As surely as you are my daughter, you must be silent now."

"Your daughter!" she said, and her gayety was gone in an instant; "am I really your daughter? The children in Gela are allowed to caress at least Domenico, but I —"

"What do you wish, Micaela, what do you want?"

They looked at one another, and their eyes simultaneously filled with tears.

"I have no one but you," she murmured.

Cavaliere Palmeri opened his arms unconditionally to her. She rose hesitatingly; she did not know if she saw right.

"I know how it is going to be," he said, grumblingly; "not one minute will I have to myself."

"To find the villa?"

"Come here and kiss me, Micaela! Tonight is the first time since we left Catania that you have been irresistible."

When she threw her arms about him it was with a hoarse, wild cry which almost frightened him.

# THIRD BOOK

*"And he shall win many followers"*

# I

## THE OASIS AND THE DESERT

*I*n the spring of 1894 the Etna railway was begun; in the autumn of 1895 it was finished. It went up from the shore, made a circuit round the mountain in a wide half-circle, and came down again to the shore.

Trains come and go every day, and Mongibello lies subdued and makes no sign. Foreigners pass with amazement through the black, distorted lava streams, through the groves of white almond trees, through the dark old Saracen towns. "Look, look! is there such a land on earth!" they say.

In the railway carriages there is always someone telling of the time when the Christ-image was in Diamante.

What a time! What a time! Each day new miracles were performed. They cannot tell of them all, but he brought as much happiness to Diamante as if the hours of the day had been dancing maidens. People thought that Time had filled his hour-glass with shining sands of gold.

If anyone had asked who reigned in Diamante at that time, the answer would have been that it was the Christ-image. Everything was done according to his will. No one took a wife, or played in a lottery, or built himself a house without consulting him.

Many knife-thrusts were spared for the image's sake, many old feuds settled, and many bitter words were never uttered.

The people had to be good, for they observed that the image helped those who were peaceable and helpful. To them he granted the pleasant gifts of happiness and riches.

If the world had been as it ought to be, Diamante would soon have become a rich and powerful town. But instead, that part of the world which did not believe in the image destroyed all his work. All the happiness he scattered about him was of no avail.

The taxes were constantly increased, and took all their money. There was the war in Africa. How could the people be happy when their sons, their money, and their mules had to go to Africa? The war did not go well; one defeat followed another. How could they be happy when their country's honor was at stake?

Especially after the railway had been finished was it manifest that Diamante was like an oasis in a great desert. An oasis is exposed to the drifting sands of the desert and to robbers and wild beasts. So was also Diamante. The oasis would have to spread over the whole desert to feel secure. Diamante began to believe that it could never be happy until the whole world worshipped its Christ-image.

It now happened that everything that Diamante hoped and strove for was denied it.

Donna Micaela and all Diamante longed to get Gaetano back. When the railway was ready Donna Micaela went to Rome and asked for his release, but it was refused her. The king and the queen would have liked to help her, but they could not. You know who was minister then. He ruled Italy with a hand of iron; do you think that he allowed the king to pardon a rebellious Sicilian?

The people also longed that the Christchild of Diamante should have the adoration that was his due, and Donna Micaela sought an audience for his sake with the old man in the Vatican. "Holy Father," she said, "let me tell you what has been taking place in Diamante on the slopes of Etna!" And when she had told of all the miracles performed by the image, she asked the pope to have the old church of San Pasquale purified and consecrated, and to appoint a priest for the worship of the Christchild.

"Dear Princess Micaela," said the pope, "those incidents of which you speak, the church dares not consider miracles. But you need not at all despair. If the Christchild wishes to be worshipped in your town, he will give one more sign. He will show Us his will so plainly that We shall not need to hesitate. And forgive an old man, my daughter, because he has to be cautious!"

A third thing the people of Diamante had hoped. They had expected at last to hear something from Gaetano. Donna Micaela journeyed also to Como, where he was held prisoner. She had letters of recommendation from the highest quarters in Rome, and she was sure that she would be allowed to speak to him. But the director of the prison sent her to the prison doctor.

The latter forbade her to speak to Gaetano.

"You wish to see the prisoner?" he said. "You shall not do it. Do you say that he loves you and believes you to be dead? Let him think it! Let him believe it! He has bowed his head to Death. He suffers no longing. Do you wish him to know that you are alive, so that he may begin to long? You wish, perhaps, to kill him? I will tell you something; if he begins to long for life, he will be dead within three months."

He spoke so positively that Donna Micaela understood that she must give up seeing Gaetano. But what a disappointment, what a disappointment!

When she came home, she felt like one who has dreamt so vividly that he cannot, even after he is awake, rouse himself from his visions. She could not realize that all her hopes had been a mockery. She surprised herself time after time thinking: "When I have saved Gaetano." But now she no longer had any hope of saving him.

She thought now of one, now of another enterprise, on which she wished to embark. Should she drain the plain, or should she begin to quarry marble on Etna. She hesitated and wondered. She could not keep her mind on anything.

The same indolence that had taken possession of Donna Micaela crept through the whole town. It was soon plain that everything that depended on people who did not believe in the Christchild of Diamante was badly managed and unsuccessful. Even the Etna railway was conducted in the wrong way. Accidents were happening constantly on the steep inclines; and the price of the tickets was too high. The people began to use the omnibuses and post wagons again.

Donna Micaela and others with her began to think of carrying the Christ-image out into the world. They would go out and show how he gave health and subsistence and happiness to all who were quiet and industrious and helped their neighbor. If people could once see, they would certainly be converted.

"The image ought to stand on the Capitol and govern the world," said the people of Diamante.

"All those who govern us are incapable," said the people. "We prefer to be guided by the holy Christchild."

"The Christchild is powerful and charitable; if he ruled us, the poor would be rich, and the rich would have enough. He knows who wish to do right. If he should come to power, they who now are ruled would sit in the parliament. He would pass through the world like a plow with a sharp edge, and that which now lies unprofitable in the depths would then bear harvests."

Before their longed-for plans came to pass, however, in the first days of March, 1896, the news of the battle at Adna arrived. The Italians had been defeated, and several thousands of them were killed or taken prisoners.

A few days later there was a change of ministry in Rome. And the man who came to power was afraid of the rage and despair of the

Sicilians. To pacify them he pardoned out several of the imprisoned socialists. The five for whom he thought the people longed most were set free. They were Da Felice, Bosco, Verro, Barbato and Alagona.

Ah, Micaela tried to be glad when she heard it. She tried not to weep.

She had believed that Gaetano was in prison because the Christ-image was to break down the walls of his cell. He was sent there by the grace of God, because he had to be forced to bow his head before the Christchild and say: "My Lord and my God."

But now it was not the image which had freed him; he would come out the same heathen as before; the same yawning chasm would still exist between them.

She tried to be glad. It was enough that he was free. What did she or her happiness matter in comparison to that!

But it happened so with everything for which Diamante had hoped and striven.

The great desert was very cruel to the poor oasis.

# II

## IN PALERMO

*A*t last, at last, it is one o'clock at night. Those who are afraid to oversleep rise from their beds, dress themselves and go out into the street.

And those who have sat and hung over a café table till now start up when they hear steps echo on the stone pavements. They shake the drowsiness from their bodies and hurry out. They mingle in the swiftly increasing stream of people, and the heavy feet of Time begin to move a little faster.

Mere acquaintances press each other's hands with heartfelt warmth. It is plain that the same enthusiasm fills all souls. And the most absurd people are out; old university professors, distinguished noblemen and fine ladies, who otherwise never set their foot in the street. They are all equally joyous.

"God! God! that he is coming, that Palermo is to have him back again!" they say.

The Palermo students, who have not moved from their usual headquarters in Quattro Canti all night, have provided torches and colored lanterns. They were not to be lighted till four o'clock, when the man they expected was to come; but about two o'clock one or two of them begin to try whether their torches burn well. Then they light everything and greet the flames with cheers. It is impossible to stand in darkness when so much joy is burning within them.

In the hotels the travelers are waked and urged to get up. "There is a festival in Palermo tonight, O signori!"

The travelers ask for whom. "For one of the socialists whom the government has pardoned out of prison. He is coming now in the steamer from Naples." — "What kind of a man is he?" — "His name is Bosco, and the people love him."

There are preparations everywhere in the night for his sake. One of the goatherds on Monte Pellegrino is busy tying little bunches of blue-bells for his goats to wear in their collars. And as he has a hundred goats, and they all wear collars — But it must be done. His goats could not wander into Palermo the next morning without being adorned in honor of the day.

The dressmakers have had to sit at their work till midnight to finish all the new dresses that are to be worn that morning. And when such a little dressmaker has finished her work for others, she has to think of herself. She puts a couple of plumes in her hat and piles up bunches of ribbon a yard high. Today she must be beautiful.

The long rows of houses begin to be illuminated. Here and there a rocket whizzes up. Fire-crackers hiss and snap at every street corner.

The flower shops along Via Vittorio Emanuele are emptied again and again. Always more, more of the white orange-blossoms! All Palermo is filled with the sweet fragrance of the orange-blossoms.

The gatekeeper in Bosco's house has no peace for a moment. Magnificent cakes and towerlike bouquets are incessantly passing up the stairway, and poems of welcome and telegrams of congratulation are constantly coming. There is no end to them.

The poor bronze emperor on the Piazza Bologna, poor, ugly Charles the Fifth, who is forlorn and thin and wretched as San Giovanni in the desert, has in some inscrutable manner got a bunch of flowers in his hand. When the students standing on Quattro Canti, quite near by, hear of it, they march up to the emperor in a procession, light him with their torches, and raise a cheer for the old despot. And one of them takes his bunch of flowers to give it to the great socialist.

Then the students march down to the harbor.

Long before they get there their torches are burned out, but they do not care. They come with arms about each other's necks, singing loudly, and sometimes breaking off in their song to shout: "Down with Crispi! Long live Bosco!" The song begins again, but it is again broken off, because those who cannot sing throw their arms round the singers and kiss them.

Guilds and corporations swarm out of the quarters of the town where the same trade has been carried on for more than a thousand years. The masons come with their band of music and their banner; there come the workers in mosaic; here come the fishermen.

When the societies meet, they salute one another with their banners. Sometimes they take time to stop and make speeches. Then they tell of the five released prisoners, the five martyrs whom the government at last has given back to Sicily. And all the people shout: "Long live Bosco! Long live Da Felice! Long live Verro! Long live Barbato! Long live Alagona!"

If anyone who has had enough of the life in the streets comes down to the harbor of Palermo, he stops and asks: "What place is this? Madonna Santissima, where am I?"

For he has expected to find the harbor still deserted and dark.

All the boats and skiffs in the harbor of Palermo have been taken by different societies and unions. They are floating about in the harbor, richly hung with colored Venetian lights, and every minute great bunches of rockets are sent up from them.

Over the heavy thwarts priceless rugs and hangings have been spread, and on them sit ladies, the beautiful Palermo ladies, dressed in light silks and shaded velvets.

The small craft glide about on the water, now in big groups, now separately. From the big ships rise masts and oars covered with pennants and lights, and the little harbor steam-launches dart about with funnels wreathed in flowers.

Beneath it all the water lies and shines and mirrors and reflects, so that the light from one lantern becomes a stream of brightness, and the drops that fall from the oars are like a rain of gold.

Round about the harbor stand a hundred thousand, a hundred and fifty thousand people, quite delirious with joy. They kiss one another; they raise shouts of rapture, and they are happy, happy. They are beside themselves with joy. Many of them cannot keep from weeping.

Fire, that is joy. It is good that fires can be lighted. Suddenly a great blaze flames up on Monte Pellegrino, just over the harbor. Mighty flames burst from all the pointed mountain walls surrounding the town. There are fires on Monte Falcone, on San Martino, on the mountain of The Thousands, where Garibaldi passed.

Far out on the sea comes the big Naples steamer. And on the steamer is Bosco, the socialist.

He cannot sleep that night. He has gone up from his cabin, and paces to and fro on the deck. And then his old mother, who has journeyed to Naples to meet him, comes from her cabin to keep him company. But he cannot talk with her. He is thinking that he will soon be at home. Ah, Palermo, Palermo!

He has been in prison over two years. They have been two years of suffering and longing, and has it been of any good? That is what he wishes to know. Has it been of benefit that he has been faithful to the cause, and gone to prison? Has Palermo thought of him? Have his sufferings won the cause a single follower?

His old mother sits crouched on the gangway, and shivers in the chill of the night. He has asked her, but she knows nothing of such things. She speaks of little Francesco and little Lina, how they have grown. She knows nothing of what he is struggling for.

Now he comes to his mother, takes her by the wrist, leads her to the railing, and asks her if she sees anything far away to the south. She looks out over the water with her dim eyes, and sees only the night, only the black night on the water. She does not see at all that a cloud of fire is floating on the horizon.

Then he begins to walk again, and she creeps down under cover. He does not need to talk to her; it is joy enough to have him home again after only two years' absence. He was condemned to be away for twenty-four. She had not expected ever to see him again. But now the king has showed grace. For the king is a good man. If only he were allowed to be as good as he wished!

Bosco walks across the deck, and asks the sailors if they do not see the golden cloud on the horizon.

"That is Palermo," say the seamen. "There is always a bright light floating over it at night."

It cannot be anything that concerns him. He tries to persuade himself that nothing is being done for him. He can hardly expect everyone all at once to have become socialists.

But after a while he thinks: "Still there must be something unusual going on. All the sailors are gathering forward at the bow."

"Palermo is burning," say the seamen.

Yes, that is what it must be. — It is because he has suffered so terribly that he expects something should be done for him.

Then the sailors see the fires on the mountains.

It cannot be a conflagration. It must be some saint's day. They ask one another what day it is.

He, too, tries to believe that it is some such thing. He asks his mother if it is a feast-day. They have so many of them.

They come nearer and nearer. The thundering sound of the festival in the great city meets them.

"All Palermo is singing and playing tonight," says one.

"A telegram must have come of a victory in Africa," says another.

No one has a thought that it can be for his sake. He goes and places himself at the stern in order not to see anything. He will not deceive himself with false hopes. Would all Palermo be illuminated for a poor socialist?

Then his mother comes and fetches him. "Do not stand there! Come and see Palermo! It must be a king who is coming there today. Come and look at Palermo!"

He considers a moment. No, he does not think that any king is visiting Sicily just now. But he cannot dare to think, when no one else, not even his mother —

All at once everyone on the steamer gives a loud cry. It sounds almost like a cry of distress. A big cutter has steered right down on them and now glides along by the steamer's side.

The cutter is all flowers and lights; over the railing hang red and white silken draperies, everybody on board is dressed in red and white. Bosco stands on the steamer and looks to see what that beautiful messenger brings. Then the sail turns, and on its white surface shines to meet him: "Long live Bosco!"

It is his name. Not a saint's, not a king's, not the victorious general's! The homage is for no other on the steamer. His name, his name!

The cutter sends up some rockets; a whole cloud of stars rain down, and then it is gone.

He enters the harbor, and there is jubilation and enthusiasm and cheering and adoration. People say: "We do not know how he will be able to live through it."

But as soon as he realizes the homage, he feels that he does not at all deserve it. He would like to fall on his knees before those hundred and fifty thousand people who pay him homage and pray to them for forgiveness that he is so powerless, that he has done nothing for them.

*A*s though by a special fate, Donna Micaela is in Palermo that night. She is there to start one of those new undertakings which she thinks she ought to organize in order to retain life and reason. She is probably there either on account of the draining or of the marble quarry.

She is down at the harbor; like all the others. People notice her as she pushes her way forward to the edge of the water: a tall, dark woman, with an air of being someone, a pale face with marked features and imploring, longing, passionate eyes.

During the reception in the harbor, Donna Micaela is fighting out a strange struggle. "If it were Gaetano," she thinks, "could I, could I —

"If it were for him all these people were rejoicing, could I —"

There is so much joy — a joy the like of which she has never seen. The people love one another and are like brothers. And that not only because a socialist is coming home, but because they all believe that the earth will soon be happy. "If he were to come now, while all this joy is roaring about me," she thinks. "Could I, could I —"

She sees Bosco's carriage trying to force a way through the crowd. It moves forward step by step. For long moments it stands quite still. It will take several hours to come up from the harbor.

"If it were he, and I saw everyone crowding round him, could I forbear from throwing myself into his arms? Could I?"

*A*s soon as she can work her way out of the crowd she takes a carriage, drives out of Palermo, and passes through the plain of Conca d'Oro to the big Cathedral of the old Norman kings in Monreale.

She goes in, and stands face to face with the most beautiful image of Christ that human art has created. High up in the choir sits the blessing-giving Christ in glowing mosaic. He is mighty and mysterious and majestic. Without number are they who make a pilgrimage to Monreale in order to feel the consolation of gazing upon his face. Without number are they who in far distant lands long for him.

The ground rocks under anyone who sees him for the first time. His eyes compel the knees of the foreigner to bend. Without being conscious of it the lips falter: "Thou, God, art God."

About the walls of the temple glow the great events of the world in wonderful mosaic pictures. They only lead to him. They are only there to say: "All the past is his; all the present belongs to him, and all the future."

The mysteries of life and death dwell within that head.

There lives the spirit which directs the fate of the world. There glows the love which shall lead the world to salvation.

And Donna Micaela calls to him: "Thou son of God, do not part me from thee! Let no man have power to part me from thee!"

# III

## THE HOME-COMING

*I*t is a strange thing to come home. While yet on the journey, you cannot at all realize how strange it will be.

When you come down to Reggio on the Strait of Messina, and see Sicily emerge from the sea like a bank of fog, you are at first almost impatient. "Is it nothing else?" you say. "It is only a land like all others."

And when you disembark at Messina you are still impatient. Something ought to have happened while you have been away. It is dreadful to be met by the same poverty, the same rags, the same misery as when you went away.

You see that the spring has come. The fig trees are again in leaf; the grape-vines send out tendrils which grow yards long in a few hours, and a mass of peas and beans are spread out on the fruit-stands by the harbor.

If you glance towards the heights above the town, you see that the grey cactus plants that climb along the edges of the cliffs are covered with blood-red flowers. They have blossomed everywhere like little, glowing flames. It looks as if the flower cups had been filled with fire, which now is breaking out.

But, however much the cactus blossoms, it is still grey and dusty and cobwebby. You say to yourself that the cactus is like Sicily. However many springs it may blossom, it is still the grey land of poverty.

It is hard to realize that everything has remained quiet and the same. Scylla and Charybdis ought to have begun to roar as in former days. The stone giant in the Girgenti temple should have risen with reconstructed limbs. The temple of Selinunto ought to have raised itself from its ruins. All Sicily should have awakened.

If you continue your journey from Messina down the coast, you are still impatient. You see that the peasants are still plowing with wooden plows and that their horses are just as thin and broken and jaded.

Yes, everything is the same. The sun sheds its light over the earth like a rain of color; the pelargoniums bloom at the roadside; the sea is a soft pale blue, and caresses the shore.

Wild mountains with bold peaks line the coast. Etna's lofty top shines in the distance.

You notice all at once that something strange is taking place. All your impatience is gone. Instead you rejoice in the blossoming earth and in the mountains and in the sea. You are reclaimed by the beautiful earth as a bit of her lost property. There is no time to think of anything but tufts and stones.

At last you approach your real home, the home of your childhood. What wicked thoughts have filled your mind while you have been away! You never wished to see that wretched home again, because you had suffered too much there. And then you see the old walled town from afar, and it smiles at you innocently, unconscious of its guilt.

"Come and love me once more," it says. And you can only be happy and grateful because it is willing to accept your love.

Ah, when you go up the zigzag path that leads to the gate of the town! The light shade of the olive tree falls over you. Was it meant as a caress? A little lizard scampers along a wall. You have to stop and look. May not the lizard be a friend of your childhood who wishes to say good-day?

Suddenly a fear strikes you. Your heart begins to throb and beat. You remember that you do not know what you may be going to hear when you come home. No one has written letters; you have received none. Everything that recalled home you have put away. It seemed the most sensible way, since you were never to come home again. Up to that moment your feelings for your home have been dead and indifferent.

But in that moment you do not know how you can bear it if everything is not exactly the same on the mountain of your birth. It will be a mortal blow if there is a single palm missing on Monte Chiaro or if a single stone has loosened from the town wall.

Where is the big agave at the turn of the cliff? The agave is not there; it has blossomed and been cut down. And the stone bench at the street-corner is broken. You will miss that bench; it has been such a pleasant resting-place. And look, they have built a barn on the green meadow under the almond trees. You will never again be able to stretch out there in the flowering clover.

You are afraid of every step. What will you meet next?

You are so moved that you feel that you could weep if a single old beggar-woman has died in your absence.

No, you did not know that to come home was so strange.

You came out of prison a few weeks ago, and the torpor of the prison still has possession of you. You hardly know if you will take the trouble to go home. Your beloved is dead; it is too terrible to tear your longing from its grave. So you drift aimlessly about, and let one day pass like the next. At last you pluck up courage. You must go home to your poor mother.

And when you are there, you feel that you have been longing for every stone, every blade of grass.

*E*ver since he came into the shop Donna Elisa has thought: "Now I will tell him of Micaela. Perhaps he does not even know that she is alive." But she puts it off from minute to minute, not only because she wishes to have him for a while to herself alone, but also because as soon as she mentions Micaela's name he will fall into the anguish and misery of love. For Micaela will not marry him; she has said so to Donna Elisa a thousand times. She would like to free him from prison, but she will not be the wife of an atheist.

Only for one half-hour will Donna Elisa keep Gaetano for herself; only for one half-hour.

But even so long she may not sit with his hand in hers, asking him a thousand questions, for the people have learned that he has come. All at once the whole street is full of those who wish to see him. Donna Elisa has bolted the door, for she knew that she would not have him in peace a moment after they had discovered him, but it was of little avail. They knock on the windows, and pound on the door.

"Don Gaetano," they cry; "Don Gaetano!"

Gaetano comes laughing out to the steps. They wave their caps and cheer, He hurries down into the crowd, and embraces one after another.

But that is not what they wish. He must go up on the steps and make a speech. He must tell them how cruel the government has been to him, and how he has suffered in prison.

Gaetano laughs still, and stations himself on the steps. "Prison," he says; "what is it to talk about? I have had my soup every day, and that is more than many of you can say."

Little Gandolfo swings his cap and calls to him: "There are many more socialists in Diamante now than when you went away, Don Gaetano."

"How else could it be?" he laughs. "Everybody must become a socialist. Is socialism anything dreadful or terrible? Socialism is an idyll. It is an idyll of one's own home and happy work, of which everyone dreams from his childhood. A whole world filled with —"

He stops, for he has cast a glance towards the summer-palace. There stands Donna Micaela on one of the balconies, and looks down at him.

He does not think for a moment that it is an illusion or a hallucination. He sees instantly that she is flesh and blood. But just for that reason — and also because the prison life has taken all his strength from him, so that he cannot be considered a well person —

He feels a terrible difficulty in holding himself upright. He clutches in the air with his hands, tries to get support from the doorpost, but nothing helps. His legs give way under him; he slides down the steps and strikes his head on the stones.

He lies there like one dead.

Everyone rushes to him, carries him in, runs after surgeon and doctor, prescribes, talks, and proposes a thousand ways to help him.

Donna Elisa and Pacifica get him finally into one of the bedrooms. Luca drives the people out and places himself on guard before the closed door. Donna Micaela, who came in with the others, was taken first of them all by the hand and led out. She was not allowed to stay in at all. Luca had himself seen Gaetano fall as if from a blow on the temple when he caught sight of her.

Then the doctor comes, and he makes one attempt after another to rouse Gaetano. He is not successful; Gaetano lies as if turned to stone. The doctor thinks that he received a dangerous blow on the head when he fell. He does not know whether he will succeed in bringing him to life.

The swoon in itself was nothing, but that blow on the hard edge of the stone steps —

In the house there is an eager bustle. The poor people outside can only listen and wait.

There they stand the livelong day outside Donna Elisa's door. There stand Donna Concetta and Donna Emilia. No love has been lost between them in former times, but today they stand beside one another and mourn.

Many anxious eyes peer in through the windows of Donna Elisa's house. Little Gandolfo and old Assunta from the Cathedral steps, and the poor old chair-maker, stand there the whole afternoon without tiring. It is so terrible that Gaetano is going to die just when they have got him back again.

The blind stand and wait as if they expected him to give them their sight, and the poor people, both from Geraci and Corvaja, are waiting to hear how it will turn out for their young lord, the last Alagona.

He wished them well, and he had great strength and power. If he could only have lived —

"God has taken his hand from Sicily," they say. "He lets all those perish who wish to help the people."

All the afternoon and evening, and even till midnight, the crowd of people are still outside Donna Elisa's house. At precisely twelve o'clock Donna Elisa throws open the shop-door and comes out on the steps. "Is he better?" they all cry at the sight of her. — "No, he is not better."

Then there is silence; but at last a single trembling voice asks: "Is he worse?" — "No, no; he is not worse. He is the same. The doctor is with him."

Donna Elisa has thrown a black shawl over her head and carries a lantern in her hand. She goes down the steps to the street, where the people are sitting and lying, closely packed one beside one another. She makes her way quietly through them.

"Is Gandolfo here?" she asks. "Yes, Donna Elisa." And Gandolfo comes forward to her.

"You must come with me and open your church for me."

Everyone who hears Donna Elisa say that, understands that she wishes to go to the Christchild in the church of San Pasquale and pray for Gaetano. They rise and wish to go with her.

Donna Elisa is much touched by their sympathy. She opens her heart to them.

"I will tell you something," she says, and her voice trembles exceedingly. "I have had a dream. I do not know how I could sleep tonight. But while I was sitting at the bedside, and was most anxious, I did fall asleep. I had scarcely closed my eyes before I saw the Christchild before me in his crown and gold shoes, as he stands out in San Pasquale. And he spoke in this way to me: 'Make the unhappy woman who is on her knees praying in my church your son's wife, then Gaetano will be well.' He hardly had time to say it before I awoke, and when I opened my eyes, I seemed to see the Christchild disappearing through the wall. And now I must go out and see if anyone is there.

"But now you all hear that I vow that if there is any woman out in the church of San Pasquale, I shall do what the image commanded me. Even if it is the poorest girl from the street, I shall take charge of her and make her my son's wife."

When Donna Elisa has spoken, she and all those who have waited in the street go out to San Pasquale. The poor people are filled with shuddering expectation. They can scarcely contain themselves from rushing by Donna Elisa, in order to see if there is anyone in the church.

Fancy if it is a gypsy girl who has sought shelter there for the night! Who can be in the church at night except some poor, homeless wanderer? Donna Elisa has made a terrible vow.

At last they come to Porta Etnea, and from there they go quickly, quickly down the hill. The saints preserve us, the church door is open! Someone really is there.

The lantern shakes in Donna Elisa's hand. Gandolfo wishes to take it from her, but she will keep it. "In God's name, in God's name," she murmurs as she goes into the church.

The people crowd in after her. They almost crush one another to death in the door, but their excitement keeps them silent, no one says a word. All gaze at the high altar. Is anyone there? Is anyone there? The little hanging-lamp over the image shines pitifully faint. Is anyone there?

Yes, someone is there. There is a woman there. She is on her knees, praying, and her head is so deeply bent that they cannot see who she is. But when she hears steps behind her she lifts her long, bowed neck and looks up. It is Donna Micaela.

At first she is frightened and starts up as if she wished to escape. Donna Elisa is also frightened, and they look at one another as if they had never met before. Then Donna Micaela says in a very low voice: "You have come to pray for him, sister-in-law." And the people see her move a little way along so that Donna Elisa may have room directly in front of the image.

Donna Elisa's hand trembles so that she has to set the lantern down on the floor, and her voice is quite hoarse as she says: "Has none other but you been here tonight, Micaela?" — "No, none other."

Donna Elisa has to support herself against the wall to keep from falling, and Donna Micaela sees it. She is instantly beside her and puts her arm about her waist. "Sit down, sit down!" She leads her to the altar platform and kneels down in front of her. "Is he so ill? We will pray for him."

"Micaela," says Donna Elisa, "I thought that I should find help here." — "Yes, you shall see, you will." — "I dreamed that the image came to me, that he came to me and said that I was to come here." — "He has also helped us many times before." — "But he said this to me: 'Make the unhappy woman who is on her knees praying before my altar your son's wife, then your son will be well.'" — "What do you say that he said?" — "I was to make her who was kneeling and praying out here my

son's wife." — "And you were willing to do it? You did not know whom
you would meet!"

"On the way I made a vow — and those who followed me heard it —
that whoever it might be, I would take her in my arms and lead her to
my home. I thought that it was some poor woman whom God wished
to help." — "It is one indeed." — "I was in despair when I saw that there
was no one here but you."

Donna Micaela does not answer; she gazes up at the image. "Is it your
will? Is it your will?" she whispers anxiously.

Donna Elisa continues to bemoan herself. "I saw him so plainly, and
he has never deceived before. I thought that some poor girl who had
no marriage portion had prayed to him for a husband. Such things have
happened before. What shall I do now?"

She laments and bewails; she cannot get away from the thought that
it ought to be a poor woman. Donna Micaela grows impatient. She takes
her by the arm and shakes her. "But Donna Elisa, Donna Elisa!"

Donna Elisa does not listen to her; she continues her laments. "What
shall I do? what shall I do?"

"Why, make the poor woman who was kneeling and praying here
your son's wife, Donna Elisa!"

Donna Elisa looks up. Such a face as she sees before her! So bewitch-
ing, so captivating, so smiling!

But she may not look at it for more than a second. Donna Micaela
hides it instantly in Donna Elisa's old black dress.

*D*onna Micaela and Donna Elisa go together into the town. The
street winds so that they cannot see Donna Elisa's house until they are
quite near. When it at last comes into view they see that the shop
windows are lighted up. Four gigantic wax-candles are burning behind
the bunches of rosaries.

Both the women press each other's hands. "He lives!" one whispers
to the other. "He lives!"

"You must not tell him anything about what the image commanded
you to do," says Donna Micaela to Donna Elisa.

Outside the shop they embrace one another and each goes her own
way.

In a little while Gaetano comes out on the steps of the shop. He
stands still for a moment and breathes in the fresh night air. Then he
sees how lights are burning in the dark palace across the street.

Gaetano breathes short and panting; he seems almost afraid to go further. Suddenly he dashes across like someone going to meet an unavoidable misfortune. He finds the door to the summer-palace unlocked, takes the stairs in two bounds, and bursts open the door to the music-room without knocking.

Donna Micaela is sitting there, wondering if he will come now in the night or the next morning. Then she hears his step outside in the gallery. She is seized with terror; how will he be? She has longed so unspeakably for him. Will he really be so that all that longing will be satisfied?

And will no more walls rise between them? Will they for once be able to tell each other everything? Will they speak of love, and not of socialism?"

When he opens the door she tries to go to meet him, but she cannot; she is trembling in every limb. She sits down and hides her face in her hands.

She expects him to throw his arms about her and kiss her, but that he does not do. It is not Gaetano's way to do what people expect of him.

As soon as he could stand upright he has thrown on his clothes to come to see her. He is apparently wildly gay when he comes now. He would have liked her to take it lightly also. He will not be agitated. He had fainted in the forenoon. He could stand nothing.

He stands quietly beside her until she regains her composure. "You have weak nerves," he says. That is actually all he says.

She and Donna Elisa and everyone is convinced that he has come to clasp her in his arms and say that he loves her. But just for that reason it is impossible for Gaetano. Some people are malicious; it is their nature never to do just what they ought to do.

Gaetano begins to tell her of his journey; he does not speak even of socialism, but talks of express-trains and conductors and curious traveling companions.

Donna Micaela sits and looks at him; her eyes beg and implore more and more eagerly. Gaetano seems to be glad and happy to see her, but why can he not say what he has to say?

"Have you been on the Etna railway?" she asks.

"Yes," he answers, and begins quite unconstrainedly to speak of the beauty and usefulness of the road. He knows nothing of how it came to be.

Gaetano is saying to himself that he is a brute. Why does he not speak the words for which she is longing? But why is she sitting there so humbly? Why does she show that he needs only to stretch out his hand

and take her? He is desperately, stormily happy to be near her, but he feels so sure of her, so certain. It is so amusing to torture her.

The people of Diamante are still standing outside in the street, and they all feel as great a happiness as if they had given away a daughter in marriage.

They have been patient till now in order to give Gaetano time to declare himself. But now it surely must be accomplished. And they begin to shout: —

"Long live Gaetano! long live Micaela!"

Donna Micaela looks up with inexpressible dismay. He surely must understand that she has nothing to do with it.

She goes out to the gallery and sends Luca down with the request that they will be silent.

When she comes back, Gaetano has risen. He offers her his hand; he wishes to go.

Donna Micaela puts out her hand almost without knowing what she is doing. But then she draws it back; "No, no," she says.

He wishes to go, and who knows whether he will come again on the morrow. She has not been able to talk to him; she has not been able to say a word to him of all that she wished to say.

Surely there was no need for them to be like ordinary lovers. That man had given her life all its life for many years. Whether he spoke to her of love or not was of no importance; yet she wishes to tell him what he has been to her.

And now, just now. One has to make the most of one's opportunities when Gaetano is in question. She dares not let him go.

"You must not go yet," she says. "I have something to say to you."

She draws forward a chair for him; she herself places herself a little behind him. His eyes are too gay tonight, they trouble her.

Then she begins to speak. She lays before him the great, hidden treasures of her life. They were all the words he had said to her and all the dreams he had set her to dreaming. She had not lost one. She had collected and saved them up. They had been the only richness in her poor life.

In the beginning she speaks fast, as if repeating a lesson. She is afraid of him; she does not know whether he likes her to speak. At last she dares to look at him. He is serious now, no longer malicious. He sits still and listens as if he would not lose a syllable. Just now his face was sickly and ashen, but now it suddenly changes. His face begins to shine as though transfigured.

She talks and talks. She looks at him, and now she is beautiful. How could she help being beautiful? At last she can speak out to him, she can tell him how love came to her and how it has never left her since. Finally she can tell him how he has been all the world to her.

Words cannot say enough; she takes his hand and kisses it.

He lets her do it without moving. The color in his cheeks grows no deeper, but it becomes clearer, more transparent. She remembers Gandolfo, who had said that Gaetano's face was so white that it shone.

He does not interrupt her. She tells him about the railway, speaks of one miracle after another. He looks at her now and then. His eyes glow at the sight of her. He is not by any means making fun of her.

She wonders exceedingly what is passing in him. He looks as if what she said was nothing new to him. He seems to recognize everything she says. Could it be that his love for her was the same as that she felt for him? Was it connected with every noble feeling in him? Had it been the elevating power in his life? Had it given wings to his artistic powers? Had it taught him to love the poor and the oppressed? Is it once more taking possession of him, making him feel that he is an artist, an apostle, that nothing is too high for him?

But as he is still silent she thinks that perhaps he will not be tied to her. He loves her, but possibly he wishes to be a free man. Perhaps he thinks that she is not a suitable wife for a socialist.

Her blood begins to boil. She thinks that he perhaps believes that she is sitting there and begging for his love.

She has told him almost everything that has happened while he has been away. Now she suddenly breaks off in her story.

"I have loved you," she says. "I shall always love you, and I think that I should like you to tell me once that you love me. It would make the parting easier to bear."

"Would it?" he says.

"Can I be your wife?" she says, and her voice trembles with indignation. "I no longer fear your teachings as I did; I am not afraid of your poor; I wish to turn the world upside down, I, as well as you. But I am a believer. How can I live with you if you do not agree with me in that? Or perhaps you would win me to unbelief? Then the world would be dead for me. Everything would lose its meaning, its significance. I should be a miserable, destitute creature. We must part."

"Really!" he turns towards her. His eyes begin to glow with impatience.

"You may go now," she says quietly; "I have said to you everything I wished to say. I should have wished that you had something to say to me. But perhaps it is better as it is. We will not make it harder to part than it need be."

One of Gaetano's hands holds her hands firmly and closely, the other holds her head still. Then he kisses her.

Was she mad, that she could think that he would let anything, anything in the world, part them now?

# IV

## ONLY OF THIS WORLD

*A*s she grew up everybody said of her: "She is going to be a saint, a saint."

Her name was Margherita Cornado. She lived in Girgenti on the south side of Sicily, in the great mining district. When she was a child her father was a miner; later he inherited a little money, so that he no longer needed to work.

There was a little, narrow, miserable roof-garden on Margherita Cornado's house in Girgenti. A small and steep stairway led up to it, and one had to creep out through a low door. But it was well worth the trouble. When you reached the top you saw not only a mass of roofs, but the whole air over the town was gaily crowded with the towers and façades of all Girgenti's churches. And every façade and every tower was a quivering lace-work of images, of loggias, of glowing canopies.

And outside the town there was a wide plain which sloped gently down towards the sea, and a semicircle of hills that guarded the plain. The plain was glittering red; the ocean was blue as enamel; the hillsides were yellow; it was a whole orient of warmth and color.

But there was even more to be seen. Ancient temples were dotted about the valley. Ruins and strange old towers were everywhere, as in a fairy world.

As Margherita Cornado grew up, she used to spend most of her days there; but she never looked out over the dazzling landscape. She was occupied with other things.

Her father used to tell her of the life in the sulfur mines at Grotte, where he had worked. While Margherita Cornado sat on the airy terrace, she thought that she was incessantly walking about the dark mine veins, and finding her way through dim shafts.

She could not help thinking of all the misery that existed in the mines; especially she thought of the children, who carried the ore up to the surface. "The little wagons," they called them. That expression never left her mind. Poor, poor little wagons, the little mine-wagons!

They came in the morning, and each followed a miner down into the mine. As soon as he had dug out enough ore, he loaded the mine-wagon with a basket of it, and then the latter began to climb. Several of them met on the way, so that there was a long procession. And they began to sing: —

"One journey made in struggling and pain,
    Nineteen times to be traveled again."

When they finally reached the light of day, they emptied their baskets of ore and threw themselves on the ground to rest a moment. Most of them dragged themselves over to the sulfurous pools near the shaft of the mine and drank the pestiferous water.

But they soon had to go down again, and they gathered at the mouth of the mine. As they clambered down, they cried: "Lord and God, have mercy, have mercy, have mercy!"

Every journey the little wagons made, their song grew more feeble. They groaned and cried as they crawled up the paths of the mine.

The little wagons were bathed in perspiration; the baskets of ore ground holes in their shoulders. As they went up and down they sang: —

"Seven more trips without pause for breath,
    The pain of living is worse than death."

Margherita Cornado had suffered for those poor children all her own childhood. And because she was always thinking of their hardships, people believed that she would be a saint.

Neither did she forget them as she grew older. As soon as she was grown, she went to Grotte, where most of the mines are, and when the little wagons came out into the daylight, she was waiting for them by the shaft with fresh, clean water. She wiped the perspiration from their faces, and she dressed the wounds on their shoulders. It was not much that she could do for them, but soon the little wagons felt that they could not go on with their work any day that Margherita Cornado did not come and comfort them.

But unfortunately for the little wagons, Margherita was very beautiful. One day one of the mining-engineers happened to see her as she was relieving the children, and instantly fell very much in love with her.

A few weeks after, Margherita Cornado stopped coming to the Grotte mines. She sat at home instead and sewed on her wedding outfit. She was going to marry the mining-engineer. It was a good match, and connected her with the chief people of the town, so she could not care for the little wagons any longer.

A few days before the wedding the old beggar, Santuzza, who was Margherita's godmother, came and asked to speak to her. They betook themselves to the roof-garden in order to be alone.

"Margherita," said the old woman, "you are in the midst of such happiness and magnificence that perhaps there is no use speaking to you of those who are in need and sorrow. You have forgotten all such things."

Margherita reproved her for speaking so.

"I come with a greeting to you from my son, Orestes. He is in trouble, and he needs your advice."

"You know that you can speak freely to me, Santuzza," said the girl.

"Orestes is no longer at the Grotte mines; you know that, I suppose. He is at Racalmuto. And he is very badly off there. Not that the pay is so bad, but the engineer is a man who grinds down the poor to the last drop of blood."

The old woman told how the engineer tortured the miners. He made them work over time; he fined them if they missed a day. He did not look after the mines properly; there was one cave-in after another. No one was secure of his life as long as he was under earth.

"Well, Margherita, Orestes had a son. A splendid boy; just ten years old. The engineer came and wished to buy the boy from Orestes, and set him to work with the little wagons. But Orestes said no. His boy should not be ruined by such work. Then the engineer threatened him, and said that Orestes would be dismissed from the mine."

Santuzza paused.

"And then?" asked Margherita.

"Yes, then Orestes gave his son to the engineer. The next day the boy got a whipping from him. He beat him every day. The boy grew more and more feeble. Orestes saw it, and asked the engineer to spare the boy, but he had no mercy. He said that the boy was lazy, and he continued to persecute him. And now he is dead. My grandson is dead, Margherita."

The girl had quite forgotten all her own happiness. She was once more only the miner's daughter, the protector of the little wagons, the poor child who used to sit on the bright terrace and weep over the hardships of the black mines.

"Why do you let the man live?" she cried.

The old woman looked at her furtively. Then she crept close to her with a knife. "Orestes sends you this with a thousand questions," she said.

Margherita Cornado took the knife, kissed the blade, and gave it back without a word.

It was the evening before the wedding. The parents of the bridegroom were awaiting their son. He was to come home from the mines towards night; but he never came. Later in the night a servant was sent to the Grotte mines to look for him, and found him a mile from Girgenti. He lay murdered at the roadside.

A search for the murderer was immediately instituted. Strict examinations of the miners were held, but the culprit could not be discovered. There were no witnesses; no one could be prevailed upon to betray a comrade.

Then Margherita Cornado appeared and denounced Orestes, who was the son of her godmother, Santuzza, and who had not moved to Racalmuto at all.

She did it although she had heard afterwards that her betrothed had been guilty of everything of which Santuzza had accused him. She did it although she herself had sealed his doom by kissing the knife.

She had hardly accused Orestes before she repented of it; she was filled with the anguish of remorse.

In another land what she had done would not have been considered a crime, but it is so regarded in Sicily. A Sicilian would rather die than be an informer.

Margherita Cornado enjoyed no rest either by night or by day. She had a continual aching feeling of anguish in her heart, a great unhappiness dwelt in her.

She was not severely judged, because everyone knew that she had loved the murdered man and thought that Santuzza had been too cruel towards her. No one spoke of her disdainfully, and no one refused to salute her.

But it made no difference to her that others were kind to her. Remorse filled her soul and tortured her like an aching wound. Orestes had been sentenced to the galleys for life. Santuzza had died a few weeks after her son's sentence had been passed, and Margherita could not ask forgiveness of either of them.

She called on the saints, but they would not help her. It seemed as if nothing in the world could have the power to free her from the horror of remorse.

At that time the famous Franciscan monk, Father Gondo, was sojourning in the neighborhood of Girgenti. He was preaching a pilgrimage to Diamante.

It did not disturb Father Gondo not to have the pope acknowledge the Christ-image in the church of San Pasquale as a miracle-worker. He had met the blind singers on his wanderings and had heard them tell of the image. Through long, happy nights he had sat at the feet of Father Elia and Brother Tommaso, and from sunset to sunrise they had told him of the image.

And now the famous preacher had begun to send all who were in trouble to the great miracle-worker. He warned the people not to let that holy time pass unheeded. "The Christchild," he said, "had not hitherto been much worshipped in Sicily. The time had come when he wished to possess a church and followers. And to effect it he let his holy image perform miracle after miracle."

Father Gondo, who had passed his novitiate in the monastery of Aracoeli on the Capitol, told the people of the image of the Christchild that was there, and of the thousand miracles he had performed. "And now that good little child wishes to be worshipped in Sicily," said Father Gondo. "Let us hesitate no longer, and hasten to him. For the moment heaven is generous. Let us be the first to acknowledge the image! Let us be like the shepherds and wise men of the East; let us go to the holy child while he is still lying on his bed of straw in the miserable hut!"

Margherita Cornado was filled with a new hope when she heard him. She was the first to obey Father Gondo's summons. After her others joined him also. Forty pilgrims marched with him through the plateaus of the inland to Diamante.

They were all very poor and unhappy. But Father Gondo made them march with song and prayer. Soon their eyes began to shine as if the star of Bethlehem had gone before them.

"Do you know," said Father Gondo, "why God's son is greater than all the saints? Because he gives the soul holiness; because he forgives sins; because he grants to the spirit a blessed trust in God; because his kingdom is not of this world."

When his little army looked tired, he gave them new life by telling them of the miracles the image had performed. The legends of the blind singers were like cooling drinks and cheering wine. The poor wanderers in the barren lands of Sicily walked with a lighter step, as if they were on their way to Nazareth to see the carpenter's son.

"He will take all our burdens from us," said Father Gondo. "When we come back our hearts will be freed from every care."

And during the wandering through the scorched, glowing desert, where no trees gave cooling shade, and where the water was bitter with salt and sulfur, Margherita Cornado felt that her heart's torments were relieved. "The little king of heaven will take away my pain," she said.

At last, one day in May, the pilgrims reached the foot of the hill of Diamante. There the desert stopped. They saw about them groves of olive trees and fresh green leaves. The mountain shone; the town shone. They felt that they had come to a place in the shadow of God's grace.

They toiled joyfully up the zigzag path, and with loud and exultant voices sang an old pilgrims' song.

When they had gone some way up the mountain, people came running from Diamante to meet them. When the people heard the monotonous sound of the old song, they threw aside their work and hurried out. And the people of Diamante embraced and kissed the pilgrims.

They had expected them long ago; they could not understand why they had not come before. The Christ-image of Diamante was a wonderful miracle-worker; he was so compassionate, so loving that everyone ought to come to him.

When Margherita Cornado heard them she felt as if her heart was already healed of its pain. All the people of Diamante comforted her and encouraged her. "He will certainly help you; he helps everyone," they said. "No one has prayed to him in vain."

At the town-gate the pilgrims parted. The townspeople took them to their homes, so that they might rest after their journey. In an hour they were all to meet at the Porta Etnea in order to go out to the image together.

But Margherita had not the patience to wait a whole hour. She asked her way out to the church of San Pasquale and went there alone before all the others.

When Father Gondo and the pilgrims came out to San Pasquale an hour later, they saw Margherita Cornado sitting on the platform by the high altar. She was sitting still and did not seem to notice their coming. But when Father Gondo came close up to her, she started up as if she had lain in wait for him and threw herself upon him. She seized him by the throat and tried to strangle him.

She was big, splendidly developed and strong. It was only after a severe struggle that Father Gondo and two of the pilgrims succeeded in subduing her. She was quite mad, and so violent that she had to be bound.

The pilgrims had come in a solemn procession; they sang, and held burning candles in their hands. There was a long line of them, for many people from Diamante had joined them. Those who came first immediately stopped their singing; those coming after had noticed nothing and continued their song. But then the news of what had happened passed from file to file, and wherever it came the song stopped. It was horrible to hear how it died away and changed into a low wail.

All the weary pilgrims realized that they had failed in their coming. All their laborious wanderings had been in vain. They were disappointed in their beautiful hopes. The holy image would have no consolation to offer them.

Father Gondo himself was in despair. It was a more severe blow to him than to anyone else, for each one of the others had only his own sorrow to think of, but he bore the sorrows of all those people in his heart. What answer could he give to all the hopes he had awakened in them?

Suddenly one of his beautiful, childlike smiles passed over his face. The image must wish to test his faith and that of the others. If only they did not fail, they would certainly be helped.

He began again to sing the pilgrim song in his clear voice and went up to the altar.

But as he came nearer to the image, he broke off in his song again. He stopped and looked at the image with staring eyes. Then he stretched out his hand, took the crown and brought it close to his eyes. "It is written there; it is written there," he murmured. And he let the crown fall from his hand and roll down on the stone floor.

From that moment Father Gondo knew that the outcast from Aracoeli was before him.

But he did not immediately cry it out to the people, but said instead, with his usual gentleness, —

"My friends, I wish to tell you something strange."

He told them of the Englishwoman who had wished to steal the Christ-image of Aracoeli. And he told how the image had been called Antichrist and had been cast out into the world.

"I still remember old Fra Simone," said Father Gondo. "He never showed me the image without saying: 'It was this little hand that rang. It was this little foot that kicked on the door.'

"But when I asked Fra Simone what had become of the other image, he always said: 'What should have become of him? The dogs of Rome have probably dragged him away and torn him to pieces.'"

When Father Gondo had finished speaking, he went, still quite slowly and quietly, and picked up the crown that he had just let fall to the floor.

"Now read that!" he said. And he let the crown go from man to man. The people stood with their wax-candles in their hands and lighted up the crown with them. Those who could read, read; the others saw that at least there was an inscription.

And each one who had held the crown in his hand instantly extinguished his candle.

When the last candle was put out, Father Gondo turned to his pilgrims who had gathered about him. "I have brought you here," he said to them, "that you might find one who gives the soul peace and an entry to God's kingdom; but I have brought you wrong, for this one has no such thing to give. His kingdom is only of this world.

"Our unfortunate sister has gone mad," continued Father Gondo, "because she came here and hoped for heavenly benefits. Her reason gave way when her prayers were not heard. He could not hear her, for his kingdom is only of this world."

He was silent a moment, and they all looked up at him to find out what they ought to think of it all.

He asked as quietly as before: "Shall an image which bears such words in its crown any longer be allowed to desecrate an altar?"

"No, no!" cried the pilgrims. The people of Diamante stood silent.

Father Gondo took the image in his hands and carried it on his outstretched arms through the church and towards the door.

But although the Father had spoken gently and humbly, his eyes had rested the whole time sternly and with compelling force on the crowd of people. There was not one there whom he had not subdued and mastered by the strength of his will. Everyone had felt paralyzed and without the power of thinking independently.

As Father Gondo approached the door, he stopped and looked around. One last commanding glance fell on the people.

"The crown also," said Father Gondo. And the crown was handed to him.

He set the image down and went out under the stone canopy that protected the image of San Pasquale. He whispered a word to a couple of pilgrims, and they hurried away. They soon came back with their arms full of branches and logs. They laid them down before Father Gondo and set them on fire.

All who had been in the church had crowded out. They stood in the yard outside the church, still subdued, with no will of their own. They saw that the monk meant to burn their beloved image that helped them so, and yet they made no resistance. They could not understand themselves why they did not try to save the image.

When Father Gondo saw the fire kindle and therefore felt that the image was entirely in his power, he straightened himself and his eyes flashed.

"My poor children," he said gently, and turned to the people of Diamante. "You have been harboring a terrible guest. How is it possible for you not to have discovered who he is?

"What ought I to believe of you?" he continued more sternly. "You yourselves say that the image has given you everything for which you have prayed. Has no one in Diamante in all these years prayed for the forgiveness of sins and the peace of the soul?

"Can it be possible? The people of Diamante have not had anything to pray for except lottery numbers and good years and daily bread and health and money. They have asked for nothing but the good of this world. Not one has needed to pray for heavenly grace.

"Can it really be? No, it is impossible," said Father Gondo joyfully, as if filled with a sudden hope. "It is I who have made a mistake. The people of Diamante have understood that I would not lay the image on the fire without asking and investigating about it. You are only waiting for me to be silent to step forward and give your testimony.

"Many will now come and say: 'That image has made me a believer;' and many will say: 'He has granted me the forgiveness of sins;' and many will say: 'He has opened my eyes, so that I have been able to gaze on the glory of heaven.' They will come forward and speak, and I shall be mocked and derided and compelled to bear the image to the altar and acknowledge that I have been mistaken."

Father Gondo stopped speaking and smiled invitingly at the people. A quick movement passed through the crowd of listeners. Several seemed to have the intention of coming forward and testifying. They came a few steps, but then they stopped.

"I am waiting," said the Father, and his eyes implored and called on the people to come.

No one came. The whole mass of people was in wailing despair that they would not testify to the advantage of their beloved image. But no one did so.

"My poor children," said Father Gondo, sadly.

"You have had Antichrist among you, and he has got possession of you. You have forgotten heaven. You have forgotten that you possess a soul. You think only of this world.

"Formerly it was said that the people of Diamante were the most religious in Sicily. Now it must be otherwise. The inhabitants of

Diamante are slaves of the world. Perhaps they are even infidel socialists, who love only the earth. They can be nothing else. They have had Antichrist among them."

When the people were accused in such a way, they seemed at last to be about to rise in resistance. An angry muttering passed through the ranks.

"The image is holy," one cried. "When he came San Pasquale's bells rang all day."

"Could they ring for less time to warn you of such a misfortune?" rejoined the monk.

He went on with his accusations with growing violence. "You are idolaters, not Christians. You serve him because he helps you. There is nothing of the spirit of holiness in you."

"He has been kind and merciful, like Christ," answered the people.

"Is not just that the misfortune?" said the Father, and now all of a sudden he was terrible in his wrath. "He has taken the likeness of Christ to lead you astray. In that way he has been able to weave his web about you. By scattering gifts and blessings over you, he has lured you into his net and made you slaves of the world. Or is it not so? Perhaps someone can come forward and say the contrary? Perhaps he has heard that someone who is not present today has prayed to the image for a heavenly grace."

"He has taken away the power of a *jettatore*," said one.

"Is it not he who is as great in evil as the *jettatore* who has power over him?" answered the father, bitterly.

They made no other attempts to defend the image. Everything that they said seemed only to make the matter worse.

Several looked round for Donna Micaela, who was also present. She stood among the crowd, heard and saw everything, but made no attempt to save the image.

When Father Gondo had said that the image was Antichrist she had been terrified, and when he showed that the people of Diamante had only asked for the good of this world, her terror had grown. She had not dared to do anything.

But when he said that she and all the others were in the power of Antichrist, something in her rose against him. "No, no," she said, "it cannot be so." If she should believe that an evil power had governed her during so many years, her reason would give way. And her reason began to defend itself.

Her faith in the supernatural broke in her like a string too tightly stretched. She could not follow it any longer.

With infinite swiftness everything of the supernatural that she herself had experienced flashed through her mind, and she passed sentence on it. Was there a single proven miracle? She said to herself that there were coincidences, coincidences.

It was like unraveling a skein. From what she herself had experienced she passed to the miracles of other times. They were coincidences. They were hypnotism. They were possibly legends, most of them.

The raging monk continued to curse the people with terrible words. She tried to listen to him to get away from her own thoughts. But all she thought was that what he said was madness and lies.

What was going on in her? Was she becoming an atheist?

She looked about for Gaetano. He was there also; he stood on the church steps quite near the monk. His eyes rested on her. And as surely as if she had told him it, he knew what was passing in her. But he did not look as if he were glad or triumphant. He looked as if he wished to stop Father Gondo, to save a little vestige of faith for her.

Donna Micaela's thoughts had no mercy. They went on and robbed her soul. All the glowing world of the supernatural was destroyed, crushed. She said to herself that no one knew anything of celestial matters, nor could know anything. Many messages had gone from earth to heaven. None had gone from heaven to earth.

"But I will still believe in God," she said, and clasped her hands as if still to hold fast the last and best.

"Your eyes, people of Diamante, are wild and evil," said Father Gondo. "God is not in you. Antichrist has driven God away from you."

Donna Micaela's eyes again sought Gaetano's. "Can you give a poor, doubting creature something on which to live?" they seemed to ask. His eyes met hers with proud confidence. He read in her beautiful, imploring eyes how her trembling soul clung to him for support. He did not doubt for a moment that he would be able to make her life beautiful and rich.

She thought of the joy that always met him where-ever he showed himself. She thought of the joy that had roared about her that night in Palermo. She knew that it rose from the new faith in a happy earth. Could that faith and that joy take possession of her also?

She wrung her hands in anguish. Could that new faith be anything to her? Would she not always feel as unhappy as now?

Father Gondo bent forward over the fire.

"I say to you once more," he cried, "if only one person comes and says that this image has saved his soul, I will not burn it."

Donna Micaela had a sudden feeling that she did not wish the poor image to be destroyed. The memory of the most beautiful hours of her life was bound to it.

"Gandolfo, Gandolfo," she whispered. She had just seen him beside her.

"Yes, Donna Micaela."

"Do not let him burn the image, Gandolfo!"

The monk had repeated his question once, twice, thrice. No one came forward to defend the image. But little Gandolfo crept nearer and nearer.

Father Gondo brought the image ever closer to the fire.

Involuntarily Gaetano had bent forward. Involuntarily a proud smile passed over his face. Donna Micaela saw that he felt that Diamante belonged to him. The monk's wild proceedings made Gaetano master of their souls.

She looked about in terror. Her eyes wandered from face to face. Was the same thing going on in all those people's souls as in her own? She thought she saw that it was so.

"Thou, Antichrist," said Father Gondo, threateningly, "dost thou see that no one has thought of his soul as long as thou hast been here? Thou must perish."

Father Gondo laid the outcast on the pyre.

But the image had not lain there more than a second before Gandolfo seized him.

He caught him up, lifted him high above his head, and ran. Father Gondo's pilgrims hurried after him, and there began a wild chase down Monte Chiaro's precipices.

But little Gandolfo saved the image.

Down the road a big, heavy traveling-carriage came driving. Gandolfo, whose pursuers were close at his heels, knew nothing better to do than to throw the image into the carriage.

Then he let himself be caught. When his pursuers wished to hurry after the carriage, he stopped them. "Take care; the lady in the carriage is English."

It was Signora Favara, who had at last wearied of Diamante and was traveling out into the world once more. And she was allowed to go away unmolested. No Sicilian dares to lay hands on an Englishwoman.

# V

## A FRESCO OF SIGNORELLI

*A* week later Father Gondo was in Rome. He was granted an interview with the old man in the Vatican and told him how he had found Antichrist in the likeness of Christ, how the former had entangled the people of Diamante in worldliness, and how he, Father Gondo, had wished to burn him. He also told how he had not been able to lead the people back to God. Instead, all Diamante had fallen into unbelief and socialism. No one there cared for his soul; no one thought of heaven. Father Gondo asked what he should do with those unfortunate people.

The old pope, who is wiser than anyone now living, did not laugh at Father Gondo's story; he was deeply distressed by it.

"You have done wrong; you have done very wrong," he said.

He sat silent for a while and pondered; then he said: "You have not seen the Cathedral in Orvieto?" — "No, Holy Father." — "Then go there now and see it," said the pope; "and when you come back again, you shall tell me what you have seen there."

Father Gondo obeyed. He went to Orvieto and saw the most holy Cathedral. And in two days he was back in the Vatican.

"What did you see in Orvieto?" the pope asked him.

Father Gondo said that in one of the chapels of the Cathedral he had found some frescoes of Luca Signorelli, representing "The Last Judgment." But he had not looked at either the "Last Judgment" or at the "Resurrection of The Dead." He had fixed all his attention on the big painting which the guide called "The Miracles of Antichrist."

"What did you see in it?" asked the pope.

"I saw that Signorelli had painted Antichrist as a poor and lowly man, just as the Son of God was when he lived here on earth. I saw that he had dressed him like Christ and given him Christ's features."

"What more did you see?" said the pope.

"The first thing that I saw in the fresco was Antichrist preaching so that the rich and the mighty came and laid their treasures at his feet.

"The second thing I saw was a sick man brought to Antichrist and healed by him.

"The third thing I saw was a martyr proclaiming Antichrist and suffering death for him.

"The fourth thing I saw in the great wall-picture was the people hastening to a great temple of peace, the spirit of evil hurled from heaven, and all men of violence killed by heaven's thunderbolts."

"What did you think when you saw that?" asked the pope.

"When I saw it, I thought: 'That Signorelli was mad. Does he mean that in the time of Antichrist evil shall be conquered, and the earth become holy as a paradise?'"

"Did you see anything else?"

"The fifth thing I saw depicted in the painting was the monks and priests piled up on a big bonfire and burned.

"And the sixth and last thing I saw was the Devil whispering in Antichrist's ear, and suggesting to him how he was to act and speak."

"What did you think when you saw that?"

"I said to myself: 'That Signorelli is not mad; he is a prophet. Antichrist will certainly come in the likeness of Christ and make a paradise of the world. He will make it so beautiful that the people will forget heaven. And it will be the world's most terrible temptation.'"

"Do you understand now," said the pope, "that there was nothing new in all that you told me? The Church has always known that Antichrist would come, armed with the virtues of Christ."

"Did you also know that he had actually come, Holy Father?" asked Father Gondo.

"Could I sit here on Peter's chair year after year without knowing that he has come?" said the pope. "I see starting a movement of the people, which burns with love for its neighbor and hates God. I see people becoming martyrs for the new hope of a happy earth. I see how they receive new joy and new courage from the words 'Think of the earth,' as they once found them in the words 'Think of heaven.' I knew that he whom Signorelli had foretold had come."

Father Gondo bowed silently.

"Do you understand now wherein you did wrong?"

"Holy Father, enlighten me as to my sin."

The old pope looked up. His clear eyes looked through the veil of chance which shrouds future events and saw what was hidden behind it.

"Father Gondo," he said, "that little child with whom you fought in Diamante, the child who was merciful and wonder-working like Christ, that poor, despised child who conquered you and whom you call Antichrist, do you not know who he is?"

"No, Holy Father."

"And he who in Signorelli's picture healed the sick, and softened the rich, and felled evil-doers to the earth, who transformed the earth to a paradise and tempted the people to forget heaven. Do you not know who he is?"

"No, Holy Father."

"Who else can he be but the Antichristianity, socialism?"

The monk looked up in terror.

"Father Gondo," said the pope, sternly, "when you held the image in your arms you wished to burn him. Why? Why were you not loving to him? Why did you not carry him back to the little Christchild on the Capitolium from whom he proceeded?

"That is what you wandering monks could do. You could take the great popular movement in your arms, while it is still lying like a child in its swaddling clothes, and you could bear it to Jesus' feet; and Antichrist would see that he is nothing but an imitation of Christ, and would acknowledge him his Lord and Master. But you do not do so. You cast Antichristianity on the pyre, and soon he in his turn will cast you there."

Father Gondo bent his knee. "I understand, Holy Father. I will go and look for the image."

The pope rose majestically. "You shall not look for the image; you shall let him go his way through the ages. We do not fear him. When he comes to storm the Capitol in order to mount the throne of the world, we shall meet him, and we shall lead him to Christ. We shall make peace between earth and heaven. But you do wrong," he continued more mildly, "to hate him. You must have forgotten that the sibyl considered him one of the redeemers of the world. 'On the heights of the Capitol the redeemer of the world shall be worshipped, Christ or Antichrist.'"

"Holy Father, if the miseries of this world are to be remedied by him, and heaven suffers no injury, I shall not hate him."

The old pope smiled his most subtle smile.

"Father Gondo, you will permit me also to tell you a Sicilian story. The story goes, Father Gondo, that when Our Lord was busy creating the world, He wished one day to know if He had much more work to do. And He sent San Pietro out to see if the world was finished.

"When San Pietro came back, he said: 'Everyone is weeping and sobbing and lamenting.'

"'Then the world is not finished,' said Our Lord, and He went on working.

"Three days later Our Lord sent San Pietro again to the earth.

"'Everyone is laughing and rejoicing and playing,' said San Pietro, when he came back.

"'Then the world is not finished,' said Our Lord, and He went on working.

"San Pietro was dispatched for the third time.

"'Some are weeping and some are laughing,' he said, when he came back.

"'Then the world is finished,' said Our Lord.

"And so shall it be and continue," said the old pope. "No one can save mankind from their sorrows, but much is forgiven to him who brings new courage to bear them."

THE END